Alexandr's Reluctant Submissive

A Submissive's Wish Novel

By
Ann Mayburn

Alexandr's Reluctant Submissive copyright © 2015 Ann Mayburn

Published by Fated Desires Publishing

All rights reserved.

ISBN-13: 978-1-62322-220-8

Cover Art by Scott Carpenter

This book is a work of fiction. The names, characters, places, and incidents are products of the author's imagination or have been used fictitiously and are not to be construed as real. Any resemblance to persons, living or dead, actual events, locals or organizations is entirely coincidental. All rights reserved. With the exception of quotes used in reviews, this book may not be reproduced or used in whole or in part by any means existing without written permission from the author

Author's Note

Dear Beloved Reader,

'Alexandr's Reluctant Submissive' is part TWO of a two part story. Please read 'Alexandr's Cherished Submissive' first so you get the full enjoyment of the rather complex story. My Iron Horse MC series crosses over with my Submissive's Wish, so if you want the background on some of the characters from Iron Horse that make an appearance, check out the first book in the series 'Exquisite Trouble'.

As always I would like to thank my Beta readers Lisa Simo-Kizner, April Symes, Angela Plumlee, Diana Sandvik, Kara Belseth, and Meghan Dickinson for their tireless efforts to wade through my illiterate first draft crap. I would also like to thank my editor Kelli Collins for not making me cry. And to you, my beloved reader, thank you as always for giving me the chance to entertain you. Now buckle up your seatbelt and grab a cold drink and a fan because you are in for a hell of a ride.

Ann

Glossary

a mhuirnín- Irish for 'my darling'

blyads- Bitch

bogger- An Irish term for someone outside the city, a farmer, someone country/redneck

Bratva- The Russian Mafia, more specifically it's often used to denote the different organizations. For example, the Novikov Bratva, or the Sokolov Bratva.

Devushka milaya- Russian for 'Sweet girl'.

dorogoya- Russian for dear/darling

Eto piz`dets- This is fucked up

Gobshite- A variation of shit, especially in Ireland and the United Kingdom

Krasavitsa- Russian for beautiful

Laskovaya- Russian for Sweetie

Lyublyu tebya vsem sertsem, vsey dushyu- Russian for 'I love you with all my heart, with all my soul'.

Malyshka- affectionate form of 'little girl' in Russian

Pizda- Russian for pussy.

prinsessa moya- Russian for 'My princess'.

Radost moya. Moya krasivaya. Ya lyubblyu tebya vsem sertsem, vsey dushoyu. Ya budu vsegda lyubit tebya. Vsegda- Russian for

'My joy, my beauty. I love you with all of my heart and soul. I will always love you, always.'

radost' moya- my joy

Sinn Féin- is an Irish republican political party active in both the Republic of Ireland and Northern Ireland.

Sladkaya moya- Russian for 'My sweet'.

Sovietnik- ("Councilor"), is the advisor and most close trusted individuals to the Pakhan, similar to the Consigliere in Italian-American Mafia crime families and Sicilian Mafia clans.

To, chto ty delayesh' so mnoy- Russian for 'What are you doing to me?'

Ti takaya krasivaya- Russian for 'You are so beautiful to me."

Ti tak velikolEpna - You are so beautiful

Ya palyubIl tebyas pervava vzglyada- Russian for 'I have loved you since the first moment I saw you'.

ya lyublyu tyebya fsyei dushoj- I love you with all my soul

Chapter 1

Solid warmth blanketed Jessica, a soul-healing scent flavoring each slow breath she took. She floated in divine comfort, her hands roaming over the expanse of a man's cloth-covered chest, the softness of his jacket pressed to her cheek. God she loved the feeling of a high-quality suit perfectly fit over hard muscle. Rubbing her nose against his solid pectoral muscle, she soaked up his essence and sighed. Her body rose and fell with his deep breaths, and she relaxed further, perfectly content to let him pet her, knowing nothing would ever be able to harm her while he held her so tenderly.

Big, strong hands stroked her as gently as could be, running up and down her body, over and over again, warming her from the inside out. Those long fingers were familiar; the scarred, tattooed, massive hands that could kill a man yet barely skimmed her body in a controlled sweep. Everywhere he touched, her skin tingled with little sparks of heat, even where his caress was hindered by her clothing. And he stroked her everywhere except where she wanted his clever fingers the most.

She frowned at that thought, stiffening, then the soothing petting motions stopped for a moment and someone tenderly kissed her forehead, someone with facial hair and pillow-soft lips.

The need to see who held her tried to surface from her overtaxed mind, but he'd resumed his cuddling and she abandoned herself to his body-melting touch. She'd forgotten how good it felt to be with a man who worshiped her, who did everything he could to bring her pleasure because it made him happy. The more he touched her, the more aware of him she became. Her skin grew sensitive and she wanted to explore more of his intriguing body. The muscled expanse of his chest under her fingertips trembled for a moment as he let out a shuddering sigh. The smooth weave of his open suit coat slid like silk against her skin and she took a moment to relish the erotic promise of his muscled torso covered by his thin dress shirt.

His scent filled her, an exotic blend of key lime, bergamot, and cedar wood that worked with his natural scent in a way that was divine.

Whoever this dream man was, his heart pounded so hard she could feel it drumming against her palm like a hummingbird's wings. He fairly trembled with tension while she continued to hold her hand against his body, absorbing his heat. His stroke lingered on her side, then his thumb brushed her breast and a hard bolt of desire shot straight to her pussy, dampening her panties in a rush of longing.

His light touch skimmed every part of her body he could reach, over and over again, as if he was memorizing the feel of her. Every once in a while he'd stop to lightly kiss her somewhere. Once he did it on both of her cheeks, then the pulse point of her wrist and each of her fingers.

What an odd dream.

Her thoughts surfaced a bit more from her sleep and she flinched, her gut filling with dread.

God no, she was dreaming of *him* again. The man she was forbidden to think about. Her illicit craving. A shocking sense of loss filled her and she curled in on herself, so terrified to let this fantasy take root, to let her sick mind abuse her broken heart with things she could never have again. While awake, she could guard herself from these delusions that felt so real. The dreams themselves were wonderful, stolen moments reliving memories of her past where she reveled in his love. Unfortunately, when she woke up, they always left her with the heart-bruising sensation of having lost him all over again.

Fuck, she hadn't had one of these dreams in weeks. Like a junkie, she was unable to force herself wake, her resistance only intensifying the feeling of being with him. A shudder worked through her as she raised her hand to his face, not daring to open her eyes. Sometimes, when she was dreaming of Alex, not looking at him somehow seemed to extend her time with him. God, how she treasured those stolen moments, when her waking mind couldn't block her bittersweet memories. They cut like glass and she craved the numbing pain.

Her fingertips encountered the prickle of a beard and she paused momentarily, trailing her fingers along his jawline. When he'd been her husband he'd had a goatee. He'd started growing a beard two years ago but she'd never dreamed of him with one.

"*Jessica*," he said, with such painful emotion that the tears threatening her eyes finally escaped and flowed hot down her cheeks, their salty wetness dripping over her chin.

"Alex," she sobbed without shame, his name broken by her hitching breath.

How could she ever forget the power of his voice? Even if she was just imaging it, the deep sound rippled over her skin like a caress, making her aware of her body being cradled on his lap. Audio caramel, sticky-sweet and sinful.

The longer this dream went on the more intense it became, and she found herself daring to open her eyes. Oddly enough, even in her dream her vision was blurry from crying with her contacts still in. With a practiced blink, she quickly removed her colored contact lenses, putting them without thought into the pocket of her jacket.

As her gaze focused, she realized right away that she was in terrible, terrible trouble, because this was not some harmless fantasy.

This was reality, hard and unbearably cruel.

With her body frozen, she stared up at Alex and died a thousand deaths as she drank in every inch of his face with a starved desperation, both terrified and elated.

No, this had to be some desperate fantasy her mind made up. There was no way she was in Alex's arms, on a brown leather couch in the middle of an enormous Mediterranean-style bedroom. It was merely a dream.

Trying to refuse the reality of her situation, she looked everywhere but at the man holding her. She'd dreamt of Alex more times than she could count, enough to quickly realize that the situation she was in right now was different from even her most vivid imaginings. She'd never have dreamed of an older Luka staring at her with such intensity that she almost became trapped by his mesmerizing hazel-green eyes.

The reality of her situation came crashing down around her as she stared at her old friend, barely breathing, her gaze locked with his. Luka had changed, his face harder than it used to be, his eyes blanker, and he had a stillness to his entire being that kind of freaked her out. Instantly her mind went to the most likely—and prayed for—explanation as to why she was here.

Hope filled her and her voice came out shaky as she said, "Luka, did Krom send for me? Is it safe?"

He gripped the back of the nearby brown leather chair he was standing next to, sagging as if she's slapped him, his full lips parting in shock. "What?"

At his baffled look, her heart plummeted. "Is it safe!? Krom said if it was safe he'd bring me back to Alex. Is. It. Safe?"

He couldn't have looked more puzzled, more shocked, if he'd tried. "I do not understand."

"He promised me," she near shouted, aware of Alex watching her as she lifted a little from his arms, unable to process him on any level at the moment and doing her best to ignore him entirely. "He promised he'd come get me when it was safe. He swore it! Is it safe?"

With a shaking hand, Luka ran his fingers through his thick light-brown hair. "*Eto piz `dets*, Krom does not remember anything from that night, no matter how hard he tries."

Her lower lip trembled and she hated how broken her voice sounded. "He forgot?"

"Yes, from being shot in the head. Jorg's men found him near the back of the house. He was near dead from blood loss." Luka shook his head repeatedly. "All this time he's been thinking he was responsible for your death, when he saved your life. I swear to you, Jessica, he didn't know that you weren't really dead. He would have moved heaven and hell to come for you, we all would have."

Another male voice captured her attention from across the room, one she'd desperately yearned to hear. "Jessica, sweet lass, we're so glad you're alive."

Her breath hitched in her chest as she slowly turned toward the sound of that familiar brogue. The sight of her uncle Peter had her blinking as fast as she could to try to keep her tears at bay. Her uncle had a lot more wrinkles than when she'd last seen him, and more white in his hair, but other than that he was still the robust man she remembered. He moved as if to come to her, but the arms gripping her tightened and the man she'd forbidden herself to think about growled that familiar growl.

Letting him go once had nearly destroyed her; letting him go twice would kill her, but she had no choice.

If nobody knew about her conversation with Krom, that meant she was breaking Mr. Novikov Sr.'s rules and it wasn't safe. She had to get out of here before Jorg found out she'd somehow stumbled onto Alex. A stinging sweat broke out over her skin, prickling and sensitizing as the compulsion to run filled her.

Panic had her heart thumping painfully as her frantic gaze darted around the room, not daring to look at the man who held her so securely yet meeting his gaze was too hard.

She couldn't.

If she looked into his haunting gray eyes again, she didn't know if she could be held responsible for her actions. His mere presence had her yearning for him so intensely that the thought of doing what she had to do was terrible, yet she couldn't let herself hesitate. Not with her daughter's life at stake.

She had to face him, but she couldn't make herself meet his gaze.

Staring at his chest, she closed her eyes as she shuddered and placed her hands on his shoulders, trying to keep herself from caressing all that hard muscle. "Alex, please release me. It is vitally important that I leave as soon as possible, with as few people as possible ever knowing I was here."

"Leave? *Nyet*."

That one word held so much anger, so much contempt wrapped up in pain, that she wanted to hide from him, knowing she deserved every bit of his disgust. "Alex, listen to me, if you ever loved me, if you ever loved our daughter—"

"You are *not* leaving me again, ever!" he growled, and she tried to push her way out of his arms, getting nowhere. "I forbid it!"

"I don't have time for this! You have to let me go before he knows I saw you." Finally she looked up and met his beloved eyes; hurt on a scale she couldn't even fathom weakening her until she sagged against him. Her voice came out in a broken murmur as she said, "He'll take her from me, Alex. Your father will take her and give her to one of his men to raise. I can't let that monster have her."

A hot flash of anger dissolved his sorrow in an instant, vaporizing it and leaving devastation in its wake. "Is that what he threatened you with? That he would steal our daughter and give her to someone else?"

She clasped her hands over her mouth, then lifted them enough to speak, her lips trembling against her fingertips. "Please don't say anything. He can't know I'm here. Please, he can't know. I stayed away from you, I did, please, if he finds out you must let him know that I didn't seek you out. *Please*!"

He closed his eyes and held her so tightly to him she could barely breathe. "I will kill him for this, for how he has destroyed our lives, for doing this to us."

"Alex—" her uncle Peter murmured from behind her.

"Out," Alex snarled.

"But—"

"Everyone get out. I allowed you to speak to her, and I will now put a bullet in the heart of any man stupid enough to be here in thirty seconds."

The door slammed not long after that, leaving her alone with him.

A rush of adrenaline gave her the strength to push out of his arms, and she stumbled as she rolled off the sofa then stood on her high heels. For the first time, she gave the room a good look, vaguely noting the fabulous view of the water and the cathedral ceiling. To think how excited she'd been on the drive up the long, winding drive that led to this fantastic palatial residence; how eager she'd been to start a new phase of her life in this veritable palace that Tatiana would adore.

Alex's voice was positively feral as he nearly snarled, "Jessica, come here."

The hair on her arms stood up and she backed away from her husband as quickly as she could in her heels, sensing the rising danger radiating from him like a blast furnace. No, she had to make him see sense. If he understood the situation, he'd let her go. "Alex, please, you can't protect me from him! He can find me anywhere, take me at any time, and nothing will stop him."

He let out a roar that she swore shook the windows and scared the hell out of her. This was not the same man she'd married. The pissed-off male standing before her was a stranger, a frightening one at that. Deep down she knew he would never hurt her, but the fire in his eyes was no longer sane. Something had broken inside of him and at this moment, she didn't recognize the cold, hard man coming at her like an enraged bull. The sunlight caught the silver in his temples as he stalked past a bay of windows and she took another shaky step backwards, almost stumbling when her heel hit the edge of a throw rug.

She held out a shaking hand. "Stay away from me!"

"Never."

When he was almost on her, she reached out and snatched a slender crystal vase that held a single orchid before smashing it against the dark wood table it had stood on.

Holding the razor-sharp glass before her, she brandished it in Alex's direction while shaking so hard she could barely maintain her grip. "Don't you understand? I will kill anyone, even you, to protect her. Please don't make me hurt you, I wouldn't survive it."

He strode forward so swiftly she almost accidentally impaled him, only flinging the vase away at the last second. The moment his lips crashed down on hers, he robbed her of all rational thought, of the ability to do anything but feel the brush of his beard against her face, revel in the caress of the lips she worshiped, and taste him on her tongue. God, he tasted just like she remembered. No, almost the same, but richer.

Better.

Once again her tears fell, but this time the salt bathed their lips and Alex let out a low, tortured moan that tore at her, lending a desperation to their embrace that sent spirals of arousal through her. Urgently she ran her hands over him, touching every part she could as he did the same, their movements rushed and jerky.

She damned herself for being weak even as she clung to him.

With the last of her willpower, she managed to break their kiss but couldn't make her arms release him. "Please don't make me decide between you."

"Jessica, listen to me very carefully." His accent thickened with his raspy words. "Jorg was the one who gave Peter information on you. I do not know what happened that night, and we will discuss, but right now I need you to understand you have nothing to fear from my father."

"What are you talking about?"

She sagged against him, desperately searching his face, her mind pinging over the differences between how he looked now and how she remembered him. The shiny scar going from his cheek to his upper lip was the first thing, a token left behind by Jorg's torture master. Hatred flared deep in her gut as she reached up and trailed her trembling fingers over his scar, the visible reminder of his suffering tearing at her already shaky hold on herself. It was all she could do not to break down into hysterics as she tried to process his words.

His voice lowered to a soothing croon while he crouched down a little bit, the thick muscles of his thighs straining the fabric. "I do not understand yet what exactly has happened, but my father, for his own insane reasons, must have decided it was time for me to know. And of course he went about giving me the information in the worst way possible. Knowing that he watched me suffer and did nothing..."

Rage like she'd never experienced trembled in the back of her mind as the ramifications of what he'd just said sunk into her.

She wondered how hard it would be to gain access to Jorg Novikov so she could shoot him in the head.

It was a violent, tempting thought and she realized that maybe she wasn't handling this all too well. In fact, little black dots began to dance around the edges of her vision as her heart continued to race. The fabric of his suit jacket began to fade beneath her fingertips as numbness tingled through her extremities. She'd gone into emotional overload and knew if she didn't snap out of it, she'd soon have a panic attack.

It took a great deal of effort, but she managed to jerk her gaze back up to Alex, seeking something to hold on to before her rational mind went on vacation. It had been almost a year since her last panic attack; she'd gotten them occasionally after the kidnapping by Jorg's goons, and she'd been hopeful those episodes were over. Instead a harsh sweat stung her skin and she began to pant.

Alex grasped her face between his calloused hands and forced her to meet his gaze, easily trapping her with his natural dominance that had only increased during their years apart. "*Dorogoya*, he will never hurt you again. I swear it."

The fierce desire to believe him battled with her need to protect Tatiana.

She forced her lips to form words she could barely whisper. "But what about the rest of the world, Alex? The Curse..."

"The Curse is no more."

She startled. "How is that possible?"

"With much work and help, we made it happen. Though you were already lost to me, I did it for my brother and sister-in-law. Dimitri has married an American girl, Rya. He loves his wife the way I love you. I did everything I could to help guard their love. She is so protected not even someone suicidal would try to hurt her, and they are very happy together. The Boldin women are safe as well. We have strong truce. Your...death helped to bring peace to the Novikov and Boldin *Bratvas*."

She'd read something about Dimitri being engaged, but at that point she'd been trying to break her habit of checking up on the Novikov men and hadn't allowed herself to research it any further.

The gentle tone of his voice seduced her and she fought his hold, trying to remember the millions of excuses to stay away from him that were as fragile as spider's silk in a hurricane. She had to remember that her wants came second to her daughter's safety. By not running as fast and far as she could, she might be betraying Tatiana. Yes, they might be safe from Jorg—though she doubted it—but Alex's life was filled with danger. When it came down to it, he was a crime lord and she'd be bringing her daughter into a world where she would be in constant peril.

The thought of anyone harming her bright, loving little girl made her stomach clench in a sour ball. Taking a deep breath, she forced herself to go against her natural inclination to give in to Alex's desires and instead challenge him with the truth. She wasn't some twenty-year-old girl anymore, dazzled by her husband's overwhelming charisma. She was a woman who'd vowed never to be a naïve, trusting little fool again.

"Rya, she's under constant guard, like I was, right? I'd bet her life is so hazardous that she can't go to the store without her own security detail." The way his lips tightened confirmed her suspicions. "Alex, I can't raise our daughter in an environment like that.

Tatiana deserves to be free to just be a little girl. To have playmates as companions, not bodyguards. The moment the world knows she exists, she becomes a target."

The switch from a gentle, comforting Alex to a pissed-off man happened so fast, she got emotional whiplash from trying to follow his shifts in temper. "I could have *protected* you all those years ago if you'd simply come to me instead of running away. All you had to do was trust me to take care of you like I had sworn to do."

She jerked back, his words hitting her like a fist. The side of her leg bumped a chair as she regained her balance. When she stumbled, he took a step forward as if to steady her but she held her hand out and snarled, "Trust you? Seriously? You lied to me about everything, over and over again. And I betrayed you by saving our daughter's life? You have lost your mind."

He ran his hands through his still thick hair and began to pace. "You should have told me. I would never have allowed him to hurt you. Never."

"How could I? Alex, people were coming to kill me, they fucking shot Krom in the head and killed our guards. Even if your father hadn't contacted me, those men would still have come for me. I would still be dead."

"I could have protected you!" His voice turned anguished and her heart bled for his pain. "If you had just trusted me a little more, I would have destroyed *anyone* for you. Do you not understand? I would rather have died with you than lived without. No torture in the depths of Hell could compare to the pain of living without you at my side. You were dead to me, Jessica, and my heart died with you."

His words struck her right in the chest and she gasped at the pain in his hot silver eyes, in every line of his strong, scarred body. All the horror and agony he'd endured was displayed before her and she whimpered for him, torn apart by how much he hurt. Her body ached with guilt, and anger, and fear, all mixed up into a dizzying cocktail that left her thoughts scrambled. Right now her emotional side ruled and her stupid soft heart couldn't stand to see him suffering.

"I did have faith in you, and faith in Krom. He said he would come get me when it was safe, and I believed that he was working on a way to *make it* safe. Every day I prayed he would be there, I'd look for him in crowds and hope. I had to stop doing that because as the days passed and I never saw him, it...it hurt. Bad. I-I had difficulty dealing with knowing how much our deaths hurt you, all too aware that if I really tried I could probably find a way to contact you. But at what price? When your father had me kidnapped—"

"What?" Alex said in a low, deadly murmur.

A hitch in her breath stole her voice for a moment, but she forced herself to continue. "He had me kidnapped just to show me that he could, and to reinforce the consequences of what would happen if I returned to you. That...that bastard made me watch a tape of Oleg's daughter's funeral."

An anguished sound escaped him and he ran his hands into his hair again, this time gripping it with his fists.

"Fuck!" His snarl startled her and she flinched, and he grit his teeth. Closing his eyes, he breathed hard enough that his nostrils flared with each deep inhalation.

Knowing he was on the edge of losing it entirely, she quickly said, "They didn't hurt me, at all, just scared me."

Hands trembling, he visibly struggled to control himself. "I failed you."

She ducked her head and tried to keep her cool so she didn't burst into hysterical tears of sorrow and guilt. Misplaced or not, she couldn't help but hate knowing that she was responsible for so much grief, so much agony. But even as guilty as she felt, the alternative would have been to have Jorg steal Tatiana from her in the middle of the night like some gruesome troll from an old fairy tale.

"No, no you didn't, not at all." Desperately, she tried to make him understand why she went along with his father's scheming. "If I had stayed, thousands of people would have died, Alex."

Before he closed his eyes, she watched him struggle to hold back tears. The sight of her proud man so exposed, so raw, was for no one but her. He was giving her a gift by showing his open vulnerability and she understood that, understood a lot of things about her husband that had been a mystery to her before. Now she treasured the intimacy of this moment, fully appreciating it and realizing what an honor it was that he sought comfort from her.

She closed the distance between them then stroked his face gently and he turned into her touch, his eyes closed so tightly the faint lines around them had deepened into crevices. When he whispered her name, it was filled with a heartbreaking mixture of love and sorrow.

She was scarcely aware of her surroundings, could have been in the middle of a circus and the only thing she would be able to see was Alex. The entire situation was so surreal, and her mind was beginning to sort out the convoluted events that led to this moment, but she was still confused. First she needed to hear again what an evil, manipulative, powerful genius Alex's father was. If she was thinking right, he'd played her with ease. Knowing just what to say to her younger self to make her flee, how to pray on her fears and weaknesses.

"You left me," he murmured, his voice breaking.

"I didn't want to leave you, it almost killed me, but your father made me believe some terrible things would happen if I stayed. I can't understand why he gave you the information on me when he worked so hard to keep me from ever going back to you. It just doesn't make sense." Her breath hitched. "Why would he do this to us? Alex? Why? I never did anything to that man to justify this cruel game he's played with our lives. How could he be so brutal? How could he deny Tatiana her father? And me my husband? Who the hell does he think he is?!"

He cupped her face in his rough hands as she fought back her tears and drank in the harsh, masculine beauty of his face. Right away she noted the scars that had been added to his handsome visage while they'd been apart, the worry lines. Even his gaze was duller beneath the anger and she longed for those gray depths to glow like they used to when he'd look at her. The memory of meeting all those years ago in her uncle Peter's bar swamped her, and her breath hitched again and a tear spilled down her cheek.

"Alex. I've missed you so much."

"*Eto piz`dets.*" He let out a low sigh and again closed his eyes, hiding his emotions from her. "You need to know that you are never leaving me. Ever. And neither is our daughter. We will be the family we are meant to be."

She jolted and a small burst of adrenaline went through her. Right now Tatiana was vulnerable back in the States with just her nanny, Gwen, and a good security system to protect them. All too easily she could imagine a group of thugs sneaking their way up to the house, ready to kidnap or kill the vibrant and loving little girl. The need to physically hold Tatiana consumed her and she grasped the edges of Alex's jacket, her worry evident in her voice. "Alex, we have to get Tatiana! We can't leave her alone."

"She is safe, I already have men loyal to me guarding her, unseen, and Krom is on his way to retrieve her." His jaw clenched and his body tensed as well. "Besides, you were never alone. My father had men watching you. In the packet my father gave to Peter there were details from various security reports, including one where they had to stop a thief who had thought to target you."

She blinked rapidly. "A thief? I can't remember anyone trying to rob me."

"Of course you do not. Your bodyguards did their job and you were never aware of the danger."

The headache worsened and she pressed her fingertips to her forehead, trying to will it away. She'd been under so much stress lately and without fail, it triggered migraines. At first she'd been freaked out she had a tumor, it would be just her luck, but after extensive testing, her team of doctors had chalked it up to a hormonal shift that had happened after she gave birth. All she knew was that she had to get a grip on herself in a situation that she had utterly no control of.

Striving to find some way to mellow out, she took a seat on the deep couch and folded her shaking hands in her lap. It took two or three deep breaths, but by the time she'd regained her composure Alex had joined her, his warmth pressed up against her, distracting her in an entirely pleasant way.

He placed his large hands over hers, holding them beneath his strength. "I hate why they were there, but I am thankful they kept you safe, both of you, for me. You have no idea how overjoyed I am that you are here, really here, with me. *Prinsessa moya,* I thought you were lost to me forever."

Now *she* was the one closing her eyes against the terrible beauty of the moment, overcome with emotion as his pet name for her rolled off his tongue, the adoration in those two words suffusing her chest with a pressure that was at once painful and good. How she'd yearned for those words, for his touch, for his everything.

Instead of giving him a chance to speak, she merely lifted her face to his and he lowered his head, his lips passing gently over hers. He exhaled just as she inhaled and she gratefully took his breath into her, tasting him on every level when he licked along the lower curve of her lip. In less than three heartbeats she was ravenous for him, eagerly stroking his tongue with hers, trying to devour him while he hummed with pleasure against her lips.

Chapter 2

The taste of his wife exploded on his tongue, the crisp bite of apples mixed with a more sophisticated perfume teasing his senses. A low growl rumbled through him as he shoved her jacket off her shoulders then tore the thin silk of her shirt, stripping her as quickly as possible while she moaned into his mouth.

When his hands met the bare, smooth skin of her back, he paused for a moment, caressing the slender curve of her spine, the perfect sweep of her waist. Her nails dug into his pectoral muscles beneath his dress shirt as she sucked on his tongue then she shoved her skirt off without breaking their kiss. Greedy, she was so desperate for his touch that she silently screamed her need for him with every inch of her body. They tumbled back onto the wide leather sofa together, their movements hungry and rough.

For a moment he wondered if she'd been with anyone else, then decided he didn't care. None of that mattered. She was here now, and she was never leaving him again. He'd gladly die first and spare himself the agony of losing her twice. Those dark thoughts twisted their kiss and he narrowed his eyes at her when she broke away, panting, her wide blue eyes searching his face as that familiar blush heated her cheeks.

Her gaze darted away then back to him, timid and vulnerable. "You need to know my body has changed. I don't look the same as I did five years ago."

The shame and apprehension in her low voice put him on alert. "What has happened?"

His fears of some type of maiming or torture raced through his thoughts while she scooted so she sat next to him in a beautiful amethyst-lace panties and bra set.

The first thing he noticed was that her breasts were a little bit larger and her belly softer. His cock throbbed as he took in her new curves, the lushness of her hips, the adorable bump of her small pooch. She would never be considered buxom, but she had filled out into a woman better than he'd ever imagined. There were some silvery lines on her hips that hadn't been there before, and a few on her belly, but that was what being a mother sometimes did to a woman's body. *His* child had made those marks, and they didn't deter his interest in her one bit.

She made a nervous sound as her hands tried to cover the cute little roundness of her tummy. "We can turn off the lights if you like."

"*Ti tak velikolEpna*," he murmured, his gaze once again devouring her pale skin, the freckles that he so loved. "As if I would not gladly have you naked around me at all times. I used to think I imagined your beauty, that your loss had made everything better in my memory, but is untrue. You stun me with your exquisiteness. Give me privilege of pleasuring you, Jessica."

Her hands shook on her belly and he forced himself to look away from the bounty that was his. As he met her apprehensive gaze, he placed both of his hands on her abdomen, loving how soft she was now, imagining how it would feel to sink between her slender, yet shapely legs. Easing her back on the couch, he looked down at her and his heart did a hard thump at the mixture of joy and pain that filled him. When he lay atop her now, he did not risk bruising himself on her hipbones. This fuller body of hers was driving him mad.

Her hands twitched beneath his and he was drawn from his mental worship of her. She nervously chewed her lower lip and he became aware of how uncomfortable she as. In a way, her unsure reactions reminded him of when they were first together and learning each other. During those early days in Rome she'd needed a lot of verbal reassurance, so he tried that tactic again.

"I remember when this belly was round with my child." He leaned down and kissed along the side of her neck, unable to stop himself from licking and biting at the spot he knew made her aroused. "We will make it that way again."

"Alex—"

"Later, we will discuss all of that later. Now is time to fuck. I must feel you around me."

Her pupil's dilated just as her hips jerked up and he loved that she was still responsive to his look, his voice. His touch. Moving her hands to her sides on the soft cushions of the couch, he growled out, "Keep them there."

She nodded, her breath coming in short pants as a lovely blush suffused her chest. That had always fascinated him, the way her pale skin could reflect her desire. He leaned back and freed his cock from his pants, moved his shirt out of the way and gave his aching dick a quick stroke. Jessica made a decidedly hungry noise and reached for him, only to have him capture her hands. If she touched him he would explode, and he didn't intend to do that anywhere but inside of her.

"I said keep them there. Or I will secure you."

When he said that, he tightened his hands on her wrists, judging her reaction to the threat of bondage. He'd had enough time now that reality was finally setting in and he planned to handle things very carefully with Jessica. He had changed in their time apart and he could only hope that Jessica would embrace this new side of him that needed to own her pleasure, to give her so much she'd remember how good things were between them.

They had played with BDSM when they were together, but he'd done some things after her death that were so deep into edge play he hoped she never heard about it. He'd been desperate to feel something, anything other than emotional pain, and had gone through a phase where he'd needed the physical release of a good beating. He knew his craving to own her completely probably wasn't healthy, but the fact that he wasn't having a mental breakdown right now was a miracle.

Jessica licked her lips then purred, "Take me, Alex, any way you want. Tie me up, fuck me, spank me, anything. I need you, all of you."

His cock jerked, eager to be inside her pussy that was so wet he could smell it, the familiar tang of her arousal bringing back a surge of memories of their times together in the past.

Memories that had been as dead as his wife.

That thought staggered him to a momentary halt. His breath hitched and he closed his eyes to fight the burn of tears he would not shed. The sorrow he still carried inside of him refused to accept that she was alive, but his body knew she was here. He could smell her in the air, taste her on his lips. His fingers touched impossibly soft freckled skin and she had a slight tan. When he had enough control over himself to look at her again, he found her amazing tilted blue eyes staring back into his own with such intensity that it stole his breath. The familiar tingle racing along his skin sizzled along his nerves like an electric caress. Her gaze promised passion, heat, love, and the wild arousal that he only got from his wife made his balls draw up tight as his body shuddered.

Something inside of him snapped, some control he'd never lost with any other woman, and he tore her panties from her with a rough shout. The sight of her neatly trimmed auburn pubic hair made his cock jerk, and with a shaky hand, he stroked those dark-red curls, damp with her arousal. Her nipples puckered against the lace of her bra, tempting him. A shiver worked through her, raising goose bumps along her skin while the fading sunlight cast shadows over her mesmerizing curves.

Unable to resist her any longer, he fit the aching head of his shaft against her wet entrance, then began to slowly push in.

They both gasped and he had to force his eyes to stay open as her tight sheath surrounded him, squeezing him in the way only she could. It was so good that sensual fire wrapped around his spine, the urge to come already pushing at him. Jessica was the only woman who tested his control like this. She arched and rolled her hips into his, taking him all the way to the root and sobbing with pleasure. Knowing he wasn't going to last, he began to fuck her with a punishing rhythm, her cries as she swiftly came on his cock driving him wild.

She pulled him down for a kiss, sucking on his lips and tongue while she met him thrust for thrust, tears trailing down her cheeks even as she tightened around him again, her hands running over his shirt-clad back in a frantic manner. With a low growl he wrapped his arms around her and pulled her off the couch, then turned and sat with her astride.

With a cry of relief she slid down on his shaft, then rode him hard, their hips slapping together. The sight of her, his beloved wife, with her eyes closed and her head thrown back in ecstasy was too much for him. To his shame, tears fell down his scarred cheeks but he couldn't stop them any more than he could stop the earth from turning. His long-suppressed emotions burst free from his iron-willed control and he surrendered himself to her. When her sheath tightened around him again he didn't bother to try to hold back this time, instead clutching her as close to him as he could, her pussy sucking the cum right out of him with the tight, rippling contractions of her orgasm. Sublime contentment filled him and he couldn't help the relaxed grin lifting the corners of his mouth. Erotic bliss, pure and clean.

As the last of his climax left him, he managed to lift Jessica off his cock and onto the couch next to him. He then pulled her into his arms, her slight frame conforming to his while she panted against his neck. Sweat trickled down his temple and he rested his head back against the couch, his whole body surging with an electrical charge that made him feel reborn. Slowly, ever so slowly, his mind began to surface from the unthinking contentment that blanketed him and he opened his eyes, drinking in the sight of his lovely Jessica.

Fuck, his wife was alive and in his arms.

Up this close, the sight of her familiar freckles filled his vision and he let out a slow breath, then reached out and stroked his thumb over the high apple of her cheek.

"I missed you so much," she whispered as her tears wet his neck and the collar of his shirt. "I'm so sorry I left you. More sorry than you'll ever know. I thought Krom would come for me. I waited and waited for him to come for me."

The sorrow in her words brought his attention into razor-sharp focus, chasing away the lingering relief his release had brought him. His woman needed him; he could lose himself in her presence later. It didn't matter how crazy this situation was, or how much he was struggling to keep his volatile emotions under control, the pain in those words cleared his head. As he studied her face, he didn't like the guilt that lay over her like a heavy cloak so soon after the pleasure of her orgasm. Of course his sweet girl would feel like she was to blame, and his earlier outbursts hadn't helped the situation. It shamed him that he'd lashed out at her and he vowed to keep better control of his emotions.

She'd been so masterfully manipulated by his father that it was a wonder she was still sane.

"You humble me," he murmured before he brushed his lips over hers. "Bravest, most selfless woman I have ever met. So loving, your light warms everyone around you. I cannot tell you how cold and dark my world has been without you. You have nothing to be sorry for. Nothing."

"I felt dead inside." She reached out and clutched her hands in his hair, bringing their foreheads together while she whispered in a harsh voice, "Every minute of every day I ached because a piece of my heart was missing. If it wasn't for Tatiana I wouldn't have survived."

"I did not want to live," he admitted, and ran his hands over her. "If it wasn't for my brother and the people that needed me, I would have tried to join you in death."

"Oh Alex." She blinked back tears. "I'm so sorry."

"Do not be. It is not your fault, Jessica."

"If I had just..."

Hating his father more than ever, he placed his hand beneath her rounded little chin and met her red, swollen eyes. "You did what you were forced to do. You did what you had to do in order to save our daughter. Thank you, my brave, strong girl."

She began to cry again and he held her, wanting her to find some kind of relief in her tears. Burying his face in her soft hair, he whispered to her in Russian how much he loved her, all the things he'd yearned to have the chance to say. Over and over he confessed his utter fascination with her, his appreciation for her kind nature, his thankfulness for the difference she made in his life. Eventually she stopped crying and he took a deep breath, then rubbed his hands gently down her smooth, soft arms, needing to somehow ease her grief.

Almost right away she responded to his touch, her body relaxing against him as she took in a deep, watery breath. He leaned back, keeping her close so he could rest on one arm and pet her with the other. The way she moved into his touch with a liquid grace reminded him of a cat, and he made a note to introduce her to pet play. The mental image of her with a black leather collar with a bell on it, a pair of black cat ears, and a cat-tail butt plug made his dick twitch and he tried to banish it from his mind. Right now his woman needed comfort, not sex, and her needs would always come first. She took a deep breath again and slowly let it out, her body melting beneath his.

After a few moments she wrapped her arms around him, stroking her fingers through his hair with a dreamy expression. Energy seemed to spark between them as he leisurely cupped her breasts then leaned down and captured her mouth. Their tongues rubbed against each other and pleasure rolled through him in a strong wave, helping to push back the darkness clouding this moment. His cock ached like he hadn't just been buried inside of her and his craving for her grew with each beat of his heart.

With a low moan, she began to unbutton his shirt. By the time she got to the fourth button he'd tensed, and when she finished they were no longer kissing. The look she gave him was confused, but he reached up and cupped her chin, stroking her lips.

"*Prinsessa moya*, my body has changed as well. Prepare yourself."

"Prepare myself?" She frowned, the passion clearing from her gaze. "You're bigger than you were before—seriously, you put on like sixty pounds of pure muscle—and you're older, but you're still the sexist man I've ever seen."

He sat up then shrugged off his shirt then turned to face her fully, shoulders back, and he braced himself for her reaction.

"What...what..." She knelt before him where he sat on the couch, her hands frantically running over the thick mass of scars from the iron burn, the long slicing cuts done in neat lines down his abdominals, a new bullet wound, and various other testaments to violence that now decorated his body.

"I did not know of your...death until five days after the fact."

Confused, she looked up at him, searching his face. "What happened?"

"I will tell you, but not right now." She frowned, and he flashed back to how often he'd had to say that to her during their marriage and quickly amended his statement. "Not because I wish to hide it from you, but because I need to fuck you again. I understand why Maks does this now, why he is driven to seek the reassurance of sex. Nothing proves to me that you are alive more than to be buried deep inside of you, to feel your life."

After studying him for a long, tension-filled moment, she leaned forward and placed a gentle kiss to his chest over her name, her lips rubbing against the hair on his right pectoral. "You have some new tattoos."

Relief filled him as he realized Jessica wouldn't push him. He'd almost forgotten how generous her nature was, how just being around her was a balm to his broken soul. He took her hand in his own and ran it down his chest, her gaze following their fingers until they got to the roses. "This one is for you and Tatiana."

Her trembling fingertips traced the entwined roses over his heart, one in full bloom and one just a bud.

"Alex, it's beautiful. Thank you."

Leaning forward again, she placed a kiss over the tattoo, then slowly trailed her mouth over to his nipple and latched on, sucking hard and making his whole body seize. Just like that, she released the beast inside of him that had an endless craving for her. With a low growl, he wrapped his fist in her hair and pulled her head back, then captured her jaw with his hand and kissed the hell out of her. She responded with equal lust, their teeth clicking as they ate each other alive, her hands stroking him, even as he controlled her every move with the tight grip he had on her hair.

They broke apart long enough for Alex to kick off his shoes then pants and he fell back onto the couch, his cock so swollen with need that he was afraid that he would come the moment he was in her. With a deep exhalation that carried the edge of a growl, he pulled her up so she was straddling him and almost spurted when her soaking-wet, hot center rubbed over his shaft.

Before he could move, Jessica lifted enough to grab his dick then sank down on him, her body fighting his intrusion as they both gasped in unison.

"Look at me," he barked, and was rewarded with her glowing blue eyes, filled with lust, focusing hazily on his.

Gripping the edges of her bra, he jerked it down, freeing her breasts for his greedy mouth. The moment he took her nipple between his teeth she began to orgasm, with his cock not even halfway inside of her. The strong ripple of her inner muscles had him yelling out, then thrusting his hips up into her while she arched back, shoving her breast into his mouth. Hunger ripped through him and he grabbed her nipple and pinched it hard, his nostrils flaring as her pussy clenched on him. One more thrust and he was buried deep inside of her still-rippling sheath, each tweak of her nipple bringing a new shiver and moan.

She lay limp against him but he didn't care, more than ready to take what he wanted from his woman.

He pulled out then flipped them over so she was on her knees with her hands braced on the back of the couch, the colors of the sunset painting her skin in rose and gold, turning her into a creature of light.

She looked so ethereal, so sensual and feminine.

It made him want to defile her in the best possible ways.

With a grunt he slammed back into her, his balls drawing up tight as he fucked her through another orgasm. By now his body was slick with sweat and her hips bore red marks from his grip that would no doubt turn into bruises tomorrow. He loved that his marks would be on her and as he stared down at the gentle curve of her lower back, he wondered if he could talk her into getting a tattoo denoting his ownership on her, like Gia and Rya had for their men. He could see it now, his name in Cyrillic on the top curve of her left ass cheek.

Feeling savage, he slapped that creamy cheek hard, instantly rewarded with the sensation of his cock being milked.

"Do you like that?" he growled.

"Master," she whimpered and reared back at him.

The heat blasted down his spine and his balls tightened until he was slamming into her, his head thrown back and his body tensing hard enough that his muscles shook. For one long moment he hung suspended there, hovering on the verge of orgasm. Jessica's cry of release pushed him over into his own climax and he crashed down on top of her, his hips pumping mindlessly into her as he came and came, each release scouring him from the inside out. By the time the last shudder worked through him, a peace had sunk into his bones that left him exhausted.

After pulling gently out of her, he turned her unresisting body around. Jessica's makeup had smeared, her hair was a mess, and her face was puffy from crying, but he'd never seen anyone more beautiful. It took some effort, but eventually he stood and managed to stumble over to the phone. After talking with security, he made sure they would be undisturbed. No one was allowed in until late tomorrow morning. He didn't care if the world burned down; they were to be left alone because he wasn't sharing his wife with anyone. To get his point across, he let them know that he would geld anyone foolish enough to test him.

As soon as he was done Jessica gave a soft, sleepy laugh. "I forgot how scary you can sound when you come."

His heart thumped hard. "You fear me?"

She blinked at him. "Of course not. You'd never hurt me."

Seeing that she meant that, he made his way back across the room to her, then picked her up in his arms by the hips so she was suspended above him. Laughing softly, she looked down at him, her hair falling forward in a dark curtain around his face as he slowly lowered her. "Glad you told everyone to leave us alone, though threatening to cut their balls off was a bit extreme."

He frowned, sure he'd spoken in Russian on the phone. "How did you know what I said?"

Her plump, warm lips pressed against his neck as she whispered, "I learned how to speak passable Russian with a private tutor. After spending all that time with you and your men, I'd picked up a lot of it already so it wasn't that hard to figure out."

"Why?"

He was carrying her out of the sitting area now but he scarcely noticed, too busy staring at her, drinking in her beauty. He almost didn't want to blink just in case this was some come kind of intense dream brought on by one of his drinking binges. Unable to help himself, he paused for a moment to lift her closer so he could give her a slow, lingering kiss that brought him a bone-deep satisfaction.

Her voice was breathy when he broke their kiss, then continued walking. "Why what?"

"Why did you wish to learn Russian?"

Her nails dug lightly into his back and she looked away. "I wanted Tatiana to know her heritage. I hoped that someday, maybe, Krom would come for us and I wanted her to be ready. I wanted to be able to talk to you in your own language, to tell you *ya lyublyu tyebya fsyei dushoj.*"

The sorrow in her voice as she told him that she loved him with all of her soul in Russian tore at him. He somehow managed to keep his emotions in check while he took them into the bathroom together, determined to be strong for his woman. They were silent as they both washed up and Alex left first to get his bed ready for them. Jessica had always loved it when he turned down the covers for her then tucked them both in. His hands shook as he tossed decorative pillows into the corner, then drew back the thick pale-green and beige comforter and cream sheets. By the time he was done, Jessica had wandered into the bedroom, watching him as she meandered and explored. The simple sight of her towel-drying her hair entranced him.

"There's not much of you here," she murmured while examining a blue glass vase that complimented the dark waves beyond the floor-to-ceiling windows. "It looks like a bedroom you'd see in some magazine spread."

Despite their perfect view, no one could see into the house thanks to the special coating on the windows, so he kept the curtains back, letting the last of the setting sun illuminate her beauty. As soon as they got back to Russia, he was going to have an appointment made with the best colorist in Moscow to return her dark hair to its former burning glory. When she raised her eyebrows at him while returning the vase to its spot on the dresser, he realized she'd made a comment.

"No, there is not much of me here. It is merely place to sleep. Not my home."

She paused in her examination, her gaze focused on the pale wood floors before she closed her eyes. "Where is home?"

"I have not had a home in five years."

She swallowed hard, twice, before bracing her hand on the wall for a moment. "I'm so sorry."

Growling deep in his throat, he snapped his fingers and pointed to the bed. "Here, now."

When she looked up there was an indignant cast to her refined features. "Pardon me?"

"You heard me. I want you in our bed, now."

Her little huff of annoyance eased something deep inside of him and his rusty sense of humor began to reawaken.

When Jessica had been gone from his life, his emotions had faded away until it seemed as if he only felt the shallow ghost of feelings. Well...all feelings except anger. His rage had rushed in to fill those empty spaces left by the loss of his family. Now his chest ached with the reemergence of tenderness, of the need to be gentle and loving with his woman. Yes, he'd cuddled his submissives, but never because he particularly desired to. He did it because it was what they wanted and he needed their bodies and submission to remind himself that he was alive.

His wife's breathing grew shallow while she slowly slipped nude into the bed, and she lay flat on her back, staring at the ceiling with her hands clasped on her chest. Letting his instincts guide him, he turned out the lights then joined her in bed and lay on his side facing her, propping his head up on his hand so he could see her clearly. Her eyes were closed, and her lower lip trembled as she held back tears.

Part of him knew his tenderhearted girl cried when her emotions became too strong, but he hated seeing her struggle.

"Jessica," he whispered before placing gentle kisses all over her face, worshiping her with his touch. "What has made you so sad?"

"Not sad, stressed." She took a hitching breath, which came out in a rough laugh that made him wince. "Well, let's see, I want to kill your father, like really kill him, and I'm trying to talk myself out of it. Then there is the thought of how I'm going to tell my family in the States I'm alive, or if that would just endanger them, along with Tatiana's safety and how to ease her into her new life. And I'm not even going to go into my feelings regarding you."

"What feelings?"

Her mouth snapped shut and in the dim lighting coming from an outdoor porch light below his windows he studied her exquisite profile. In the shadows she looked the same as he remembered and he couldn't stop himself from tracing his fingers down her throat, over her racing pulse. She still refused to look at him, but turned her body enough to rub her cheek against his chest.

"I used to wonder if I imagined how good things were between us, if I'd somehow tricked myself into seeing an idealized image of our relationship. Living with you was so intense, so passionate. I enjoyed every moment of it because I got to share my life with you. Now I'm back with you and it scares the hell of me to know the truth."

"What truth would that be, *dorogoya*?"

"Being with you is even better than I remembered, and I underestimated how damn sexy you are," she muttered against his throat.

He couldn't help but laugh at how disgruntled she sounded. "This is bad?"

"No, not really. Just annoying because I'm helpless to resist you." She sighed, then snuggled closer, curving into him in a way that had him closing his eyes so he could savor this moment. "No more talking. I really need to sleep."

The soft scent of her perfume filled him as her breath warmed his skin. She gave him a little hip wiggle followed by a soft sigh, and soon settled down. She wrapped her arms around his biceps, drawing him closer until he was practically on top of her. Once he was positioned to her liking, she slowly softened beneath him, her exhausted body falling into a deep sleep.

For a long time Alex stayed awake, planning, plotting, and savoring the joy of his wife cradled safely in his arms.

Chapter 3

A loud pounding on the door roused Jessica from a deep sleep and a man grunted next to her. She turned then buried her face against the warmth of his wide back, cuddling into a body she knew as well as her own. With a smile, she placed a kiss on the smooth skin over his spine, the smile growing bigger when he groaned and stretched as she continued to rain kisses on him. Disbelief raced through her that he was really here in bed with her, but before she could decide if she wanted to ride him until he was speaking in tongues, or have him pound her into the mattress, a knock on the door again interrupted her.

Alex grabbed her hand that was on his ribs and pulled it closer so she was holding him as he shouted out in Russian, "Unless the world is burning down, fuck off."

There was a few seconds of silence, then the knocking came again.

Jessica and Alex both rolled out of bed on a sharp indrawn breaths then grabbed some clothing. She quickly dug through her luggage, absently wondering why it looked like someone had put a huge hole in the dry wall, then donned her gray stretch pants and a black silk t-shirt that partially slid off one shoulder. Not even bothering to put on a bra, she shoved her arms through the shirt while attempting to follow Alex to the door. Clad in only a pair of black trousers that hung low on his heavily muscled hips and lower abdominals, he turned and faced her, his body broad enough to completely block the door.

She bounced off his chest, totally not ready for him to stop her. Before she could lose her footing, he caught her gently. "Jessica, stay here."

"What?" She frowned as someone took a heavy fist to the door. "No, I want to know what's going on."

"No, you stay here. We do not know who is there, what is intention."

"Alex—"

With a gentle move, he set her away from him, deeper into the room. "Please, for me. Stay safe. Trust me."

There was a fine tremor going through his large frame that made her bite her tongue, then nod stiffly. "I'm trying."

His eyes tightened with pain and she wanted to apologize, to take the words back, but he was already shutting the door.

When she pressed her ear to the wood and the crack around the frame, she couldn't hear anything and sighed. Damn well-built homes with their solid wood doors. Nervous energy filled her as her mind raced through all the awful things that could have happened. There was no such thing as a worst case scenario anymore; her overactive imagination liked to outdo itself with terrible images of death and destruction. By the time Alex returned, on the phone with someone, she was pacing the large room in an effort to work off some of the adrenaline spiking through her blood.

She searched his face as soon as he looked at her, and his grim expression made her freeze mid-stride.

"I understand," Alex said in Russian. "We will be there as soon as possible."

He spoke for another minute or so, brief words that told her nothing, before thanking the person on the phone and asking whoever it was to give Dimitri's love to the stranger's family then hanging up.

Tossing the phone onto his unmade bed, he quickly crossed the room before hauling her into his arms and squeezing her tight.

"Alex? What's going on?"

His warm breath stirred her hair as he spoke. "We must return to Russia as soon as possible."

His strong arms flexed around her, the muscles tightening as she ran her hands over his biceps, unable to be near him without touching him, absorbing his heat. "Why?"

"There is a delicate situation happening within the *Bratvas* that I must attend to."

"Does it have anything to do with me and Tatiana?"

The corner of his mouth twitched. "Not directly."

She sagged against him, realizing he wasn't going to share. Damn him. Back when she still held out hope that Krom would come for them, she'd sworn to herself that when she reunited with Alex, their relationship would be different. That he would treat her like an equal. Instead he was still doing that "because I said so" bullshit that irritated the hell out of her.

"Stop with this double-talk crap and tell me the truth."

"Is truth. The situation indirectly impacts you because of association with me, not because direct threat to you." He sighed, his big body slumping into hers. "Is not good."

"Then what's going on? I don't need all the details, but tell me something. Please."

He cupped her face and stroked her cheeks with his thumbs. "My uncle Petrov has summoned me."

Petrov Dubinski, a very nice man who adored his nephew, and the head of what was rumored to maybe be the most powerful *Bratva* in Russia. They'd never met, but his wife and daughters had attended her wedding. From what she could remember, they were nice women who clearly adored Alex and Dimitri. During their time apart, she'd read up on the various Russian mafias and the men who ruled them. Petrov Dubinski was a living legend in the criminal world. He was ruthless, terrifying, but inspired a great deal of loyalty and even love among his people. The Dubinski *Bratva* was linked to the Novikovs' by marriage; one of Petrov's sisters was Alex's mother.

All these thoughts raced through her mind as she gripped his shoulders. "Your uncle summoning you…is this bad?"

"I do not know. My uncle would not reveal what he wanted to discuss, only that needs me. He apologized for interrupting our reunion and asked me to tell you that he will make it up to you, and that he would also like to meet you as soon as possible."

"Why?"

Darkness filled his gaze, an endless pit of emptiness that chilled her. "Because he was there for me when I thought I had lost you and my daughter. He was one of the people who gave me the unwavering support I needed. We spent many, many nights talking about you together."

"Oh."

A stillness filled him as he stared at her, and she sucked in a trembling breath, undone by the open pain in his gaze. "Did you think about me while we were apart?"

It took all of her strength to tell him the truth. They couldn't start their relationship again built on lies. No, she would be honest with him, even if it hurt to admit what she'd had to do in order to survive. "At first I did constantly, every moment of every day, but as the years went on with no word from Krom, I-I tried not to. I tried to pretend you didn't exist."

The pain in his gaze doubled and his whole body sagged. "Why?"

"Because it killed me to see you on the Internet and know that I would be sacrificing our daughter's safety if I ever approached you. I yearned for you, Alex, my entire being mourned without you. Holding on to hope year after year was beginning to destroy me, mentally and physically. Did you know that I'm on two different kinds of anti-depressants? I don't take them to feel good or get high. I have to take them in order to be able to function like a normal human being. My loss of you was so great that it was destroying me. The only way I could be the kind of mother Tatiana deserved was to cut you out of my thoughts as much as I could. And seeing you with all of those women...I used to throw up when I saw an image of you kissing one of them." She sucked in a gasp and couldn't believe she'd just decided to let it all hang out.

One of the things she'd regretted over the years was not being upfront about her needs and emotions. Including her now irrational, raging jealousy. He studied her closely, and she inwardly sighed when she saw the familiar wall in his gaze, the one that blanked out all emotions. Despite the slightly bored look on his face, his attention on her had sharpened to the point where it felt like a touch as he slowly examined her. Then he took a step closer and cupped her neck with his large hands, his thumbs slowly stroking her jaw.

"I understand why you needed to protect your mind from the loss. Many times I tried to forget you as well, to move on as my friends and family were begging me to, but I could not. Even when you were dead and all hope was lost, I never stopped loving you and only you. *Prinsessa moya*, do not doubt for a moment that I would not have given anything,

anything to just have one more minute in your presence." His voice thickened and her eyes stung with tears. "I will treat every moment I have with you like it is precious, because it is. Those women served a physical need, my emotions were never involved. They were all aware of this, and fine with it for their own personal reasons. Until I held you in my arms mere hours ago, I thought I was still a widower, and always would be."

"Damn it," she grumbled in a choked voice, "I'm mad at you. Why do you have to make sense? It's hard to argue with you when you're being all logical."

"So you would rather fight with me?"

"Yes—no, I don't know! You make me crazy."

Sighing, he gently kissed her lips. "I missed your temper."

"I think you need to see a psychiatrist."

"I missed the way you like to verbally lash me."

"Now I'm wondering if you're an emotional masochist."

"Your body gets hot when you are angry. Is easy to redirect that energy."

"What in the hell—"

Her protest abruptly cut off as he palmed her breast, teasing the already erect nipple with his thumb. Little stinging tingles of pleasure radiated down to her clit when he pinched it, hard. Her gasp was swallowed by his hungry kiss and he caressed her tongue with his own, inviting her to play. Unable to resist him, she threaded her fingers through his hair, drinking him in as he broke their kiss to bite the side of her neck. Another rush of painful tingles seared through her and she moaned, rubbing her hips against his.

"I remember everything about how to pleasure you. Even when my memory of what our bedroom in Ireland looked like had faded, I still knew every inch of you like I had just held you in my arms."

He bit her again, deeper this time, and she cried out as he sucked on the spot hard enough to sting. Wrapping her fingers in his hair, she tried to tug him off, but he was like some predator intent on devouring her and refused to budge. Only when she had what she was sure was a world class hickey on her neck did he pull back. She was ready to scold him, but the feral look in his eyes made her knees weak.

"I do not care if you were with a thousand men while we were apart—"

"I wasn't with anyone else, ever."

That seemed to throw him. "Not once?"

"Never. While you believed you were widowed, I was always still married to you in my heart and mind."

Closing his eyes, he rested his forehead against hers. "I do not deserve you."

Tired of the constant emotional fireworks between them, she rubbed her nose against his. "No, you don't. You're lucky I let you hang around."

His shoulders straightened and he seemed to grow bigger as he wrapped one large fist in her hair, tilting her head back enough that it strained her neck. An immediate burst of arousal struck her and she automatically arched into his touch. She remembered he liked it when she did that and melted inside when he gave her a pleased smile. Their eyes met and the strong, no-nonsense Master she knew so well gave her a very possessive look.

"This," he stroked her neck where he'd sucked with a rough fingertip, chills skating down her spine, "will show everyone who looks that you belong to me."

She stiffened. "I can't let Tatiana see a giant hickey. She'll think I've been hurt and it will upset her."

His grip on her hair loosened and warmth flooded his expression like nothing she'd ever seen. "Do you think she will like me? I will not scare her?"

The insecurity in his voice drove her to soothe him and she ran her palm over his bristly cheek. "Of course she'll like you. She is such a happy little girl and loves almost everyone she meets. I mean she's still a four-year-old, so there are the usual tantrums and drama that you'll have with any little kids, but I'm sure she'll have you wrapped around her little finger in no time."

Their embrace turned gentle again and she felt as if she was riding waves with Alex, one moment cresting with anger and hurt, the next rocking together in absolute bliss.

Dimly, the ringing of her phone came to her, the song she'd assigned Gwen filling the air. "Shit! Gwen!"

He released her and she dove across the room, fumbling through her bag until she got to her phone. "Gwen?"

Her nanny and best friend's voice came shouting through the speaker. "What the hell is going on, Jessica?"

"Gwen, wha—"

The pissed-off woman continued on like she hadn't even spoken. "It's the butt crack of dawn am I have a giant scary dude who says his name is Krom—what kind of name is that?—sitting at the kitchen table telling me he's come to take me and Tatiana to meet you and your *husband* in Russia."

"Where's Tatiana?"

"She's fine, sleeping safe and sound, but I'm about five seconds away from shooting the asshole glaring at me."

Sighing, she rubbed her forehead. "Gwen, put the gun away. Krom is there to help you. It's all very complicated, but I need you not to shoot him please. He's there to protect you and he can't do that if he's dead."

Gwen was silent for a moment. "Protect us? From what? Jessica, this is really fucked up. Are you sure you're okay? Do I need to call the police?"

"No!" She took a deep breath and continued in a calmer voice, "No. I need you to do exactly what Krom says and help get Tatiana to Russia as quickly as possible. This is very important, honey, you have to trust me, please. I promise I'll explain everything once I see you in person."

"Are we in danger?"

"No—well, yes. I can't have this conversation with you on the phone."

Krom's deep voice came from the background and Gwen snapped, "No one asked you, Wolverine, for your opinion. You go back to just sitting there and looking scary. And stop scowling at me. Didn't your mother ever teach you that your face would freeze that way?"

"Gwen," Jessica groaned. "Please don't give him attitude."

"Tell him to stop being such a dick and I won't have to."

Someone pounded on the door to Alex and Jessica's room, then yelled in Russian, "The helicopter is here."

Alex looked up from where he was texting into his phone. "Come, Jessica, we have long travel day ahead of us and must go."

"Crap. Gwen, I have to go. I'm so so sorry about all of this and I promise I'll explain everything to you when you arrive. I know that's lame, and you don't have to come if you don't want to, but—"

The stubborn streak Jessica knew so well filled Gwen's voice, "Oh, I'm coming. Do you think I'd send *mi flora* off with a group of strangers? No way in Hell."

"Thank you, sweetheart. I owe you big time."

"Yeah, you sure as heck do."

She hung up the phone and sprinted to her suitcase, digging through it until she found a bra and a decorative silvery-blue scarf trimmed with lace. After putting her bra on and wrapping the scarf around her neck, she turned to go find Alex, only to run right into him.

She met his gaze and her pulse fluttered at the stern look he was giving her. With very deliberate, tight gestures, he unwound the scarf from her neck.

"Do not cover my mark."

Sure her cheeks were bright red, she tried cover the hickey again, but he wouldn't allow it. "Alex, I can't parade around with a love bite on my neck!"

"You do not wear my ring or my collar," he growled. "No man will look at you without knowing you are taken, that you are mine. I must have this, Jessica."

She blinked at him and hesitated. "I don't want people to think I'm a slut."

He closed his eyes, and to her surprise, laughed before opening them again. "You came back from dead; I do not think my mark as big of deal."

The absurdity of the situation made her lips twitch, but she didn't fight Alex when he tossed the scarf to the floor. "We must leave now."

She slipped on her ballet flats then glanced at her luggage. "What about my stuff?"

"Personal shopper has already stocked closet for you at our home."

"Um—okay."

Before she could question him further, they were out in the hallway where Luka and Maks waited for them, with two more unfamiliar people. The guy blended in with the rest of Alex's bodyguards—big and scary—but it was the woman who caught her attention. Built like an Amazon, the female bodyguard had to be close to six feet tall and she was all muscles and curves. With her black hair, blue eyes, and no-bullshit attitude, she kind of reminded Jessica of Wonder Woman.

Maks and Luka just stared at Jessica, clearly not listening to Alex as he gave them instructions in Russian.

Her heart ached at the pain in her friends' gazes and she tugged away from Alex then stood a pace away. What if they didn't want her to touch them? What if they were mad at her that she'd followed along with Jorg's wishes and hated her?

Lifting a hesitant hand in their direction, she said, "Can I have a hug, please?"

She didn't even have a chance to draw a breath before she was enveloped by both of them, Luka pressing his face to one side of her head, Maks to the other. The men shook against her and she dimly heard Alex telling the other two guards to wait for them outside. Maks trembled against her back and Luka gripped her tight enough that she was struggling to draw a breath.

Thumping on his thigh, she said, "Hey, fragile human here. You two behemoths are going to squish me."

Right away Luka's grip loosened, but he didn't step away. Maks had every inch of his body pressing into hers, and she was trying to ignore the fact that he was becoming aroused. She'd expected this reaction from him, given their past history, but it still made her uncomfortable—and if she was being honest, turned on. She couldn't help it; he was a very good-looking man who she knew was great in bed, but his feelings for her went beyond friendship. Feelings she could never return.

Not wanting to tempt Maks with what he couldn't have, she gently stepped away from them, brushing back tears.

"I missed you guys, so much."

Maks gripped her by the back of the head and laid a kiss on her before she was even aware he'd moved. It was a brief kiss, but his erection now pressed into her as he groaned against her lips. Before she could twitch to push him away, Luka had her face cradled gently in his big hands. She studied the new scars that gave his handsome face a dangerous cast and wondered how he'd gotten them.

Maks was still at her back, but she ignored him as she nuzzled her face against Luka's big hand, something she used to do when she was trying to be cute and get her way with him.

His voice came out rough, like boulders sliding against each other, as he said, "I thought I had failed you."

Meeting his gaze, she held it and allowed him to see the truth of her words. "No, you didn't. None of you failed me. I'm here, I'm alive, and I'm so happy to see you again."

The large man sagged forward and if Maks hadn't been bracing her body, she probably would have staggered beneath his weight. Luka was a big, solid man but he seemed unable to stand on his own for a moment. The sight of her proud friend struggling to deal with his intense emotions sent her into mother mode. She'd forgotten how much she enjoyed taking care of these men in her own way, how much she'd loved their company. They were her constant companions, friends many times over bonded together through tense situations and just hanging out together. She'd missed coffee with Maks, going to clubs with Luka, and shopping with Oleg.

Not to mention the loss of Catrin and Nico, two people who had become family to her.

The list of people who Jorg Novikov had stolen from her mounted by the moment, and she asked God to forgive her for wishing to end his evil life.

Scraping herself together, she gave them each a hard hug before returning to Alex's side. The proud look in his deep gray eyes warmed her from within and she had to look down to hide her smile. Part of her argued that she shouldn't fall back into her old habits of living to please Alex, but she couldn't help how making him happy made her feel fulfilled. Maybe it was just part of who she was, something she couldn't change that had been hardwired into her DNA. At this point in her life, she was old enough to acknowledge that she had a taste for submission, that she loved taking care of a powerful man.

Holding out his hand, a look of open relief briefly flitted across his handsome, scarred face before she slipped her hand in his. Right away he raised her knuckles to his lips and kissed her fingertips softly. The scruff of his beard brushed against her skin, reminding her of how it felt against more delicate areas of her body, and she couldn't help her besotted-sounding sigh.

The men chuckled behind her, while Alex gave her a roguish wink. "Is good to know I have not lost my touch."

Rolling her eyes, she was about to make a good comeback when the door at the end of the hall burst open. The Wonder Woman-looking chick yelled out in Russian, "We have uninvited guests on their way, ETA fifteen minutes. We need to leave, Mr. Novikov, now. Plan Green has been engaged."

Panic froze Jessica in place but Alex never even paused, simply scooped her limp form into his arms and practically sprinted down the hallway. The world blurred by in a rush of bodyguards swarming the building and guns everywhere. She clutched Alex's jacket and shivered, her nightmares coming true already. Jorg must be behind this somehow, testing her, punishing her for seeing Alex again. The thought made no sense, but her default mode was to fear her father-in-law, greatly.

Bright sunlight blinded her as they moved out onto the helicopter pad/gigantic terrace. Men surrounded it while more seemed to be checking the chopper over. With her heart in her throat, she noticed a black helicopter with what looked like fucking missiles hovering not far away. Her scream was lost in the whine of blades and then she was practically thrown into the plush backseat of some crazy-luxurious corporate helicopter. Alex lunged in after her, along with Luka. Maks stayed behind, in full-on badass mode now as he directed people on the ground with hand gestures while holding a big, big gun.

She gasped in a breath of air then said in a voice loud enough to be heard over the faint hum of the helicopter blades, "There's a black helicopter with missiles pointing at us."

He gently placed her onto the long padded bench and strapped her in, seating himself right next to her. Luka sat across from them, with what looked like a submachine gun in his grip and cold murder in his gaze. She clutched Alex's hand tight while he gave her a soothing murmur.

"*Dorogoya*, there are four of those black helicopters out there. They are watching over us."

"You mean they're on our side?"

"Yes."

"That's crazy."

They began to lift off and she gave a little gasp at the sudden movement.

Luka didn't look away from his window as he said, "Is not so crazy now that you actually need them, is it? Bet you are thinking right now that you are very lucky woman to have smart man like your husband here to protect you."

That wry observation almost startled a laugh out of her. "Yes, yes I am."

Alex turned her gently in his arms and pulled her into a hug, raining soft kisses over her face. "I am sorry, but I must do this. I can only pray you will forgive me. Is for your own good, I swear."

"What?"

Something stung her upper arm, and she went to reach up to touch it when Alex grabbed her wrist. "No, let it work. You will sleep, safe and sound, and when you wake we will be in Moscow."

Already her eyelids were fluttering, but she forced herself to say, "Fuck you," before the darkness took her.

Chapter 4

The scent of cleaning supplies stung her nose as Jessica looked around the small bathroom/changing area of whatever airport they were at. She'd woken not too long ago, held in Alex's arms as he spoke with his men in Russian too rapid for her still woozy mind to grasp. That numbness was quickly fading, burned away by her rage.

Jessica snarled at Alex as he tried to touch her, angrily shoving her still oddly numb and tingly limbs into a pair of clean black dress pants he'd provided her with. She already wore the top he'd given her, a chocolate-brown silk blouse that consisted of artfully draped panels of fabric accenting her lean frame. Add the giant diamond stud earrings he'd insisted she put on and she actually would have felt rather stylish and sexy, if it hadn't been for the huge hickey on her throat. Purple and black now, the bruise stuck out like a neon sign on her pale skin and she hated the way some people smirked when they saw it. Like it was the badge of being a loose woman.

Fucking slut-shamers.

When Alex had the gall to actually try to touch her again, she smacked his hand away with a scowl. "I said, do *not* fucking touch me. You lost that privilege, asshole."

"I understand you are upset—"

"Oh no, I don't think you understand anything. If you understood, you would know that drugging me against my will is about the worst thing you could do to me. You drugged me, Alex! Not even a full day with you and you've already betrayed me."

"Only to keep you alive. I told you, I had high-level meeting on plane. Not enough room to keep you from being noticed on such small aircraft. It was either make you unconscious or stay at the hangar until we could find and access a bigger plane. Getting in the air was more important."

"I don't care what your excuse is," she hissed. "When we get to Moscow I want a divorce."

He had the gall to laugh. "That will never, ever happen. You are angry, you are right to be, I understand."

The condescending tone of his voice made her see red. Regardless of the fact that she was changing in the stall of a small regional European airport with Alex, she yelled at him, "You don't understand shit!"

For a moment he seemed surprised, then determined. "No, you do not understand shit, and that is my fault. I should have told you what was going on before I put you under."

His words disarmed her and she frowned at him. "No kidding."

The grit of his highly polished shoes on the grungy tile floors was loud as he closed the distance between them with a few determined strides. "This place is not secure, what I have to say to you will have to wait. Please, Jessica, I beg you, trust me little longer."

"But you will tell me?"

"I will. First we need to provide united front before my men. Dimitri said all of Moscow is abuzz with rumors that I have remarried a woman who looks a lot like you, and rumors that you have returned from the dead."

"Shit, how do they know?"

"News like this is impossible to contain." He shrugged. "It does not matter. I will let everyone know that you are my Jessica, my wife, the only woman I have ever loved. Let me speak for you."

"Speak for me?"

"Is better if you remain silent."

Oh no he didn't. "So I'm supposed to just stand there like arm candy and look pretty?"

He grit his teeth. "No, you are going to trust me and help me keep us alive."

"By not talking?"

"Yes."

"And you'll tell me why?"

"I swear it."

She tried to find patience for this impossible man. "And if I don't like your answer I can kick you in the balls?"

"Do that and I will chain you to my bed and tease you until you are out of your mind with the need for my cock. But you will not get it."

Pissed at his threat, and unwillingly turned on, she glared at him in the smudged large mirror above the concrete sinks. "Try it and you better never fall asleep again."

His laughter only irritated her more; she hated how handsome he was when he smiled. "I have missed your claws."

Twisting her hair back into a quick braid, she secured it with a ponytail holder that Zoya, the Wonder Woman-looking bodyguard, had provided her with. Zoya had long black hair that she kept in a tightly braided bun, so Jessica had bet the woman carried a spare hairband around with her. When

Jessica has asked to borrow one from Zoya in Russian, the intimidating woman merely raised a brow, then pulled a black band from her back pocket. It was nice to have a woman on her security detail and she was glad it was someone she hadn't known before her "death". Since Zoya had never met Jessica, she didn't look at her with the same weird mix of awe and sometimes fear that other people did.

She turned and glared at a stone-faced Alex, pulling together her shields to try to lock her unflappable public persona tightly in place before she faced the world. Blocking everyone out was a technique she'd picked up while working for the bank in order to deal with the bitches in marketing. Those women had it out for her for whatever reason, and anytime she had to pass by their cubicles, the whispers would rise like hisses. She'd developed the ability to ignore them and planned to use that skill to get through public gatherings at her husband's side. Not that she imagined any paparazzi would be here, but it never hurt to get in the habit.

Alex said this was a private field that belonged to the Russian government, but he had a friend who let him use it. Translation—someone owed Alex, or wanted to kiss his ass, and did it by letting them land their private plane on government property. There was even a couple of what she assumed were Russian soldiers here, men wearing camouflage and toting guns. They'd stared at her when she'd disembarked the plane on Alex's arm, her gait unsteady as she'd tried to shake off the effects of the drugs.

The tingle still hadn't fully left her hands and feet when she turned and faced Alex. "Well, this is about as good as I'm going to get."

The soft fabric of his suit brushed over her bare arms while he pulled her into an unwilling hug. "You are perfect, and I am sorry to put you into this position. If I had control of the universe we would still be in bed at my home in Spain, making love until you passed out. Please forgive me for dragging you into this world."

Unable to reply in a way that wouldn't bring yet more drama, she opted for silence and let her body do the talking instead. In response to the desperation in his tone, she gave him a long, warm, soft kiss, worshiping his mouth with her own. It felt very odd to kiss Alex with her taking the lead, but it was still heavenly.

Soon the ember of arousal was heating the skin between her legs, her clit sensitizing with each stroke of his tongue. But when he turned the kiss carnal by grabbing her ass with his big hands and lifting her up so she could wrap her legs around his waist, she caught fire. Pouring all of her anger, her fear, her confusion into the kiss, she tried to show him how desperate he'd made her, how much she'd missed him. He might be good at saying it with words, but she wasn't.

So she gentled the kiss again and he allowed it, but still seduced her with his mouth. Emotions built between them and she reveled in the feeling of being connected to him, in allowing herself to love him, and believe that this time she wouldn't be torn away. It may not be the total devotion he wanted, but it would take time for her mind to accept the reality of her life and convince her reluctant heart to trust him again.

He lightly broke their kiss, nuzzling his nose against hers before pulling back altogether.

"Come, *prinsessa moya*, it is time to go to our home in Moscow. Tatiana will be here tomorrow and I would like you well rested before you see her again. It will help her adjust if you have energy and help your body get used to a new time zone. I want her to be happy here, badly, but I fear the only practice I have had with little girls was my sister, and that was long ago."

His voice thickened and she could practically feel him battling tears. "Alex, it will be all right. You have no idea how much I've wanted to introduce you to our daughter."

"What does...does she know who I am?"

"Not really. When she asks about you, I always tell her that you have important business far, far away helping people and can't come home until it's done." She swallowed nervously, knowing he wouldn't like the next part. "To the rest of the world, I was a widow. You were dead, slain by a tragic heart attack at a young age right before I had Tatiana. My—my nanny Gwen, who's the closest thing I had to a family, thought you were dead as well, so she may be a bit freaked out when she sees you."

She tensed, waiting for his outburst, but he merely rubbed his fingertips over her cheek as he smiled. "Then I will know what it feels like to be you, yes? To my friends you are dead, and to your friends I am dead. Between the two of us we will cause quite the sensation."

Unexpected laughter escaped her and she gazed up into his light-gray eyes, warm and delicious love filling her. "I've missed you."

"I have been missing half of my heart for five years, and it has finally returned to me. The love I have for you consumes me, makes me feel alive. It has been so long since I've done anything more than exist merely to protect my brother and people." He lowered his head and brushed his lips ever so gently over hers, making her breath come out in a shaky exhale. "We must leave this place before I disgrace you by fucking you in this disgusting room."

The throb of her clit argued that they could maybe have a quickie without touching any surfaces, but her mind insisted she didn't want to give all the men outside the thin walls of this room a show with the sounds Alex always wrenched from her. "Yeah, I'd rather not."

He held her hand tightly in his as they left the room, keeping her close to his side. Their bodyguards fell into place, Zoya in the front, Maks and Luka in the back on either side. They formed an odd triangle of protection around them, and she would be lying if she didn't admit having them there made her feel better. Alex gave her hand a small squeeze before he led her out into the warm—by Russian standards—evening, which meant it felt frigid to her. Miami's heat had thinned her blood and she already missed the fiery sunshine on her face.

The moment they cleared the front door, they were hustled to the waiting black SUV-like limo and Jessica shivered as soon as they were inside. Before she had a chance to situate herself, Alex had her pulled tight against him. His warmth was more than welcome and she burrowed close.

"You are shivering."

"To me, it's freezing outside. I just spent the last almost five years in the tropical heat, this is fucking cold."

He kissed her brow. "When things are safer, I will take you to island my family owns in the Caribbean and warm you back up. I think you will like."

She smiled and tipped her head back so she could look at him. "I would."

A man's voice cut through the air from the speakers. He spoke in Russian as he said, "Sir, there is an ambush up ahead. Krom has devised a new route for us that is secure. Our teams are moving into place, Orange protocol."

Alex didn't appear alarmed at all, but she was panicked enough to push out of his arms and roll off his lap while frantically looking through the windows. It was hard to tell what time of day it was, the overcast sky was dim enough to conceal any hint of the distant sun. In the dim ambient lighting of the limo, Alex appeared dark, intimidating, and powerful. An odd combination that she found arousing as hell, but she shoved down her ill-timed hormonal reaction to him.

"Did I hear that right? An ambush was waiting for us? Does it have to do with whatever we were fleeing in Spain?"

"Do not fear, is under control." He grit his teeth, his nostrils flaring before he muttered, "Now, I am not so glad you learned Russian."

She slumped back into the smooth leather seat, her silky clothing sliding against her skin as she stared up at the ceiling, trying to compose herself. "Who wants to ambush us?"

Opening his phone, he read a couple messages before responding in a distracted voice, "Take your pick. Rival *Bratva*, someone seeking revenge, someone seeking to make a name for themselves, or perhaps a bounty hunter. There is large price on my head for any foolish enough to attempt it."

"Do you think this is happening because of me? I mean, these attacks started after I reappeared. That is, unless this is normal for you."

"Is not normal." He frowned and looked at his phone, his thumb moving across the screen. "Is not abnormal, but I do not think it has to do only with you."

She clutched at his biceps, needing him to pay attention to her. "I want a gun."

That made him look away from his phone, his arched eyebrows raised high, the silver glints at his temples catching the light. "What?"

"A gun. I want one. If you're in this much danger, I want to be armed."

"No one will ever get close enough to you to touch you, I swear it."

Resisting the urge to roll her eyes, she spoke slowly, knowing she needed to tread carefully with Alex in regards to her safety and his pride. "Still, if the world comes to an end around us, I'd rather be armed. Look, I've been practicing over the years. At first because I wanted to hone my skills for when we reunited, then to protect myself and Tatiana. I'm a really good shot, even won a couple trophies in the amateur women's division back in Miami. Plus I've gotten used to carrying one with me. You don't have to worry about me accidentally shooting anyone."

His lip twitched. "Maybe I do not want to give you one in case you get tired of me one day and decide to put a bullet in my head."

She snorted. "If I was going to kill you for pissing me off, you'd have been dead a long time ago, buddy."

Laughing, he gripped her by the back of the neck and pulled her forward for a kiss. "So malicious."

She nipped his lower lip, enjoying the brush of his beard on her face. "You like it when I'm mean to you."

"I also like it when you are sweet. Like when you are on your knees before me, your ass red from my hand, your nipples poking out from my attentions, and your eyes are pleading with me to fuck your mouth. So adorable, so eager to please her Master. I cannot wait to feel you come all over my cock."

A strangled whimper of need escaped from her that made Alex chuckle and broke the mood between them. She gave him a smack on the arm and tried to pretend she wasn't ready to screw his brains out. Sheesh, her panties were already soaked.

Looking out the dark window, she frowned at the sight of buildings in the distance getting closer. Tension was starting to build in her again and she tried to distract herself. Freaking out about what might happen wasn't going to help her survive anything they might face. Years of being reliant only on herself gave her a deeper well of strength than she'd had when she'd been married to Alex.

"So we're in Moscow?"

"Small city on outskirts. What I believe Americans call suburbs. Will be at our apartment in forty minutes. Had to take detour."

"Because of the ambush?"

"Yes."

Her stomach growled and without looking up from his phone, he pointed at the side of the limo. "Food is there, and drink."

While she munched on a ham sandwich that was surprisingly good, and fed Alex bits of food when he could take a bite, she listened to him talking on his phone and noticed that he didn't seem to be holding anything back. In fact, as he spoke about questioning one of the men that had been in the attempted ambush, he ordered his men to torture the would-be assassin. She'd sucked in a breath at the easy way those evil words rolled from his lips, but her conflicted guilt eased when he talked to who she thought was Maks about using the instruments of torture they'd found in the van their enemies had been driving, along with shackles. Knowing that a fate worse than death had probably been their intent, she didn't feel all that bad about the same devices they'd planned on harming her with being used on them instead.

He also talked to his uncle Petrov a great deal, but those conversations didn't make much sense to her. She had a feeling a lot of what he said was code and gave up trying to figure out what they were talking about. Dimitri called as well, and she'd even had a chance to chat again with a very pissed-off Gwen. Her nanny had freaked out on her for a good ten minutes about what an asshole Krom was and how he wouldn't tell her anything about what was going on, before she calmed down enough for Jessica to explain the truth about Alex. When she did, Gwen let out a scream that was lound enough to make Jessica almost drop the phone, then asked her a million questions before their conversation got cut off by an incoming call for her husband.

She hadn't been able to talk to Tatiana because her daughter was sleeping while the plane refueled, but Gwen sent her a picture of the little girl curled up, surprisingly enough, on Krom's lap and covered in a pink blanket while the large man held her with obvious affection.

Gwen also added the following caption to the image: *Despite the fact that he looks like an evil version of Wolverine and is a complete and utterly bossy dick, Tatiana adores him and vice versa.*

Alex had lingered with fascination over the image, enlarging it so he could study their daughter's sleeping face.

"She is so beautiful," he murmured. "Like an angel."

Snorting, she shook her head then ran her fingers through his hair, unable to stop touching him. "Remember that you called her that. Your little angel has quite a temper on her when she doesn't get her way, and can manipulate adults like you wouldn't believe by being cute. She can also be a right stubborn pain in the butt. Wonder which side of the family she gets that from?"

The droll but warm look he gave her vanished when his phone rang again. He answered it, speaking once again to Petrov, but this time he kept her close to his side, stroking her arm lightly and sending pleasant little tingles through her body. The fresh scent of his key lime and cedar cologne filled her as she rubbed her cheek against the shoulder of his jacket. They had entered the city by now and the streets were crowded with trucks, cars, and tons of mopeds, along with a few motorcycles.

She rested against Alex, gratefully using his silent strength to bolster her own as she took in the chaos of her new world.

Chapter 5

Driving through an upscale neighborhood filled with an odd mixture of old mansions and modern high-rises, Jessica marveled at the beauty of some of the buildings and leaned closer to the glass to try and get a better look. Yeah, almost everything was unfamiliar, and she was freaked out by their entourage and the attention it attracted, but she tried to be positive about things. Tatiana would get to live in a city that had been the home to generations of her ancestors, and she'd have an extensive family to grow up with. Something she'd thought her daughter would never have. Alex had said that Petrov had many grandchildren for Tatiana to play with, and there were what seemed like an endless amount of cousins of all ages. It sounded wonderful, but she worried her daughter would feel like a stranger in a strange land.

Like Jessica did.

In an effort to hide her homesickness from Alex, she smiled wide and continued to look out the window of the sleek car and tried to sound excited. "Wow, this place is amazing! I never imagined this many people would just be out and walking around. What part of the city are we in? Will we be able to come back here sometime? That outdoor restaurant looks really nice, the one with the tulips out front. I love tulips; they always remind me of spring."

He obviously saw through her pathetic attempt at being happy. "Easy, *prinsessa moya*, the threat has been eliminated. You are safe. Please, do not be nervous."

She sighed, the turned away from the lure of the city to face Alex's worried expression. "It's not my safety that has me antsy." He gave her a blank look and she reminded herself that he wouldn't know the slang she'd gotten used to using. "Antsy means full of energy and nervous."

"Then what has you antsy."

The way he said the word, as if testing it out and finding it not to his taste, made her smile. "I'm worried about how I'll fit into your life, how you'll fit into ours. It's going to be hard with Tatiana because I've never had to share the responsibility of raising her. All decisions were mine and things went the way I wanted. I know that it won't be that way anymore and I worry."

"My wife, we will do what parents do, compromise."

"You make it sound so easy."

He rubbed his fingers over the back of her hand, sending tingles up her arm. "There is nothing that we cannot overcome, Jessica."

"You really believe that?"

"I am sitting next to my wife, on the way to our home, to prepare for our daughter's arrival tomorrow. *Nothing* is impossible."

Mollified, she placed her free hand on his thigh and gave the solid muscle a squeeze.

Alex spoke quietly beside her. "You do not know how many times I wished I had a chance to show you my real hometown before I lost you."

Biting her lip to keep from crying—she was going to dehydrate at the rate she'd been bursting into tears—she forced a smile. "Well, I'm here now, so tell me about our new place."

The gray of his eyes lightened and he smiled, clearly pleased at her "our place" comment. He quickly filled her in on the details of the high-security building and she wasn't sure if she was relieved or nervous to find Dimitri and Ivan had apartments in the same building, along with a couple dozen bodyguards and staff who lived in the smaller apartments on the lower floors. Evidently their place was four floors above where Ivan and Dimitri lived with their wives. The thought of those two playboys marrying anyone was peculiar to her, but she supposed the years had changed them as well. In an odd way, she almost expected everything to be the same as when she'd left, as impossible as that thought was.

They pulled up to a set of seriously intimidating wrought iron gates and drove through what had to be an eleven-foot-high concrete walls reinforced with spikes and thick metal wires on the top. The guards were all daunting men who stared in the direction of the limo as they drove past, they eyes covered by dark sunglasses that hid their gazes. Alex leaned forward, his bulk pressing into her side, then pointed through the window.

"This building sits on three acres of land. There is an enclosed garden and a play area for children. I do not pay attention to such things, but Rya has said there are a good amount of little girls around Tatiana's age that live in the building. Across the street is the private school where many of the children of employees from the US Embassy attend. I think we shall enroll Tatiana there when it is time. Like this building, the school is also very safe. In Russia, times of great unrest are not so unusual, and security is often our priority. Is one of many reasons *Bratvas* are such a part of daily life. We help stave off anarchy, bring order to chaos, in ways that the government cannot."

She blinked at him, slightly stunned by how grave his voice was. "So, uh, is the apartment kid-proof as well as bombproof?"

"Is not bombproof. There is a bunker deep beneath the ground in the basement. Is like bomb shelter...what is word...group. We share portions of it with other owners. The Novikovs' portion is very big, enough to house and supply thirty people for five years."

Staring at him, she slowly shook her head. "I meant did you move any breakable stuff, anything that she might pull down and destroy. Your girl is very inquisitive, but a little clumsy. She's managed to break three, count them, three televisions so far. And a washing machine. And destroyed a blender. Not to mention pouring a bottle of vegetable oil on the neighbor's dog we were watching while he was on vacation. Ever try and wash canola oil out of a Golden Retriever's long coat? Good times. So, that's great to hear we have some crazy hideout in the basement, but if I were you, I'd be more concerned about anything that she can reach."

Leaning forward, he nuzzled his nose against hers. "Only you can instantly lift me from the darkness. I cannot be around you and be unhappy. Is physically impossible. I forgot how good it feels to simply be in your presence. I love you, Jessica Novikov, never doubt that for a moment."

Whatever response she might have had, other than bursting into tears at the pain still haunting his voice, was quickly lost on a small gasp. The intimidating sight of armed men and women guarding the entrance to the enormous glass building, each scanning the area with a professional detachment, took her mind off their emotional issues and back to the present with a snap. To think, when she'd been with Alex previously, this life had been one step away from becoming her reality, blocked only by his will. She realized now just how much he'd done to protect her from this harsh truth.

But it wasn't just the guards who had silenced her; it was the sight of an older Dimitri standing near the curb next to a small, very attractive and curvy woman with lots of long dark hair. The woman wore a soft-green trench coat that fluttered around her black boots in the brisk wind, and Dimitri's green tie complemented her outfit. Together they were a striking couple, and she couldn't help but feel an enormous burst of happiness and pride for her brother-in-law. From what Alex had told her, Dimitri loved Rya to distraction and the feeling was entirely mutual.

At the sight of her old friend, her lower lip began to quiver and she tried to fight off the tears, but lost the battle when Dimitri yanked her door open then pulled her out with a happy shout, lifting her by the waist and spinning her around while she clung to his shoulders. Unable to help herself, she laughed while he practically tossed her into the air then caught her in a giant hug.

Crushing her to his chest, he whispered in her ear, "Welcome home, little sister."

"I missed you so much," she managed to get out in a choked voice.

"Never again, Jessica. Do you understand? We will never let you be taken from us again." His voice lowered to barely a whisper. "I am glad you are alive, *dorogoya.*"

From next to them she could hear Dimitri's wife speaking with Alex, but her attention was on the big man who gently set her on her feet. Dimitri had indeed grown up in their time apart and she barely recognized him with his full beard. The teasing sparkle was also gone from his eyes, and a new seriousness seemed to radiate from him.

Plus, he was huge.

Pressing her lips together in an effort to regain her self-control—she really didn't like crying before a crowd of strangers—she shook her head. "No mushy stuff, Dimitri. Be a dick so I don't feel like crying. You know how weird and blotchy I get."

Alex came up behind her and looped his arm around her waist while Dimitri laughed. Right away her hands went over his and she cuddled into him, the movement as natural as breathing. For a moment Alex stilled against her, then placed a lingering kiss on her temple. Dimitri's wife watched them with tears in her golden-brown eyes.

Stepping forward, the small woman held out her hand, the massive yellow diamond of her engagement ring throwing rainbows in the bright light. "Jessica, it is...I'm glad...that is— I'm Rya, welcome home."

Before Jessica could react, Dimitri stepped behind his much smaller wife and swept her up into his arms, giving her a sound kiss on the lips before setting her on her feet again while she blushed. "Forgive my horrible manners. Jessica, this is Rya Novikov, my wife. She is nervous to meet you."

"Shush," Rya muttered as she elbowed Dimitri in the side until he released her from his hold with a scowl. "I'm sorry, normally I'm not like this."

"I understand," Jessica said with a small smile. "I'm like seeing a ghost."

"No, more like meeting a legend." She smiled up at her husband, so tiny compared to him, but her spirit burned like fire as she gazed up at him with pure adoration. "Dimitri has told me a lot about you. I kind of feel like I know you already."

Alex clasped her wrist, cutting off her reply, and tugged her after him so abruptly she almost stumbled. "Come, let us go inside."

Dimitri tensed as well and Rya exchanged a worried look with Jessica. Neither woman resisted as the men ushered them into the massive, almost fortress-like building. She got a brief tour of the main floor, making note of the salon so she could finally go back to her natural color, then she was whisked into a waiting elevator. As they went up to the nineteenth floor, Rya talked about people living on the different floors they passed, making mention of a few families with children around Tatiana's age.

She appreciated Rya filling her in on everything, but right now her mind was having a hard time doing anything more than living in the moment. The interior of the elevator was made up of mirrors and she stared at the reflection of her standing there with Alex to her side. He was looking down at her, studying her face, and the expression of utter worship on his made had butterflies tickling her lower belly.

Keeping her gaze locked on the mirror, she pulled him behind her and whispered, "I forgot how good we look together."

"I did not," he whispered back.

She had to close her eyes for a moment from the heartbreaking intensity of his gaze, a choked sound escaping her, and was saved from further embarrassing herself by the elevator dinging at their floor.

Rya's eyes were suspiciously wet as she wiped at their corners, and Dimitri's face might as well have been carved from granite.

Maks was waiting for them outside the elevator and she blushed when he winked at her, but was relieved that he wasn't giving her that hot stare that made her antsy.

Rya began to talk in a fast, excited voice. "Okay, so I wasn't sure what to do for Tatiana's room, but the girl is set for clothes for like the next ten years. I went shopping with Gia, that's Ivan's wife, and a couple of Alex's cousins. Alex...well, Alex is the first one among our group of close friends to have a child so we might have gone a little crazy. Anything that you don't want, please let me know, I won't be offended if something isn't to your or her taste. There are a couple shelters in the area that could use whatever you don't like, so nothing will go to waste."

They reached a set of black double doors with curving steel handles and what looked like a thumb pad next to the door.

Catching the direction of her gaze, Alex said, "We will set you up in the system later. Right now I want to show you our home."

To her surprise, Dimitri and Rya stayed in the hallway. With a small smile, Rya tugged on Dimitri's hand. "Well, we're going to, uh...do some stuff that we have to do. It's been so nice meeting you, Jessica, and I cannot tell you how happy I am that you and Alex are back together."

"Thank you." She barely got the words out before Dimitri snatched her up into another huge hug.

He released her then pressed a kiss to her cheek. "Do you think I could meet my niece tomorrow?"

"Only if she's not too tired," Rya quickly added. "I know how cranky kids can get during travel and she'll probably be wiped out."

"I think she would love to meet you, but Rya's correct, she might need a day to settle in after all the excitement."

Alex began to slowly close the door. "Goodbye, Dimitri. I need to make love to my wife, so fuck off."

It shut on their laughing faces while she turned to scold Alex. "That was rude."

The words died in her mouth as she caught sight of the short double staircase leading up to what looked like a huge sitting area with an amazing view of Moscow through the floor-to-ceiling windows. One wall was dominated by a large bar with elegant white cloth and black wood chairs, along with two huge and comfortable-looking sofas, which had been set up on a giant Persian carpet. The sitting area was separated by some neat-looking curved black coffee tables inlaid with strips of white. The room managed to somehow be modern and inviting, something probably achieved with the help of a killer interior designer and an unlimited budget.

"Holy moly," she murmured and held Alex's hand, pulling him with her as she walked up the stairs, taking in the artwork tastefully adorning the open space, the sculptures on the low coffee tables, and all the delicate things an active little girl would accidentally destroy.

She bit her lower lip, trying to figure out how to approach the need to child-proof his home.

"Alex, this is all so beautiful, but…"

"You do not like? We have other options if this does not please you."

She turned to find him studying her and knew she was doing a shitty job of hiding her apprehension. "No, no, it's magnificent. It's just that there are so many…fragile things. I-I'm afraid Tatiana might break them. I'd try and keep her out of this room, but there really isn't anywhere to put a baby gate on those big stairs."

He took a step closer, crowding her with his body. Alex was like a massive tiger, all muscle and bulky grace. He gently cupped her face then rubbed his firm lips against hers. "I will have anything removed that could be a danger to her. I do not give a shit if she destroys every inch of this home, it is just things, but I do not want her hurt."

It was hard for her to let go of the habit of being the only one who could protect Tatiana. She battled with the need to double check the rest of the house, but then caught sight of the eight-foot-tall bulletproof glass barriers going up around the porch. They would still get fresh air from above, but would be surrounded on all sides. Alex had said that special glass could withstand a direct RPG attack, but she'd rather not experience that fact firsthand. The panels were massive and she wondered how he'd gotten this done so quickly. Then again, if this apartment was anything to go by, Alex wasn't hurting for money. If he just sold the modern art masterpieces scattered about he'd be set for a couple lifetimes.

His fingertips brushed her cheek. "Come, sit. As I have promised you, we must talk."

Shit. Part of her wanted to just ignore the outside world and live in a little bubble of ignorant bliss with Alex. That was kind of how their marriage had been and she wondered if she was falling back into bad old habits or if she just naturally felt comfortable with Alex making the majority of the decisions in their relationship. Either way, if he was attempting to be honest with her, she needed to pay attention.

After they sat together on the damask couch facing the floor-to-ceiling windows that looked out over Moscow, she picked at the bright red-and-blue throw blanket on the curved back of the couch. "Okay, what's going on? Why did you drug me? What was that ambush about?"

"I drugged you because my uncle Petrov has made a...change in his will."

"Is that supposed to make some kind of sense to me?"

His gaze darkened and he gave her that "irritated Master" look that instantly had her nervous. "If you will listen, I will tell you. I was not finished."

She pantomimed zipping her lips and he shook his head with a smile.

"I have missed your impertinence." Taking her hand in his, he tugged her closer until she was almost in his lap. "It was well known that my uncle Petrov's son-in-law was going to inherit the Dubinski *Bratva*, but he was shot in the head yesterday and is slipping in and out of a coma."

"Oh no! Is he okay?"

"Will probably make full recovery in time, but is no longer fit to lead the Dubinski *Bratva*. That means there will have to be a new successor to my uncle's empire, and there are many of my friends and associates being considered for the position. Petrov never had any sons, only daughters, and the youngest is unmarried. Even if she were married to suitable man, she has expressed a desire to stay as far away from the *Bratva* life as possible."

"So what does this have to do with you?"

"My uncle has requested me at his side as part of his council for choosing his heir. Timing is bad, I want to spend every moment I can with you, but I cannot refuse this. He needs me and I owe him more debts than I could possibly repay in a lifetime. Beyond my personal reasons for attending, whoever heads the Dubinski *Bratva* will have control of the majority of not just Moscow, but Russia as well. He will have to be smart, wise, brave, and ruthless man—but not monster. If my uncle choses poorly, it could endanger you as well as my people and that is unacceptable. Dimitri and I have worked hard to give our people and those they love safety, and a life worth living, like my uncle does with his people. I will not allow that safety to be taken from them or you." He took a deep breath, his hands clenching. "There were people at the meeting that I do not want even catching one glimpse of you. And there were things said that if you had heard, they would have viewed you as a threat to be eliminated. That will never, ever happen."

She closed her eyes, unable to stand the pleading look on his face, as if he was begging her to understand. The selfish part of her just wanted to rage at him for already getting her messed up in this criminal bullshit, but this situation was not her husband's fault. He had done his best to protect her, gone to insane lengths to keep her well-guarded and happy. Looking back, she now appreciated how hard he'd worked in order to win her heart when he already had a life filled with so much stress and responsibility.

But knowing what was in the balance if her husband failed felt like a physical burden, and she sagged beneath the weight of once again having to put her desires on the back burner for the sake of other people. If only God had made her just a little more selfish, she could have insisted that Petrov could go fuck himself, that she and Alex had just reunited, and that they deserved time together—uninterrupted as a family. But there was no way she could live with herself if people died because of her selfish wants. Perhaps it was better they have a little time apart to process each other, to come to grips with the monumental shifts in their lives.

She tried to tell herself that her heart wasn't breaking at the thought of leaving his side for any amount of time.

Tracing the lines in his forehead that she'd never seen before with her fingertips, she let out a soft sigh. "Do what you need to do in order to keep us safe. I know you wouldn't leave me if it wasn't important."

"Leave you?" He surprised her when his nostril's flared in anger before growling out, "No, is unacceptable. You will come with me. While you may not be able to sit on council with me, you could learn much from my aunt Vera. She is greatly admired in the world of the *Bratva* for being a woman of worth—smart and loyal. I know she will like you because you are very similar."

Flushing beneath his praise, she couldn't help the little happy thrill that he wanted her with him. Hell, he could have said his aunt had PMS and hated Americans and Jessica still would have gone with him. The thought of being more than a few rooms away from Alex was unacceptable.

"I would love to go with you."

Closing his eyes, he let out a frustrated growl. "That means I do not have time to fuck you properly."

"Why not? Though right now, I'd even take an improper fuck from you."

His fingers wrapped around her waist and tightened. "Where we are going, there will be many influential and famous people. It is important you look good, not just because I wish to show off your beauty, but because you will be a walking legend among them. The woman who came back from the dead."

Groaning, she buried her face against his throat. "Do you think they'll be mad at me that I let Jorg chase me off?"

"*Nyet*. Every person there knows how my father operates. His cruelty has been felt by them all in one way or another. My uncle Petrov lost his beloved sister to the Novikov Curse. He revealed to me in our late-night talks after I'd thought I lost you, that there was not a day that went by where he did not feel guilt for not protecting her well enough. If it turned out his sister had actually been hiding, not dead, all these years, he would have been nothing but happy. You will be welcomed by them with open arms."

"Yeah, 'cause everyone wants to hang out with Lazarus at a party," she muttered into his chest.

"We do not have to face them until tomorrow, but I have a favor to ask of you before I fuck you to sleep."

A shot of heat went straight between her legs and she squeezed her thighs together as blood rushed to her sex. "What is it?"

Taking a strand of her dark-brown hair between his fingers, he held it up and curled it with a distant look softening his harsh features. "There is salon downstairs. I would like them to dye your hair back to its original color."

Heat rose to her face as she ducked her head. "Does brown look bad on me?"

"Nothing could look bad on you, but do not wish to return to red?"

"No, no, I can't wait to stop dying my hair. Seriously, having red roots with dark hair is weird. And if I don't color in my eyebrows I almost look like I don't have them. It's just that, I wonder if Tatiana will be upset by the change. I mean, I'll look different."

"You will have hair that matches your daughters. I think she will be all right. Please, Jessica, do this for me."

"Why do you want my hair back so bad?"

"I hate the fact that this color you wear is not something you chose to do, but rather because my father forced it on you. His visible stamp on your body is abhorrent to me." His dark brows drew down and he did a quick scan of her body. "I will be back, *dorogoya*."

"Huh?"

He left her sitting on the couch, her gaze following him as he went up yet another flight of stairs to the left of the sitting area.

Puzzled and tired, she pulled a lock of her hair forward and studied the color. The dark brown, which she hadn't minded for years, suddenly drove her crazy. Great, every time she looked at herself now she'd think of Jorg Novikov. The urge to get her hair done as quickly as possible filled her and she sat on the edge of the couch, her gaze darting in between examining the apartment then watching as Alex quickly crossed the room with a subdued smile.

He held a rectangular case that was embossed with the familiar BVLGARI stamp.

"After your death, I thought of selling your collections, but I could not bear to part with something that had touched your skin."

With her heart in her throat, she could barely swallow as Alex knelt before her. "I kept all of your jewelry in the hopes of someday giving it to Rya and Dimitri's children. I thought you would have wanted that."

"Oh, Alex," she managed to choke out, reaching for him.

"Hush, *radost' moya*. No tears. I need you to wear something for me."

Her eyes and nose burned as he opened the lid to reveal her Winter's Night sapphire set. The snowflake necklace made up of diamonds and sapphires sparkled in the sunlight and she sighed, caught up in the memory of wearing this set in Paris. They'd still been new to each other at that point and she'd been drunk on his love the entire time they were there. Spending a week with Alex in the City of Lights, and making love until dawn broke over the fabulous view of the River Seine from their luxury hotel suite, were some of her most treasured memories. The night after going to a decadent Parisian BDSM dungeon, he'd taken her dancing at an old and exclusive jazz club, where they'd swayed together for hours together, oblivious to the world and utterly wrapped up in each other.

The smoky scent of the club filled her mind for a moment and she smiled when Alex plucked the ring from the black-velvet setting. It was a lovely five-carat sapphire with diamond baguettes flanking it on either side. She'd always loved the depth of the stone, the way it could almost seem black with wisps of a deep, radiant blue swimming inside. With it was a sparkling eternity band of tiny white diamonds.

With a soft sigh, he slipped the rings onto her finger, then kissed them. "Do you know why I picked this one for your new wedding ring?"

Not wanting to think about the fact that her old wedding set was probably buried with the burned corpse of someone Jorg had killed to take her place in the car bombing, she tilted her head and admired the sparkling ring. "No, why?"

"Because Krom informed me that among your possessions in Miami, he found your sapphire heart collar in a safety deposit box."

"I-I couldn't bear to leave it behind."

The firm set of his mouth as he examined her made her want to kiss him until he softened once again.

Looking him in the eye so he knew she meant it, she said, "I want you to wear a wedding ring as well."

He held up his hand, the hammered gold band she'd given him five years ago gleaming on his finger. "I never got rid of it. Sometimes when I was very lonely I would wear it to feel closer to you."

She held her fingertips up to her mouth and rolled her eyes to the ceiling, struggling to regain her calm. There had been enough damn tears in her life during the past forty-eight hours. At this point she could either mourn over his statement, or try to make it into something positive. She loved Alex to death, but he was far too serious most of the time. One of the things that she'd loved about their relationship was knowing that she was the only person he ever completely relaxed around, other than Dimitri. That Alex could rely on her unconditional love.

And she was determined to make him feel that way again. "I stole a bottle of your cologne. I used to spray my pillow with it until it ran out. I'm surprised you didn't notice."

He blinked at her. "Our room had been ransacked, twice, before Oleg arrived. Once by representatives of the Boldin *Bratva*, and once by an unknown group. The Boldin *Bratva* claimed the home had been looted when they arrived to kidnap you. Plus, things were taken, and the Boldins would not degrade their reputation by stealing during a revenge abduction. Your jewelry at our home in Ireland was taken, except for a few pieces that had been hidden away, and they also took some guns and cash. We eventually traced the guns to a local gang, but they knew nothing about the men that had sold them. Your jewelry was never recovered...so I am very glad that you took your collar with you, that it didn't end up in the hands of some thief."

Her determination to look on the bright side of things suffered another blow as she tried to think of a way to put a positive spin on those horrible events. Unfortunately she couldn't think of anything to say, and she hated the pain that had reentered Alex's stormy gray eyes. His jaw tensed and the scar on the side of his face twitched while his anger built. No words of comfort would come to her, so instead she let her body and emotions guide her.

She wrapped her arms around his neck, buried her fingers in his lush hair, and pressed her mouth to his, kissing the corners of his lips, tasting him with a soft moan.

A tortured sound came from him as he delicately returned her kiss, butterfly-soft strokes of his lips that had her pressing her hips into him. The brush of his beard over her face was a tactile sensation she was still getting used to, but his taste was the same and she was starving for him. Before she could slide her hand between them and grip his erection, he tore his mouth from hers then proceeded to place a gentle kiss on her forehead before stepping away.

He stared at her mouth, then let out a tortured sigh. "Come. The salon downstairs is expecting you. I will take you there, but will be waiting in private club on another level of the building with my men."

Smirking, she stroked his bearded cheek. "What, afraid you'll get girl cooties by hanging out in the salon?"

"There is business that must be done, and I would rather deal with it while you are busy, so we can spend every moment we can steal from the world together."

She nuzzled her nose against his, kissing away the tension in his lips. "Someday, I have no idea when but someday, you and I are going to spend the whole day being lazy and doing nothing except eat and sleep."

"And fuck."

"Mmm, no, not fucking. That's too energetic. We'll make love."

His breath hitched. "I have not made love since I lost you."

Uncomfortable with the mention of him being with other women, but not wanting to be a crazy bitch and yell at him for moving on when he thought he was a widow, she forced a smile. "Let's go get my hair done so we can come back here and take a nap before Tatiana arrives. Trust me, you're going to need your energy to keep up with her. And you get to meet Gwen. She's staying, by the way. I don't care what you have to offer her, just encourage her to stay on as Tatiana's nanny, but don't force her. For the past few years, she and her mother have been more like family than anything else. I love her, and Tatiana loves her, but...she speaks her mind and she is very defensive of me. I also want her to be able to take some art classes, which means she'll need a bodyguard to go with her that can be discrete. And she'll need a translator."

She took a deep breath, then slowly let it out.

He kissed along her jaw. "Whatever you want. I will build this Gwen a castle if she wishes. If my daughter loves her then she must be a good woman."

Ha, she'd remind him of those words the first time he locked horns with Gwen. Her friend may look cuddly and cute, but she had sharp teeth when needed. If she felt someone or something was a threat to Jessica she wouldn't hesitate to say something. Jessica just hoped she didn't try to take on Alex.

"No, not a castle, but she'll need an apartment here. Maybe down on the same floor as the bodyguards so she'll be safe. And make it a nice one, please. She deserves something decent for coming out here probably against her will. And please let her decorate it."

"It will be done."

"And we'll both need Russian lessons. Mine is okay but it could be better, and I don't want her to be unable to talk with the locals. She can be a bit of a spitfire so she'll want to be able to communicate on her own."

"What is spitfire?"

"She's small and round, cuddly even, but when her temper gets riled you better step away because she spits fire."

"Ahhh, hot temper."

"Yeah, but only with adults. She has endless patience for Tatiana."

Alex's phone beeped and he read the screen with a frown. "Come, there is much to be done so I can savor you properly."

She wasn't sure what he meant by that, but she was all for anything that involved Alex slowly tasting her.

Chapter 6

In an isolated circular booth at the back of the Novikovs' private club, Alex forced his mind to stay in the present. He focused on the sight of his reflection in the mirrors lining every wall of this opulent, yet cutting-edge modern space. Everything was clean, simple, and perfect. He wished his life was the same way, but everything would be dealt with in time.

He needed to be patient, even when it went against every primal urge he had.

To his right, Ivan lounged on the pale-tan velvet sofa, his arm stretched across the back in a deceptively relaxed pose. His gold watch gleamed in the faintly blue-toned lighting and the masculine diamond wedding ring he wore had Alex running his thumb over his own band. Memories of touching the band for strength and patience tried to intrude on his thoughts, but with an iron determination he focused on the present.

Only two waitresses were working the bar, but as always the service was impeccable. The willowy brunette that took their earlier drink orders returned with her tray filled and her gliding walk would have looked perfect on some fashion runway. Dressed in a sexy, but tasteful little black dress, she gave each man at the table a sample of her bright smile without coming off as too flirtatious. Gia and Rya liked to bring their girlfriends here to party, so the staff knew their value was in their service, not in spreading their legs. If his guests wanted pussy, he'd send them to one of the many bordellos the Novikov *Bratvas'* owned where the women were willing and discrete.

But now his wife had returned and he couldn't wait to wake up with her warm and safe in his arms again.

Dimitri snapped his fingers before Alex's face while Luka chuckled. "The quicker we get this meeting over with, the quicker you can return to Jessica."

Kostya Boldin looked bemused in a cocky way as Alex met his hard gaze. He was still a young man in his early twenties, but the heir to the Boldin *Bratva* had been raised much as Alex had, but with a much better father. He was blonde like most of the Boldins, and he had his tongue and ears pierced along with his septum. It was an unusual look among the more conservative upper ranks of the various *Bratvas*, but Kostya had the balls to pull it off.

Alex didn't care if the little shit pierced every inch of his body, with his father Gedeon's influence, Kostya was going to be a good leader someday and Alex liked him.

"Alex, we understand the less than ideal circumstances, but time is of the essence. My uncle Efim says that Petrov is moving swiftly to appoint his replacement, that he's already having paperwork drawn up for shifting over the *Bratva's* assets into the new heir's name, so he is wasting no time. This is a delicate situation for all of Moscow—hell, for all of Russia, and many are scrambling to figure out who Petrov will select. It has created unrest and my uncle and I agree that the potential for violence hangs thick in the air. Whoever Petrov chooses will inherit a volatile *Bratva*. They will be tested, again and again, until they establish power. He will need to be a strong man, someone people will think twice about crossing. My uncle said there is much fighting within the Dubinski *Bratva* about who should rule."

The urge to rub his face with frustration was huge, but he couldn't let Kostya see his worry. Efim was Kostya's great uncle and the man had been a part of the Dubinski *Bratva* for over 40 years. He was one of Petrov's most trusted advisors and a key player in arranging for Alex and Dimitri to meet in secret with the Boldin *Bratva*. Alex trusted Efim, and wished he was here to shed some light on the situation, but right now his uncle Petrov needed Efim, so Alex met with Kostya instead.

"I agree." Sometimes it was necessary to be blunt and honest. Holding the other man's dark gaze, he said in a low voice, "The Boldin *Bratva* has as much to lose as the Novikov if the wrong man is named as heir."

"This is true." Kostya nodded slowly. "It is no secret that the Dubinski *Bratva* is among our closest allies and we would not endorse a bloodthirsty, spoiled fool to lead it. And we certainly do not need another psychopath like Cozir Sokolov."

Tapping his fingers on the gleaming rosewood table, Alex nodded in agreement. "That would be unfortunate."

They all grimaced at the mention of the sadistic animal who led the Sokolov *Bratva*. So far he hadn't messed with the Novikovs' people, but Alex didn't trust him at all. The man was still angry about losing his prostitution business to the Novikov *Bratva* and Alex knew that loss of income had hurt the fractured Sokolov *Bratva*. Fractured because when Cozir took over years ago, many of the Sokolovs who did not want him as a leader fled for the United States, taking their money and influence with them. Those who remained were corrupt men Alex wouldn't trust to guard a pile of dog shit.

Ivan took a drink before setting his glass down with a controlled, precise movement. "The man who will run the Dubinski *Bratva* must understand that peace is better than war. I do not want some idiot getting us all killed. He must understand that the safety of our people comes first. It is no secret that the Dubinski *Bratva* helps keep my wife alive, as it does with your mother, aunt, and female cousins, Kostya. No man at this table wants anything but peace for his family. That is why we are here."

The younger man curled his upper lip in a warning snarl. "I know why we are here."

Instead of engaging in a pissing contest with the suddenly volatile young man, Ivan shrugged. "I do everything I can to ensure my Gia's safety, but I am only one man. It is my circle of friends and family that have built a wall of protection around her. That wall includes the influence of the Boldin *Bratva*. I am grateful for that protection; it has allowed me to build a good life. The kind of life that I want to continue to live. The kind of life I want not only my children to have, but yours as well."

Alex considered Ivan as he expertly handled the prickly young man. While he knew his old friend did not want to inherit the Dubinski *Bratva*, he also knew Ivan would be his choice. It was selfish of him; he understood that Gia, Ivan's wife, wanted nothing to do with the criminal world, but Ivan would make a good *Pakhan* and Gia would fulfill her duties as the leader's wife well. After all, it wasn't just the man who would be running the *Bratva*, but also the woman working hard behind the scenes at his side. It used to baffle Alex that the Dubinski *Pakhan* would consult his wife on *Bratva* matters, but he now understood the need to seek his woman's opinion. Jessica was highly intelligent and she often helped him look at things in a way he normally wouldn't.

Kostya sighed. "Agreed. Come, let us speak of lighter things. Alexandr, on behalf of myself and my family, we congratulate you on your wife's return. As is our agreement, she is now under the Boldin *Bratva's* protection, as well as your daughter. My mother would like to meet them, sometime in the future when the world is a little less insane. I must say, not many women could do what Jessica did in order to survive. You should be proud."

"Thank you, I am."

Unexpected warmth softened Kostya's normally cold expression for a moment. "Will I get to meet her at some point?"

Alex glanced at his watch with a frown, noting that it had been almost two and a half hours since he'd sent her into the salon. "Yes, she should be arriving soon."

Luka kept his eyes on the front door to the club, his posture agitated. "How long does it take to dye a woman's hair?"

Alex was wondering the same thing. He was getting a gnawing sensation in his stomach as time stretched on. Logically he knew his wife had Maks rabidly guarding her every move, and that this building was incredibly safe, but he wondered if he'd ever feel completely calm without her by his side. His heart began to speed up and he had to fight down a feeling of panic that urged him to go to her, now, to rescue her before something bad happened while she was out of his sight. The emotions were so powerful that his hands trembled, and he gripped them into fists. Dimitri caught his gaze with a questioning look but Alex couldn't reassure him. Not when his mind screamed that his wife was about to be taken from him again.

Movement caught his attention as the front doors to the club opened and Jessica shuffled in with a wounded look on her face that had him bolting upright from his seat.

As soon as she spotted them, she schooled her features into a pleasant but strained smile and began to make her way across the room at a more normal pace. Her deep auburn hair flowed down her back in a straight sheaf and his heart stuttered at the sight of his beautiful wife. Seeing her true hair color soothed something inside of him, some jagged edge that kept poking at his heart. Memories of that glorious fire spilling over his thighs as she arched her back and rode him hard had his cock twitching. As she got closer, he noticed the little line between her eyebrows was there, a sure sign she was irritated. Maks trailed behind her, a furious scowl twisting his thin lips, and all of Alex's internal alarms began to go off.

Before he could say anything, Luka let out a loud whoop and leapt from the table, his light-brown hair in a disarray of spikes from constantly running his hands through it. Jessica's smile became real when Luka swooped her up, his hands at her waist as he twirled her around before giving her a huge hug. Her feet dangled off the floor as she wrapped her arms around his necked and hugged him back.

Jessica squeaked when Ivan grabbed her from Luka, placing two loud, smacking kisses on her cheeks before stealing one from her lips. She laughed and shoved playfully at his chest, her smile fading as Ivan said something to her. With a soft expression, she cupped his cheek and nodded, her gaze holding his while they spoke. It took a great deal of restraint to keep from going over there and taking her from them. Rationally Alex knew he was acting like a fool, but on some level he still felt like she could be snatched from him at any moment.

They laughed over something before Ivan set her on her feet, then Dimitri stepped in and gave her a big hug. He held up a long strand of her hair and she batted his hand away, her giggle warming Alex's heart.

When she turned to face their table again, her titled blue eyes, glowing like neon, caught his and he arched a brow at the anger that tightened her lips and narrowed her gaze. The look she was giving him was far from happy and he could practically see the flames of her Irish temper burning below the surface of her porcelain skin.

Confused by what the hell was going on with his mercurial wife, he moved quickly to her side. She saw him coming and stepped away from Dimitri, her shoulders going back and chin up before she marched in his direction. When they reached each other, she stopped and gave him that fake smile he hated. It was all teeth, no warmth. More like a snarl than a smile.

Her voice practically dripped ice as she gave him a sarcastic, "Hi, honey."

Not even bothering to hide his concern he said, "What is wrong?"

"Nothing." She spit the word out at him and he was pretty sure she was grinding her teeth.

"You are upset."

"Not at all, *darling*."

The way she said "darling" was far from endearing, more like a curse. "Jessica, you are not being honest with me."

"No, I'm choosing not to discuss this right now because if I do I'll end up screaming at you in your little club, and that wouldn't look good in front of your friends. While we were apart, I brushed up on proper *Bratva* etiquette so when Krom came for me, I'd be ready to be a better wife to you."

"You are already perfect wife for me." He wanted to reach for her, but with her temper up she was apt to bite him. "Please, tell me what has upset you."

"I told you, we'll talk about it later. You say that to me all the time, how does it feel when I say it to you?"

Lowering his voice, he stepped close enough that he could smell the unfamiliar scent of the salon's shampoo. "I do not speak of things in order to keep you safe."

"Yeah, well, I'm not speaking of this in order to keep from kicking you in the balls in front of your company. I haven't forgotten the lecture you gave me about the role I need to play in public. I'm not stupid and I'm pretty sure that us fighting would not be good for your image."

She was correct, but he was having a very hard time giving a shit who was there. Something wasn't right and she was going to tell him, now. Before he could respond, she unclenched her jaw and turned on her heel, her voice bright as she said, "Isn't that Kostya Boldin? He's much better looking in real life. Kinda has that rock-star vibe going for him with that hair and those piercings."

Maks, who'd joined them at some point, grunted. "Dimitri, get our girl a couple shots."

Turning her anger on her bodyguard, Jessica snarled out, "I'm fine."

"Either you go and drink, or I spank you for not allowing me to take care of those *blyads*."

She flinched as if struck, then glared at him. "I said I'm fine and you will not do anything to those women. I'm a big girl and I can handle myself. It'll take more than a couple catty bitches to hurt me."

Rage filled Alex as Jessica's lower lip trembled.

Ivan stepped between them and looped his arms around Jessica's neck while giving Alex a look that clearly said "back off". "Come, is time to celebrate, to drink. My wife is out with Rya right now, buying things they claim are essential to any little girl's bedroom. Like a four-story dollhouse or maybe a pony. They did mention going to Tusya's estate to look at his Gypsy Vanner herd. Beautiful horses, intelligent. Would be good gift for little girl. You had horse growing up, yes?"

"What?" Jessica blinked. "Uh…yeah. But horses require a lot of care and upkeep. And they won't fit in an apartment building."

"Do not worry, my Gia is smart. If she buy you horse, she buy you stables and workers to go with it."

By this point they were at the table, where Jessica snatched up one of the full shot glasses and slammed it down before shaking her head at Ivan.

"What happened?" he asked Maks in Russian as they moved closer to the now empty bar. The servers were long gone, having been no doubt ushered out by Dimitri the moment he caught Jessica's mood. Alex glanced at the armed men standing guard at the front doors before looking back at Maks.

The muscle in his solid jaw twitched and he smoothed his hand over his dark-blue tie, something Alex knew he did to help soothe his temper. "Evidently one of your ex-mistresses was there, along with a friend you had also fucked, and they talked about you. They did this in an area of the spa that men were not permitted in, otherwise I would have stopped them. Jessica tried to pretend it did not upset her, but she is a bad liar."

Guilt assailed him at the thought of his wife hurting because of his actions. "Who was it?"

"Ulyana, and that woman she brought to your yacht with her."

"Fuck."

She'd been his mistress for a few months last year, but he'd quickly tired of her obvious manipulations to be something more than his submissive. A stunningly beautiful woman from an old Russian family, she'd had delusions that she could seduce him into making her his wife. Worry consumed him as he considered how catty Ulyana could be and his skin prickled as anger tightened his chest at the thought of Jessica having to endure that bitch.

"I told you to stay with her at all times. You should never have left her alone. What were you thinking?"

A conflicted look crossed Maks' hard face as he smoothed his tie again and shifted. "She ordered me to stay out. Said I could search the rooms first, but that she would not have me 'lurking around like a serial killer' while she got a body wrap. We argued, but eventually she convinced me to compromise. After making sure the back rooms were secure, I gave her the privacy she needed. It never occurred to me that the women there could be a danger in more ways than one. I know I should not have left her alone, but I did not want to push Jessica. She has had much to deal with and I wanted to give her some time to process all that has happened. It is our job to protect her when she is fragile, to guard her and make her feel safe. In this, I failed."

Alex knew his friend hadn't really done anything wrong, but his anger was once again straining his strict control. As he struggled with the need to throttle Maks, he realized having Jessica back in his life was a double-edged sword. She brought his long-dead heart and emotions back to life, but it had been so long since he'd had to deal with them that he was becoming overwhelmed. He had to be strong, for both their sakes, and while he'd like to explode at Maks for being so unwise, he managed to keep his stance relaxed, aware of Jessica watching him closely.

"This will not happen again."

"Do not be foolish, of course it will happen again." Maks raised his hand, quickly adding in a hushed whisper, "I do not say that to be cruel, but it is true. There have been many women in your life, and you have not avoided sleeping with women who move in your social circles. You need to talk to Jessica about the women you've been with during your time apart. Be honest with her, prepare her for the inevitable bitches who will resent her, envy her. They will seek to hurt her just to fill their own empty lives, to drive you apart for the sheer spite of not being able to capture your heart. Women can be cold, cruel creatures who can eviscerate a man's soul. Just look at my own mother."

The thought of anyone as venomous of Maks' mother getting near Jessica made his hands clench into fists as adrenaline fed into his bloodstream. "I will kill anyone who tries to hurt her. Male or female, I don't care."

Studying Alex, Maks titled his head to the side and gave him a half-smile. "While I appreciate your idea, it would be in bad form to kill off all your ex-lovers. Now, if Jessica were to want someone taken care of, I would be more than happy to help her get rid of the body."

Alex snorted at Maks' droll tone, the anger slowly draining out of him. "This is true."

With a sigh, Maks shook his head, his green eyes an odd color in the blue-tinted lights, then turned slightly so he could watch Jessica. Alex followed his line of sight and his chest hurt as shame pierced him. While he knew that he had nothing to feel guilty over—he'd thought she was dead and had never loved any of his sexual partners—he couldn't help but know the idea of him being with another woman hurt her.

He really did not want to discuss his active sex life over the past few years, but Maks was right. They would run into more of his ex-lovers and he didn't want Jessica caught unprepared. Besides, if she'd checked on him at all over the years, she would have seen pictures of him with various women on his arm. None for more than three months, but an endless parade of women who he'd mindlessly fucked. BDSM had been the only way he could connect with a female, and even then he'd had rules set in place before he took any woman, the number one being that they must never mistake his friendship for love. Their affairs would be a mutual satisfaction of their lust between friends, nothing more, nothing less.

Somehow he had to make Jessica see that those women were his dark past, and she was his glorious future.

After doing another shot, Jessica smacked Dimitri on the arm while Ivan roared with laughter at something his brother had said. He studied his wife's face, the fall of her hair, the ways she'd changed yet still remained the same. When their gazes met across the bar, her smile slipped a little bit and she lifted her chin, blatantly snubbing him to the point that Maks chuckled.

"It is nice to see that she still has her strong spirit."

Turning back to the table, Jessica nodded as she listened intently to something Kostya said. Whatever the other man was talking about irritated Ivan and Dimitri, but they didn't interrupt the young Boldin heir. When Jessica snarled something at the other man, Alex was at the table before anyone else in the room could twitch, hauling Kostya out of the booth by his shirt.

"Alex!" Jessica shouted in a shocked voice. "What the hell are you doing?"

When Alex looked over at her and saw her staring at him with fear, he immediately dropped Kostya, who jerked at his suit while holding his hand up to his bodyguard, who had materialized from the back corner of the room. "What did he say to you that made you jerk back like that?"

Her lips narrowed and that familiar determined look came over her exquisite face. Without regard to his size, she shoved at Ivan's shoulder. "Move. I need to have a word with my husband."

Barely hiding a smirk, Ivan moved out of her way with an elegant bow. She ignored him, her angry attention totally focused on Alex. Without raising his voice, he said, "I want everyone out. No one comes in until I give the all clear."

Maks' smug look would have normally been enough to irritate him, but his attention was totally captured by the ethereal creature clenching her fists as she stared up at him. "You have anger management issues."

The hard tips of her nipples pressed against the fabric of her shirt and he didn't care if they were stiff because of arousal or anger, either way it made his blood rush through his body, a heated wave that awoke the beast inside of him that was ravenous for her.

He didn't dare look away from her to check if they were alone yet. "What did he say to you?"

She flushed but continued to hold his eyes. The electricity built, small sparks exploding along his skin. He wanted to close the distance between them, but his woman was wound up to the point of snapping. His heart ached that he hadn't been there to care for her, to help her deal with her stress, to share her burdens. Nostril's flaring, he took in a deep breath of her scent then wrapped his fist in her glorious Irish hair, determined to show his woman that she could rely on him to give her everything she needed.

For a brief moment, a blissful look of relaxation took her over and she melted against him, her body fitting to his so perfectly his dick throbbed with need. Being inside her was perfection, watching her come apart beneath him then drift deep into subspace made him feel powerful. As if he could give her the world. The visible proof of the pleasure he brought her was an aphrodisiac like no other. A soft moan came from between her pink lips.

"What did he say, *dorogoya*?"

With a flash, her eyes opened wide and she tried to wiggle out of his arms. "Get your hands off of me."

"Jessica, either you tell me what he said to upset you or I will hunt him down and make *him* tell me."

"You're overreacting. He was telling me about some of the women in the Boldin family that had perished because of the curse, women your father and grandfather killed." She took in a deep breath and her nostrils flared as she blew it out, some of the anger leaving her. "He also promised that he would do everything he could to protect myself and Tatiana, so don't be mad at him."

Studying his wife, he resisted the urge to pull her close again, seeing that her temper was still on edge. "I will never let anything happen to you."

"I know." She closed her eyes and rubbed her temples. "This is just...all of it is so much to take in right now."

Unable to help himself, he drew her into his arms and pressed his lips to her hair, trying to tell her without words how much he loved her, and how sorry he was for the pain and worry he brought to her life.

Chapter 7

Jessica's temper strained its leash as she struggled against the urge to strangle her husband. The hurt, the almost shameful feeling suffusing her, was more than unhappiness. It almost felt like her depression was returning and she wondered if she needed to conference call with her psychiatrist or something. The ache in her belly deepened as she thought about Tatiana and worry rushed to fill the void of her daughter's absence.

Alex's erection pressed into her stomach, and a tingle raced through her, distracting her from her dark thoughts. The scar on his lip twisted when he frowned as he turned her fully to study her face. Right away Alex's expression softened and he made a gentle hushing noise that soothed her beyond reason. "I forget myself. You are exhausted, have been through much. Come, we will go back to our apartment. I will show you Tatiana's room, then we shall rest. You have no idea how often I have dreamed of having you in my bed, how many times I have woken in the middle of the night, my dreams of you so intense I expected to be able to reach out and touch you."

"I know what you mean. I both hated and loved those dreams because for one moment I'd be in your arms again, feel your love again, only to wake up and realize I was still so terribly alone."

His grip on her tightened just short of pain and a tormented look flashed over his stern face before he placed a kiss on her forehead. "You will never be alone again."

They stood there for a long moment, just holding each other as their bodies fit perfectly together, their breath synching, and she swore the beat of their heart was the same. "Come, *prinsessa moya*, let us return home."

Instead of allowing him to release her, she clutched him close. "Okay."

"Jessica." His husky voice held a trace of amusement. "I cannot move until you let go of me."

She simply nodded against his chest and continued to cuddle close. With a low rumble of pleasure, he scooped her into his arms. He'd always loved to carry her and she couldn't help her no doubt besotted sigh of contentment. It was so nice having someone else she could lean on, literally. Pressing one of her hands against his chest, she found herself soothed by the beat of his heart, strong and steady.

When they reached the door, he knocked three times then it opened, revealing a stone-faced Maks. It would take her a bit to get used to his serious bodyguard expression again. Her strongest memories of the time spent with her friend were mostly of those few occasions she'd made him laugh or smile. Life would enter his dead eyes and she liked to see the real Maks come out from behind his formidable walls. His expression reminded her that they were in a semi-public part of the building, a VIP floor of sorts, but she still found herself glancing around to see if those evil bitches from the salon had somehow followed her here.

It had taken a great deal of effort to keep her expression blank as those two hags had whispered to each other in Russian about Alex's exploits after they learned where she lived in the building. It had been one thing to have seen pictures of Alex's sexual conquests online, but to meet two of those women in the flesh had hurt. The fact that he'd been with other women went from an abstract concept to reality and her jealousy had been almost impossible to control. She'd needed every ounce of her willpower to keep form either breaking down into tears as the stunning blonde woman, Ulyana, had gone on and on—in detail—about her time as Alex's submissive.

Even worse, they speculated on who Alex would take as a mistress, talking about it as though it was a given that her husband would keep a woman on the side. Ulyana had been very, very interested in the position and Jessica had silently vowed that if the other woman even got near Alex, she'd beat her so bad even her plastic surgeon wouldn't recognize her. While she was worldly enough to know that most powerful men had a mistress or two, the thought of Alex keeping a woman to fuck made her physically ill. When Jessica's attendant returned, the other women started talking about fashion and Jessica had somehow managed to scrape her pride together enough to say goodbye to them as she left. The last thing she was going to do was let that bitch know she'd hurt her.

They'd reached the elevator before she knew it and she absently watched how the men piled in with military precision. Maks and Zoya, looking intimidating in her dark suit, joined them. Zoya didn't bat an eye as she took in Alex carrying Jessica, merely positioned herself in front of them and pushed the button for what she assumed was their floor. Her brain was done trying to process any new information and she yearned to find some bed, any bed, and just curl up beneath the covers and hide from the world for a while.

Closing her eyes, she rested her head against Alex's chest, the low murmur of his voice blending in with the heavy beat of his heart. She had no idea how long it had taken them to get to the apartment, but when Alex began to climb a set of stairs, it jarred her enough to drag her from the doze she'd been in. Turning to look around, she found that they were almost at the top of the stairs leading to a wide landing. Six doors lined the long hallway, four on one side and two on the other. He stopped before the second door on the right and gently lowered her to her feet.

"Is our daughter's room."

The unexpected thickness in his voice made tears threaten so she forced herself to suck it up and turn the brass knob of the dark wood door. It swung open easily and she took in a deep breath, the faintest hint of paint the only thing betraying the fact that this room and everything in it was brand new. As she took in the beautiful space, she realized she totally, totally owed Gia and Rya—huge—for doing this for her.

Instead of pink and super girly, the room was done in a neutral beige with splashes of jewel-tone color everywhere. The big canopy bed had a deep amethyst comforter and cranberry silk throw pillows, some furry, some silky, all adorable. Her gaze went to the small bedside tables with their bohemian-looking pierced brass lampshades, then she took another step into the room and smiled at the sight of child-sized bookcases lining the entire wall, filled with books and toys, as well as a comfortable couch and pair of massive papasan chairs.

A door across the room had been left open with the light on inside, revealing an amazing closet that was half filled with little girl clothes and shoes of just about every color and variety she could think of. On the other side of the room there was a bathroom that appeared to have a clown fish theme, and thick white velvet curtains embroidered with a rainbow of whimsical silk flowers graced the windows.

In a smaller room all these colors and textures might have been too busy, but this room was huge and Jessica let out a low breath as she turned in a slow circle.

"You do not like?"

Realizing he'd misunderstood her sigh, she shook her head. "No, I love it. Are you kidding me? Tatiana is going to lose her mind when she sees this room. She loves bright colors and this room is much bigger than her old one...so much bigger. Wow."

He cleared his throat then gestured to the far wall, where a daybed covered in even more pillows sat near the window. "A guest bed has been installed. Gia told me story once about spending the night at her friends' homes when she was a little girl. I assumed this was something common for American girls and I do not want Tatiana to miss out on anything by having to move here and live with me."

The wistfulness in his gaze had her slipping her hand into his. "Come on, time for bed."

He led her to their room across the hall and she looked down at her feet to hide her smile that he wanted to be as close as possible to their daughter. That was so Alex. Always protective, even when it drove her crazy. His thumb stroked her hand, sending tingles spinning through her blood. Warmth tightened her lower abdomen and she barely noticed the room when they stopped moving, her focus more on his touch than anything else. She'd forgotten how immense his hands felt when he held hers, how strong and solid they were. After being stuck in Mommy mode for so long, she reveled in the sensation of being a sensual woman.

She'd missed this feeling, the feminine power that rioted through her body like an electrical storm, reminding her how good it felt to desire and be desired.

"Jessica," he murmured as he closed the door behind him and locked it.

When she looked up at him, she faintly noted that the room they were in was done in shades of navy, tan, and gold. To be honest, she barely noticed anything other than the intense look Alex was giving her. There was anger in his gaze, mixed with lust, and a thousand other emotions that flashed by so quickly she couldn't make sense of them. The silence around them took on a heavy weight as they stared at each other.

When he finally spoke, what he said was like a punch in her gut. "I have fucked many women while we were apart. I wish it was not true, but it is."

God, she'd rehearsed this conversation so many times, debated how she'd want to handle this. It all came down to the fact that to Alex, she'd been dead and he'd been a widow. There was nothing wrong with what he'd done, no matter how much it hurt her. The thought of him kissing other women, fucking them, sleeping with them made her ill, so she banished those thoughts from her mind.

"I understand."

He frowned. "You understand?"

"Yes." She realized her voice was stiff, but it was the best she could do to keep her tone even. "I understand."

"No, I do not think you do."

"Oh—trust me, I do. I used to do searches for you on the Internet, starved for anything I could find that would reassure me that you were alive and well. Thankfully the press loved to take pictures of you and your latest girlfriends. You had quite the variety. And that Ulyana woman was lovely. You do have a thing for leggy blondes."

Well, that didn't come out quite as calm as she'd hoped.

Evidently, Alex didn't think so either.

"I *fucked* them, never loved. Ever. My heart died with you. I was bastard to many of them, blatantly using them after I told them they would never be anything more than a brief sexual plaything for me. It is not something am proud of, but is truth."

"How many have you fucked here?" Shit, it was like she was suffering from emotional Tourette's, one moment determined to let the past go, the next obsessing about it. "I'm sorry, I'm being cruel. Please forgive me. This has been a stressful day."

"*Prinsessa moya*, I have never brought a woman into any of my homes since I lost you. Always at hotels, or their places, or homes I bought for them. Never into my bedroom. This space belonged to you even though you were gone. This is your room. Turn around and look above the fireplace."

It took her a moment to look beyond the large sitting area to a deep-gold and blue marble fireplace, and the painting above it.

She took a step forward then pressed her fingers to her lips as her heart raced.

Alex's deep voice came from right behind her, the warmth of his body burning into her. "Do you remember this night?"

Unable to find her voice, she nodded. Oh, she remembered the evening captured in this huge picture. It was the night they'd found an outdoor jazz club in Paris and had danced together for hours. Her collar gleamed in the soft, almost impressionistic image and their bodies flowed into each other perfectly as they hovered on the edge of kissing, their mouths inches apart. Whoever the artist was, he'd managed to capture their love almost like an emotional photograph, her face so soft with open adoration for the handsome man dancing with her.

"Every time I look at that picture, I can perfectly remember the way you smelled that night, how warm you felt beneath that poor excuse of a dress Catrin picked out for you. It was indecent and I fucking loved how everyone watched us, how the men hungered for you. They could not have you, because you are mine, just like I am yours."

She leaned back into him and let out a soft sigh. "I remember that night. It was warm for Paris in the spring, and it seemed like everyone in the city was out celebrating being alive. You sang to me while we danced."

"I did," he said in a surprised voice. "I had forgotten about that."

She yawned and leaned back into him more until he was fully supporting her weight. "I'm going to fall asleep standing up."

His soft chuckle rumbled against her back before he lifted her into his arms and kissed her. "Then let me take you to bed, give you an orgasm, and let you sleep."

"Perfect."

Chapter 8

Alex's heart pounded so hard he was hardly able to draw a breath as he took his wife to his bed. All these years he'd tortured himself by imagining her here in the room with him, but now that he was touching her, smelling her, tasting her in the air, he struggled to control himself. He wanted to devour her because in the back of his mind, in a dark place he didn't like to examine too closely, his inner demons whispered that she could be taken from him again at any moment. That he had to savor every second with her because just like a phantom, she could be gone again, ordered away on the whim of his father.

Invisible bands tightened around his chest as she ran her hand over the comforter, her gaze rising to the mound of pillows.

"I love this bed."

He'd decorated this room with her in mind, just as he did with all of his homes. "I am glad you like, now take off clothes then bend over and clutch the bed. You are going to come, hard—many times, and I do not want you to shred my back with those wicked nails of yours."

She froze, then turned to look at him with the same wide-eyed shock that had never failed to drive him crazy. "Yes, Master."

"Assume the position, *lyubov moya*."

The fear that nipped at his heels began to recede as she slowly surrendered to him, giving him the control he needed. Right away a smile curved the side of his mouth and she beamed at him, the love radiating from her healing him bit by bit. He was still a fractured man, but he no longer had to struggle against losing himself to the darkness like his father had. Thankfully his friends had done anything and everything they could to keep him together. Now, more than ever, he was glad they had fought so hard to keep him sane. He owed them all an enormous debt and would never forget it.

The rustle of fabric caught his attention and his cock throbbed to life at the sight of his beautiful submissive. She cast him an almost shy glance over her shoulder, biting her lower lip before she stepped forward and bent over the bed. The endless expanse of her slender legs drew his gaze to her pert ass and his dick throbbed with pleasure. After stretching her arms out in front of her, she spread her legs wide and tilted her hips. The sight of her wet and swollen cunt making his dick ache. Satisfaction filled him as he removed his clothing, the need to touch her silken skin tormenting him. He paused when he was a breath away from caressing her, scolding himself for forgetting his duty to his woman.

She came to him needing her Master, and her Master she would get.

"Safe word is butter?" he asked in a low voice while hovering behind her.

Her back rose and fell as her breathing deepened and she arched her hips farther, exposing herself to him. "Yes, Master. But you won't hear me saying it tonight."

Without thought he smacked her heart-shaped bottom, reveling in her sharp gasp. Right away his handprint burned red on her pale skin and he rubbed the mark, his cock dripping pre-cum at the way she tensed. He could see the bud of her clit poking out from its hood and knew that just this small amount of play had her near orgasm. She had always been so responsive to his touch and he was glad that hadn't changed.

"So brave. Perhaps you need something to remind you not to challenge me."

"Bring it."

He couldn't help but laugh at her bratty smirk. "Rest assured, I will give you everything you need, always. I *am* your Master."

She stilled, then moaned low in her throat when he grabbed his dick and rubbed the swollen head between her slick labia. The sensation was so good that he had to grit his teeth to hold back the urge to plunge into her.

To his surprise, when he moved his shaft against her clit she had a small orgasm, her quick gasp and the wetness that soaked his cock attesting to her release. Now it was *his* turn to suck in a quick breath when she ground her pussy against his shaft like a cat in heat.

With a low growl, he stepped back, clenching his hands into fists in an effort to keep from grabbing her. "Do not move."

He considered getting his toy bag from the closet, but quickly decided against it. Never would he use something on Jessica that had been used on another woman. Among the thousands of things that needed to be done, he needed to place orders with all of his suppliers for new toys. Thousands of kinky scenarios flashed through his mind and he had to take a moment to gather himself before he went into his bathroom and grabbed his silver hairbrush. It was a hefty item expertly crafted in a flat, modern design that was perfect for spanking.

When he returned to the bedroom he inwardly groaned at the tempting sight she made, all aroused and silently begging for him. The gleam of her honey shone on her inner thighs and she made a low, almost whining noise as he ran his hand over her hip loving the new curves her body had developed. Not many, but enough to give him something to hold on to. When she tried to rub her hot cunt against his straining erection, he gave her bottom a brisk smack with the flat side of the hairbrush, earning a sharp squeal.

"Such a pretty little ass," he said absently as he continued to warm up her skin with a series of soft blows. "I love how pink it gets for me."

Her only response was to whimper into the bedspread and tilt her hips even more until he marveled at how flexible she was. With one hand he continued to spank her, but with the other he ever so gently began to pet the curls on her mound, his hand glancing off her slippery sex. Soon she was chanting his name and shuddering, her impending orgasm flushing her body. Her eyes were closed and her brows were drawn down with tension as she visibly strained for her release.

The sight was so arousing that he tossed aside the brush, then stepped behind her and slammed into her willing body. She was tight, but wet enough that he slid in deep, his body lying atop hers so she was pinned beneath him, helpless to do anything but take his cock. The skin of her buttocks was much warmer than the rest of her body and he groaned in satisfaction.

"Perfect," he choked on a breath when her pussy quivered around him, then clenched his cock so hard it was like being grabbed by a strong fist.

When she began to rhythmically contract her sex around him, his eyes rolled back in his head at the sensation. Little minx, she could undo him like no other. He was helpless to resist the primal demand that he fuck her, now, hard. An animalistic snarl rose from somewhere deep in his chest as he reared up and grasped her hips, easily lifting her slender body and plunging into her with hard slams of his hips.

She went wild for him and he had to grip her hard to keep her on his cock. Fuck, no woman could bring him to the edge as quickly as his Jessica. Her next orgasm struck while just the tip of his cock was in her and he swore her pussy sucked him back in, tugging on him hard enough that when he tried to pull back it was a struggle. Gentling his thrusts, he eased her back down from her intense release, running his hands up her sides, the light mist of perspiration on her skin turning that movement into an easy glide. When he reached her shoulders he paused to trace the delicate bones beneath her fragile skin, to devote himself to learning her body all over again.

Soon enough she grew restless with his slow movements, whispering for him to fuck her, begging him to take her.

He leaned down and brushed her hair from her ear before kissing the pink shell, tasting the salt of her skin as he took in a deep inhalation of her scent. "Remember that I love you, because I am about to fuck you like I hate you."

A shuddering sigh escaped her before she tossed her hair back and met his gaze, her pupils huge. Ahh yes, his little girl was flying deep in subspace. She looked dazed, like she was drunk, and he reveled in his power to bring her to that place, to give his submissive, his wife, what she craved.

Rearing back into him hard enough that her buttocks smacked against his groin, she cried out, "Please!"

He grabbed both of her wrists in his hands and pulled her slowly up until her upper torso was suspended from the bed, her breasts shaking in the air while she was pinned onto his cock. All she could do was take his dick any way he chose to give it to her. The angle of his thrusts changed and she keened when he hit her G-spot, a wide smile breaking out on his face as she screamed her way through another orgasm. During her contractions he kept up his punishing pace, slamming into her now hard enough that she let out a sharp gasp of air each time he bottomed out. Somewhere in the rational part of his mind he knew he was fucking her too hard, that she wasn't used to his cock yet, but he couldn't stop himself.

His sane mind had receded and he operated on instinct and raging emotions. The harder he fucked her, the more alive he felt, and her screams only goaded him on. He almost stopped, then she came so hard she went limp after. Bracing his arms on either side of her head, he fucked her wilted form, grinding deep as the fire burning at the base of his spine exploded into his balls. The world went white, then black as he came harder than he ever had in his life.

Slowly, bit by bit, sanity returned as his chest heaved and his body burned from the energy it had taken to fuck Jessica into submission.

When he turned to look at her, he found that her eyes had shut and she appeared fast asleep. They were both a sweaty, sticky mess so he went to the bathroom and got a washcloth and towel after he cleaned himself up for Jessica. She let out a grumpy protest when he put the washcloth between her legs but soon fell back asleep. When they were both clean enough, he scooped her beneath the sheets and curled his body around hers.

Burying his face against her damp hair, he let out a shuddering sigh as the darkness inside of him raised up like a striking snake, biting him and filling him with a venom of fear and grief. He was helpless against the tears that burned his eyes, against the way he clutched at Jessica like she might be taken from him at any moment. The tears wouldn't stop and a sense of impending doom grew until he was fighting the urge to leave the bed and double check all of his security. It was only through sheer force of will that he pushed back the crippling panic.

Jessica whimpered and tried to pull away from him. It took him a moment to realize he was gripping her too tightly and shame filled him as he eased his hold. Fuck, he was going to hurt her if he did not get control of himself. For a moment he considered that he might be going crazy like his father had, that he was destined to turn into a monster, and he wondered if Jessica would be safer without him in her life.

As soon as that thought raised its ugly head, he tore it from his mind.

No, for her, for their daughter, he would fight with everything he had against the emotions threatening to turn him into a psychotic beast.

Forcing himself to focus on something other than his irrational dread and desolation, he leaned back enough that he could see Jessica's bare shoulder in the dim illumination through the heavy curtains. There was just enough light for him to make out her freckles and he began to count them. It took him until he reached forty, some were so tiny they were no more than specks of cinnamon on her skin, but his heart had finally stopped racing and he was back in control of himself. As he drifted he once again buried his face against the side of her neck after arranging her hair over the pillow and relaxed into the perfect comfort of holding his wife.

The next day, Jessica slipped her hand into his as the light lunch they'd eaten churned in his gut. He rarely got sick but right now his anxiety was so intense he was fighting to keep the contents of his stomach down. She gave him a squeeze, forcing his eyes off the doors to his apartment and onto her.

Wearing an elegant black blouse and a new pair of jeans that hugged her curves, she was beautiful in a fresh, genuine manner that he'd almost forgotten. He'd grown used to the high-maintenance women he'd taken as mistresses and submissives, and the great deal of effort it took for them to look the way they did. His Jessica wore only a light-pink lip gloss for makeup and her glorious hair hung in a long, straight sheaf down her back, yet she was the most beautiful woman he'd ever seen. Just looking at her brought him pleasure, made his body light up and his anxiety ease.

"Don't be so nervous, it'll be okay," she whispered in a low voice. "She'll love you."

He glanced around the room, meeting Maks' gaze for a moment. It reassured him in a fucked-up way to see his own worry reflected back in his friend's face. His daughter was going to walk through his front door at any moment and he was inwardly terrified that she would not like him. He had to prepare himself for the fact that she would view him as a stranger, would probably be scared of him, and would not want anything to do with him despite their genetic bond. He'd not had much experience with children before Jessica's...disappearance, and had avoided them after. It hurt too much to look at children and imagine his own daughter alive and growing up as they were.

"I am not nervous," he growled back.

She grinned at him, impudent woman, then wrapped her arm around his waist. "Really? Then why did you change your outfit four times?"

It was true, he had changed his clothes four times. He couldn't decide on what tone to set for his first meeting with Tatiana. Did he wear a formal suit so she would know how important the occasion was for him, how he cared enough to look his best for her, or did he wear something casual so she would not be as intimidated by him? It was only when Jessica chose an outfit for him that he finally settled on his broken-in jeans and button down deep-purple shirt. Jessica said their daughter's favorite color was purple so he figured it didn't hurt to stack the deck in his favor.

Maks' voice came from the doorway leading to the library off the foyer. "They are exiting the elevator now."

He gripped Jessica's hand, needing her support as he focused his considerable willpower on remaining calm. If he didn't keep an iron grip on his control, he was bound to grab the little girl up the moment she walked through the door. Memories of placing his hand on Jessica's rounded belly, on learning about her pregnancy, of planning their future together, rushed over him as he stared at the door, which had begun to open.

All he had was a glimpse of Krom's large body before a streak with deep-red hair barreled past the man and shrieked, "Mommy!"

Jessica released his hand and crouched down to catch their daughter, who threw herself at her mother with a happy squeal. Tatiana's face was hidden by her long, ember-dark hair as she hugged Jessica, and Alex's heart thundered. A moment later she pulled back and Alex's heart threatened to burst with love as he took in the features of his little girl. From her rosebud lips to her big gray Novikov eyes, she was the most beautiful child he'd ever seen. Chills raced down his spine and he had to swallow back the tears that wanted to escape as he looked at a miracle. While she didn't share her mother's freckles, Jessica's ancestry was all over their daughter's face, but he could see himself in her as well. She had his dimples and when she frowned, he recognized the stubborn jut of her little chin.

"Mommy, what happened to your hair?"

Looking self-conscious, Jessica laughed. "You don't like it? I went to a beauty salon and had the color changed."

The little girl frowned deeper. "Why?"

"Well, this is my real hair color. I used to make it brown because I thought it was pretty, but I thought it might be a nice change."

Tatiana picked up a strand of Jessica's hair then let it drop and smiled. "I like it. You look like Ariel." Her eyes went wide and she bounced in place. "I flew on a plane with a bed for a long time and Krom sang me songs! He watched *Beauty and the Beast* with me four times, and by the end he could sing along with the *whole* movie."

Jealousy spiked him at the openly admiring tone in his daughter's voice for his friend, but he quickly squashed that feeling. Tatiana would need all of the protection she could get and if Krom loved her, nothing in the world would harm her. He looked over at his friend, biting back a surprised laugh at the sight of the big, menacing man clearly flushing.

Next to him stood a short, very curvy woman with deeply tanned skin like Gia's and long black hair she had secured back in a French braid. She was pressing her lips together while looking at the floor, clearly holding back a laugh as she cupped her hands over her mouth in a fake cough.

Krom stiffened, then looked down at the woman with a glare that would have made some men piss themselves.

Alex was about to intervene when the busty woman looked up at Krom from beneath her lashes, then poked him in the ribs and whispered, "Oh, pull your panties out of your rear end and stop glaring at me. I promised I wouldn't say a word, and I didn't. You forgot that Tatiana was thrilled beyond belief when you sang to her, so of course she'd mention it to her mother. Despite the fact that you're a D-I-C-K, she adores you, so stop pouting."

"Gwen," Jessica snapped. "That's enough."

Before Alex could get in a word, Gwen snapped back, "No, he *is* a—a you know what. And you would not believe the bull-puckey I've had to put up with while this Neanderthal ordered me around like he's a sultan and I'm some seventh-century concubine who'll bow and scrape to him like all of his peons."

"Concubine? Peons?" Jessica asked in a faint voice, her expression wavering between amusement and exasperation.

Gwen seemed to ignore her question and looked up at Krom with narrowed eyes. "And I won't even go into how damn bossy he is. I mean really, would it kill you to say please?"

An odd look came over Krom's face when she put her hands on her hips and glared at him.

It took Alex a moment to realize one of the coldest bastards in the world was smiling.

He hadn't seen his friend smile since Jessica's death.

Maks stared as if he were seeing a ghost while Zoya blinked rapidly then rubbed her eyes. It only took a moment for Krom to realize they were all staring at him before the smile vanished like smoke and his normal blank face returned.

A soft little voice said, "Excuse me?"

He looked down and found his daughter peering curiously up at him and his heart skipped a beat. "Hello, Tatiana."

Her little nose scrunched up and she gave him an expression he'd seen on her mother's face hundreds of times. "You say my name funny, like Krom."

Vaguely aware of his wife still arguing with the nanny while hugging Krom, he knelt before his daughter, his body aching to hold her. Even on one knee he was still taller than she was and he marveled at how someone so tiny could have such a big presence. He had no idea how big an almost-five-year-old girl would be, but to him she appeared petite and unbearably delicate. Her fingers were so little, and he marveled at her reddish-brown lashes.

Realizing that she was waiting for him to respond, he cleared his throat. "It is how you say your name in Russian."

She tilted her head. "What's your name?"

"Alexandr Novikov."

He waited for some sign of recognition even when he knew there would be none. "Do you like movies?"

Jessica picked that moment to intervene, placing her hand gently on Tatiana's shoulder. "Don't answer that, it's a trick question. If you say yes, she'll guilt you into watching cartoons with her. If you say no, she'll also guilt you into watching cartoons with her. Either way you're doomed."

Nothing in the world sounded better than sitting down with his family, watching a child's show with them. "I would be honored to watch a movie with you, Tatiana."

His daughter turned the full force of her big gray eyes on him and he knew in that instant that she did indeed have him wrapped securely around her tiny finger, just like Jessica had predicted. "Really? You'll watch a movie with me?"

"Of course."

The way Tatiana smiled at him filled him with a kind of love he'd never experienced, just as deep as his love for Jessica, but different. Hell, he'd give her the world if she kept looking at him like that. His own lips curved into a wide smile and he swore he could feel one of the bleeding wounds on his soul finally healing, leaving him almost whole.

"Later," Jessica said in a firm voice. "Right now it's late and I need to show you to your new room."

Tatiana spun to face her mother. "I have a new room? But what about my old room?"

"You will have that as well," Alex said in a soothing tone. Hell, he'd buy her whole neighborhood in Miami if it made her happy. "You will have both homes. Here, in Russia, and in America."

He could see that some of what he said went over her head and Jessica clarified. "We're going to be living with Alex, here in Russia."

Tatiana's brows drew down. "But I don't want to live in Russia."

His heart broke, but right away he began to plan how they could live in the United States at their old home in Miami. Jessica must have seen something on his face that tipped her off to his musing, because she rolled her eyes at him before looking back to their little girl. "We'll worry about that later. Right now, I want you to see the room that your aunt Rya and Ms. Gia decorated for you."

Tatiana followed her mother, her expression rapt. "I have an aunt? Like Gwen's aunt Marisol?"

"Yes, but a little different. Your aunt Rya is much younger, but she's just as nice."

By this point they'd reached the top of the stairs where Zoya waited. She kept her gaze professionally distant, but the moment Tatiana passed her, a small smile curved the normally dour woman's lips. Jessica chatted with their daughter about Rya, and also mentioned her uncle Dimitri. As soon as they opened the door to the little girl's room, that conversation stopped as Tatiana let out a shriek. "Oh my goodness!"

Afraid that something was amiss, he rushed into the room, only to find Tatiana spinning around with her arms wide out in the center of the room, a huge smile lighting her face. Abruptly she stopped and ran to where a massive dollhouse sat in the corner, half-opened. The little girl let out a soft, almost cooing sound as she opened the dollhouse the rest of the way, revealing an interior decorated with tiny replica furniture of the highest quality. Dimitri had it specially made in record time, and had no doubt spent a fortune, but the end result of his daughter's joy was worth any amount of money.

"Mommy, look! Everything is so pretty!"

"It is, isn't it?" Jessica slipped her arm through Alex's, then leaned up and gave him a gentle but lingering kiss on his lips.

A shocked gasp came from across the room and they both gave each other a guilty look before turning to face Tatiana, who was now staring at them. "Why did you kiss my mommy?"

All of the advice to take things slowly with Tatiana flew out the window when he replied, "Because I love her very much. We are married now, Tatiana. Do you know what that means?"

Jessica gave him a pissed look before her expression smoothed over and she went to the small green sofa beneath an oil painting of fairies cavorting in a summer field. "Sweetheart, come here."

Giving Alex a suddenly shy glance, the little girl crawled onto her mother's lap. Once there, her gaze darted to Alex, then back to Jessica. "You're married? Like Gwen's mama and papa?"

"Yes, honey," Jessica said in a low voice, her free hand smoothing back their daughter's hair from her little face. "Do you remember how I showed you pictures from Mommy's wedding before you were born? The handsome man that Mommy was kissing while we danced was Alex."

The little girl abruptly stilled and her eyes grew even wider. "Is he my papa?"

Jessica visibly trembled and tears filled her eyes, but she managed to blink them away. "Yes, he is."

The little girl's lower lip quivered and she hid her face against her mother's chest. Right away, Jessica held their daughter close as Alex longed to do. It felt like the world was drowning in darkness as Tatiana began to cry. Fuck, he had totally screwed this up with his eagerness.

When Jessica shot him a hard look, he flinched and took a step back, intending to remove himself from the situation before he could do any further damage. Maybe it was best if he watched his daughter from afar until she was more comfortable in her new home. With his chest hurting like he'd been kicked in it, he took another step back, unable to tear his gaze away from the sight of his tiny little girl crying because of his selfish need to be her father in truth.

"Stop," Jessica said in a firm voice, her watery gaze on him. Both he and Tatiana followed her order and stared at her. At that moment, she radiated the quite inner strength that all women had and he marveled at the way his daughter instantly calmed. "Tatiana, why are you crying? I can't help you if I don't understand what's wrong."

Reaching up, his daughter pulled Jessica down so she could whisper in her ear. His wife blinked in surprise, then placed a dozen kisses on the little girl's head. "Of course he wants you, very much."

"Where was he?" Tatiana rubbed her cheeks against her mother's shirt, wetting it with her tears.

Alex desperately tried to remember what Jessica used as a cover story for his absence but before he could form some type of response, she answered for him. "Your father was doing some work that helped to save a lot of people's lives. He couldn't come home until it was done."

"Like Batman?"

"Yes, kind of."

"He's a superhero?"

"He's my superhero."

Their whispered conversation lanced the festering wound of doubt trying to form and his tense muscles relaxed, sending both a physical and emotional relief through him.

Giving him another shy look, his daughter turned back to Jessica. "Does he have a cape? He shouldn't, capes are dangerous."

That odd comment startled a laugh out of him and he wondered if he translated her words correctly.

"No, honey, no capes." Jessica gave him a small, mischievous smile and his relief deepened that she was no longer angry with him. "But he does have race cars, motorcycles, and even a jet."

"Wow," Tatiana breathed and turned all the way on Jessica's lap to face him, her lips pursed while she carefully examined him. "Is he in disguise?"

"What?"

Tatiana flapped her hand in his direction, a perfect mimic of her mother's gesture. "He isn't wearing his superhero costume. He must be in disguise."

Alex took a couple steps closer, then knelt at the other end of the couch, not wanting to crowd Tatiana's personal space. An unexpected lightness filled him as he studied up close the beautiful results of his and Jessica's love. He was wrong, Tatiana had a light smattering of freckles on her nose, but they were much paler than Jessica's. It was like God took all the best parts of them both to create this perfect little girl, and his chest swelled with pride as he took in the beauty of his wife and daughter.

Leaning close, he lowered his voice, "You are right, Tatiana. I am in disguise. No one but you and your mother know who I am. Will you keep my secret?"

In many ways that was true, they got to see a side of him no one else did, a tender and caring side that most people who knew him would swear did not exist in his cold, dead heart.

But he wasn't dead inside anymore and the strength of the emotions coursing through him were hard to process.

Looking around as if someone might be lurking in the corners of her bright and happy room, Tatiana whispered back, "Yes, I'll keep your secret."

A knock came from the door, interrupting their conversation.

Instantly the need to protect his family hardened his muscles in a rush of adrenaline. He stood and crossed the room, his mind already descending into the space where only actions mattered. There was a brief moment after he answered the door where he almost didn't recognize Krom, but soon his thoughts cleared enough for him to really see the other man, and the silver tray he held.

"What is it?"

Krom's face remained closed down, but his eyes kept darting over his shoulder to where Tatiana and Jessica still sat on the couch, giggling at each other.

"I have brought meal for Tatiana." He grimaced for a moment. "Gwen insisted and I did not want her interrupting you, so I brought it."

"Gwen insisted?"

Frowning, Krom nodded. "You should know now that she is like a rabid mother bear when it comes to Tatiana. She loves your daughter very much and has considered herself both Tatiana and Jessica's protector for a long time. While she will never be a formidable fighter, that does not mean she is not a formidable woman."

If he didn't know better, he'd say the emotionless man was interested in Gwen. Right away Alex knew that situation would be a disaster and he'd be stuck with a woman scorned as his nanny. The thought of exposing his daughter to such tension made his voice come out with a snap that made Krom's shoulders stiffen.

"You will keep your relationship strictly professional, am I understood? Since you will both be in close contact with my daughter and each other, as Tatiana's main bodyguard and nanny, I will expect you to find other women to fuck. The last thing I want is to have to face Jessica's wrath when you break that woman's heart."

The dishes on the tray rattled faintly for a moment and Alex was shocked to see that Krom actually looked angry enough to hit him. "You have nothing to worry about."

"Good. Give me the tray and I will take it to them."

Krom shook his head. "Your uncle Petrov called; he said it was important that you call him back as soon as you could."

He turned back to find Jessica and Tatiana watching them. "I must make a phone call. Krom has brought you dinner, Tatiana. I promise I will not be long."

Jessica smiled at him, but the worry was evident in her gaze. "Take your time. We'll eat, then take a swim, I mean a bath, in that giant tub and relax."

His phone rang and he looked down, noticing his uncle Petrov's number. Jessica blew him a kiss and he left the room, his daughter's excited chatter filling the air behind him. As soon as the door was shut, he answered the call.

"Hello?"

"Alex, I am sorry for interrupting you now of all times, but I have some information that you need."

"What is it?" Maks met him at the top of the stairs and together they descended to his lower-level office.

"Word has spread that Jessica has returned and," Petrov sucked in a harsh breath and when he spoke again, his voice faintly trembled with anger, "there has been a bounty put on Jessica's head. It was on a mercenary site one of my men monitor. They want her alive, not dead, so that would mean someone seeks to use her as leverage against you. This is not a surprise, but I did not expect it so soon."

His fingers went numb as he clenched his phone hard enough that the case squeaked in protest. He wanted to rant and rave, to throw things then go out tonight and slaughter whoever had done this. Someone had a death wish that he was going to fulfill.

"Who do I have to kill?"

"If only it were that easy. First we need to discover who offered the bounty, and who may be stupid enough to take the job. My men took the posting down as soon as they found it, but you and I both know that in this age, once information is out there is no taking it back."

He placed his phone onto the mount on his desk, hitting a button so it was on speakerphone. "How much is the bounty?"

"Five million." Petrov gave a humorless laugh. "Should I be offended that it is higher than the price on my head?"

Alex struggled once again to contain his emotions, gripping the edge of his desk so hard his hands ached. Even if he was being torn apart inside by his fear and rage, he must keep his cool in front of his men. Maks had been joined by three other Black Tier members and they all had their laptops open and were typing furiously.

"Everything is secure." Maks glanced up at Alex, then back down on his screen. "I will die before anyone touches them, Alex."

He ignored the other man, focusing his attention on Petrov. "She is safe for the moment."

"Of this I have no doubt. We both knew it was inevitable, she is too big of a target, but I was hoping for a little more time. That is a luxury we no longer have. Come to my home tomorrow morning with your women. There is something we must discuss in person, a way to make sure the people we love are safe."

He'd planned on spending all day tomorrow with his family, on not letting them leave the nearly impenetrable fortress that was their home, but he could not ignore his uncle's request. "We will be there."

"Thank you. Now, go enjoy your family and tell Jessica I very much look forward to meeting her tomorrow."

Chapter 9

Jessica sighed as Tatiana fidgeted around in her car seat in the Bentley that had basically been turned into an armored tank. They were flanked on either side by men on motorcycles, and in front and behind by behemoth black SUVs that were stuffed with bodyguards. It was still early in the morning, barely past nine am, but Jessica's jet-lagged body made her feel like it was the dead of night. She was so damn tired and wished she could go back to bed, but Alex had said his uncle needed to see them this morning, and Petrov Dubinski was not the kind of man anyone, even her husband, crossed.

The smatterings of silver glitter on Tatiana's pretty dress caught the light streaming through the windows, throwing random patterns of speckles onto the ceiling of the car. She wore her favorite sneakers with the dress, the scuffed black shoes that lit up when she walked. Jessica had wanted her to wear the cute shoes that came with the outfit, but Tatiana had thrown a hissy. She cut her eyes over to her husband, who was busy texting. Normally she would have nipped

Tatiana's fit at the bud—the little girl was beginning to test her boundaries and Jessica knew better than to give in to her demands—but Alex had right away said that Tatiana could wear anything she wanted.

Irritation still clenched her gut at the way he'd casually overruled her, like she had no say in what her daughter did now that he was here. Already she could see signs that Alex would majorly spoil Tatiana, but they would have to deal with that later. Right now she was trying to puzzle out the bits and pieces of information she'd picked up this morning about some kind of increased threat level. When she'd asked Alex, he'd merely shrugged, his face as closed down as could be, then told her that there was nothing to worry about in a rather condescending manner.

She shifted and crossed her legs, briefly admiring the pretty knee-high suede teal boots that went with her black, teal, and white block dress. Just like Tatiana had a complete wardrobe in record time, Jessica had the same. A whole spare room had been turned into a giant closet for her and she'd been overwhelmed by it all. Hell, she'd been overwhelmed since the moment she'd walked through the doors of that villa in Spain and had seen Alex.

"Mommy, are we almost there?"

"I'm not sure, honey. I've never been to Uncle Petrov's house before."

Alex glanced up as Tatiana bounced in her seat. "We are almost there. Be good and I will have a surprise for you when we return home."

Her daughter beamed at Alex and she watched him visibly melt like a sugar cube left out in the rain.

Shoot, she didn't want to interrupt this special bonding time between them, but she and Alex had to get some things straight. She was not going to have Tatiana turn into one of those spoiled socialites who expected the world to lay itself at her feet. Despite her ill-gained wealth, Jessica had managed to raise Tatiana in as normal a way as possible, which meant the little girl didn't get everything she wanted, and didn't get a prize for behaving like she should.

After counting slowly to ten, she said to Alex in stiff Russian, "You are going to spoil her."

He didn't even look up from his phone. "It is my right as her father."

Patience, she needed to have patience with him. "And it is my right as her mother to keep you from turning her into an entitled little beast."

Now he looked up and his expression was not happy. "Do you think I would allow that to happen? What is wrong with giving her nice things? I have the money, is of no concern."

Aware of Tatiana watching them with wide eyes, she kept her tone light. "It is not about the money, it's about raising her to be a good person."

"Are you saying I am a bad influence on my daughter?"

This time she had to count to twenty before she spoke again. "I am *saying* that I would ask that you respect my wishes on this matter and stop buying her things."

"No," he snapped. "End of discussion."

Furious, she clenched her hands into fists to keep from throttling him. "End of discussion? Are you for real?"

"Mommy," Tatiana whispered, cutting through their tension. "Please don't fight."

Right away the bubble of her anger was pricked and she forced herself to calm down, to save this conversation for behind closed doors. "We're not fighting, honey. Just talking about adult things."

The car slowed as it approached an elegant four-story townhome in a gorgeous section of Moscow, surrounded by a concrete wall with black wrought iron spikes on top. Mature trees lined the street and the wealth of those who lived here was obvious. Tatiana turned in her seat to watch the gates slide smoothly open, admitting their entourage.

The home that they stopped in front of was painted a dark hunter green with gray accents, a very classic yet modern vibe. Alex tried to take Jessica's hand in his but she shook him off and ignored his hurt look. No, she was not holding hands with him when he'd been so openly disrespectful to her.

He was lucky she didn't stamp on his foot.

Maks opened their door and gave Alex a nod before helping them out. When he held her hand to escort her from the car, his gaze was decidedly heated and his thumb rubbed her palm before he released her. She glanced over at Alex to see if he'd noticed Maks' hot look, but he was busy helping Tatiana from the car.

With the little girl between them, they turned to face the double doors at the top of the small set of stairs leading to the home. As if on cue, the doors opened, revealing Petrov and his wife Vera.

If she hadn't known that Petrov was one of the most powerful people in the world, she would have dismissed him as an attractive older man, with dark hair like Alex's that had been liberally shot with silver. Dressed in a pair of black slacks and a crisp white button down shirt, he certainly didn't come off as a ruthless killer, but that is indeed what he was.

Her instincts were to shield her daughter from this dangerous man, but she wouldn't dare insult Petrov like that.

His wife, Vera, was probably in her late sixties but still exuded class and beauty, dressed in a tasteful blush pink pantsuit with her hair up in an elegant bun. What Jessica assumed were rather large diamonds sparkled at her wrist and ears. Her face didn't have the stretched and pulled look of Botox and facelifts and her blue eyes were kind but reserved as she met Jessica's gaze. For a moment they all stood there, examining each other, before Petrov smiled.

"Jessica and Tatiana, it is my utmost pleasure to welcome you to my home."

She couldn't help returning his smile, utterly disarmed by his charm and charisma. "Thank you so much for having us."

His gaze flickered to the bodyguards surrounding them, then he held out his hand. "Please, come in. I must steal your husband away for a little bit, but Vera will take care of you and your lovely daughter."

As soon as they were inside, Jessica found herself being led away into the elegant home by Vera, with Maks and a man she wasn't familiar with trailing after them like a pair of dark wolves.

They reached a room on the second floor with Vera pausing now and again, usually to show Jessica a picture of Dimitri and Alex when they were younger, among the other framed photos decorating the walls. Each image came with a story, and while Vera was still standoffish with Jessica, she was sweet to Tatiana and told her tales about her father when he was a little boy.

"Tatiana," the formal woman said in lightly accented English. "I would like to introduce you to some of your cousins. They have been awaiting your arrival and are in our playroom. Come, we will take you to them so your mother and I may talk."

Her daughter gripped her hand. "Mommy, I don't want to go. I want to stay with you. Please."

Alarmed at her daughter's sudden ashen look, Jessica gave Vera an apologetic smile. "Would it be possible for her to stay with me? At least in the same room?"

"Of course, but why don't you take a look at the playroom first, Tatiana? Would be shame for you to miss out on the wonderful chocolate cake chef made for you as snack."

An unfamiliar, exasperated voice came from Jessica's right. "Mother, you know Lani is going to kill you if you keep feeding the kids sugar."

They both turned to watch a curvy, glowing and very pregnant young woman in a stylish black-and-pink dress waddle down the hallway. Jessica absently noted that the woman's bare feet were very swollen, and that it looked like her belly had dropped. She bore an amazing resemblance to Vera, but her smile was wider, her gaze less guarded.

The woman looked at her and welcoming look. "My name is Polina and I am Petrov's youngest daughter."

Tatiana shifted, then took a couple steps and placed her hand on the woman's belly. "Are you having a baby?"

Polina startled at the slight touch, then shifted so she could look around her rounded stomach and smiled. "Yes, darling, I am. A little boy. Soon you will have new cousin."

"A cousin," Tatiana said in a wondering voice and Jessica's heart constricted. "I've always wanted a cousin. Gwen has a bunch and they're all so nice."

Polina smiled and stroked Tatiana's hair. "Now you have many, many cousins, who are so happy to have you here."

"Jessica," Vera said in a low voice, "it is important we talk in private."

She looked between Vera and her daughter, still chattering away with Polina. "I don't know if I'm comfortable having her away from me."

Vera nodded. "I understand your reluctance to be parted from Tatiana. Would you feel better being in the room next door to the children with an adjoining door that would be closed? You will be able to see her through a two-way mirror, but she will not be able to see us. The conversation we must have is not for her tender young ears. We guard their innocence for as long as we can, so when they finally face the world is with a little bit of a brain in their head." She gave her pregnant daughter a pointed look. "Take this one, for example, pregnant and refusing to get married."

"Mama, stop." This time there was a hiss in the other woman's voice.

"What? Is true."

Feeling a full-on mother/daughter brawl coming on, Jessica quickly said, "That's fine, let's go to the room so we can have some privacy."

Once they were in what looked like a small burgundy-and-gold themed sitting room, she noticed right away there was a giant two-way mirror that looked out into what could only be described as a child's fantasyland come to life. There was a mock tree house, a corner of the room that was filled with what looked like a big rack of child-size costumes, little tables with books and puzzles on them, and in general everything a kid could ever want, along with a good many adults keeping watch over the children in an unobtrusive manner. Climbing all over and playing with the toys were three little girls and two boys ranging in age from around eight to a toddler.

Despite Tatiana's rapturous cries over the different toys, Jessica hesitated to let her join them. "Are you sure she'll be all right?"

"Of course. We are merely a door away and Krom is in there, you just can't see him because he's in the far corner reading to Nina, my seven-year-old granddaughter, with three year old my great nephew Vicktor climbing his leg."

Polina eased herself into one of the padded chairs with an audible grunt. "Actually, Krom is much loved by the children. Odd, I know, but he has a way with them."

"He sings to me," Tatiana said in a shy voice.

Both women gasped then smiled at the girl, which made Tatiana hide her face against Jessica's hip.

"He sings to you?" Vera blinked, then leaned down and gave Tatiana a quick hug before standing again and meeting Jessica's gaze, tears glimmering in the other woman's eyes. "That is good news, very good news. This may be hard for you to understand, but I care deeply for the people that protect and guard my family. For the last five years, Krom has been a ghost of a man."

"He used to sing all the time," Polina added, "in church choir with his sister, of all places, but after your...ah, separation, part of his soul died as well because it was tied to you. He allowed you to be one of the very, very few people in his life who he cared about. Your death changed him."

Giving her sleeve a tug, Tatiana asked, "Mommy, why is she saying you died?"

Struggling for some kind of explanation, Jessica exchanged a glance with Polina, who had an embarrassed flush staining her cheeks as she smiled at the little girl. "Forgive me, Tatiana, my English is not so good sometimes. I say the wrong words."

The little girl considered this for a moment before easing her hold on Jessica. "Krom is teaching me Russian."

Vera held out her hand. "I am sure he will do a wonderful job. If you will follow me, Miss Novikov, I will introduce you to my grandchildren and great nephews. I think they are getting ready to have the cake soon."

At the word "cake", Tatiana abandoned Jessica without looking back. "The chocolate cake your chef made?"

Vera looked amused as she said, "Yes."

"One piece," Jessica called out to their retreating backs.

"Yes, Mommy," the little girl said as she darted through the doors, practically pulling Vera behind her now.

As soon as the little girl entered the room, Krom came into view on the left side of the giant window and crouched down, holding his arms open for her. She threw herself at the big man and he scooped her up with a laugh, twirling her around so the skirt of her dress flared out like dandelion fluff in the wind. Vera smiled at them, then began to motion to the other children in the room.

Gingerly putting her swollen feet up on the dainty coffee table, Polina sighed.

Giving her a sympathetic look, Jessica asked, "When are you due?"

"Soon. I keep telling myself that soon I will be done with this. Soon I will be able to tie my own shoes again, will be able to sleep for more than two hours without having to get up to use the restroom."

"Is this your first child?"

"Yes, and I cannot imagine how hard life was for you to go through pregnancy with Tatiana while you were alone with only your doula, Shannon, at your side in Miami."

"What—how did you know that?"

Shaking her head, Polina glanced at the room where Vera was still making introductions. "There is very little about you that is not known now, is way of world we live in. Knowledge is power and you are a great mystery to many. Is not every day the dead come back to life, yes?"

"I guess so." She took a seat across from Polina. "What else do you know?"

"I only briefly skimmed the file my father has on you."

"Wait, Petrov has a file on me?"

"Of course. For years he tried to help Alexandr find your killer. It was one of my father's greatest regrets that he could not save or avenge you. Alex is like son to him, and brother to me, so seeing him in such...agony hurt all of us."

"My husband," Vera said in a quiet voice as she came back into the room and shut the door gently behind her, "would do anything for Alex and Dimitri. How much do you know about their relationship?"

"I know that Alex spent a great deal of time with you growing up, and that he loves you very much."

Sitting on the love seat, Vera crossed her long legs and studied Jessica. "After Jorg lost his second wife, he also lost his mind. There were some...incidents that happened before we realized just how bad he had gotten. Petrov intervened and we had Dimitri and Alex live with us for over a year while Jorg got on medications to stabilize his psychotic episodes."

"I didn't know that."

"We will always, *always* do what is best for Alex," Vera said in a decidedly warning tone. "And we will eliminate any threats to him."

"Excuse me?" Jessica bristled. "Are you saying I'm a threat to him?"

"Yes and no."

Polina started to interrupt, but Vera held up one imperious hand. "Your very existence is threat because you are now powerful weapon to be used against him. Everyone saw how Alex lost himself for years after your death, how broken he was. There are those that would be eager to see Alex destroyed, those who would love to harm him in any way possible. You are his greatest weakness."

"But," Polina added with a glare thrown in her mother's direction, "you are also his greatest strength, if you choose to be. If you have the fortitude to truly be his partner in life."

"I don't understand what you're trying to say."

"What my daughter is saying, Jessica, is that you are no longer simply mother and wife. You are part of the Novikov *Bratva*, whether you wish to be or not, and you can either embrace the role and help your husband, or you can try to fight it and only cause him more heartbreak. I have been where you are, Jessica, thrust into an unknown world, given all this responsibility without knowing what to do with it. You do not know me, but I am hoping that you will allow me to offer what guidance I can."

"What guidance *we* can," Polina added. "I have helped out as my mother's social secretary when needed, helping her see to her duties as the wife of the head of the Dubinski *Bratva*. While I have utterly no desire to become further involved in that world, I can help you navigate it."

She slumped back into her chair, her gaze wandering to where Krom was down on all fours, giving the children horseback rides while Maks and the unfamiliar bodyguard watched with impassive faces, but amused eyes. "What kinds of duties will I have?"

"You are responsible for the heart of your people." Vera must have seen her confusion because she gave Jessica a small smile. "Alex is burdened with the daily task of keeping his people not only alive and happy, but prosperous. He does a good job at it, but he is only one man. You, if you step into the roll, will be a liaison between Alex and his people, someone they can go to who has Alex's ear."

Polina nodded. "There will be dinners to host, lunch events to attend, all sorts of things. In many ways it is like being the wife of a political leader. Like your president's wife, yes?"

"I think I understand what you're saying." She rubbed the bridge of her nose as she began to consider the enormous changes that were happening in her life.

"Is much to take in, I understand, but we are not telling you these things to scare you, but rather to help Alexandr, who we love. You must understand, Alex is responsible for the lives of tens of thousands of people. His daily decisions affect not only himself, but a vast group of people who depend on him to keep them safe and happy. Is a burden that would crush most men, but you can help ease it."

The enormity of the responsibility that Alex dealt with humbled her. She couldn't imagine having to make the kind of life and death decisions he had before him on a daily basis. While in theory she'd known lots of people depended on Alex, she'd never really considered how much control he had over their fate. In an odd way it was like being married to a king. Which made her a queen, and she needed to be his power behind the throne. The normal part of her blanched at the idea of involving herself in his dangerous world, but the woman she'd become over the last five years knew she had the strength to be there for Alex.

"Where do you think I should start?"

"The first thing you need," Polina said with a brisk clap of her hands, "is a good social secretary. Someone who is fluent in both English and Russian. Someone you can trust and is familiar with the Novikov *Bratva*. If you are open to the idea, I could have a list of possible candidates sent to you."

"What about Mariel Testov?" Vera asked. "She is very well connected and sweet."

A flush warmed Polina's cheeks and she switched to Russian while darting her gaze between her mother and Jessica. "She was one of Alex's mistresses a few years ago."

Jessica swallowed hard, trying to bury the flare of jealousy twisting her stomach into a sour knot.

"Oh, yes. That will not do."

Switching back to English, Polina gave Jessica a bright smile. "Do not worry, we will find the right woman for you."

Before she could stop her bitter words, they spilled out from her lips. "It might be hard to find a woman Alex hasn't slept with."

Polina flinched, but Vera's shoulders stiffened. "Regardless of who Alex was intimate with in the past, he loves you and he is a loyal man."

"I know." She sighed and turned her attention to where a little girl in a khaki romper was crouching next to Tatiana at a small table with a box of crayons, while Krom sat in a plush chair not too far away, watching them intently. "I know it's stupid, I know it's irrational, and I know Alex thought I was dead, but can you understand that it is difficult for me to deal with the knowledge that Alex had lovers while we were apart?"

"You were dead," Vera said while Polina tried to hush her mother.

Closing her eyes, she took a deep breath then slowly let it out, trying to keep her anger under control. "Yes, I was, and no, I don't blame him for…easing tension with other women. At least logically I don't, but I can't help that the idea makes me sick."

"Then you will have to deal with your feelings, because you are bound to run into more women Alex has been intimate with. And you must be prepared for their attacks."

"Attacks?"

"What my mother means," Polina said in a much gentler voice, "is that you will be moving in the social circles that many of the women Alex has…dated are in. And there are those who still pine for him, still hope to catch his eye and heart even though is impossible. You are only woman he has ever loved, and even while you were apart, you held his heart. Will always be yours."

The other woman's words soothed her and she unclenched her fists, not even realizing how tightly she was gripping her hands until her palms stung from her fingernails. "He's the only man I have ever loved."

Vera leaned across the small table and patted Jessica's knee. "We know this. If you did not love him so much you never would have left him."

Looking down at her hands, twisting the new engagement ring sparkling on her finger, she voiced one of her private worries. "You don't hate me because I left him?"

"No, not at all." Vera sighed. "You loved him and your daughter enough to give up everything to keep them safe. A weaker person would have stayed, would have endangered their lives for her own comfort and well-being. Five years ago you were a confused young woman who did the best she could against a man who could manipulate the devil. Let go of any misplaced guilt you have over this."

Her lower lip quivered as she tried to blink back her tears. "Thank you. I'm trying, but this is a lot to take in."

Polina cleared her throat. "Truly, we do not mean to add to your burdens. We are here to offer you any help or guidance you may need. All of Alex's friends are. My older sister, Lani, wants me to give you her phone number so you can call her if you wish. She could not be here today because," Polina's voice warbled, "because she is in the hospital with Semyon."

"Her husband," Vera added with a heavy sigh. "He has woken from his coma but he has much healing ahead of him. His brain is...not right yet. The grandchildren are staying with us while she stays with him in the hospital."

Feeling incredibly selfish, Jessica gave the women a sympathetic look. "I'm so sorry."

Visibly stiffening her spine, Vera nodded. "Is a tragedy, but we are also very luck. Three of my grandchildren almost lost their father entirely. Would be easy to give in to pain, to misery of what has happened to my family and wallow in grief. But God has blessed me to be mother and grandmother. I do not have the luxury for such things when my children need me."

Thinking back to how she had to pull it together for her daughter, despite the fact that she was barely functioning, Jessica nodded. "After Tatiana was born, I went through a really bad time. If I had my way I would have stayed in my room, trying to sleep my life away so I didn't have to face the pain of being awake. I probably would have never left my room except my little girl needed me so much. She depended on me for *everything* and I was trying to do it all on my own. Thankfully my wonderful nanny started working for me and she recognized the signs of postpartum depression right away."

"What is postpartum depression?"

"It's when a woman gets very, very sad after she has a baby, sometimes violent, but not in my case."

Vera folded her hands on her lap, the gigantic diamond ring glittering on her manicured finger. "Yes, we call it something different but we know what is."

"You got better?" Polina asked in a low voice while rubbing her stomach.

"Yes. I went to the doctors and they put me on medication to help pull me out of my depression." She flushed, a hint of embarrassment heating her body at admitting to the fact that she had to take drugs to stay sane. "It took a few months, but once they started to work with my body, I began to return to my old self. So yes, I understand wanting to cry until you pass out, but our children will always come first."

Slowly nodding, Vera gave her a small smile and visibly relaxed. "It will take a strong, compassionate woman to stand at Alexandr's side. I am glad to see that he has one. Now, let us discuss who is trying to kill you."

Chapter 10

Alex shifted in the hefty leather chair he'd been sitting in on and off for the past seven hours and fought to keep his attention on the presentation. While he knew he should give all the candidates equal attention, he also knew the one being shown to them now would not get Alex's vote for *Pakhan* of the Dubinski *Bratva*.

Across the room from Alex, his friend Ivan laced his fingertips together beneath his chin as they stared at the hologram of a tall, lanky man with deep-brown hair and a dour expression.

Matvey Yemilin, one of the candidates put forward to Petrov for his consideration as heir. There were easily two dozen men in the room, all of Petrov's most loyal men and allies. Including Efim Boldin, Kostya's uncle. That sharp-eyed old man kept studying Alex as they went through the candidates, but he ignored him. Many people were watching him right now, because they knew how much Petrov valued his input. Not only was Alex loyal to Petrov, he was also adept at reading people, and he knew the men in this room well enough to decipher most of what they were thinking.

And right now, the majority was unimpressed with Matvey.

He was a good candidate, a loyal soldier, and respected member of the community. But he was hesitant at times and that was something a *Pakhan* could never be. A man who hesitated was the one who took the bullet first. That made him a good mediator, but a bad solider.

That was the running theme of the day with the nominees. Good in one area, but not versatile enough to run an empire in a violent world. Dimitri sat next to Alex, with Petrov on his other side. His uncle had a notepad before him as if he was taking down information while each candidate was presented, but in reality it was a large stack of legal documents that Petrov was signing. Alex did not allow his gaze to wander over to the papers because that would be an invasion of his uncle's privacy, and an insulting betrayal of trust. So despite his curiosity, he forced himself to pay attention to the slowly rotating hologram of Matvey and the statistics being displayed next to his image.

They'd been going over candidates with Petrov's High Council for what seemed like forever. Jessica and Tatiana had left for home long ago, and his gut twisted every time he thought of them being there alone. Well, as alone as they could be with an army of people devoted to their protection surrounding them. He wondered if Jessica was going to be upset that he'd had to stay behind, but she'd seemed pensive when they parted, yet loving. Something had happened while she'd talked with his aunt and cousin, and he could only hope that whatever they said hadn't upset her.

For a brief moment he could feel the slender arms of his daughter around his neck as she'd hugged him goodbye. While he held her, she'd whispered in his ear that Mommy told her it was time for him to do superhero stuff and Tatiana wished him good luck saving the city. The memory lifted his spirit a bit, and he had to force himself to pay attention to the auditor reading off Matvey's financial history.

A loud, exasperated sigh filled the air and from across the room, Efim Boldin stood from his elegant black leather chair and leaned forward, planting his gnarled fists on the table. In his late eighties, his once powerful frame had shrunk somewhat, but his hard gaze remained the same. He was a staunch supporter of Petrov, but had been one of the most vocal about there being no peace between the Boldin and Novikov *Bratvas*.

At least he had at first.

Through sheer will and determination, Alex wore the old man down, not giving up until he made Efim see that peace between them was possible, that letting pride stand in their way was a sin against their families. Now, while he would never consider the old bastard a friend, there was a grudging respect between them.

Curious as to what was going on, he sat up straighter and focused on every line and wrinkle of the aged man's face, calling on his memories to know what each slight change in expression meant.

"We are wasting time, Petrov," Efim announced, his lips thinned with annoyance, but his gaze was direct and clear. "There is only one man who can fulfill your role well enough to ensure the continued peace and prosperity for our people."

Voices rose in dissent, and Dimitri exchanged a glance with Alex but kept silent. It was better to let the other men show their reactions. And reacting they were, yelling at each other while Petrov tapped his pen against the stack of papers before him. Without raising his voice, he simply said, "Enough. My decision has been made."

"But—"

Petrov held his hand up and his platinum-and-diamond cufflink flashed in the light. "Come here and read this before you speak again, old friend."

Efim grumped, but he stood and made his way around the massive table to where Petrov sat. The temptation to look down at what his uncle had written tore at Alex, but now Petrov kept the papers guarded from everyone but Efim. The old man pulled out his glasses from the inner pocket of his suit, then put them on and squinted as he read whatever document Petrov had decided to show him.

After scanning his gaze over the page twice, he handed the paper back with a sharp nod. "Wise choice."

While Efim made his way back to his seat, Petrov slowly pushed his chair back then stood, his gaze focused on the documents before him. The room grew hushed, only the faint sound of breathing mixing with a few men shifting here and there. Never had the power that his uncle wielded been more evident than when a room filled with some of the most influential men in the world fell silent to hear him speak.

The hair along Alex's arms prickled and a surge of adrenaline flooded his muscles with strength. A feeling went through him, a knowing, that whatever his uncle was about to say was going to change his life forever. The unpleasant shiver that raced down his spine sent a bolt of apprehension through him, but he fought it off.

"For many years," Petrov began, "I have witnessed some of the greatest and worst men come to power throughout the world. Leaders who took their people to unparalleled safety and success, while other men poisoned and corrupted everything they touched. As my friends, you know one of my mottos is, 'Those that ignore history are doomed to repeat it'. It is when we do not learn from our past mistakes, when we do not strive to rise above the circumstances that we are born into, that we become weak and easily defeated. A strong man pays attention to the sacrifices of those that have come before him, of what he may be required to do in order to protect his family."

Murmurs of agreement filled the air while Alex watched his uncle, absorbing the man's wisdom.

"But there lies the true heart of the problem. The man who would lead my people needs to be a man of honor and compassion, but also a ruthless predator who will do what is necessary to protect those who he loves." His voice lowered, threaded with some intense emotion Alex could not name. "There will come a time, gentlemen, when the very fabric of our society will crumble. It is inevitable, look to history. We are in a time of prosperity, wealth, and unparalleled access to knowledge, but much like ancient Rome, we are crumbling from within. The place we stand in is soaked in the blood of our ancestors who fought to keep what is ours. That turn of the wheel may be on us sooner than we think, taking us from a time of prosperity to a time of strife. It will take a brave, smart, *ruthless* man to endure and thrive."

Dimitri stiffened next to Alex and the quick glance they exchanged was filled with worry. If Uncle Petrov was warning of bad things on the horizon, only a fool wouldn't pay attention. And he had a point; the history of the Russian people, of humanity in general, was filled with death and chaos. To hope that the world would be any different from now until the end of time was a foolish dream. His thoughts turned to Jessica and Tatiana, the primitive need to defend them tightening his muscles even as he strained to remain impassive.

There were other worried glances around the table, and even the bodyguards looked shocked at what Petrov had said.

"With this in mind, there was only one man who would take care of my people as I would. One man who has proven himself over and over again to be trustworthy and reliable. He knows what the loss of a loved one does to a man's soul, how it could twist his heart to hatred, but he has always chosen the honorable path...well—as honorable as we are among ourselves."

This drew some quiet laughter that broke the tension a bit. From his left, he caught the incredulous sight of Ivan grinning, wide. When he noticed Alex looking at him, the fucker winked as if he knew the secret to some inside joke. As he tried to puzzle out Ivan's reaction, he turned back to Petrov—only to find his uncle looking closely at him.

"Upon my death, Alexandr Petrov Novikov will inherit the role of *Pakhan* from me, with the condition that he change his last name to Dubinski and absolve himself of all business ties to the Novikov *Bratva*. Family ties will, of course, be permitted and encouraged."

Blood rushed through his ears in a deafening roar as his heart sped, his mind refusing to believe he'd just heard his uncle offer him the Dubinski *Bratva*, the sixth most powerful criminal organization in the world.

He'd have to give up his name, and despite his hatred for his father, that pained him deeply.

But the Dubinski *Bratva*...his family would be safe.

The course of the world changed as he stood and took Petrov's offered hand, his voice rough with emotion as he said, "I would be honored."

Cheers rose from around the room as he was suddenly embraced by his friends, the congratulations raining down on him, some sincere, some not.

For what seemed like hours, but was probably less than thirty minutes, he talked with everyone, trying to get a grasp on what had just happened without being obvious. Eager to get home and share the news with Jessica, he made his way through the small group, stopping to shake a hand quickly or accept a pat on the back, before finding his uncle surrounded by some not-so-happy men.

To his surprise, Efim wasn't among them. When Alex passed him, the old man smirked, then patted him on the back and walked away with a grinning Kostya at his side. If he wasn't misreading things, Efim had been about to suggest Alex as a nomination when his uncle spoke.

He clasped his uncle's shoulder. "I regret that I must leave, but I need to be with Jessica and Tatiana right now."

"Of course," Petrov said in a low voice as he moved them over to a quiet corner of the crowded room. "I wish I could have named you sooner, but I had to let them present their candidates. Vera was cross with me because she couldn't be as honest with Jessica as she wanted. Your wife, by the way, has a huge fan now in my wife and daughter. They adore her and Tatiana, so expect them to be in your life, meddling around constantly."

He couldn't help but laugh despite the intense nature of his day. "Like they do not meddle already?"

The smiled dropped from Petrov's face and the gravity of his expression disturbed Alex. "Someday, they will be your responsibility."

"I will always take care of them, you have my word."

For a moment Petrov looked as if he wanted to say something, but ended up shaking his head instead. They stood there for a moment, looking at each other, before Petrov shook his head again and gave Alex a gentle push. "I have so much to tell you, but it can wait. If you take away one thing from tonight, let it be my warning. Diversify our land holdings; build us sustainable colonies around the world. Make them defendable."

"Against what?"

"Everything."

The entire ride home he'd brooded about his uncle's words, that sense of impending doom tickling at him again. He wondered if he had some form of PTSD from Jessica's loss. Thanks to his father's mental illness, he was well studied on the subject and knew what signs to look for. Now that he finally had a moment to contemplate in the silence of the car, he was able to analyze his own response to the things he'd learned tonight.

Like the fact that with the scratch of a pen before he'd left, he'd ceased to be Alexandr Novikov and became Alexandr Dubinski.

Stroking his beard, he stared out at the world slipping past his window, marveling at how quickly things could change. Nothing was permanent, all he could do was enjoy the moments he had while he had them. His reflection smiled back at him as he thought about Jessica waiting for him in bed, the sheets warm from her body, the scent of her permeating the air. Across the hall from her, their daughter slept in her own bed, a miracle in itself.

The mental image of his family safe and resting soothed him enough that when he walked through the lobby of the fortress he called home, he was able to maintain his usual slightly bored look instead of reflecting the stunned way he still felt deep inside.

People murmured congratulations to him and he nodded back, resisting the urge to push them away so he could reach his home quicker. The logistics of transitioning from one *Bratva* to another, to becoming the fucking *Pakhan* of the Dubinski *Bratva*, began to set in. He was no longer a Novikov. An ache pierced his chest, and when Rya met him at the entrance to his floor, he gladly took her into his arms with a soft sigh.

She hugged him back, the thin silk of her black robe flowing beneath his fingertips, comforting him. "Look, Alex, this doesn't mean we're not family anymore. I don't care what your last name is. You will always be Dimitri's brother and my favorite brother-in-law."

Instead of laughing, he sighed again and held her close. "I am also your only brother-in-law, but thank you."

After a few more moments of hugging each other, he gently released her then stepped back. "I must go see my wife."

"Uh, about that." Rya fiddled with her robe. "She seemed a little...agitated earlier."

"What do you mean?"

"She talked a lot about either kicking you in the balls or punching them."

"That is not good. Did she say why?"

"No, but she didn't mention killing you so that's always a bonus."

Smiling, he shook his head before giving her another hug. "Thank you, Rya."

She hugged him back tight. "Goodnight."

The walk down the hall was quick, and he didn't bother to acknowledge anyone who spoke to him.

They all could wait.

First, he must remind his wife of the harsh reality of his world and pray their marriage was strong enough to survive.

Chapter 11

Jessica paced between the perfectly made bed and the comfortable mocha suede couch set, her strides long and impatient. She was so mad steam should have been coming out of her nose like an angry dragon. Her bare feet hardly made a sound on the thick, lush carpet, and a childish part of her wished she was wearing shoes on a wooden floor so she could stomp properly like she walked.

The memory of her daughter doing just that made her pause. Gee, wonder where Tatiana had gotten that lovely trait from. The thought of her little girl calmed her somewhat, and she tried to gather herself for the confrontation ahead. Arguing with Alex was the last thing she wanted to do, but this was complete and utter bullshit.

Thanks to Vera, Jessica was now aware that she had a five-million-dollar hit out on her—that Alex knew about, but didn't tell her. Like it somehow wasn't her business that professional assassins would now be hunting her. The surprise, then pitying understanding on Vera and her daughter's face had only deepened her urge to choke her husband. She may not have had much over the last five years, but she'd had her pride.

She was almost to the bed again when the door opened and Alex came into the room, his gaze finding her right away and pinning her in place.

Still wearing the same black suit he'd had on when they'd left the house this morning, he looked as tired as she felt, and she had to battle the need to comfort him. Stupid overactive nurturing instinct. "Hello, Alex."

"Rya warned me that you are upset with me."

At the mention of her sister-in-law, she flushed, feeling like a bitch for how snippy she'd been with Rya earlier tonight. Her new sister-in-law had stopped by to see if Jessica wanted to hang out while the men were gone, but she'd been in no mood for company, no matter how nice the other woman had been.

Tatiana was also being cranky at that point, the long day spent playing with her cousins catching up to her, along with all the traveling. Thankfully Gwen was there to work her magic after Jessica gave Tatiana a bubble bath filled with toys. An obscene amount of toys. She'd have to find a way to donate at least half of them. With that many things to play with, her daughter had fooled around with each one for about twenty seconds before tossing it aside in favor of a new toy. Jessica had been raised to appreciate everything she had, and she'd be damned if her daughter was going to turn out to be one of those vapid, entitled children of the super-rich.

Gwen had been rather cranky as well, but for different reasons. Like Jessica lying to her about everything. About how her scary-as-hell husband was alive. And how Gwen basically now lived in lockdown with an irritating Krom always breathing down her neck. And how Krom was a moody bitch. And how Krom had no sense of personal space.

Gwen had talked about Krom so much that Jessica had bluntly warned her away from the damaged man, not wanting her friend to get hurt by someone she knew wasn't interested in romance or love. After that, Gwen had been quiet and Jessica worried that she'd hurt her friend's feelings, but she had bigger things to think about at the moment.

Like the army of ninjas who were just waiting for her to make one wrong move so they could end her life.

"Alex, is there something you haven't told me? Something I should know? Like maybe the fact that I have a five-million-dollar hit out on my head?"

He stilled and she suddenly found herself the focus of a very intense man. "Who told you?"

Not wanting to get Vera in trouble, she shook her head. "It doesn't matter."

His shrewd look pierced right through her. "It had to be Vera."

Damn him and his mind-reading skills. "I didn't say it was."

Casting her a sideways glance, he began to take off his jacket. "That is not important right now."

"The fuck it's not. I happen to find it very important."

He shook his head, then began to unbutton his shirt. Inch by inch his broad, sculpted chest with the tattoo of her name and the memorial roses beneath came into view. At the sight of her ink on his flesh, some wounded part of her soul eased and she looked away while the tears burned her eyes.

"Is not what I meant, your safety is everything to me."

Vera had told her she would need to be direct with Alex. According to the older woman, men were blunt creatures. Give them too many details and you would lose them.

"Alex, you need to know that if our marriage is going to work, you have to treat me like a partner. I must know what is going on in the world around us, especially if it's a matter of safety. That's part of the trust thing between us. I swear you won't regret it. You always say knowledge is power, right? Well give me something to fight back with."

He began to unbuckle the gold buckle of the black leather belt holding up his pants while he slowly crossed the room. For a moment, she was distracted by the way his muscled torso bunched and flexed with his movements, but she forced her gaze back to his dark, serious face. When he came to a stop, he was less than a foot away and she leaned toward him, yearning to close the distance between them no matter how pissed off she was.

"I am trying to tell you something very important, something that will give you a great deal of power, but you will not give me a chance to speak."

"Oh." She blinked up at him while he ran the backs of his fingers over her cheek. "What is it?"

"Come, let us sit."

She allowed him to lead her over to the brown couch and gave out a little squeak when he sat, then yanked her onto his lap so that she was straddling him. "Really? We can't have this conversation without me on top of you?"

He laced his fingers together on her lower back, holding her tight. "Something I did not expect happened tonight, something that has taken me by complete surprise."

The soft hair of his chest tickled her fingertips as she stroked the delineation between his pectoral muscles. "Alex, just spit it out already. What happened?"

He took a deep breath, his big body lifting beneath her. "Tonight my uncle Petrov named me as heir to the Dubinski *Bratva*, and I accepted the position."

"What?" She stared at him, waiting for him to crack a smile. "You're kidding me, right?"

"Is no joke."

Shock slammed through her and she sagged. Alex's grip on her back tightened, the concern on his handsome face calming her even as her heart raced. Actually, he looked more than concerned, he looked panicked. Her husband rarely looked panic, but it was an expression she'd noticed a great deal of in private over the last few days. Seeing him distraught like this reminded her of Vera's warning that Alex would need her to help support him when the world wanted to grind him into dust. At the time she'd just thought it was in reference to their reunion and getting used to each other again, but now she wondered if the older woman had been trying to warn Jessica about what Petrov was going to do. She tried to calm her frantic thoughts and focus on what her husband had just said.

"I need to be clear on this. Your uncle has named you heir, which means one day you will lead the Dubinski *Bratva*? You'll be the *Pakhan,* correct?"

"Yes."

All the time she'd spent researching the world of the Russian mafia while they were apart came to mind and she frowned at him. "But you can't be the head of the Dubinski *Bratva*; you're the heir to the Novikov *Bratva*."

"Much has changed. My brother Dimitri was named heir by my father. I am—or I was—to head up the public franchises the Novikov *Bratva* owns that support our people." His thumbs stroked her lower back in a soothing motion. "I am afraid you will not like that our name will change."

"Pardon me?"

"You were right. A Novikov could not lead the Dubinski *Bratva*. That is why my name, our name, is now Dubinski. I signed the papers that my uncle had prepared, in front of many very powerful men tonight. Was essential part of taking on role of *Pakhan*. I do not regret it, because half of the blood in my body belongs to my mother's people, and it honors me to take her maiden name."

She swallowed hard. "I'm...I'm Jessica Dubinski?"

"Yes."

The unreality of this moment washed over her, leaving her feeling lightheaded.

"Do you know I'll have had four last names?" She ticked her fingers off as she spoke. "Venture, Novikov, St. Cloud, and now Dubinski. Wait—five, because I was a Cleary for eighteen months before I became a Venture." A somewhat wild giggle escaped her before she abruptly sobered. "Your father, is he going to kill you for changing sides?"

"He is a nonissue."

"Alex, he's going to be furious with you over changing your name. You know how traditional he is, how caught up in his pride. He's going to lose his mind."

"I am hoping the shock will kill him and save us all the trouble."

A startled laugh escaped her and she rested her face against his chest, soothing herself with his heartbeat. "You know what, suddenly the hit on me doesn't seem like that big of a deal."

He kissed the top of her head over and over again. "It will be dealt with, I promise."

"How? Vera said it would be next to impossible to get rid of it."

"Jessica, look at me."

When she lifted her gaze to his, she was staggered by the ferociousness of his expression. "You both underestimate me, when you should both know better."

Flushing, she looked away and fiddled with the edges of his shirt. "I'm sorry."

He gave a weary sigh. "So am I. This is not how I wish for things to occur. If I had my way, I would disappear for next twenty years with you and Tatiana. Find some quiet part of the world to raise our family where we could be safe and happy. Unfortunately, that is about as likely to happen as unicorn appearing in Red Square."

Laughing softly again, she let herself stare at him to her heart's content, gaining strength from the growing bond between them. "Honestly, Alex, I had that kind of safe life in Miami but without you, it was nothing."

"Being with me puts you both in such peril. I hate that more than anything, knowing how I have endangered both your lives."

"Hey now, enough with the melodrama." His arched brows raised high in indignation, but she ignored him. "We could sit around all day finding ways to make every bad thing that's happened in the world somehow be our fault, but I'd rather enjoy what we have."

Vera's words of wisdom came to mind, *'You are your husband's source of joy, comfort, and relief. Spoil him with love and he will move mountains for you.'*

Gentling her tone, she stroked his hair back from his temples, fingering the silver strands. "You look tired."

He gave her a weary smile. "It has been a long day."

"Mmm, if I remember right, I know the best way to make sure you sleep well...Master."

Heat flared in his gaze and the world around them began to slip away as she fell beneath his sensual spell.

"And what is it that you remember?"

With a slow grind of her hips, his semi became a full-on erection. "How much I enjoy serving you in all ways. How much I love to suck your cock. You remember that, don't you? All those times I took you so far into my throat it burned, and held my breath while you flooded my mouth with your cum."

"My filthy girl." His low growl seared through her. "I want Maks to eat your pussy while you swallow my cock. Feeling your mouth on me as you orgasm, the way you sigh against my dick, is one of my favorite memories of you. Will you allow that?"

"What? You want Maks to join us?"

Startled, she almost shifted off his lap before he caught her and hauled her back with a blank expression. "Forgive me, I was wrong to assume that you would want him to pleasure you."

She chewed her bottom lip. In truth she missed the excitement of the lifestyle they'd enjoyed together, but right now she was still feeling out her relationship with her husband. "Alex, we kind of need to ease back into all of...that."

"We never have to do any of that ever if you do not wish it, Jessica." He grasped her face between his hands, his silver eyes bright with emotion and a hint of fear. "I am sorry I brought it up. You must think I am depraved to suggest such a thing."

"No, no, I don't think you're depraved." She sighed, hating to think that Alex would hide his desires from her in the future for fear of offending her. "I'm just...possessive of you right now. I want to drown myself in you, to revel in being able to touch you, taste you, enjoy you. Anything or anyone else would be a distraction from who I really want and need. My beloved husband."

"I am possessive of you as well, but your happiness is my satisfaction. I want you to drown in pleasure, to give you anything and anyone that you desire. That has not changed."

Closing her eyes, she shook her head. "Only you could make permission for me to have an orgy sound romantic."

"Is gift."

"I love you."

"I love you so much, *dorogoya*," Alex whispered before he captured her lips in a gentle kiss. "You hold a piece of my soul, keep safe and clean for me even when the world coats me in its filth. Most amazing woman I have ever met, and also most beautiful."

She boldly licked his lips, loving the way his hips thrust up slightly. "Come with me. I want to show my Master just how much I missed him."

With a small smile she led him to the bed, then ran her hands over his chest. "Permission to undress you, Master?"

His gaze was incendiary, and he barely nodded. "*Da.*"

She couldn't help but smile as she ran her hands over his body. "You wouldn't believe how much time I've spent these past five years dreaming about touching you like this."

"Jessica—"

The pain in his voice had her placing her fingertips gently against his lips.

"No, I'm not sad, I'm grateful." She slowly bit her lower lip, then released it, knowing it drove him crazy. "Grateful and incredibly horny. God, I can't be around you without wanting to be as physically close as possible. Just touching you sends chills through me."

She ran her fingers through his soft hair, loving the heat of him against her body, enjoying the intense pleasure that she got from just being with him. Through her actions, she wanted to show him how much she cared. The need to submit to him, to give him everything he desired, burned through her clean and pure. There was no conflict in her heart about serving her Master; it was as natural to her as breathing.

Turning so her back was to him, she removed her own clothes slowly enough to tempt and tease him, to test his self-control. Energy thrilled through her as he gripped his cock and gave it a hard squeeze once she was nude and facing him again. With him watching her like this, she became hyperaware of her body, sinking into the first warm layers of her subspace. By the time she reached him again, her moves were languid, flowing, every touch a seduction. The smooth skin of his shoulders was revealed to her and she instantly rubbed her cheek against his warm skin. With a sigh, she leaned up on tiptoe to kiss a thin, white scar going over the meaty curve above his collarbone then kissed her way down. His crisp chest hair tickled against her face and she rubbed her lips over the hard bump of his nipple. Giving into an impulse, she moved on and rained gentle, lingering kisses over his torso, loving him with her touch.

"You have the most amazing lips," he murmured and stroked his hand affectionately down her cheek. "Nothing like them in the world. They soothe me when nothing else can, give me hope when all of mine is lost."

She dropped her hands to his belt, smoothly removing it before unbuttoning his pants. The sensation of the firm muscles of his lower abdomen against the backs of her fingertips was heaven. Once they were loose, he quickly stepped out of them, stripping off his socks and giving her a hell of a view of his massive body. As soon as he stood, she plastered herself against him, rubbing her body over his and creating a torrent of sparks that lit her blood. Need pulsed through her sex, but she was enjoying the moment too much to rush it.

"I always loved how big you were," she whispered as she met the rolling thrust of his hips, moving almost as if they were grinding against each other on the dance floor. "The first time I saw you, I noticed how massive your hands were. I'd never been attracted to that before in a man, but as soon as I saw your fingers all I could think about was how they would feel inside of me. So long and thick."

He made a pleased sound when she raised one of his fingers to her mouth and slowly sucked on the tip.

"All the better to touch you with, my dear."

She released his digit with a loud pop of her lips, then smiled. "Are you the big bad wolf?"

"Yes, and I am going to eat you."

"You can't be serious."

"You better run, because I am coming for you."

"You don't scare me."

"Last warning."

"Am I supposed to be afraid of you now?"

She was openly taunting him and she had a feeling he was about to end her little game then remind her who was in charge.

Her clit pulsed at the thought.

"You are mine now, *prinsessa moya*. Perhaps it is time I remind your *pizda* who it belongs to."

Her laughter rang out through the room as he picked her up, then tossed her on the bed. The joy of being with Alex felt so damn good on all levels that even as he buried his rough face between her thighs, all she could do was smile and grab on to his hair. His clever, blessed tongue danced over her clit, flicking and rubbing against the little bud until she was moaning softly. In response, he cupped her bottom and suckled her, growling when she tensed and her back arched, the first waves of her orgasm tightening everything deep inside. Then he began to rhythmically suck her clit and she broke, pulses of ecstasy crashing through her.

He licked at her, his touch incredibly soft and tender. Fuck, Alex didn't just make love with his cock; right now his mouth was definitely making love to her pussy. The breath escaped her lungs in a long, pleasure-saturated sigh that made Alex look up at her and smile. He rested his chin on her pubic mound and she lovingly traced her fingers over his face.

"That was amazing."

"I know."

Laughing, she helped him up the bed until his body was covering hers, both of them smiling despite Alex's rock-hard cock pressed between them. The muscles of his arms flexed enticingly as he pushed himself up over her and her legs naturally fell open for him. They both looked down as he slid the flushed head of his big dick between her puffed-up labia, teasing her clit until she once again panted beneath him, dying for his cock deep inside of her.

"Alex, please," she whimpered.

"What is it, *dorogoya*? What do you want?"

"I need you to shove that big dick of yours inside of me, now, and fuck me until I come all over you."

A low, deep groan vibrated through his body into hers and he did just as she asked, gripping the thick base of his erection and lining himself up before pushing into her with all his strength. She screamed out in discomfort as he pressed somewhere deep inside of her that sent shocks of painful electricity through her nervous system. The urge to safeword out hovered on the tip of her tongue, but before she could say it, he leaned down and sucked gently on her nipple while he rubbed her clit with his thumb.

Twisting beneath him, she whimpered, unable to separate the discomfort from the gratification of being stuffed absolutely full with dick. In marked contrast to his initial vicious thrust, his next moves were slow and gliding strokes that rubbed her just right. Wrapping her hands in his hair, she held him to her breast while he worshiped her body with his, surrendering to him as she let herself totally go.

"That's it, baby, give yourself to me," he purred.

Unable to form a thought coherent enough for words, she responded with her body by clasping him with her internal muscles. Right away he stiffened, then picked up his pace. Squeezing him every time he went deep, she felt her belly begin to tighten with her impending orgasm. It hovered just out of reach, but came closer with every thrust of Alex's body into hers. When he raised his lips to hers, she met him in a soul-consuming kiss, their bodies as intertwined as they could possibly be.

When her climax hit her, she cried out into his mouth, her hips jerking against him while he threw his head back and roared out his release. The thick pulse of his cock inside of her had Jessica twitching, her body so overstimulated by this point that just the brush of his skin against hers was almost too much. Tucking her against him, Alex rolled them so she was on top, still connected by his dick slowly softening inside of her.

Stroking her damp back, Alex let out a rumbling hum of pure contentment. "Just when I think there is no possible way that I will be able to relax enough to go to sleep, you fuck the tension right out of me."

She snorted a laugh against his chest. "You're welcome, I think."

When he leaned over to turn off the light, he slipped out of her and she scampered out of bed to grab some baby wipes that she'd started keeping nearby. By the time he had the pillows adjusted to his liking, she was clean enough to slide back into bed with him, happy little sighs escaping her as she cuddled close. The heavy weight of his arms wrapped around her and she rubbed her nose against his chest, unable to get close enough to him as the sound of his heartbeat lulled her to sleep.

Chapter 12

The next morning Jessica slept in late, and it took her longer than usual to get ready. Today she was a different woman...with a new last name. And with that name and status change came a great responsibility. Her mind still wasn't sure how to accept the new realities to her world, but she was managing to keep her panic at bay. With bodyguards and cameras watching her at what felt like pretty much all times, she knew she needed to project a certain appearance if she wanted their respect. And hyperventilating while saying "Oh my God" over and over again probably wasn't the impression she was going for. The meds her doctor had prescribed her helped a great deal, leaving her clearheaded but not as jumpy, and she was thankful for them.

With the need to at least look the role she'd been thrust into, she'd donned a fabulous purpely-gray knit dress and paired it with some amazing silver snakeskin Gucci heels. Impressive diamond-stud earrings surrounded by platinum filigree went in her ears and a matching bracelet on her wrist. The big sapphire wedding set still glittered on her finger, and she added a thick serpentine platinum choker with a filigree of diamonds. She felt as if she was dressed for a fabulous New Year's Eve party instead of going to breakfast, but she needed to get used to the new culture she found herself in.

Plus, it was fun to play dress up with the jewels Alex had designed for her all those years ago. In a way it felt like she was reclaiming a part of her past, and not just in a physical sense. Each piece of jewelry held a memory, a perfect snapshot of the moment Alex had given her the different pieces. The earrings she wore today were new, but he'd given the necklace to her at their home in Ireland before going out and playing in the snow. Well, she played while he watched her with a predator's intent, but it had been fun.

Touching the now warm metal of the necklace fondly, she still wondered if it was too much.

Vera had said that in the social circles Jessica would now move in, it was the normal thing for the women to wear small fortunes in jewelry in public. It was a statement of both Alex's wealth and protection that she could wear such audacious bling without fear of getting mugged. No one, not even the world's best jewel thief, would be tempted to steal from Alexandr Dubinski.

A shiver raced down her spine, momentary apprehension urging her to stall, but she forced herself to walk to the door of her bedroom and face the day.

As soon as she was in the brightly lit hall, Zoya caught her attention. The woman wore a charcoal-gray suit that was of a severe cut, but the pale-green blouse beneath added a feminine touch that kept the statuesque woman from appearing too butch. Yesterday she'd seen a few of the male bodyguards giving Zoya appreciative looks behind her back, but none to her face. Jessica didn't blame them; Zoya could break balls with a glance.

"Good morning, Mrs. Novikov...my apologies, I mean Mrs. Dubinski."

"I wish you would call me Jessica. That's the only part of my name that hasn't changed a hundred times."

Zoya gave her a faint, wry smile as they moved down the hallway together. "As you wish, Jessica."

More bodyguards stood off to the side while they made their way downstairs. Voices filled the air and grew louder as Zoya led her to the elegant and modern dining room walled off from the kitchen and living room. A simple ebony wood table stretched almost the length of the large space, and it was filled with people. They all turned as one when she entered the room and she almost froze beneath all the attention. Some of the faces she didn't recognize, but Vera was there, along with Petrov, who was currently talking to Gwen seated next to him. Ivan and Gia sat next to Dimitri and Rya, but it was Tatiana who captured her attention.

"Mommy!"

Everyone chuckled as Tatiana sprang from her chair and darted across the room to Jessica. Today her daughter wore a pair of bright-pink and orange striped tights along with a jean skirt and a white sweater. She thought it was ambitious to dress her daughter in white before breakfast, but Tatiana looked so cute with her braided pigtails that all Jessica could do was catch her daughter in a big hug. The sweet smell of maple syrup hit her as she kissed Tatiana's cheek.

"Good morning, honey. Did you sleep well?"

"Gwen had a sleepover with me last night. We painted our nails!" She proudly displayed her tiny fingernails, now sporting a bright-pink polish that matched her tights.

"Oh, I'm jealous, it looks so pretty."

"And Papa gave me this," Tatiana said proudly, pointing to a glittering white stone on a fine gold chain that Jessica hadn't noticed before.

"That's beautiful," Jessica murmured as she examined the necklace, pretty sure her not-yet-five-year-old daughter was wearing a two-carat diamond around her neck.

"You don't like it?"

Aware that she wasn't masking her reaction from her daughter very well, she hooked her hair back behind her ear to show Tatiana her earrings. "I love it. Your papa got these for me. We match."

Tatiana pouted, "I want my ears pierced."

"Not until you're older."

Alex's deep voice rumbled from behind her. "Let her have her ears pierced, Jessica. She would look beautiful."

Tightening her jaw, she stood and turned so she was facing Alex, not allowing herself to be distracted by how edible he looked in his black suit and pale-silver tie. "She is too young."

"What harm would it do? I will find the best person in Moscow to pierce them for her."

Tatiana skipped over to her father and gave him a beaming smile. "Thank you, Papa."

Jessica could feel her eyes growing wide as she took in the indulgent smile Alex gave her. "Anything for you, my sweet Tatiana."

She swore she snapped a couple of her back molars while gritting her teeth in an effort to keep from snarling.

People around the room shifted uncomfortably, then Petrov rose from the table, wiping his mouth with a burgundy cloth napkin. "Jessica, it is so good to see you again, thank you for the wonderful breakfast."

It took a lot to contain her need to drag Alex out of the room by his ear, but she managed to turn her gaze to Petrov and attempt a smile. "You are welcome anytime, Petrov, it is always my pleasure to have you in my home."

Vera, dressed in a chic peach crushed-silk dress, gave her a little nod of the head, as if approving of the way she was handling the situation.

The elegant older man graced her with a small wink. "As delicious as this meal has been, I am afraid I must steal your husband from you so that we may attend to some business."

"Of course." She darted away before Alex could touch her, not pausing as she made her way to the sleek chrome and metal table against the wall that held the coffee service. "Have a good day."

She almost dropped the coffee cup she'd grabbed when strong hands gripped her shoulders. After she was spun quickly around, Alex pressed his mouth to hers and ravaged her in a most pleasant manner, all the while ignoring her attempts to discreetly shove him away. Those pushes soon turned into gropes as she felt up his solid abdominals beneath his shirt. The little moan that escaped her would have been embarrassing if Alex hadn't growled as well and deepened the kiss. Their tongues stroked against each other and she was lost in him, the hard press of his body, the key lime and cedar of his cologne, and his lovely taste flavored with coffee.

A shattering sound made her jump with a small shriek, but to her embarrassment she realized she'd been so caught up in the kiss that she'd dropped her coffee cup.

Without missing a beat, Alex swept her into his arms, stepped over the shards of the cup, and gently placed her into an empty seat.

"Be safe, my wife. I love you."

It had all happened so fast that by the time she'd remembered why she was angry, he was gone and she was left looking at a table full of bemused women.

Glancing around, she looked for Tatiana but didn't see her. "Where's my daughter?"

Rya was obviously fighting a grin as she said, "While Alex was busy asserting his dominance over you, Gwen took Tatiana to her playroom."

She groaned and heat flooded her face as embarrassment spiked through her. "I'm sorry about the PDA."

Laughing, Gia shook her head. "If I had a dime for every time Ivan has shut me up like that in public, I'd be a billionaire like my husband."

"Besides," Rya added while smoothing down her crimson off-the-shoulder shirt with a grin, "I'm impressed that you didn't kick Alex right between the legs. He was being a complete douchebag."

"Indeed," Vera said in a dry voice, giving the two younger women a look of amusement and exasperation.

Jessica sighed, then leaned back and tapped the edge of the table with her fingertips. "We haven't even had a chance to talk about it, but he's already spoiling her rotten."

"Are you surprised?" Gia asked while spearing a piece of melon with her fork. "Think of how much they spoil us. Ivan is going to be *dreadful* when we have children. I can only hope we have boys."

"Amen," Rya muttered.

"So," Vera clapped her hands together, "we also have much to discuss. Gia, Rya, I asked you to join me today because the three of you must work together with your husbands to save the world."

Rya choked on a piece of toast and Gia pounded her on the back while saying, "I beg your pardon?"

While Rya drank some juice, Vera smiled. "Maybe not so literally, but have you really considered how much influence you wield between the three of you? How many ties of friendship you have to other powerful women? Thankfully my nephews were wise in their choices of wives, because they will need you in the days to come."

A frown twisted Gia's full lips. "What are you talking about?"

Jessica's stomach growled and she got up to make herself a plate from the elegant buffet while listening to Vera speak.

"There are many changes happening right now, and the world is destabilizing as we speak." Vera sighed, then traced the edge of the table with her fingertip. "It is nothing Petrov and I can put our finger on, nothing that would indicate one problem that could be fixed, but rather a combination of things all happening at once. Wars, climate change, governments being overthrown and technology advancing faster than we can keep up. My husband, if he was not head of the Dubinski *Bratva*, would have made an excellent historian. He loves to read about the rise and fall of various empires and has developed an eye for how things might fail, and when. It has made him a very successful man. After much discussion over the last few years, we are afraid that there are signs all across Russia, all across the world, of a change coming. The empires that currently rule are beginning to rot from within and the world will seek to restore the balance of power once again."

Gia spoke in a quiet voice as Jessica came back to the table. "Like a revolution, or World War Three, or something else?"

"We do not know." Vera shrugged. "Of course this could all be the ramblings of a crazy old man and his wife."

Rya snorted, then leaned back in her chair, her warm amber gaze sharp on Vera. "In the time I've known Petrov, he hasn't exactly struck me as the hysterical type. If he feels that something wicked this way comes, we'll try and help our husbands to be ready for it."

"Good, now let us discuss your party, Jessica."

"Party?" Jessica asked after hastily swallowing a mouthful of scrambled eggs.

"Of course. We must introduce you and Tatiana to society."

"Uh—is that a good idea with a bounty on my head?"

All the women laughed and Gia gave her a small smile. "Darling, we all have bounties on our heads."

"What?"

Rya nodded and reached out to Gia, grabbing the other woman's hand and giving it a quick squeeze. "Different assholes would love to get their hands on us for a variety of reasons. Gia because she's the wife of one of the richest men in the world, Vera because she is Petrov's wife, and me either because my stepdad is the vice president of an outlaw MC back in the States or because of Dimitri. There isn't a moment of our lives, since we met our men, that we haven't been in some kind of danger."

"She's not trying to freak you out," Gia added.

"Yeah, I'm not trying to scare you. I wanted you to know that just because someone or something threatens you, doesn't mean you have to live your life afraid. When I first came to Russia with Dimitri it took me a while to adjust to my new reality, which included a loss of the freedom that I've always taken for granted. You have no idea how much I'd love to just hop on my motorcycle and go cruising around Russia, but that will never happen. At least not without a discreet helicopter escort."

Gia snorted. "Or go for an early morning swim in the ocean without six other people joining you and more guards in scuba gear on jet skis patrolling offshore."

"But," Vera added with a wry look at the two younger women, "the rewards are well worth the sacrifice. You also need to remember that you chose this life. Right now you could be living with some normal, boring man in some normal, boring small town, where your biggest worry is what to make for dinner. All three of you had the opportunity to give up your husbands, but you chose to stay with them. Everything comes with a price."

"If it was just me, I wouldn't be so worried about my loss of freedom, but I worry about what this will do to Tatiana."

"Having raised children myself, I can tell you it will not be easy, but being a mother never is, no matter where you live or what the circumstances are."

She sighed and picked at her food. "I know. I just worry so much about Tatiana."

"Is perfectly normal to feel that way," Vera agreed. "But you have to trust in your husband to protect you both, or life will drive you insane."

"I do, but I'm not the kind of woman who can just sit back and let someone else do all the work. Not now, not after doing it on my own for so long. I can't just relax and eat chocolates, ignorant of the danger around me. If someone is threatening me, I want to know so I can be ready to kick their ass."

"You must trust your husband to handle these situations."

Gia leaned back in her chair and crossed her arms. "So if someone is trying to kill me, I tell them to hold on, I need to contact my husband first?"

"I'm not exactly the 'princess waiting for a rescue' kind of girl either," Rya muttered.

"Ditto," Jessica added.

With an exasperated sigh, Vera threw her hands in the air. "No one is asking you to be a sacrificial lamb. I am telling you that is easier to trust your husband and work with him to protect you, than to do it on your own. Work together or this world will tear you apart."

"Oh, well that's different," Rya said with a slight flush coloring her cheeks.

Once again in control of the room, Vera focused her gaze on Jessica. "Back to what I was saying earlier, we must prepare you for the party."

"Like what to wear?"

"Not exactly. We will need to go over who to invite, and why. Then we will gather biographies on the guests and go over them. We will need at least few weeks before we send out the invitations, and then another few weeks to throw the party together and give people time to arrive. Gia, Rya, I know this is short notice but would benefit you to attend our planning. I know you have both done this kind of thing before, but I can help you figure out some of the undercurrents of our world. There will be people there who would kill you as easily as look at you if they had chance."

Rya twirled her ponytail with a bemused and slightly uneasy smile. "I'm not sure if I should be excited we're throwing a party, or terrified that we're throwing a party."

"It is," Vera said with a knowing look, "entirely up to you on how you choose to live your life. Do you wish to live like you are at a festival, or a funeral?"

"Festival," Rya said instantly and released her ponytail. "Definitely a festival."

A loud knock came from the door, followed a moment later by Zoya peeking her head in with a flush coloring her pale cheeks. "Forgive the interruption, ladies, but Mr. Dubinski wishes to speak to his wife."

Jessica watched Vera, waiting for the other woman to stand and leave the room to take the call, but the older blonde merely looked back at Jessica with an arched brow. "I believe she means you, Mrs. Dubinski."

Flushing, Jessica stood and smoothed down her dress. "Oh, right. That's going to take a bit of getting used to."

The corner of Vera's lips turned up in amusement. "If I have not mentioned before, I am honored to have you and your daughter as my family now, Jessica."

"Thank you." She would have said more but Zoya thrust a cell phone at her. "Hello?"

"Jessica," Alex said in a low, serious voice. "Catrin is on her way up to see you."

She took an unsteady step back, waving away Zoya when the other woman went to steady her. "Catrin's here? I thought you said she was with Nico in Madagascar."

"Word reached them that you had returned."

"Oh my God," she whispered while her heart began to pound. "Oh my God. They're here? Oh, Alex, I've missed them so much."

"I must go, but you have my permission to enjoy anything you wish with them. Am I clear, *prinsessa moya*? Catrin has missed you as well and I know she will want to devour you. I want you limp with satisfaction when I come home so I can slide into your already wet, tight *pizda*."

Conscious of the other women standing from around the table, she said quickly, "Yes, I understand."

"It eases my worry to know that you will be with two people who love you almost as much as I do. You, my sweet girl, are starved for affection, and I will feed it to you however I choose until I think you are satisfied."

Sure her entire body was flaming red with an intense blush, she whispered, "Okay. Goodbye, Alex. I love you."

He hung up and she turned to find Rya and Gia moving past her with a surprised Vera sandwiched firmly between them. Giving Jessica a small smile, Rya said, "I'm sure Catrin and Nico would like privacy for seeing you again. Gia and I are good friends with Catrin and she has spoken very fondly of you."

"Very fondly," Gia said with a soft laugh while Vera looked confused.

"We will talk later," Vera said over her shoulder as she was carried out the door.

"Thank you," she told the other women, grateful that they were removing the elegant lady from a potentially awkward situation.

Then again, maybe Catrin had changed. The vibrant, exuberant, bubbly and energetic woman she knew five years ago may have vanished, leaving a stranger in her place. It wouldn't be that unusual, hell it was part of growing up, but she still hoped that the woman that walked through her front door bore at least some resemblance to her best friend. As much as she'd mourned Alex, she'd also mourned the loss of the unorthodox relationship she'd had with Nico and Catrin, the connection that was always a source of comfort and strength for her.

She could use comfort and strength right now.

Walking quickly from the dining area to where she thought the front door was—this place was huge—she tried to ignore the growing trail of bodyguards who followed her, spearheaded by a no-nonsense Zoya.

"Maks has informed me of the nature of your relationship with Catrin. I have pulled the security out of the apartment. We will be nearby, but you will have complete privacy. Maks will be manning the cameras to ensure you will not be disturbed." She gave a blushing Jessica a wry grin. "Your husband is a very, very protective man."

"I—well, yes."

Zoya looked up at the sound of two faint beeps. "I must go. Gwen has Tatiana down in her apartment with Krom. She will keep her until you are ready for Tatiana to return. I will be joining them as well."

"Thank you," Jessica said in a faint voice.

A pounding came from across the foyer and Maks looked over at her for permission to open the front door, his expression carefully blank, but she swore she saw the hard glint of jealousy in his eyes before he turned away. Fuck, his lingering looks were getting more lingering by the day, and she so did not have time to deal with his confused feelings. Giving him a nod, she rubbed her shaking hands on her hips.

"Maks, please let them in."

Chapter 13

"Jessica?" Catrin's familiar voice shouted as she came barreling through the front doors, followed closely by Nico.

Time stood still for a moment as she drank in the sight of her much-loved friend, a silent exhale leaving her while admired the stunning, mature woman Catrin had grown into. Her hair was now shoulder length and carefully styled into tussled golden waves shot here and there with champagne-blonde highlights. She wore a white blouse edged with black that dipped low in the front, revealing a ruby pendant that glowed against her fair skin, and a short skirt that showed off her legs. The curves that Jessica had so loved were still there, still lush, and still made her tingle.

She bit her lower lip when Catrin's familiar paleblue eyes met hers and she took a hesitant step forward. "Hello, Catrin."

With a scream, the woman sprinted across the foyer on her black high heels, launching herself at Jessica, who staggered back, sure they were going to fall to the hard marble floor, but in an instant Nico was there.

His long arms encircled both Jessica and Catrin, holding them tight while he whispered, "You are really alive."

Grasping at both of them as best she could, she and Catrin burst into tears while Nico murmured soothing nonsense. By the time he managed to maneuver them onto one of the red leather sofas in the den, they'd managed to compose themselves enough that they were both struggling to calm their hitching breaths. With a shaking hand, Catrin reached up and wiped her thumb gently beneath Jessica's eye.

"You look like a blind hooker put your makeup on, darling."

She giggled, rubbing her fingertips over Catrin's black mascara, now streaking down her cheeks. "You look like you should be in a clown porno."

Catrin's lower lip quivered, but she blinked rapidly. "I—Jessica, I have missed you so much."

Reaching out, Nico grasped his wife's hand. "We were out of communication at our vacation home. We came as soon as we heard."

"What the hell happened?" Catrin asked while wiping at her makeup with some clean tissues that Nico had pulled out of her purse. "I've heard many rumors, but I need to know the truth."

After Jessica finished her story, she found herself held between Catrin and Nico, her friends cuddling her close. She breathed in their scent, resting her cheek against the soft cotton of Nico's mustard-yellow shirt. He'd removed his jacket and tie when Catrin had kicked off her heels to be more comfortable while listening to Jessica. Reveling in the feeling of immense comfort her friends offered her, Jessica unburdened herself, telling two people who understood her what she'd been through.

Catrin placed a gentle kiss against Jessica's forehead. "I wish I was there to help."

"But we understand why you did what you felt was necessary," Nico added in a low voice, his long fingers gently stroking up and down Jessica's arms.

She shifted between them, her bare legs draped over Catrin's silk-clad ones. When the blonde shifted, Jessica could see the edges of the black garters that held her stockings in place. All three of them were holding hands, and Jessica felt totally safe in the cocoon they created for her.

"I was so miserable," she whispered. "I missed all of you so much. If it wasn't for Tatiana, I think I would have given up."

Catrin stiffened, something Jessica noticed because of how intertwined their bodies were. "Your daughter."

"Yes." Puzzled by Catrin's reaction, she glanced over to Nico, but he was watching his wife closely. "She's almost five, a handful but so loving."

"Much like her mother." Nico nuzzled against Jessica's cheek.

She laughed, then ran her hand over the short, rough curls covering Nico's head. "I have no idea what you're talking about."

Catrin stared across the room, her voice unusually grave as she said, "Do you like it, being a mother?"

Now Nico tensed as well, and she wondered what the hell was going on. There were strong emotional undercurrents she couldn't decipher. The only thing she knew for sure was that Catrin's expression suddenly seemed so fragile.

"It is the most fulfilling thing I have ever done, and even when my world was so dark I wanted to end my life, her light was strong enough to lead me back out of my depression. I can't express in words how much I love her. It's a different kind of love than what I feel for Alex, but just as strong, if not stronger in some ways. I'm Alex's mate, his loving partner, but I'm her mother."

Abruptly, Catrin stood and gave Jessica a bright smile while refusing to meet her eyes. "I must use the restroom, please excuse me."

After she disappeared around the corner, Jessica turned on the couch to fully face Nico, their knees touching as they studied each other. "What's going on?"

A pained look crossed his dark, handsome face. "Catrin does not want children."

"Oh...I see."

"Not because she does not like them, but because she is afraid of what will happen if someone hurts them. When she lost you, Catrin also went into very dark place. It was months before I could get her to leave the house." He sighed and patted her knee. "I am not blaming you for any of this, but you need to understand why she may be a bit hesitant about Tatiana. She loved your daughter from the moment she knew about her and the combined loss hurt her, changed her."

She felt like bursting into tears again, but bit her inner cheek and nodded. "I understand. I won't mention Tatiana around Catrin."

"No, please, do not do that. I am hopeful that if my wife sees the love you have for your daughter, she might help her heal enough to consider having children of her own."

"Nico, if she doesn't want kids, I don't know if she'll ever change her mind."

"I know this, and I have made peace with it. If I did not know my wife so well I would be happy spending the rest of my life with just her, but she yearns for children. I see it every time we are around our friends with babies, how she holds them with such longing. And I will not lie; I would be overjoyed if she changed her mind." He took a deep breath, then pressed a soft kiss to her lips that was all warmth and acceptance tinged with sadness. "Your return gives me hope for something I have wanted since the moment I met

Catrin and pictured her as my wife and mother of my children."

This time she couldn't fight her tears as she rained slow, gentle kisses on his sharp-boned face. Seeing such a powerful man fighting to keep his composure made her heart ache and she clearly took in Nico for the first time since they'd reunited. Other than a series of fine lines around his mouth, and new ones around his eyes, he didn't appear to have changed. At least he didn't until his eyes opened and the man who looked back at her wasn't the same one she remembered. There was a darkness inside of him now that hadn't been there before and she mourned its presence, mourned the loss of innocence that had fed the monster now inside of her old friend.

She wanted to take that dark look from his eyes, to give him back any happiness her absence had stolen from him. "I will help you."

"Help him what, sweet girl," Catrin purred from behind her.

She watched Nico look at his wife and the love that consumed his face chased away any lingering sorrow. He stared at Catrin as if she was the most fascinating thing he'd ever seen. She followed his gaze to find the lovely blonde woman standing next to them, her face once again serene after her outburst. Jessica was tempted to poke at the fragile mask that guarded Catrin's emotions, but she decided to let it be. Hell, she'd spent the last five years wearing a mask and still marveled at the immense sense of freedom she had at being able to just be herself.

"Not what you're thinking." She tugged at Catrin's hand, pulling her down into the small space between Jessica and Nico.

Nico rubbed his lips against Catrin's blonde waves. "You always want to spoil your surprises."

A fake pout curved the other woman's red-stained lips, and mischief glittered in her blue eyes. "You must be mistaking me for someone else."

Jessica gave Catrin the same firm look she gave Tatiana when she wanted the little girl to behave. "I cannot believe you're going to sit here and lie like that. You do remember that I was with you when you were trying to snoop through Nico's things, looking for some hint of what he got you for Christmas."

Relaxing, Catrin laughed and stroked Jessica's cheek. "You know, I had trouble imagining you as a mother, but that voice you just used? Reminds me of being scolded by my mama."

Conscious of how closely Nico was watching his wife, she smiled. "Would you like to meet Tatiana?"

Visibly stiffening, Catrin looked away then said in a soft voice, "I would, but I am not ready yet."

"What do you have to be ready for?"

Reaching out blindly, Catrin grasped her hand and held it hard. "Jessica, you asked me to be her godmother. I...wanted to be that so badly, and I was so honored you had asked me. There were so many things I imagined doing with Tatiana, so many plans, and when both of you died I felt a little like I had lost my own child."

The deep timbre of Nico's voice filled the silence in a soothing wave. "But that is the past. Right now Jessica is very much alive and we need to appreciate the gift God has given us."

Hating the sight of her friend so distraught, she leaned forward and rested her head on Catrin's shoulder while hugging her tight. When Nico wrapped his long arms around them, both she and Catrin melted with matching sighs. That made the women giggle while he began to gently stroke them, his large hands roaming their bodies, calming them with his touch. She'd forgotten how easily she responded to Nico as a submissive. The handsome black man was such a strong Master that it felt natural for her to yield to his control, especially when her Mistress did as well. That odd dance of Dominance and submission began to move through them, the energy rising into a slow-building spiral of sensuality.

Catrin wiggled a bit so she could stroke the side of Jessica's face, cuddling her closer.

"I missed this," Jessica whispered against the soft, fragrant skin of her friend's slender neck. "It's like a drug to me, one taste of it and I'm instantly addicted to flying deep in subspace. The only thing better than flying alone was to have you there with me while our Masters sent us soaring."

"*Milaya devushka*," Catrin murmured before gently tugging at Jessica's hair.

Raising her head off her friend's smooth shoulder, she slowly closed the distance between them, the sugary bubblegum scent of Catrin's perfume teasing her memories. She closed her eyes and rubbed her nose against the other woman's in a slow slide. Their lips barely brushed and warm sparkles of electricity sent a tingle through her. Her nipples hardened and she shifted farther so she could press her small breasts against Catrin's ample ones.

Nico continued to pet them in a slow, sensual rhythm that helped keep her grounded in the moment. There was so much going on in her life right now that she needed the release of submitting to Nico and Catrin, to give control to people she absolutely trusted. Handing herself over to their care brought her relief on a soul-deep level.

The blonde woman nipped at Jessica's lower lip, and she moaned into Catrin's mouth. She ran her hand up the curve of Catrin's waist to just below her breast. Cupping the soft weight, she kept her thumb just on the very edge of Catrin's erect nipple tenting the fabric over her breast. Looking up at the other woman, she let the intense need she had for them both rise to the surface, knowing how it would affect the lush blonde.

"Mistress, may I pleasure you?"

Catrin moaned low in her throat, the sound so sexy Jessica almost came from a brief press of her thighs.

Instead of the other woman answering Jessica's question, it was Nico who said, "You may play with her, but do not let her come. She gets vicious when denied orgasm and I want her to take out that frustration on you. It has been too long since I have seen your tight ass turn red from my wife's attentions."

Chapter 14

Alex glanced down at his phone again, stealing glimpses of his wife and friends via the security system set up in his home. To his surprise they were still all clothed, but the women were making out in an utterly decadent, unhurried manner while snuggled on Nico's lap. He could see the love the women still had for one another in the way they smiled and gazed into each other's eyes. Jessica looked radiant and he couldn't help but zoom in the camera on her face. Right now she was gently biting, then sucking on Catrin's neck. In response, the blonde woman's lips curled up into a sensual snarl of need and he had to stop himself rearranging his raging hard-on.

With an internal pang of regret, he turned his phone off and focused on the room. His uncle had arranged for him to meet with an interesting mix of people this morning, friends from his past and people he knew by reputation. There was only one woman in the room, but she had such a presence about her that his gaze had automatically gravitated her way when he'd arrived. Mimi Anderson, aka Mimi Stefano, aka Lady Death, who was still a classic Italian beauty, smiled at him, and the big salt-and-pepper-haired man she was with followed her gaze with an unhappy expression.

"Well, well, well," she said with laughter in her voice. "Congratulations, Alexandr Dubinski. I am very pleased with Petrov's decision."

"Mrs. Anderson," he said in difference to the man now glaring daggers at them. Rumor had it Mike Anderson wasn't exactly stable, and Alex believed it. "Is always a pleasure to have you in my city. And I assume this is Mr. Anderson?"

"Yes." She placed her hand gently on the glowering man's chest and his gaze instantly softened, eased by his wife's touch. Alex knew how that felt. "This is my husband, Mike. He's heard a lot about you over the years."

"Like the fact you tried to seduce my wife," Mike growled out.

Alex laughed at the man's pissed-off glare. "Who told you that?"

"Are you calling my wife a liar?"

Ignoring the way Mike's body went still, much the same way he would ignore a tiger about to pounce, he shrugged. "No, no is true, I tried my hardest to win her heart. But did she mention that I was twelve at the time? My seduction skills were...not so good."

Mike's mouth twitched and he relaxed enough to hold out his hand. "Call me Mike—and no, my wife didn't mention your tender age."

With a sigh, Mimi smoothed the sleeve of her husband's black suit, her red nails a stark contrast against the dark fabric. "Details, details. Either way, we were glad to come when Petrov invited us."

"By invited she means summoned," Mike muttered. "We were gonna have our granddaughter for the weekend, instead we gotta fly halfway around the damn world without knowing why Petrov needs us."

"Why is it," came Petrov's smooth voice from Alex's left, "that whenever we meet, you are always complaining?"

Mike lifted his chin in Petrov's direction with a wry smile. "Why is it every time you're around I end up getn', shot, stabbed, or thrown out of a helicopter?"

Walking past Mike, Petrov gently grasped Mimi's hand and placed a kiss on the back of it. His uncle still had a way with women and he wasn't surprised to see Mimi, feared assassin and knife expert, blushing like a teenage girl. She shook her head, then pulled him into a quick hug.

"Thank you for your help with my daughter's situation. Did you or Jorg ever find out what that shiny stuff the Israelis wanted so badly was?"

Puzzled, Alex glanced at Petrov, but he found his uncle giving Mimi an unexpectedly grave look. "Is not a discussion for now, but we are beginning to have our suspicions. I will talk to you about it later. Alex is missing his wife and I do not want to keep him any longer than necessary."

"Of course he is. And on a side note, Alex, we are so happy that your wife and daughter have returned. Jessica is a wonderful woman and I look forward to seeing her again and meeting your daughter." Mimi tossed her deep black hair over her shoulder. "Now, let's get down to business. We have much to discuss."

The meeting ended up being about places the Andersons would recommend around the world for building survivalist colonies. Petrov claimed he was getting into the business because he expected people to become more and more interested in luxurious, yet self-sustaining fortress compounds, but Alex knew it was more than that. The other people at the meeting had been geologists, meteorologists, as well as an astronomer, sociologist, and an expert in energy sources.

ALEXANDR'S RELUCTANT SUBMISSIVE

It had been an interesting conversation, and Alex had learned a great deal, but his mind kept returning to the luscious image of his wife kissing Catrin. He wondered if they were naked by now, if Nico was having his cock sucked by them. Alex waited to see if any feelings of jealousy stirred at the thought, but it was only hot arousal that warmed his blood. While he would much rather do nothing except daydream about different kinky scenarios with his wife, he forced himself to listen to the meteorologist drone on and on about shifting wind patterns, the rapidly thawing tundra, melting icebergs around the world along with sea level rises and global temperature increases over the next century.

He didn't need to listen to the scientist talk about what was happening in places like Siberia; he'd witnessed it firsthand. Green where there had been nothing but eternally frozen dirt, birds and animals venturing farther north than ever before. Alex hadn't really dwelled on the changes, he had about a million other things to worry about, but he listened with a little more interest as the scientist talked about which areas of the world would theoretically have the most stable environments in the years to come.

Once the scientist took a breath, Petrov interrupted him. "Thank you, Mr. Daniels, for your input."

"You're most welcome, Mr. Dubinski."

"Time for a break. Meet back here in fifteen minutes. There are refreshments set up in the salon across the hall."

As people shuffled out of the room, Petrov drew Alex aside. "Dimitri called earlier to say that word of you leaving the Novikov *Bratva* is spreading. Many of your current staff wonder where their loyalties lie, who they should work for. Maks is having a hard time dealing with it, but Krom has already indicated that he will go with you and your family, wherever you may be. Luka is also on the fence, but that has more to do with the fact that if he leaves, there is no one he trusts to take his place. The Novikov *Bratva* depends on him as their negotiator, but he has been with you since you were boys."

Alex had been trying to ignore the fact that he would have to cut professional ties with longtime friends in the future. They couldn't be loyal to both the Novikov and Dubinski *Bratvas*, and he absolutely did not want his leaving to weaken the Novikov *Bratva*, and in return his brother. They would always be his people, and even as he worked to keep the employees of the Dubinskis safe and happy, he would do the same for the Novikovs. No matter what, Dimitri would always be his brother and Alex knew that, together, with the backing of two powerful criminal syndicates, they would be a formidable force.

As he always did when he was unsure, he asked his uncle for his opinion. "How would you handle this?"

Petrov thought for a moment before answering. "I would only take a few men, and leave the essential ones behind with Dimitri. You know all of my bodyguards, but you need to pick three or four from the higher-ranking men on my staff to serve on your personal escort. To do otherwise would be an insult to them."

Recalling Jessica's positive reaction to Zoya, he asked, "I know you have some female bodyguards on your staff. Do you have any that you think would be good with Jessica and Tatiana?"

"I do, let me think on it."

Alex placed his hand on the older man's shoulder, giving it a gentle squeeze. "Thank you."

"Do not forget tonight that we have a web conference with Japan tomorrow. My niece Irina and her husband Hiroto will be there representing the Nakamura *Yakuza*."

Insulting the *Yakuza* was one of the last things he wanted to do. "I will be there."

Petrov grasped the back of his neck, giving it a squeeze as he said, "I am proud of you. A lesser man would not be able to deal with all of these changes in your life. When you go home tonight, think about how lucky you are to have such a good woman waiting for you, and an adorable daughter. Speaking of your wife...I would offer the advice that you talk with her about how she has been raising Tatiana. Listen to her reasons for doing things the way she does. I say this not only because of the cultural differences, but because if you ever disrespect her like you did this morning at breakfast in public again, she might take a knife to you."

Frowning, he stepped back when his uncle released him. "What are you talking about? She was a little upset about Tatiana getting her ears pierced, but I'm sure she's forgotten it."

"I would not count on that." Petrov gave him a wry smile while making his way back over to his laptop. "And even if she has, she will remember it the instant you make her angry. Women are funny like that. You think you're forgiven then BAM, out of nowhere, they're bringing up shit from twenty years ago like it happened yesterday."

Alex couldn't help but laugh, having experienced that himself a time or two. "I will take your advice."

"It wouldn't hurt for you to show her some extra attention, maybe buy her something nice."

"Something like that," Alex said as a plan began to form to give his woman a gift that she would truly appreciate.

Maks met him at the entrance to his floor, standing off to the side of the elevator. His black suit was impeccable as always, but his tie was loosened and there was a hard flush high on his cheekbones. Having watched Maks fuck many, many times, he noted the look of arousal on his friend's face, and his hard cock tenting his pants despite his efforts to hide his erection with his jacket.

"What has you in such a state?"

Glancing around them, Maks made a subtle hand gesture that dismissed the remaining bodyguards. The floor was completely secure at the moment and as Alex shrugged off his coat, Maks gripped his cock. A look of frustration filled his friend's face and for a second Alex thought he saw burning envy with a touch of jealousy in the other man's eyes, but the look was quickly gone as they approached the sleek mahogany door leading to his apartment.

"I've spent the past four hours watching Catrin and Jessica slowly seduce each other. Nico insisted that they wait to go any further until you came home. It's got Catrin in a state and she is going to Dominate the hell out of Jessica if you allow it." Maks hesitated, then laid a hand on Alex's shoulder. "Catrin needs this, Alex, needs to feel that connection with Jessica. Tonight, for the first time in a long time, she began to talk about having children again. Teasing Nico about being a father."

Alex let out a low breath of air as he entered his home. "Where are they?"

"In your bedroom, taking a nap."

"They are sleeping?"

"Jessica and Catrin have been drinking."

Smiling, Alex began to loosen his tie then took it off and handed it to Maks. "Ahhh, I see my girl still can't hold her alcohol."

"That, and I think she is emotionally exhausted. They talked about how much Jessica wanted to fly in subspace again with Catrin."

He began to unbutton his shirt, taking the stairs two at a time. "Tatiana is safe and happy, yes?"

"Of course. Between Krom and Gwen, she is practically worshiped. It is very good for Krom to be around your daughter, heals a part of him. We have all noticed and believe he should go with you when you officially cut all ties with the Novikov *Bratva*."

Alex froze, then turned and looked down at Maks standing in the middle of the foyer, a deep pang going through his chest as he clearly read the sorrow in the other man's eyes. "Do you?"

"Yes." He took a deep breath, sorrow showing in his regretful expression before he once again met Alex's gaze. "I, however, will be remaining with Dimitri and the Novikov *Bratva*."

He wanted to question his old friend, to try and get him to stay, but he had to respect Maks' decision. "You will be missed."

"It's...it's better this way." Abruptly he stiffened. "Please tell Jessica goodbye for me."

"You do not want to tell her yourself?"

Rubbing his face, Maks stared at the ground as he said in a shamed whisper, "Alex, the feelings I have for your wife are...not right. I have always considered you my brother, but now I am lusting after your wife in a way that disgraces me. It is best if I remove myself from the temptation. I pray you understand."

"Thank you for being honest with me."

Maks' shoulders stiffened and he lifted his chin. "When I see her in the future, I shall avoid her."

"Please, do not do that. Jessica values your friendship greatly and when you get your head on straight and find the woman you're really meant to love, you will want that friendship again."

"Perhaps I have to look harder then for my perfect woman."

Such a proud man, and such a good friend. "Maks, take this advice. You will never find a perfect woman. You like to put them on pedestals so high, no mortal could ever survive the fall. I understand why you are keen to avoid marrying the wrong woman, your mother is enough to make any man question even looking at a female, but it is time for you to move on. Someday, you will make a wonderful father, and a good husband."

"Goodbye, Alex." A small smile curved his tension-thinned lips. "I pray that you are right."

"Of course I am. Now, go to the club and find your relief in some sweet little submissive to take your mind off things."

"If only it were that easy," he murmured as he walked out the door.

The seconds ticked by as Alex remained halfway up the stairs, an unexpected pang of hurt ricocheting through his chest. Logically he knew why and approved of his friend's reasons for staying with Dimitri and Rya. While his brother threatened Rya with letting Maks do things with her, he'd never let it happen. And while Maks flirted with Rya, it was far more innocent than the consuming looks he gave Jessica. Yes, it was better that Maks stay with the Novikov *Bratva* and keep Dimitri's family safe than torment himself around Jessica with misplaced guilt.

By the time he reached his bedroom, his shirt was totally unbuttoned and his belt was off. He entered his bedroom, unsure what he would find, then shut the door with a smile. There, on his big bed, were three of his favorite people in the world. Catrin lay in the middle of Nico and Jessica, her hands flung over her head with her large breasts exposed by the lowered blanket.

His wife wore a miniscule pink negligee, Catrin's favorite color, and one of its thin straps had slid down her freckled shoulder. Her leg was thrown over both Nico and Catrin's hips, the slender limb so pale against Nico's dark flesh. Memories of nights spent sleeping together like this, in a satisfied heap, filled him and he marveled at how full his life was now that Jessica was back. He'd indulged in orgies while they were apart, but all the sexual excess in the world wasn't as powerful as standing over the people he loved.

Catrin stirred, turning on her side so she was cuddled into Jessica. The women fit so perfectly together and he was tempted to run his hand up their thighs, to tease them awake. But he was unsure as to what his wife's expectations were so he would let her set the limits.

That didn't mean he wasn't going to try to get her to decide in his favor.

The moment his hands hit the bed, Nico's eyes flashed open, ready for battle, then mellowed as soon as his brain registered that Alex was a friend. He was gratified that he had such a good man guarding his woman, one Alex knew would die to save them. And he would do the same.

"My cock is about to explode," Nico hissed. "Thank fuck you're home. Do you know what it's like to have these two kissing and rubbing on your lap?"

"Actually, I do. Exquisite torture."

Both men chuckled and the women stirred. When Catrin and Jessica slept together they always slept deep. They waited until the females in their arms relaxed, then started talking again.

Nico drew the sheet down the pronounced curve of Catrin's full hip, also revealing the top of Jessica's pert buttocks where her short nightgown had risen up. They were nicely red, and Alex moved out of bed long enough to get naked, then slowly pressed his body against his wife's, the contact of her skin sending sparks of pleasure over his entire body. He shivered, aware of Nico watching him with a grin as Alex fit his aching cock between Jessica's ass cheeks. Her bottom was slightly bigger now, and the new softness hugged his dick just right.

"Are you going to come all over her before you even get inside?"

"Fuck you, her ass is amazing."

Nico let out his own small shudder as he grasped Catrin's breast, the pale flesh and pink nipple looking so appetizing in his grip. Jessica began to stir as Alex did his best not to grind into her, and her sleepy mumbled words made no sense. He allowed his hands to roam up her body until he grasped her nipples, reveling in how nice and thick they were. She had the perfect nipples for clamps and his stomach clenched at the thought, his dick jerking against her.

Catrin moaned softly, then the men grinned while Jessica lifted her head from the pillow, looking over her shoulder at Alex. "Are you real?"

"Yes, *prinsessa moya*, I am real."

She frowned slightly, then looked back over at Nico and Catrin. "So you're real too?"

"Yes, Jessica," Nico said in an unexpectedly serious voice. "We are real."

He leaned up on his elbow so he could watch Jessica's face while her gaze slowly drifted down over Nico and Catrin's bodies, her ass pressing back into him while her legs clenched. "May I touch her?"

Unsure who Jessica was addressing, Alex answered, "You may do whatever her Master desires, but only if you want it as well. Never will we do more than you are comfortable with, but know that nothing is off limits when it comes to your pleasure. Now ask Master Nico nicely if you can touch his submissive."

With a low moan, Jessica shifted out of his arms and crawled to the foot of his gigantic bed. Once there, she knelt and spread her legs wide, revealing the swollen pink of her sex. She'd trimmed the auburn fluff over her mound at some point and the lips of her sex were shaved bare. Moisture glistened on her thighs, and as he watched, she clenched.

Lowering her head and placing her hands palms-up on her thighs, she whispered, "Master Nico, may I touch your submissive?"

Catrin's pale-blue eyes were barely open at this point, but she smiled at the sight of Jessica. "When you touch me I am not your submissive, Jessica. I am your Mistress. Do I need to spank you some more to remind you?"

"No, Mistress." Another clench from her exposed pussy, begging him to slide his cock in deep.

Nico slid the sheet completely off of Catrin, revealing her bare sex, already glistening with arousal. "But I am always *your* Master, my lovely wife."

Jessica took in an audible breath. "I forgot how beautifully made your pussy is. Dusky rose, and your clit is deep pink when it's begging for me to suck it."

It took a bit of effort, but Alex managed to hide his shock at Jessica's frank talk. When they were together before their separation, he'd had to coax filthy words from her. Now she said them with a confidence that threatened his self-control, making him want to fuck her cross-eyed.

No, he'd had her all to himself and she needed to renew this connection with Nico and Catrin. Hell, he'd missed the special bond they'd had, missed doing normal couples things together with his friends. They made Jessica so happy and, evidently, bold. They also gave her the confidence to extend her boundaries because she trusted them, and it made Nico and Catrin the best gift he could give her.

"You will suck her *pizda*," Nico murmured, "but you will also put your delicate little fist inside of her pussy while I fuck her ass."

Jessica's neon-blue eyes widened and she almost toppled off the bed before throwing out an arm to steady herself. "What? That's impossible. We won't fit—we'll hurt her."

Catrin gave a sweet groan of pleasure while Nico pinched her nipples. "You've seen her fuck myself and Krom at the same time, one in her ass and one in her pussy. Do you think your little hand is bigger than my cock?"

"I-I don't know."

"Come here," Catrin purred and rolled over so her ass pressed into Alex's side. "Maybe you do not remember my husband's lovely cock so well. Maybe sucking on it will help remind you of its size."

Jessica gave Alex a quick look, some of the apprehension slipping from her face when he winked at her.

Nico scooted up, then reclined back on the padded silk headboard of the mammoth bed, his dark skin gleaming where the light seeped in around the edges of the bedroom curtains. "Come here, *milaya devushka*, and pleasure your Master."

Jessica crawled forward, but Alex pulled her into a quick kiss then whispered against her lips, "Remember, you can say no at any time."

She pulled back and gave him a look so sultry he had to bite his lower lip to hold back a groan. "Why would I do that when all I want to say is *da*?"

Giving her still-pink buttocks a smack, he sent her over to a smiling Catrin, who was propped up against Nico's chest. Alex moved up the bed and threw some pillows aside before he arranged himself next to Nico, the women's mouths meeting in a decadent kiss over the tip of Nico's cock. The sight turned him on and he fisted his shaft, pinching the base to try to control himself. He lived in the moment, celebrated the bounty of love in this room with them tonight. For so, so long he'd been starved for this kind of affection, but had denied it at every turn because nothing in the world was as good as Jessica when she let go of her inhibitions.

Soon he found himself kissing his wife while Nico began to finger-fuck Catrin, no doubt stretching her out to accept Jessica's fist. The mental image was so hot that a spurt of pre-cum wet Jessica's waist. She broke their kiss, her face rubbing gently against his as she said, "Will you fuck me while I pleasure Catrin and Nico, please, Master?"

"Anything for you, *prinsessa moya*."

He teased her hard nipples, pinching the tips and squeezing them firmly enough to make her gasp. Abruptly she stiffened in his arms, her long legs spreading and tangling with Catrin's plump thighs.

Catrin had her hand busy between Jessica's legs, tormenting his wife until she trembled in his arms and he growled with anticipation of the pleasures yet to come.

Chapter 15

Warmth blossomed inside of Jessica, the indescribable joy of reuniting with loved ones filling her heart. She rubbed her face against Catrin's soft cheek, reveling in her husband's firm touch behind her. In this perfect moment in time she simply floated, drunk on the endorphins making her tingle from the inside out. Heat flushed her sex when Catrin's smooth lips met her own, silken and slow kisses that drove her crazy.

Alex slipped his hand between her legs, his big knuckles barely grazing her labia. "So wet. You want to be fucked, don't you?"

She broke her kiss with Catrin and looked over her shoulder, letting him see how much she wanted him. "Please, Master."

His body tightened as he balanced himself over her, enclosing her completely with his much bigger frame while keeping most of his weight off of her. The heavy length of his cock twitched against her back, leaving a hot kiss of pre-cum. Beneath her, Catrin moaned while Nico slid his long, dark fingers through her golden hair, quietly worshiping her with kisses. Usually the lovely blonde was wild with desire by this point, but Nico had been tempering the evening to a gentler tone, making it about love instead of pure lust. Oh, Jessica was plenty hot and bothered, but every time she met Catrin's gaze she couldn't help but smile at the happiness she found sparkling in her friend's blue eyes.

Alex swept her hair to the side, then reached past her to pinch Catrin's nipple. "I will only fuck you when you've given your lovely Mistress what she wants, your fist in her cunt and her husband's cock in her ass."

She bucked against Alex, her hips tilting up in a silent pleading gesture. Just when she was sure he couldn't shock her any more, he'd say something so raw that it was as if he was already filling her pussy. The crisp hair of his body rubbed over hers and she writhed beneath him, her torso pressing into Catrin's.

"Do it, sweet girl," Catrin murmured between kisses with Nico.

She licked her lips, hesitant to hurt her friend even as the wild part of her that had been sleeping for so long hungered for the experience. "Are you sure?"

"Very," she purred. "Normally it makes me orgasm hard, but with you it will likely kill me with pleasure."

"But Nico's so...not small."

Nico chuckled. "Catrin's body, for whatever blessed reason, was built to take big dick."

The mattress dipped as Alex leaned over and opened the drawer next to the bed, pulling out what she guessed was lube. Her suspicion was confirmed when he began to pour it onto his fingers, but she was quickly distracted by Catrin rubbing her thumb over Jessica's hard clit with a slow, steady touch. A gasp of pleasure was torn from her throat when Catrin began to play with the hood of her clit in a way that made her toes curl.

"Mmmm, you respond so nicely." She gave Alex a glance as he passed the lube to Nico, then returned those dreamy blue eyes of hers to Jessica. "I would like to make you come all over my hand like the filthy girl you are, but then your Master would take away my fun."

Little bolts of excitement tightened her nipples to the point that she wanted to rub them on something, anything, to ease the ache.

The scruff of Alex's beard brushed over her skin as he feathered kisses along her back. "Play with Catrin's pussy while Nico takes her ass."

Still braced against the headboard, Nico helped his wife crouch above him while Jessica knelt between his legs, with Alex behind her. She took in the amazing sight of the beautiful Catrin, her face suffused with want and passion, slowly easing the pink-tipped head of Nico's dark shaft into the small ring of her anus. With a low growl, Alex lifted her hand and used their fingers to gently pet Catrin's swollen, dusky sex. Her clit was a hard line and her creamy arousal already coated Nico's slick shaft.

At the first good rub of their fingers, Catrin arched and said in Russian, "Permission to come, Master?"

"*Nyet.*"

Jessica tried to hide her grin at Catrin's snarl, knowing all too well how it felt to be denied the need to do what her body wanted.

Craved.

When Nico was halfway in, and Catrin's thighs were shaking, Alex took his free hand and wrapped her hair around his fist, directing her mouth to Catrin's quivering sex. "Her greedy *pizda* has dripped all over Nico's dick and balls. Clean them."

"Oh God," Catrin moaned out, sliding down farther on Nico's cock and making him groan. "Yes, clean him, my sweet girl."

It wasn't like she had much of a choice; Alex's firm grip on her hair made her his puppet to do with as he wished. With a low rumble in his voice that was unbearably sexy he said, "Stick your tongue out."

The taste of Catrin's pussy, Nico's musk, and the vanilla-flavored lube all hit her tongue at once and she moaned hard enough that Nico's long thighs clenched repeatedly.

Alex released her hair once he deemed Nico cleaned, only to grab her hand instead. "I've seen you finger-fuck her with three fingers in her cunt. Get them in there, now."

She blinked, taken aback by his harsh tone, but she noticed his gaze was on Catrin. The other woman seemed to be in heaven and she stretched her arms back and braced them on Nico's broad chest, her breasts thrust out as she gave herself to them completely.

Biting her lip, Jessica did as her Master ordered and slid three fingers into the groaning blonde, marveling at how she could feel Nico's erection in her friend's ass. The skin separating the two entrances to Catrin's body was incredibly thin and she wondered if guys got off on the fact that their cocks were rubbing together while inside a girl. It must feel amazing...for everyone involved.

"Now four," Alex ordered. "Bring your fingers together a bit, like this, so goes in on a point instead of wide. Work it in slowly. Stretch her as you go. You are doing so well, *prinsessa moya*."

She copied the way he shaped her hand and began to slowly thrust her fingers in and out. While she was doing that, Alex had begun to play with her pussy again, his knowing touch driving her to distraction, making her want to climax so damn bad. The release would be big, she could tell already by how tense her body was, and the thought of doing it with her husband inside of her was bliss. He kept her safe while she abandoned herself to hedonistic pleasure.

The head of his cock brushed her entrance as she got her hand in Catrin's pussy up to her knuckles, the fit tight, but by the look on the pink-cheeked blonde's face, the feeling must have been divine.

"Push," Alex whispered as he did the same thing with his hips, filling her slowly with his perfect dick. "Give her what she needs."

A sense of power filled Jessica as she slowly forced her hand in until the entrance to Catrin's stretched sex clasped her wrist.

With a scream, the curvy woman came, her inner muscles milking Jessica's hand while Nico began to slowly move in and out of his wife, his thick grunts feeling like a physical touch. Alex caught Nico's rhythm and soon he was fucking her at the opposite pace, his plunging hips moving her hand in Catrin's soaking wet heat in perfect counterpart to Nico's thrusts. Once again her thoughts were consumed by the idea of taking two men at once like this, of their cocks plunging in and out of her.

Alex ran his thumb over her anus and she contracted around him. "So good."

His growl of agreement blended with Catrin's scream of relief as she came again, her pussy sucking on Jessica's hand. Sex surrounded her, the air so thick with it she swore she could taste their pheromones. Rolling her hips, the lush blonde worked herself on Jessica and Nico, her expression one of dreamy bliss. It was so hot and Jessica strained to keep from climaxing, her pussy clamping down on Alex thrusting inside of her.

When Alex plunged his thumb into her bottom and said, "Come for me," she gladly complied.

Stiffening, Catrin orgasmed at the same time and their cries filled the air.

The moment Jessica regained her senses enough to move, Alex growled, "Remove your hand."

As soon as she was free he dragged her to the edge of the bed and turned her over onto her back.

At the sight of his disheveled hair, damp with sweat, and her tattoos on his body, she couldn't stand him not being inside of her. "Please."

He slid into her with one perfect thrust, his wide chest tempting her. She sat up enough to take his nipple between her lips and moaned against his skin when he did this move where his whole body seemed to rub against hers with each thrust. Their gazes met and she had to force hers to remain open, refusing to lose sight of her husband's eyes filled with such love for her for even a second. They found their mutual orgasm like that, and when they collapsed into an exhausted heap, she wrapped her arms around his neck with Catrin and Nico cuddling against her back and fell asleep, surrounded by love.

Chapter 16

Sheer panic raced through Alex and his skin prickled painfully as he stared at his wife. "What do you mean you are leaving?"

With a sigh, Jessica gathered up her pink purse from the table in the foyer and looked inside. She wore a cream suit that fit her slender figure perfectly and made him want to jerk her dress up and bury himself inside of her. At least it normally would if his daughter wasn't there, watching her mother pull some lip gloss out of the purse.

"I mean I have to go have lunch with Rya and a few of the wives of your men. I want them to feel comfortable enough with me to come to me with their concerns." She smoothed on a raspberry color over her lips, making them even more kissable than usual. "Gwen is over at her Russian tutor's house, and I know your schedule is clear for at least the next six hours, so you'll have to watch her for me."

He swore his dry throat clicked as he swallowed, all too aware of Tatiana's trembling lower lip and sad expression. "Jessica, this is not good idea."

She arched one auburn brow at him. "And why would that be?"

Switching to Russian, he took a step closer and lowered his voice. "I do not know what to do with her."

"Alex, you've been around each other for a few weeks now. Yes, you're still new, but she sees you every day. You're a part of her life and yes, it may take time for her to get used to you, but it won't happen unless you spend some time alone with her." The firm look on her face didn't soften, but the compassion in her gaze soothed some of the ragged edges of his nerves. "If you need him, Krom will come help you, but I told him that Tatiana was your daughter and that I trust you completely with her."

Before he could protest, she moved away from him and knelt before Tatiana. The little girl was dressed in bright-pink tights with a black dress and a sparkly pink headband that held back her long hair. His wife hugged their daughter, gently prying the little girl off of her. Pain ricocheted through his chest at the sight of Tatiana's tears.

"Be good for your Papa."

In a soft whimpering voice, Tatiana said, "I don't want you to go."

"I'll be back before you know it. I love you."

The door shut behind her before Alex could protest and he stared at Luka, his panic reflected in the other man's eyes. Tatiana's sniffles became louder, drawing his attention back to his daughter. His mind raced as he stared at the little girl wiping her face with the back of her hand, dejection making him sick. She didn't like him; it was obvious by the way she'd begun to cry in earnest.

Even though he knew he was the source of her unhappiness, he was helpless to resist the need to make her feel better.

"Shhh, Tatiana, do not be sad, my darling girl."

He knelt before her like her mother did and she gave him a wounded look. "I want my mommy."

Fuck, he could run a billion-dollar mafia, but couldn't figure out what words to say to a little girl to make her feel better. "She had to go out, but she will be back soon."

"I want her now."

She jerked away when he went to reach for her, intending to give her a hug, with a rebellious look twisting her sweet little face. He tried to ignore the lance of agony that slashed at his soul, to hold back his rage that he was a stranger to his daughter. The only thing that kept him from ending his dying father's life was the fact that it would endanger his women even more than they already were.

Scrambling to find a way to pacify her, he said, "What would you like to do? We can do anything you want."

She blinked at him, her sobs quieting enough that she could say, "Can we have ice cream?"

"Of course we can."

Luka cleared his throat. "Jessica does not permit ice cream until after dinner."

Looking up at him through her wet lashes, Tatiana said in a sweet voice, "Daddy, can we please have ice cream? I promise I'll eat all my dinner and I won't get any on my clothes."

In the back of his mind, he knew Jessica would be irritated with him, but surely she would understand this was a special circumstance. "Then let us have ice cream."

"Can we watch a superhero movie after?"

"Nap time," Luka muttered but Alex ignored him again.

"Of course. Why don't we have our ice cream in the theater room? Come, we will tell the chef what kind of ice cream we would like then you can pick out any movie you want."

She beamed at him then threw her arms around his neck. "You're the best Papa ever. Thank you!"

His eyes burned as he held the precious little girl in his arms, a sweet and warm joy filling the hollow parts of his soul. "And you are the best daughter."

After wiggling out of his grip, she held her hand out to him. "Papa, can Mr. Luka have some ice cream too, please?"

He exchanged a bemused look with the bodyguard. "Of course."

"Thank you, Papa!"

Taking her small hand, he carefully held her with a delicate grip and thanked God that he had lived to see this day.

For the first time in two and a half weeks, Alex hoped to make it home before dinner, and he couldn't wait to get this meeting with Nico, Dimitri, and Petrov over with. When Nico had asked to meet with them as soon as possible, Alex's internal alarms went off and he was once again delayed in leaving for home. It would be nice to see his family sometime other than at breakfast, occasionally dinner, and almost always bedtime for Tatiana. The way she smiled at him, the feeling of her little arms wrapping around his neck, the way she loved with her whole heart, all of those things and a thousand others had him completely enraptured with her. He knew he was spoiling her, but he deserved the chance to do something that was stolen from him, something he'd always dreamed of doing.

"Alex?" Dimitri said with a chuckle "Are you with us?"

Petrov looked up from the documents he'd been studying. "Just a little longer. We'd all like to get home to our wives, but we must discuss this 'Silver Wood'. I need to know why it is so important that Jorg Novikov would agree to any terms Lady Death demanded in order to get it, and then why he asked Dimitri to guard it with his life. I have heard whispers of Silver Wood, but never what it is or why some very important people want it so badly. And when I mean important people, I mean the ones currently ruling the world. The Israelis are still looking for it, but they're keeping tight-lipped on why. And I know for certain the Russian government is looking for it as well. Yes, we have a large supply, but without the knowledge of what it does it is useless to us. With this in mind, I have had Nico and his lab work on giving us some answers. If you will, Nico."

Standing, Nico tapped on his laptop and Luka dimmed the lights. Yesterday he'd told Alex that he'd talked with Dimitri, and that Luka would be joining the Dubinski *Bratva* as Alex's right-hand man. It felt good to have his old friend guarding his back, even if he did catch the handsome bastard flirting with his wife on a regular basis. It was cute the way he made her blush, and Luka's interest in Alex's wife was purely sexual, which allowed Alex to find the situation humorous instead of deadly.

No one upset the wife of Alexandr Dubinski, this lesson had already been taught in some brutal ways Jessica would never learn of. Like the torture of those who had tried to ambush them when they arrived back in Moscow. Or having his ex-lovers who'd gossiped in front of Jessica at the salon evicted from the building. They were lucky he hadn't ruined them while he was at it.

The first image popped up, a bunch of chemical formulas that Alex didn't understand or even bother trying to. He had his strengths, and scientific formulations and biochemical compounds were not among of them. Fortunately for him, Nico was able to unlock the secrets of the universe one element at a time, and Alex had faith in his friend's brilliance.

"I am honestly baffled."

That made Alex sit up and pay attention. "You could not identify the substance?"

"Yes...and no. You see, what you have—it should not exist. It is impossible, a paradox, yet there it sat before me, as real as could be. I am explaining this badly. What you have is five gallons of a liquid that almost looks like mercury, but isn't. In fact, it isn't a chemical at all. It's a bacteria; a bacteria that has been extinct since before the Ice Age, swimming in a silver pulp made from trees that no longer exist."

"What?" Dimitri leaned forward, his gaze studying the next slide showing what Alex assumed was an image of the bacteria. "Where the hell could it have come from?"

Nico clicked his laptop again and a drawing of a tree came up with some long Latin name beneath it. "We know from fossil records that the bacteria grew on this species of tree, and this tree only, which has also been extinct for thousands of years. In fact, great temperate forests of this tree used to grow in what is now far northern Siberia and Canada. So the fact that you have five gallons of this bacteria tells me that someone went to an enormous amount of energy to produce it, something that should be impossible. But why?"

"Is it different from any normal bacteria in any way? Modern bacteria, that is," Petrov asked in a distracted voice while he stared at his computer screen.

"Not that we can find. We're running more tests with the sample you gave us and hopefully we'll get some more answers as we narrow it down. What I *can* tell you is that it is not harmful to humans and it is highly resistant to all modern antibiotics. It also appears to not harm animals, but we cannot tell if this is true with all species or simply the ones we have access too."

"Continue testing," Petrov said in a distracted voice. "I have very recently managed to attain some of this Silver Wood as well. I will send you some samples to see if perhaps it is a different strain."

"Of course."

The meeting didn't last that much longer and by the time Alex made it home, Tatiana and Jessica, along with Rya and Gwen, were finishing up their dinner. His wife treated Gwen like a friend more than an employee, so he wasn't surprised by the sight of his nanny eating dinner at his formal dining table. If Jessica considered the woman family, he would accept her into his home and do everything he could to make Gwen happy.

"Papa!" came the squeal from somewhere behind him and he turned just in time to catch Tatiana as she threw herself at him. He lifted her then spun her around, her silky hair tickling his nose. After giving her a firm kiss on the forehead, he turned to find Jessica glaring at him.

"What is wrong?"

"Your daughter was playing in an area of the apartment I restricted her from and she broke a lovely, and no doubt very expensive, set of vases while shooting the new foam bow and arrow you got her. When I punished her for this, she told me that she was going to tell her papa and he wouldn't make her stay in her room, that he would let her out whenever she wanted." Her nostrils flared as Tatiana cuddled into his neck. "I told her there would be no dessert tonight and she would be going to her room. Your daughter then proceeded to tell me that she would have dessert because *you* would give it to her. She also said that you give her cake, and pie, and cookies all the time before dinner, despite the fact that she's only allowed one dessert a day—and that you say I'm silly for not letting her have whatever she wants."

The other women quietly set their silverware down and left the room while his wife continued to glare at him.

He wanted his daughter to like him, and he was sure punishing her for minor things wasn't necessary while they were still getting to know each other. And he had to admit that even though he knew he was going against Jessica's wishes, he didn't see the harm in Tatiana having sweets, and they made her so happy.

Still, he didn't appreciate his daughter using him to annoy her mother. "Tatiana, if your mother said no dessert, then there will be no dessert tonight."

His adorable little girl pulled back, her big gray eyes studying his face. "But Papa, I'm hungry."

"Then you should have eaten your dinner," Jessica said in a firm voice.

"But it had yucky vegetables and no macaroni and cheese!"

Part of him wanted to give in to the tears already welling in his daughter's eyes, but he had a feeling Jessica would kill him in his sleep tonight if he did not back her up. "I am sorry, but your mother is right. If you want to grow up big and strong, you must eat balanced diet."

"But I'm not hungry for vegetables, I'm hungry for cake. Get it for me, Papa. Please."

He arched a brow at the stubborn set to her little chin. "No."

"I said please!"

"And I said no."

Tatiana squirmed out of his arms so fast he almost dropped her. She took a step away, put her little hands on her hips, and glared at him with the frown line she'd inherited from Jessica prominent between her dark-red brows. Even when she was angry she was adorable.

"I want cake!" she screamed loud enough that he had to steel himself from wincing as her cheeks flushed.

Okay, maybe she wasn't adorable when she was angry.

"No."

Her entire face turned red. "Give me cake!"

Stunned at the abrupt change in her demeanor, he gave her a stern look. "No. Now you will behave in a respectful manner and not raise your voice at me."

"Cake!" she screamed in his face.

To his astonishment, his delightful little girl threw herself to the floor and began to thrash her arms and legs as if she was having a seizure. He looked to Jessica to see if she was alarmed, but to his surprise, he found her calmly eating her dinner. After taking a sip of her wine, she returned to nibbling her carrots, completely ignoring Tatiana's increasingly shrill screams.

When she noticed him looking at her, she yelled over the wails, "Come, eat with me. We have a plate for you."

He looked down at Tatiana, who was now banging her feet on the wall, then back at Jessica.

She gave a subtle shake of her head, then pointed at his plate.

There had been many difficult things that he'd had to do in his life, but walking away from his distraught daughter was one of the hardest.

The moment he began to move, her fit doubled until he was worried she might hurt herself.

Handing him his glass of wine, Jessica shook her head. "Ignore her."

He leaned in so he could say into her ear, "What if she harms herself?"

"She won't. This isn't the first time she's thrown a hissy fit. The one that she had at the zoo when I wouldn't get her a giant stuffed tiger was the worst. I had to physically carry her out of the place over my shoulder with her kicking and screaming the whole way."

He numbly ate some of his dinner, his entire body on edge as his sweet daughter continued to shriek like she was possessed.

"How long will she be like this?"

"Normally? Varies, but the longest she's gone was around twenty minutes before she cried herself to sleep. I'm going to cut this one short so you can eat without the dinner theater."

The plate before him should have held humble pie, because that was what it tasted like as he steeled himself against his innocent daughter's pissed-off screams. Perhaps Jessica had a point when she warned him against spoiling Tatiana. The girl was so happy and delightful, he thought it would be all right. The way his ears and mind were bleeding from her screams begged to differ.

"Are you sure we should not take her to a doctor? This is not natural."

His wife actually laughed then said in a low voice, "Oh, Alex, trust me, tantrums are a normal part of growing up. All kids have them. You may not have seen one before, but believe me, nothing's wrong with her other than a stubborn little girl with a temper not getting her way."

Jessica calmly set aside her silverware then turned to face Tatiana, slowly rising from her chair until she looked down to where the little girl continued to thrash but also watch her mother out of the corner of her eye. It pained Alex to realize that once again, Jessica was right about Tatiana manipulating him. The very idea that someone so young could be so adapt at getting him to do what she wanted was crazy, yet he had not just been wrapped around her finger, but dancing on her string. In an odd way, he was proud. His daughter would be a formidable woman one day and he pitied her future husband. When Tatiana got married, he'd be sure to give the man a case of his liquor of choice in preparation for dealing with her temper.

Taking a drink of the rich red wine, he set the glass down carefully and turned back to find Tatiana's screams had turned into high-pitched shouts instead of the sound of dolphins being killed.

"You have until the count of five to calm down, or you will be standing in the corner with your nose to the wall. This is unacceptable behavior and it will not be tolerated."

Tatiana started to scream again, but by the count of three she'd wound down to hiccupping sobs, and by one was almost quiet. Her lower lip quivered and it killed him not to go to her and soothe her. Christ, who knew being a father could be this hard? He'd been in hostage situations easier than this. The last thought made him almost chuckle, but he managed to swallow it back.

"Better. Now, we're going to wash up, put your pajamas on, and you are going to bed early tonight. Obviously you've had a long day and you need your rest."

Tatiana's voice warbled pitifully and Alex had to force himself to not interrupt. "But Mommy—"

"No," Jessica said in a tone that would have made a Domme proud as she led Tatiana out the door. "Bedtime. That's it. End of argument. Now say goodnight to your father. If you do a good job of brushing your teeth, he'll come to say prayers with you."

Though he didn't particularly believe in any religion's view of God, he enjoyed praying with his daughter. Her earnest little face, eyes squeezed tight and lips pursed, as she silently said her prayers filled him with so much love that for a moment, he understood just a small portion of the kind of love God had for mankind. Only an adoration that intense would allow humanity to live on as it tried to destroy itself over and over again.

He was snapped out of his melancholy thoughts by the door opening again and Luka strolling in, his bronze tie askew and the lines around his green-brown eyes deeper than usual.

"Have a seat, my friend, you look tired."

Luka slumped next to him and ran a hand with a thick gold ring on it through his light-brown hair. "There is so much to be done. I need to go tour the Dubinski training facilities in Siberia sometime in the next month or so with Kozar and his men. Thankfully their camp is within a seven-hour snowmobile ride from the Novikov compound, so I've been there before. Pisses me off, it's going to be cold as fuck up there, everything frozen solid, just when it's warm in Moscow."

"I apologize for having to send you up there, but it is not just a training facility that you are going to." Alex stood, then retrieved a clean glass from the walnut sideboard and filled it with the aromatic red wine before handing it to Luka.

The man took a sip, then gave an appreciative sigh. "Very good. What else is up there?"

"Deep beneath the earth, Petrov has a factory of sorts that is ready to produce any weapon he might need. Including chemical. I want you to check out the security for the place and make sure no one can break in and arm themselves with nerve gas."

"Interesting. I will see what I can find."

"Do not mention to Kozar that you know there is more to the place than meets the eye. See what he volunteers, how honest he is with you. Do not offend or agitate him, but test his loyalty."

After taking another drink of wine, Luka leaned back and sucked in a breath through his teeth. "Loyalty, that will be a sticky point, won't it? So hard to say who is going to have your back, and who will try to stab it."

Shrugging, Alex grinned. "You say that like people haven't been trying to kill me from the cradle on."

"Good point."

His mind drifted back to the meeting they'd had with Nico. Something about the whole situation bothered him, kept gnawing at the back of his mind. It was a mystery, and he hated not knowing things. Knowledge was true power and a smart man hoarded it like a dragon with gold. He knew they had something important, something that shouldn't exist, but he wanted to know what the fuck it was for and how the hell it was made.

"This Silver Wood, what do you think?"

"I think," Luka set his glass down, then leaned forward with his elbows braced on his knees, "that it is trouble. Have you seen it? Is it as Petrov described?"

Over a year ago the canisters had arrived from the United States under much secrecy on Jorg's orders. Mimi Anderson had traded the canisters in exchange for Jorg getting her twin daughters out of some mess back in the States involving weapons stolen from the Israeli and Russian mafias, and mixed up with American outlaw motorcycle gangs. Alex had been genuinely surprised at all the favors his father had called in on the women's behalf to save the Anderson twins, but he'd chalked it up as his father owing Mimi. Even if Jorg hadn't agreed to help her, Alex would have, because she was the one who'd helped rescue him from Jorg's torturers all those years ago and he considered her a good friend.

Dimitri had met with Mimi personally during the exchange and he'd said she had no idea what was in the canisters, only that the Israeli Mafia had wanted it badly. When they'd opened the container, they'd found giant plastic sealed tubes inside, like massive pills filled with liquid silver. It had been odd, but nothing that Alex hadn't dealt with before. In the world of the Russian *Bratva*, odd things were a daily occurrence so he hadn't given it much thought at the time.

Alex nodded while loosening his tie. "Yes, I saw the contents, and they were very carefully packed, like the most delicate of eggs instead of massive plastic capsules. Unfortunately, there was nothing in the packing material to indicate any kind of origin or use."

"Do you think your father knows what it is?"

"If he does, he hasn't said anything or tried to access the Silver Wood...at least that I know of. That tricky old bastard could be up to anything."

A light knock came from the door, followed a moment later by Jessica peeking around the edge. "Okay, guys, wrap it up. Luka, the world will just have to continue to spin without my husband there to guide it for a few hours. Love having you here, wish you could stay, get out."

With a chuckle, Luka stood and stretched out, then nodded to Alex with a wry grin. "It seems I have been given my orders."

"Indeed," Alex said in a low voice as he caught the bright gleam of desire in his wife's eyes. "Now get out."

Jessica held the door open for Luka with a grin, halting him for a second to whisper something in his ear, making him laugh as he left.

Shutting the door behind her, Jessica sauntered up to him, all willowy grace and ethereal beauty. "Ready to go tuck Tatiana in?"

He gave her a wry look, remembering the earlier hysterics. "Is she still screaming?"

"No, but impressive, wasn't it?"

He grabbed her hand and pulled his wife closer, unable to be in the same room with her without touching her. "I believe I owe you an apology."

"For what?" she asked in a sugary-sweet fake voice while batting her lashes at him.

Pinching her pert bottom, he smiled at her little yelp. "It could be that I might have been spoiling Tatiana more than I should have. I did not realize how good she was at manipulating me."

"Don't feel bad, honey. Children are born knowing how to manipulate. It's part of our evolutionary makeup. I mean think about it, if kids didn't know how to be cute and get their way, our ancestors would have died out long ago. Trust me, this is normal little kid behavior and tantrums are a part of growing up." She stroked his bearded cheek and his whole body seemed to tighten at her touch. "And she is incredibly adorable, so don't feel bad."

"Like her mother," her murmured before catching her mouth in a quick, hot kiss. "Let us put our adorable daughter to bed, then I will apologize to you properly in our bedroom."

Chapter 17

After three weeks of exhausting work trying to learn the world of the Dubinski *Bratva*, Jessica was so glad she and Alex finally got to go out and have some fun, even if it was kind of business related. She cuddled Tatiana and smiled at Gwen as her friend complimented her outfit. Tonight they were going to some kind of dance club the Dubinski *Bratva* owned as a pre-party for the big coming out event planned next week. She was all glitzed up for the night and had to admit she felt good about how she looked. One of the spare bedrooms had been turned into a salon of sorts, and she'd been primped and pampered until she felt like a million bucks.

Then again, the chandelier diamond earrings she wore, along with a platinum-and-diamond choker, were probably worth near that so maybe she had a right to feel pretty. Her dress was certainly amazing, a couture Dolce and Gabbana black-lace cocktail dress that revealed a hell of a lot of leg, but showed off her black Giuseppe Zanotti black sparkly stilettos nicely.

Tatiana smiled up at her and Gwen let out a low whistle. "Wow...you look amazing."

Flushing, she ducked her head. "Thanks. Amazing is what six hours with a four-person stylist team can do."

With a smile that held a touch of sadness, Gwen fingered her braid. "Maybe that's what I need. Think I should let them loose and maybe finally get this mess cut?"

"I love your hair!" Tatiana declared. "It's so pretty, like a princess. Don't cut it."

"You look wonderful," Zoya said from behind Jessica, and she twirled around, an automatic smile turning her lips.

She looked behind Zoya to the empty doorway. "Where's Krom?"

The female bodyguard moved across the room to the small sitting area, her gaze scanning the space as if she expected a bad guy to leap out from behind the giant stuffed bear propped up in the corner of the room. "He needed to visit with his sister, she just had a baby and he is eager to meet his new nephew."

"Oh, she had the baby?" Gwen said in a happy voice as she tidied up the play area. Her friend had cleaning OCD and it came in handy around kids. "I'm so excited. I know Krom was freaking out about it."

Zoya's voice held an unusual note of surprise. "He told you? Krom is usually very...how to say in English...private about his family."

A hot flush bloomed over Gwen's face and Jessica narrowed her eyes as her nanny stammered out, "Well, what do you think we do while we take care of Tatiana? We talk like any normal adults do. Actually, we talk like normal adults with a curious little girl do. My *flora* is a very inquisitive child, and isn't afraid to ask questions. She isn't old enough to judge, and Krom understands. Look, I know he's scary and all of that, but you've never seen him alone with Tatiana. He will be a wonderful father someday."

Before she could drag Gwen to the side to question her about the obvious affection in the woman's voice for Krom, Alex strode through the door, a huge smile breaking out over his handsome face when Tatiana squealed, "Hi, Papa."

It had only been a little over a month so the novelty hadn't quite worn off for her yet, but Tatiana seemed to have accepted Alex along with the other big changes in her life. Gwen had told her over and over that kids were more resilient than adults, but Jessica had been worried that her daughter would have a hard time adjusting. Her doubts had proved unfounded because Tatiana was happier here than she'd ever seen her in Miami. After all, here she was surrounded by a throng of adults who adored her, and had the fun of having young cousins to play with.

But most importantly, Tatiana had Alex's deep and all-encompassing love for his daughter.

Tatiana bounced over to her father's arms and lifted hers with a big smile.

With a grin of his own, Alex scooped up the little girl and tossed her in the air. He of course caught her with ease but Jessica's heart still thumped hard every time he did that. Red hair flying as he spun her around, Tatiana giggled then thumped his chest. "Too fast."

Right away he stopped and placed a gentle kiss on her cheek. "Forgive me, my beautiful *solnyshko*."

He scanned the room for Jessica and when their eyes met, her belly dropped at the sight of her husband, looking dashing in a black suit and midnight-blue tie with silver dots, holding their daughter so gently. She moved close enough that Alex's familiar lime and cedar scent enveloped her then breathed him in deep. The sight of her strong, deadly husband cuddling their little girl made her heart ache with happiness. All those years, this is what Jorg had stolen from them. She'd personally kill the old man without batting a lash, but all contact between Jorg and herself was forbidden by Alex and Dimitri.

Looking down at their little girl, he said in a gentle but firm voice, "You will be good for your nanny, yes?"

Tatiana gave her father her cutest look, so sweet that sugar wouldn't melt in her little rosebud mouth. "Do I get a pony if I do?"

Alex winced, but he held strong as he said, "Your mother and I have agreed now is not time for pony."

Having heard this before, Tatiana sighed, "Yes, Papa."

With only a small pout, she walked across the small den that had been turned into her hangout room. Comfortable couches were grouped before a medium-sized television and the walls had been painted in soft pastel tones that worked well together. There were shelves and shelves of toys and books, but they were only half as full as they'd been a few days ago. Tatiana had thrown a fit because Gwen wouldn't let her take down all the dolls and play with them at once, only one at a time. Alex had been in the room with them at the time. To Jessica's surprise, Alex had put his foot down in the form of taking the toys that she didn't play with much and donating them to a local orphanage. Tatiana hadn't been happy, but Alex had stuck by his word despite her tears.

True, that night Alex had agonized that Tatiana would hate him forever, but the next morning, just as Jessica had predicted, Tatiana was her usual bubbly self.

They left after spending a little more time with Tatiana, taking their Bentley to the crazy-cool three story club that was bathed in purple, green and gold lights and sported massive white stone pillars on the facade. They were meeting some business associates of Alex's who were visiting from the United States. She'd found that, in many ways, the *Bratvas* were more like tightly run business empires than just a group of thugs selling drugs and doing petty criminal shit. Every day Alex revealed a little more to her about the inner workings of the Dubinski *Bratva*, while Petrov's wife and daughters filled her in on her role. She'd been excited to learn that she was more than a pretty smile on Alex's arm, that she would actually be in charge of some very important things, like the charity work the *Bratva* did. Evidently giving back to the community was a matter of pride among Russian men. And then there was the endless job of making sure her people were happy.

Yes, *her* people.

The thought still made her want to both giggle and wince. As Alex's wife, she was the one other women would come to with their problems and it would be her job to either help them as best she could or let her husband know if it was beyond her ability to fix. So far she'd sat in on Vera's meeting with one woman worried about her daughter being abused by her boyfriend, an older widow who was having issues with her younger neighbors disrespecting her, and a teenage girl nervously thanking Vera for helping with her education.

After that girl had left, Jessica learned she was a former underage prostitute who Petrov had rescued from a slave trader. Sometimes it was easy to forget the fact that Alex was neck deep in evil deeds with evil men, and she wondered how he managed to somehow retain his morals, twisted as they were, after all these years. Hell, her first thought after learning about the teenager's background had been to find the men who had kidnapped her and make them pay in pain before their deaths.

Shit, now she was sounding like a ruthless killer herself.

The beep of a horn next to her drew her back from her deep thoughts and to the present. Alex was quiet as well, but it was a peaceful silence between them, a perfect moment of serenity. It seemed as if the only time they were alone was in bed, and after screwing the hell out of each other they'd pass out. She let out a soft sigh, readying herself for the night ahead. She had no idea what section of Moscow they were in, but wherever it was, it was posh. The crowd milling around outside of the building was full of beautiful people dressed in clothing so finely made it could only be couture. Jewels sparkled everywhere, but her gaze sought out the tops of the buildings, where she knew Alex had snipers positioned to guard the entrance of the club. Excessive, but she had to admit it made her feel better.

As they pulled up, Alex gave her hand a squeeze, then kissed her wedding rings. "Are you ready?"

"Yep."

He smoothed a delicate curl from her eyes. "Tonight is about having fun. Catrin and Nico are waiting inside for us. As are Dimitri and Rya. Ivan and Gia couldn't make it, they are spending time with her family in the States, but said next time they look forward to having us over for dinner. I think you will like the Americans who are visiting us. Do you remember Mimi Stefano?"

"Of course." She squeezed his hand. "Laz's cousin. I met her in Rome a couple times and she rescued you from your father."

"Yes." The word was rough and she rubbed her thumb over his skin in a soothing gesture. "We helped her twin daughters out of a delicate situation a while ago. One of the twins, Sarah, is visiting with her husband, the president of a...what do you Americans call it...a motorcycle club. They had some business in the area and wanted to stop by on Mimi's behalf. She wishes she could have come herself to visit with you, but her other daughter, Swan, is due to give birth anytime now to twin boys."

She tried to imagine dealing with two newborns and laughed softly. "God bless them both."

Luka opened her door, his face set into a stern expression, then let out a low whistle at the sight of her. "Mrs. Dubinski, you must warn a man before you wear a dress like that."

She took the dashing man's firm hand and braced herself for the barrage of noise as soon as the crowd caught sight of her. Right now, unfortunately, her reappearance was a thing of great gossip. It was all over the Internet, along with some of the craziest speculation she'd ever seen, everything from alien abduction to having lived in an Arctic research lab with Bigfoot. Their official story was that she'd been in a car accident and suffered amnesia, but no one really bought it.

A few reporters had come close to the truth, but not enough to alarm her. Hell, even if they found out what really happened, no one would believe it. Her mind strayed to the grave in Ireland where some unknown woman's charred bones rested with her old wedding rings. Jorg's men had been the ones to find Krom, so she was pretty sure they'd take her rings from him while he was unconscious, to help stage her death. She didn't talk much with Alex about those dark days, but she had talked with Krom about it and they'd pieced together what had probably happened that night after she drove away to start her new life in Miami.

A shudder made goose bumps rise up along her arms and she tried to turn her thoughts from the past to the present. The paparazzi were kept far away from the club, but she could see the lights reflecting off the long-range lenses on their cameras down the street. There were so many of them, and they surged like a pile of cockroaches scurrying over each other when she looked their way.

Luka followed her gaze then murmured, "We have three of our men in that mess."

Grateful that he understood her concern, she gave him a small smile. "Thank you."

The corner of his pouty lower lip curled up, the light-brown scruff covering his jaw glinting as they stepped onto the black velvet carpet that led to the entrance of the three-story building with its opulent Roman-style columns. Alex joined them, and having the big, solid presence of the men near her gave her a much-needed bolster of courage. Her husband held out his arm and she slipped hers through his, falling naturally into step with them as they turned to face the crowd now watching them intently.

With security flanking them on all sides, they strode into the club together and she held her head high, pretending she was walking past the bitchy chicks in marketing as she ignored the blatant stares and pointing.

From behind them, Luka murmured, "Has anyone ever told you, Mrs. Dubinski, that you have amazing legs?"

Alex growled, "Do not make me kill you, Luka. Would interrupt my plans for the evening."

She recognized her bodyguard's teasing for what it was, a way to relax her, but when she glanced his way she found him scanning the area with a stern expression. Luka abruptly frowned and she followed his gaze to the front doors of the club. A tall, regal-looking brunette wearing a red leather dress was giving Alex a blatantly seductive smile as they approached. The woman was obviously some kind of authority at the club because the bouncers behind her were differential to her.

Arching a dark brow, she looked Jessica up and down, then turned her attention to back Alex. "Welcome, Mr. Dubinski," she purred in Russian. "We are honored to have you here tonight. As always, I am at your *complete* disposal for *anything* you want."

Jessica started to think about choking the bitch in the red dress but before she could draw a breath, Alex growled in a low voice and replied, "Divana, I will only tell you this once. My wife has returned to me and I will destroy anyone who threatens her happiness or my marriage. Do you understand?"

"Oh—of course. My apologies, Mr. Dubinski."

She smoothed on a bright, cheery smile that was as fake and sparkly as a cubic zirconia. The fear in her gaze, however, didn't match her expression and Jessica almost felt sorry for her. Alex was deadly when he went into protective mode and he wouldn't hesitate to eliminate anything he considered a threat. A part of her felt like she should be disturbed by this knowledge, but if she was being honest with herself, she'd kill anyone who ever tried to harm her family with no qualms, so she understood how he felt.

The pounding of a bass-filled song shook her from her thoughts as she followed Alex into the club through a neon-lined archway doorway, the woman before them slightly unsteady on her heels as she constantly glanced over her shoulder with a brittle smile.

"There you are!" a familiar voice yelled from somewhere to her left.

She turned to find Rya working her way through the crowd towards them with Dimitri in tow. Tonight the voluptuous brunette wore her hair down and loose, dressed in a figure-hugging little gold-spangled dress and decked out in a sultan's fortune of rubies. Dimitri trailed behind her, wearing a black suit and white shirt, but no tie. His expression was closed down and if she didn't know him so well, she'd be intimidated by the gigantic man stalking their way with such a cold gaze. Where Rya showed her emotions with ease, it kind of hurt Jessica's heart to see how good Dimitri had become at being unreadable.

When he caught her watching him, he smiled, then gave her a friendly wink that sent a gentle wave of relief through her.

A moment later, Rya grabbed her in a hug, the shorter woman smelling like honeysuckle and amber. "God, can you believe this place? Isn't it insane?"

For the first time, Jessica really looked around the club while Dimitri and Alex spoke in low voices behind them. The building was three stories high with women on swings and in cages dancing above the crowd. Long streamers hung from the bottoms of the swings and they twirled through the air in glittering arcs. A bar took up two sides of the room, made of smoky glass and lit from beneath with smooth ambient lighting. Staircases led up to a second floor, guarded by two big men in black suits who she pegged right away as serious muscle, then another set of softly glowing amber glass stairs led to a glassed-in third level that peered out over the club.

She studied that area, trying to see past the reflective glass that hid the revelers on the third floor from the rest of the crowd. Another pair of guards stood at the top of the stairs and they were big enough to block the entrance with their wide shoulders. She couldn't imagine being able to spot a threat in all this chaos, but then again, they were probably used to it. Luka was as alert as ever, his body language broadcasting the fact that he was not a man to be fucked with. He caught her looking at him and gave her a smirking wink.

"Do you think your husband would kill me if I danced with you later?"

Alex growled loud enough to be heard over the music and Rya led her a few steps away, giving them some privacy while remaining close enough that their husbands wouldn't freak out.

Rya laughed. "I swear someday one of our guys is going to strangle Luka. He's such a flirt."

"The worst," Jessica agreed. "I cannot tell you the number of women who have fallen victim to that dashing smile of his. Hell, he slept with two of my friends from back home and they were not too keen on sharing him."

"Pity," Rya said with a seductive little smile. "Sharing can be *lots* of fun."

She knew from Alex that Dimitri and Rya were also into kink, but they hadn't played together.

Alex came up behind her and slid her hand into his calloused one. "Follow me."

As she had suspected they would, they made their way up the stairs and it seemed like everyone in the entire club was watching them.

She had an insane urge to jump up and down while giving a good Kermit the Frog Crazy Arms dance just so they had something worth looking at.

They passed the first set of guards, then a smiling young man dressed in a white shirt and well-fitted black pants met them at the bottom of the stairs.

In almost accent-less English, he said in a voice loud enough to be heard over the booming techno, "Welcome Mr. and Mrs. Dubinski, Mr. and Mrs. Novikov. The rest of your party is waiting upstairs for you."

They soon cleared the landing to the third story and right away the noise level lowered enough so her ears weren't ringing.

At least they weren't until Catrin yelled out, "There you are! Now we can really party."

Three hours later, Jessica snorted a laugh at an outrageous story Rya was telling about doing a threesome with Luka when she and Dimitri first started dating. "Girl, it was so-so dirty wrong but I think he licked Dimitri's balls while he was eating my pussy."

"While Dimitri was fucking you?" Catrin asked with a little wiggle. "Delicious."

"Oh yeah." Rya gave a dreamy sigh. "It was sooooooo good."

After splitting two bottles of champagne, a fruity drink, and a couple vodka shots, Jessica was feeling pretty free and reveled in being around women who were just as kinky as she was. "Wait, back to the ball-licking thing. I think I find that kinda hot, the idea of two guys touching each other. Is that weird?"

Snuggling closer to Jessica, Catrin smiled. "It is very hot. Nico is not interested in men at all, but I have watched other men touch each other and it makes me so wet."

She looked over to Alex again, tempted into being very naughty by Catrin's teasing tone.

Alex glanced over at them and when his gaze went from Catrin and Rya to her, the breath in her chest hitched at the heat in his gaze. He gave her a slow, dirty smile that sent her hormones into overdrive. While he wasn't the handsomest man in the room, he drew her attention like a magnet. The music throbbed around them and she swore her blood pounded to the same beat as he continued to hold her prisoner with his stormy gray eyes. Her whole body clenched as he slowly raised his drink and rubbed his lips against the rim before taking a sip, reminding her of the way he rubbed his mouth against her pussy before devouring her.

"Wow," Rya said in a low voice, "I've *never* seen him look at anyone like that."

"Of course not." Catrin's reply was so soft Jessica had to strain to hear it. "You've never seen him in love. I told you, he is different man with Jessica."

Alex looked away and she took in a deep breath, feeling as if she'd just broken the surface of the water after jumping into a deep lake.

Laughing, Rya poured another shot, only spilling a little bit before shoving it over to Jessica. "Drink."

Before she could, a mature man's hand picked up the glass and she followed its path to find Petrov smiling at them before he tossed the shot back in a smooth motion. The other two women squealed and spilled out of the booth to give him hugs, but Jessica wasn't sure how to react around him. He seemed really nice, and when they'd spoken he'd been kind, but he was Petrov fucking Dubinski and he was so powerful that even Jorg didn't mess with him. He had

Rya and Catrin hanging off both of his arms, giving him big smiles.

"I see you have started drinking without me."

Rya slid into the booth and tugged Petrov in next to her, with Catrin sliding in next to Jessica again. This left her sitting across from Petrov and she studied the older man with drunk fascination. Being really, really buzzed helped her relax and she smiled at him.

"Is Vera with you?"

"Unfortunately, no. She does not have the patience to put up with all the noise and the overgrown, unruly children. Plus two of our grandchildren are unwell with the flu, so she is over helping our daughter care for them."

"Awww, that sucks." She reached across the table and grasped his hand. "Does Lani need anything? I can talk with her or bring some meals over, clean her home if she isn't up to it."

"That is very kind of you to offer, but unnecessary."

She shook her head, her alcohol-soaked brain insisting she could somehow help. "Really, it's not a big deal. There was a group of women from my church that would do all of that and more for anyone in our town that needed their help. Didn't matter who it was, rich or poor, if you needed someone, they'd be that someone for you. I mean doesn't everybody need somebody? Not having anyone...that's the worst."

Petrov squeezed her hand, his expression unexpectedly grave. "You are not alone any longer, Jessica. You have us and we are overjoyed to have you back in our lives.

She sniffed, blinking back tears and nodded. "Thank you."

Chuckling, he poured another full to the rim shot and handed it to her. "I am afraid I must speak to some people before I can go home and rest my old bones. Goodnight, sweet Jessica. Ladies."

They all said goodbye and watched him leave before turning back to each other.

Catrin kissed her cheek. "You will always have me, *dorogoya*."

"Me too," Rya chimed in, her gaze direct, if a little fuzzy. "I've got your back not only because I like you, but because since you've returned, both Alex and my husband have been happier than I've ever seen them. Dimitri actually jokes with people now. It's crazy."

She slammed the shot, gasped, then took another sip of her cocktail, some fruity creation in an elegant glass, then turned to Rya. "So tell me how you and Dimitri met."

The story that Rya told about how she fell in love with Dimitri had Jessica round-eyed with disbelief. "Holy shit. So there were rival *Bratva* members with this delegation as well at the lodge?"

"Yes. Initially they paid me no mind because I was with the Master who'd won me at the Submissive's Wish Auction, just another pretty face, so to speak. That lodge was crawling with beautiful women so I didn't really stand out. At least not to anyone other than Dimitri."

"But they suspected Dimitri was attached to you when you got back from your secret vacation together at the Grand Canyon?"

Taking another drink before answering, Rya nodded. "I know it sounds crazy, but Dimitri and I fell deeply in love during those few stolen days. He was everything I'd ever wanted in a man, perfect for me in every way, but I was soon to learn completely forbidden. He tried to resist his feelings for fear of what would happen to me, because of the Novikov Curse. He feared I would be taken from him like you were taken from Alex."

Empathy for the other woman filled her, fueled by a few too many drinks, and she had to blink back tears. "Oh honey, that sucks."

"It did." Rya's golden eyes went distant, tension filling her body. "When we returned to the massive lodge where the European delegation was staying with their submissives, Alex let us know that the Sokolov *Bratva* was suspicious, that there were already rumors about Dimitri caring for me in a way he'd never cared for a woman before."

"How did you keep from tipping them off?"

Rya suddenly swallowed and looked away, taking a long drink before setting her glass down. "We...ah, pretended we didn't know each other."

"And it worked?"

Rya shredded her napkin, her whole body screaming tension. "Yeah."

Standing suddenly, Catrin tugged at Jessica's hand. "Come, I have to use the bathroom."

Puzzled by Catrin and Rya's weird reactions, she allowed the petite blonde to drag her through the VIP section that had become filled with people in the past few hours. All the alcohol they'd been drinking seemed to catch up with her and she had to force a giggle back as she watched Catrin's rather unsteady walk. Wow, she'd had a *lot* to drink tonight. Aware that her every move was being watched, she focused on walking in her tall heels without tripping, glad the club lighting helped mask any wobbles. She was so determined to not fall and bust her ass that she was startled by the brighter lights of the luxurious bathroom and ran into Catrin's back.

Shades of orange, gold, and red streaked through the giant marble slabs that made up the bathroom walls. There were stalls, but floor-to-ceiling giant wood doors hid them entirely. A pleasant spice lightly scented the air, and it was almost peaceful in here after the constant noise outside.

Now that she saw the bathroom, all those shots she'd done and drinks that had gone down so easy made her have to piss like a racehorse. Catrin must have felt the same because she didn't look at or say anything to Jessica, just went into one of the stalls. Jessica used the other, and after peeing for what felt like ten minutes, she went back out into the area where the sinks were, along with a countertop filled with items a woman might need arranged on a beautiful, sleek silver tray.

She washed up and considered reapplying her lipstick, but she had a feeling putting on her makeup while drunk wasn't a good idea. God, it had been years since she'd been able to let loose like this and she couldn't wait to get back out there and find her husband. Maybe she could talk Alex into dancing with her. While the fast-paced club music wasn't really his taste, she thought she'd be able to seduce him into getting dirty on the dance floor. Just the thought of having his hard body pressed into hers sent a little tingle of heat between her thighs.

Catrin waited for her in the sitting area of the bathroom, perched on a butterscotch brown crushed-velvet settee over on the other side of the spa-like space. Her normally merry smile was totally missing, and her blue eyes, while glassy with alcohol, were also very direct. She crossed her legs, then laced her fingers together on her lap. Taking a deep breath, which made her lovely breasts swell above the neckline of her dress, she said in a low voice with just the faintest slur to her words, "Jessica, you need to know something. Someone needs to tell you before story is just thrown in your face, and I hope you love me enough to not just react, but to listen."

Unease crept through the haze of booze and she frowned at Catrin. "What?"

"Is about what happened at the lodge when Dimitri and Rya first got together. Something that occurred that you may not like. Rya and Alex have been...intimate."

She staggered back, her hand automatically reaching out to brace against the wall as all the vodka she'd drank sloshed in her suddenly queasy stomach. "What? She's having an affair with Alex?"

"No, nothing like that! It was only one time and a dangerous situation. Nico and I were there as well. Was very complicated time, not good, not for pleasure."

After listening to Catrin's explanation of the events at the Submissive's Wish Auction, she still couldn't help the sharp spike of betrayal that went through her heart. It wasn't just jealousy and hurt over Alex and Rya's actions, but jealousy that Catrin, Nico, and Rya had been together as well.

Dammit, *this* was why she didn't drink. Her emotions were all over the place as drunken, jealous rage hit her hard. Her stomach clenched like she'd been kicked in the gut. Crossing her arms over her chest, she slumped against the cool stone wall.

"Are you still fucking her?"

Frowning, Catrin lifted her chin. "I do not appreciate you being a bitch when I am trying to help you."

"Help me?" She let out a bitter laugh that made Catrin flinch. "You just told me that my husband fucked his sister-in-law."

"No, he never fucked her. He played with her while Nico and I helped, years ago."

Words fueled by irrational anger spilled from her lips. "God, is there anywhere I can go where I don't have to see someone who's fucked my husband? They're everywhere! The restaurant where we had lunch with Vera, the party at Gia's, I even ran into one of his sluts at the fucking grocery store! And now I have to know that Alex slept with his *sister-in-law*? That yet another woman knows what he looks like when he has an orgasm?"

"Stop being such a bitch and listen to me!" Catrin abruptly stood and stalked over to Jessica, tears streaking her mascara down her cheeks. "You. Were. Dead! Gone, and never coming back. I had to live through your death, as did Dimitri, and Alex would have done *anything* to spare his brother the pain of losing the woman he loves because he knew all too well what that agony felt like. So do not give me this jealous bullshit. The woman I know would never be mad at the man she loves for doing whatever he could to save another woman's life. Do you think it was easy for Rya? She loved Dimitri and was forced to do a scene in public with his brother, even though it tore her heart apart. Yes, Alex has been with other women, but it is *you* that he loves. Let go of this anger, Jessica, before it eats you alive."

She had nothing to say in response to that because guilt had swamped her, sending her to her knees as the pain, trauma, and agony she'd been carefully keeping locked away managed to get past her guards. God, every word Catrin said was true. While she'd like to blame it on all the drinks she'd had, she continued to cry in great racking sobs as Catrin held her, murmuring comforting things while Jessica soaked her dress with her tears.

When she'd finally managed to settle down enough to release Catrin, she was ashamed at breaking down like this. "I'm so sorry. You're right, I am angry, and I'm trying to let it go but it's so hard."

"No, no darling, I am sorry, I explained this badly." Catrin made Jessica lift her chin and meet her gaze. "It happened in the past and has not been repeated. While Alex loves Rya, it is as his sister-in-law. And yes, I do still play with her, but her main lover and submissive is Gia."

That made Jessica blink. "Rya's a Mistress?"

"No, she's a switch, but Mistress to Gia...much like I am Mistress to you," Catrin mused. "Now, let us clean up before someone comes in here and tells Nico and Alex we've been crying. You know that would throw them both into a panic."

She helped Jessica to her feet then led them both over to the sinks as they began to repair their damaged makeup.

Her voice still thick with tears, Jessica sighed at the sight of her reddened eyes. "I hate this insecurity, this jealousy. I wish it would just go away because it makes me so fucking pissed over things I rationally know I can't control. I'm not like this, really I'm not."

"Do not be so hard on yourself, sweet girl." Catrin turned her head and examined her hair. "Your life is not an easy one and you have been so strong, but you are also allowed also to be human."

Sighing and deciding her face was as good as it was going to get, she stood up straight and squared her shoulders. "I need to talk to Alex. We need to clear the air so this isn't hanging between us. I promised myself I'd tell him when something was bothering me, and this is bothering me."

"Wait," Catrin squawked as Jessica strode off for the door, still wobbling in her heels but determined to talk to her husband. "Jessica, you have been drinking. Now is not good time for this."

She shrugged Catrin off, the woman's protests lost in the noise of the club. Yes, the room was still spinning a bit, and she couldn't feel the tip of her nose because it had gone numb, but she wasn't that drunk. Seriously. She was fine. The crowd parted like an invisible force field extended from her, then she felt a presence behind her and found one of her bodyguards following and scanning the mass of people with a decidedly unfriendly expression.

Ignoring him, she thanked God for her height because she could see over some of the people and that allowed her to spot Alex, talking with Dimitri and a devastatingly handsome guy in probably his late thirties. He had almost shoulder length golden-blonde hair streaked with silver at the temples and held back by a leather band. A tattoo on the side of his thick neck with the name "Sarah" on it caught her attention and as she got closer and got an eyeful of the woman at his side she understood his desire to have her name on his body. Smiling up at him was a stunning young woman with long pale-blonde hair, a gorgeous face, and a body that looked as if it was right out of the pages of a swimsuit calendar encased in a little red dress. There were many beautiful women here, but the one who had to be Sarah outshone them all.

The woman was scanning the crowd and saw Jessica coming first. She elbowed the man standing next to her, who followed her gaze. Alex did as well and when their eyes locked, his narrowed. Okay, so she was a blotchy-faced mess, but he had no right to look so judgmental. She was even walking kinda-sorta straight.

Her drunken emotions swung from guilt to anger as she suddenly hated the fact that he knew what Rya looked like naked. Her chest hurt and a stinging sweat broke out over her body as she came to a stop before him, swaying in her heels alarmingly before he reached out to steady her. Anger pushed aside her hurt feelings and she glared at Alex, knowing in the back of her mind she was being totally irrational, but unable to stop herself.

"Don't touch me, you asshole! I can stand on my own two feet without any man's help."

Alex frowned, Dimitri frowned, the man with the neck tattoo frowned, but Sarah grinned.

"Jessica, compose yourself," Alex said, his warning tone loud and clear.

"I am composed." She stiffened her spine then lifted her chin, hoping he didn't notice how she had to squint slightly to focus on him in all the shifting lights.

"You are being rude to our guests."

Realizing that what he said was true, she turned to the couple watching them curiously. "I'm so sorry to be rude like this, but communication is important in a relationship and I need to let my husband know that

I'm super pissed at him. I love him very much, so he has to know he's a jerk. It's an important foundation."

The dangerous-looking man cracked a wide smile that set dimples in his cheeks and his wife burst out laughing. His deep voice was so seductive she was sure her heart skipped a beat as he growled out, "That's fine, sugar. You're right, communication is important to a healthy relationship. Sarah and I are gonna head on over to the bar and do some shots with some friends of ours so you can work on that foundation of yours. It was nice meetin' you, Jessica."

An important fact suddenly occurred to her and she reached out and pulled a startled Sarah into a hug. "Wait, you're Mimi's daughter! Please tell her thank you for saving Alex's life. I miss her. She makes really good sugar cookies for chick-flick night and she smells nice."

"That she does," Sarah gently extracted herself from Jessica's arms and grinned at her. "We have got to party together before I leave. Rya has my cell phone number, please give me a call."

"I will."

She turned back to Alex, her anger returning in an instant as she saw he was staring at her like he was really pissed off. As if he had any reason or right to be mad at *her*. Dimly she knew the majority of the VIP section was watching them, but her focus was entirely on her glowering husband. She lowered her voice, leaned unsteadily into him, then pointed her finger at his hard chest.

"Considering I just found out you've messed around with Rya, I'm really fucking calm."

"Enough," her husband growled. "I will address your concerns, but I will not indulge you acting like this in public. Stop your temper tantrum, now, or you will be punished."

Her lower lip quivered and with her filter missing, the words that she knew would hurt him tumbled from her mouth, "Maybe we need some space."

That was the last thing in the world she wanted, but her heart hurt so damn bad even though she knew she was being incredibly selfish and unfair. She was out of control, spinning within her own head and drowning herself in her fears. The instinct to sever all ties and protect herself like she'd had to do when she left him before was strong. Fucking hell, she knew she was acting like a crazy woman, but she seemed helpless to stop herself.

Staring up into his eyes, she blinked away the tears that filled hers again, hating how raw she felt at this moment, in front of all these strangers.

Why did she think confronting him here was a good idea?

He snarled, and before she knew it, she was slung over his shoulder with her ass in the air and he was striding across the room.

She would have been kicking and screaming at him to put her down, but the alcohol in her stomach was threatening to come up as his shoulder pressed into it, so all her energy was spent on struggling not to barf all over his magnificent ass.

By the time he set her on her feet she was gagging and had to sit down on a gray suede couch while struggling to keep the liquid down. If she started throwing up, she would never stop. God, she hadn't been this drunk since college. Her head spun and she sucked in deep breaths, slowly realizing in the quiet of whatever room she was in that she wasn't really that drunk, more like having some kind of emotional breakdown. A tremor started in her belly and spread to the rest of her body until she was shaking.

With a low sigh, he took a step forward then pressed her reluctant head to his muscular thigh. She resisted the comfort of his touch for all of a moment before allowing the warmth of his energy to flow over her, soothe her. As her body relaxed further, she mused that her physical reaction to him was so strong it was like a narcotic. Her heartbeat finally slowed and she rubbed her face against the silken cloth of his dress pants.

The anger that had run her mouth earlier had vanished, leaving her feeling once again guilty, but now also ashamed at her actions out there. Shit, she'd yelled at him in front of everyone like one of those crazy drunk bitches she always hated. Double shit, she'd said that stuff in front of Dimitri.

"Who told you?" Alex asked, his voice distant despite his fingers caressing her cheek.

"It doesn't matter—"

"Who told you!" he thundered.

Startling, she tried to pull away but his firm grip on the back of her neck kept her pressed to him, as though he needed to keep her there. Her voice came out breathy as she replied, "Catrin, but it wasn't in a bad way. She was trying to help."

He didn't respond, instead releasing her then holding his phone up to his ear before he said in Russian, "Nico, your wife took it upon herself to tell Jessica about what happened at the lodge when we had to throw the Sokolov's off our trail. Have Luka get my bag from the limo and bring it to me. Yes. Please take care of it. I will be dealing with Jessica's disobedience myself."

"Wait!" she said as she imagined how upset Nico was going to be. "Please, don't get her in trouble. She was trying to help."

He calmly put his phone back into his pocket, then began to take off his tie. "Do not worry, she will be getting a punishment very similar to yours."

Chapter 18

"Punishment?" She sat on the edge of the couch, glancing around the small private lounge done in shades of gray, cream, and lilac, looking for a possible escape route from the very determined man now removing his jacket.

"Yes, punishment. Your behavior was disrespectful and dangerous. Distracted me in a public place, had the potential to make me look weak in front of my men, and insulted our guests. Your conduct was not first impression I wished for you to make on Beach and Sarah. They are from the United States and were looking forward to meeting with you. Mimi has spoken very highly of you to them, about what a sweet woman you are. Unfortunately, they did not get to see that side of you tonight."

Her lower lip trembled and she looked away. "I'm sorry."

"As am I, *dorogoya*." He cupped her chin. "You are suffering. I will take you away from your worries, from your fears. It is my privilege as your Master to make you fly so deep that nothing will touch you. But I will not make it easy on you."

Her nipples hardened beneath her dress and her skin grew sensitive under his dominant gaze. "Yes, Master."

Taking a seat in a large, lilac leather wing-back chair, he motioned to her. "Remove your dress and come here."

Excitement tingled through her blood, making her nipples tightened as she slid her clothing off. If he noticed her arousal, he ignored it, looking at her in an impersonal way she didn't like. She was used to his open adoration and worship; being denied that affection hurt.

Determined to get in his good graces again, needing to renew their connection and reassure herself that he loved her, she assumed the standing submissive position that he preferred. Still wearing her heels, she widened her stance then laced her arms together behind her back with her gaze on the ground, only wobbling a little bit as she tried to find her balance. It wasn't the most comfortable of stances, but it displayed her body to her husband and she was reassured to hear his small inhalation at the sight.

"Come here, lay on my lap."

Following his commands was as natural as breathing to her. There was a sense of anticipation in the air, like when a roller coaster began to climb the first big hill, along with a small twinge of fear. When Alex punished her it was never easy or fun, but it was always an experience like no other. And afterwards she would feel renewed and energized, like she'd shed a weight from her back that she didn't realize she'd been carrying. She needed that release, and knew her husband needed it as well. They were a perfectly matched pair in that aspect. His need to own her and her need to serve him fitting together like a lock and key.

She draped herself over his lap carefully, his erection pressing into her rib cage. Yes, her husband had a bit of a sadistic streak and he enjoyed punishing her. Heat flooded her pussy as she wondered if he'd have her suck him off after he spanked her. The mental image of him climaxing while she drank him down hit her right in the pit of her belly, and she shivered when Alex began to arrange her to his liking.

His rough hand moved over her back, stroking her skin, soothing her even as she fought the urge to wiggle. Surely she couldn't be looking forward to the pain? The moisture welling between her legs begged to differ and Alex skimmed his fingertips between her nether lips, playing with the slick arousal coating her sex. He made a pleased noised and continued to toy with her until she was making breathy little moans. The big pad of his thumb pressed down on her clit and she arched her back.

Without any hint that it was coming, his free hand slapped her ass, hard.

She yelped, then moaned when his thumb pressed her pulsing nub.

"You love this, my filthy girl," he whispered.

"Yes, Master."

"So do I, but I do not think you will like what is to come."

He rained another series of spanks over her butt and upper thighs, the skin beginning to burn enough that she had to bite her lip to help her endure the hurt.

The constant hits paused and she sucked in a sobbing breath, unaware that she'd begun crying.

"You will not disrespect me or yourself like that in public again, do you understand, Jessica?"

"Yes," she said in a hitching voice.

"You will always remember that you represent the Dubinski *Bratva*, and that you will not shame your people, am I clear?"

"Yes, Master."

He gave her a harsh slap that tore a scream from her. "Are you sorry for your actions?"

"Yes, I'm sorry! Please, Master." She lifted one arm from the floor to swipe at her tears.

"What do you think, Luka? Does she appear very contrite?"

Startled, she looked over her shoulder to find the handsome man standing a few paces away, his hazel gaze roaming her body while his substantial erection pushed against his pants. "No, she looks fuckable."

"I agree, but unfortunately she acted like brat and needs reminder about self-control."

Luka's face went positively evil. "Would you like me to help you in correcting her behavior?"

Her pussy clenched and both men laughed while she blushed and hung her head. "What would you suggest?"

There was silence for a moment, followed by the sound of a zipper. Her aroused body hoped it was Luka freeing his cock so he could fuck her, but instead she found him digging through Alex's BDSM toy bag. Like a good boy scout, her husband had toy bags in all his cars, ready to be grabbed at a moment's notice so he could torment her. She loved how kinky he was, but she also tensed because Alex was introducing new toys all the time.

There could be anything in that bag.

"Ahhhh, can we use this? I have not had chance to play with in years. You and Dimitri horde all for yourself, greedy bastards. "

She went to turn her head to look, but Alex placed his hand on the back of her neck to hold her in place and she moaned at the display of domination.

"Yes, and grab the belt, the one with the cup."

Luka's wicked laugh sent a shiver down her spine. "Mmmm, this will be fun."

"Lick her," Alex ordered and she spread her legs wide, the groan ripped from her throat at the thought of Luka's reportedly talented mouth on her pussy.

Alex spread her buttocks in an obscene manner, exposing every inch of her swollen sex and ass to the other man.

The low growl that Luka gave sent shivers down her spine. The man must have knelt behind her because his breath warmed her sex as he took an audible inhalation. "Delicious."

Alex's cock twitched and she wanted so bad to stroke him, but didn't dare. Her husband loved to watch other people eat her pussy, it was one of his favorite kinks, so knowing that he was getting what was, for him, an amazing up-close show only made her hornier.

Instead of going for her sex, Luka's firm tongue licked over her anus, startling her enough that she tried to clench her buttocks together, unable to because of Alex holding her open and exposed. He licked around that dense little bundle of nerves, teasing it until Jessica was moaning uncontrollably. She'd never climax from having her ass licked, but holy shit it felt good.

Catrin had said Luka was bisexual and she wondered if Alex had ever enjoyed the talent of that man's tongue. The absolutely taboo slant to her thoughts turned her on something fierce and she swore her throbbing sex was dripping on the floor. Luka pulled back as she whimpered, allowing Alex to spank her already tender ass. With a fierce cry, she bucked and almost slipped off his lap.

Both men laughed while Alex shifted her so she was standing with her legs spread, and her head was in his lap. The temptation of his cock so close to her lips, the smell of him, was too great and she nuzzled his erection, rubbing her face on it like a cat. He groaned and stroked her cheek.

"Such a good girl, but I do not think you will be as happy with me soon."

Before she could question him, what she assumed was lubricant was spread around her rear entrance, teasing her and making her twitch. Luka's pleased murmur only aroused her more and she reveled in these two strong men taking total control of her. Right now none of her worries mattered; nothing existed except for their touch. They took her so deep into her physical self that she was free to just exist and trust her Master.

More of the lube was spread onto her pussy and she wondered why he bothered since she was already soaked with her natural arousal.

The answer came a few moments later when he spread the liquid on her nipples and a teasing warmth began to heat them almost like the sensation of a mouth sucking.

Crap.

It wasn't lube that he was using on her, it was Aphrodite's Tears. One of the world's only true aphrodisiacs. A precious liquid that made her body hypersensitive and needy, drove her mad enough with the desire to come that she'd do anything Alex wanted.

Her mind cleared a bit and she stiffened when something that felt a lot like a G-string with a metal crotch was fastened around her. She shuddered in apprehension, fearing that she exactly what her punishment was going to be—and it was going to totally suck.

"I cannot spank you," Alex murmured, "to correct your behavior because you enjoy it. In fact, most of my punishments would be things you would enjoy because you are a filthy girl. No, in order to teach you lesson, we must take something away. In your case, the ability to orgasm."

She tried to jerk upright, but he held her in place while Luka fondled the burning cheeks of her ass, the oil beginning to do its job, making her already swollen tissues enflame further. Soon that tenderness would become a physical pain until she had at least three or four good climaxes to ease it. The only other time she'd used the oil had been during the hunt at the Stefano estate outside of Rome, and the memories of that debauched night had her nuzzling Alex's cock again while Luka stroked her buttocks.

"Stand up," Alex said in a low voice as he helped her find her balance, still nude in her heels.

When she looked, she found Luka had his pants unbuckled and partially unzipped, his uncircumcised cock out and looking thick and delicious as he stroked it. Because he was fair-skinned his cock was a reddish pink and she wondered how dark the head would turn just before he came. The heavy sensual look on his handsome face had her belly clenching, and her body begged her to go bend over in front of him and get filled with that tempting dick. Alex walked up next to her, his erection still contained by his pants, and she practically melted beneath his aura of command. The chastity belt she wore cupped her sex so it got no pressure on it, no matter how she shifted.

"You will go apologize to our guests, then we are going home. Luka, help put her clothes on."

She shivered uncontrollably while Luka dressed her as leisurely as possible, caressing her needy skin the whole time, driving her into a frenzy. It was only Alex's presence that kept her from tearing the belt off and taking the other man by force. He was the consummate tease, knowing just how to bring pleasure from different parts of her and what to do in order to have her begging him beneath her breath to fuck her as he zipped her dress.

Her whole body throbbed and she was shaking so much that Alex had to help escort her out of the room. She clung to him, taking in deep inhalations of his masculine scent; the pheromones that he gave off letting her body know that there was a healthy, prime male right here, perfect for sex. It took a great deal of effort not to let her hands roam all over him and embarrass herself further, but the damn oil was driving her to distraction. Memories of the hunt at the

Stefano country mansion filled her again and she swallowed back a moan at the sight of Nico speaking with Beach and Sarah. She didn't see Catrin and wondered where the other woman was.

The handsome black man's warm, soft lips would be perfect right now on her swollen sex. The damned cup kept all pressure off of her aching flesh, leaving her feeling so empty, but the rasp of her dress over her diamond-hard nipples was almost as good as a caress. By the time they reached their group, she was half out of her mind with lust and drank in all the beautiful people around her. As she took in the American couple, Beach and Sarah, her mind drifted to fantasies of playing with them. The woman was stunning but there was something about the man's body language that spoke of danger and power. Control. Yes, he was a man who liked to be in complete control. She could see it in the way he held his wife, his grip half on her hip and half on her ass, a possessive sign that said she was taken. He had tattoos on his fingers and she bet they looked really good against Sarah's perfectly tanned and glowing skin.

Alex stopped her before them and she licked her lips while Sarah gave her a curious look.

Before Alex could say anything, Jessica breathed out, "I'm sorry for my temper earlier. I'd had a few too many shots and—well, I'm sorry I acted that way. I've known Mimi for a long time, and it truly is a pleasure to meet her daughter and son-in-law. She's an amazing woman."

"Thank you," Sarah said with a breathtaking smile, her worry replaced with amusement. "And don't worry about it. We've all had a drunken fight or two with our old man. Making up is always tons of fun. And I meant what I said earlier about getting together. Nico was telling us about a...private club that you belong to that we might enjoy playing at."

Jessica shifted, fighting the urge to rub herself against Alex as her hormone-saturated mind immediately pictured watching Beach and Sarah do some kinky BDSM fuckery. "I haven't been there yet, but Catrin said it's lots of fun."

Alex gripped the back of her neck then said to Beach, "I will contact you later about that matter we were discussing."

"I don't know much of anything, but what I do know I'll gladly share." Beach gave her a small smile, his deep, mesmerizing blue eyes twinkling. "Pleasure meeting you, Jessica."

"You too, Beach," she murmured. Totally inappropriate thoughts about coming on his wife's face filled her head and she was glad he couldn't read her mind. The longer she stood here, the more her thoughts turned inwards, forcing her to focus on a body hungry for sexual release. As the oil worked on her, she was swamped in the warmth of her arousal, all too aware of how many good-looking men surrounded her.

Luka was whispering something into Nico's ear and the ebony-skinned man's white teeth flashed in his good-looking face as he smiled at her, then winked. Holding her gaze, he ever so slowly licked his lower lip, then grinned again. Her sex-obsessed mind right away began to imagine what it would look like to see Nico's big dick stretching Luka's mouth. She'd never really thought about two guys together being something to fantasize about, but now that she thought about *these* insanely sexy men kissing, she was going crazy.

Frustrated from head to toe, she leaned into Alex. Her nipples hurt so much she had to clench her hands into fists to keep from rubbing them, tweaking them, offering them to Sarah, who was examining the stiff points of her aroused buds pressed against her dress. Just the rasp of fabric of her dress each time she took a breath was too much, yet not enough. The warm burn of her ass wasn't helping and the memory of

Luka's tongue playing with her back entrance had her squirming.

Okay, they needed to leave, right now, or she was going to hump the next stationary object she got to.

She pulled her devious husband's shoulder down and leaned up on tiptoe in her heels. "Alex, please, can we go now?"

The music throbbed around them as he moved in closer so her back was to the wall of a small alcove, his body blocking the crowd. "Does your pussy hurt, *prinsessa moya*?"

She nodded, totally captured by his stare and aware of Luka standing next to Alex with Nico, creating a barrier of muscle that made her feel as if they were in their own little private world with Beach and Sarah watching.

He trailed his fingertips up her thigh, slowly lifting her dress.

The thought of Beach and Sarah seeing her in a chastity belt embarrassed her greatly and she tried to push him away.

"Hands on the wall," Alex growled and she obeyed almost instantly, earning a chuckle from the men gazing at her with open appreciation.

Sure her face was going to melt with the heat of her blush, she closed her eyes as he resumed his slow raise of her dress until the cool air hit her hips, her pelvis exposed.

Sarah chuckled. "Oh, how I hate that fucking thing. I wonder if it has that damned vibrating feature that mine does. Or the inflatable anal plug."

Surprised, Jessica looked over at her, only to find Beach griping his wife's neck with a no bullshit expression that turned Jessica on something fierce. "With as much time as you spend in it, one would think you loved your 'bad girl' belt."

Giving her husband a sultry pout, she looked up at him through her lashes. "I try to be good, *Papi*, but it's hard."

"Brat," he growled before laying a kiss on his wife that had her sagging against his large body.

Jessica's gaze was torn from the erotic picture by Alex as he said in her ear, "Sarah is Beach's submissive as well as wife."

She was a little disturbed at the other woman calling her husband the Spanish word for Daddy, but who the hell was she to judge?

Alex tapped the hard cup of the device shielding her from his touch, sending vibrations to her pussy that had her groaning. "Please, Master."

"I wish we had more time to spend together," Alex said as he turned to an obviously aroused Beach and Sarah, "but I am afraid my wife's punishment is not over yet and I must take her home."

They made their goodbyes and when they found Catrin and Rya talking together, Jessica gave both of them a hug, whispering to the women that there were no hard feelings, she understood the situation, and that it was cool. While that wasn't entirely true, she was still grappling with her jealousy, it wasn't their problem, it was hers. The spanking had mellowed her out enough to allow her to let go of some of the irrational hostility from earlier toward a woman who'd been nothing but nice to her.

Catrin, of course, noticed her aroused state. "What did Alex do to you while he had you alone? You can barely keep still."

Remembering Alex's phone conversation with Nico, she grimaced. "I'm being punished, a chastity belt and Aphrodite's Tears."

Both women gasped and Rya looked over to where the men were huddled together, "Oh, he is an evil bastard."

"Very," Jessica agreed. "He had Luka tease me while he punished me."

Catrin's eyes glittered. "Is Luka going to play with you tonight?"

"I don't know." She glanced over her shoulder, finding Alex still talking with a group of men she wasn't familiar with. "Can I ask you a personal question?"

Arching a brow, Rya nodded. "Sure."

"Is Luka as talented in bed as I think he is?"

"Oh yeah, that man has no shame," Rya laughed. "Here comes Alex. Have fun."

Before she could respond, Alex was escorting her quickly out of the VIP section.

"Come, *prinsessa moya*, our night has just begun."

Chapter 19

Alex had to curl his hands into fists as they walked through the lobby of their apartment building, his wife looking a little worse for the wear from her evening. Her makeup had been cried off, her hair falling out of the messy bun she had it in atop her head, and she was shivering, but not with the cold. No, right now his sweet girl was so aroused that she was giving every man who looked her way hungry eyes. The aphrodisiac had been working on her for close to an hour now with no relief, and he knew his wife well enough to know she was close to her breaking point.

Once she went over the edge, she would be savage with her need to find satisfaction, and he planned to give it to her in a way she'd never had before.

He pulled her closer to his side, enjoying the way she cuddled into him while they waited for the elevator. Looking over her head, he met Luka's gaze and read the question there. The fact that Luka was giving him the opportunity to recant his invitation for the hazel-eyed man to join them reaffirmed that he could rely on his friend to give Jessica exactly what she needed without overstepping his bounds. When Luka gave him a slight grin, he couldn't help but smile back while his wife whimpered in his arms. The dark side of his nature liked knowing that she was suffering, that her body must be hypersensitive due to the oil.

The elevator opened and he stepped inside with Luka and Jessica.

Once the doors closed, Alex jerked off his tie while Luka hit the button for the top floor, where the private playrooms were that belonged to Alex and his friends.

Wrapping the blue silk tie between his hands, he looked down at Jessica and found her gaze fastened on the tie while her lovely breasts trembled with each breath she took.

"Once I blindfold you, Jessica, you will be entering a fantasy realm where you are slave to my every whim, mine to do with as I wish. This is, of course, your choice. If you do not wish to wear the blindfold, I will still fuck you until you faint, but will only be us."

She actually moaned deep in her throat like someone was stroking her pussy and he had to restrain his own answering growl. "Take me, Master, please. Blindfold me, use me, make me yours in all ways. My body belongs to you."

"All of you belongs to me," he corrected her gently as he secured his tie around her face. "Keep your eyes closed until I can place a proper blindfold on you. Do you understand?"

"Yes, Master."

The doors opened to the floor they were heading to and he had to keep his stride measured as they walked down the hall to the fourth door on the left.

Alex placed his hand on the reader next to the doorway. It unlocked and Luka opened the heavy brushed-steel door that led to a large room filled with BDSM equipment. While Alex never brought a woman home to play, Dimitri and Rya had been spending more time at home together than a club lately so the brother's had bought a playroom together. They wanted one big enough that they could have a large amount of their friends over to play without everyone being cramped without enough equipment to go around.

They still enjoyed playing with others, but it was usually here, in the safety of their home, instead of their old BDSM club. When they were bachelors without a care about propriety they'd played wherever and whenever they wanted. But now, married and completely in love, neither man wished to have their private moments with their wives observed by strangers.

Shrugging off his jacket, he handed Jessica over to Luka. "Undress her."

"Yes, Sir."

Jessica startled, her mouth opening to ask a question before she snapped it shut again.

He let his gaze roam her lovely form as he stripped down to his bare skin. Tonight he wanted her to feel him with every inch of her body. Her fair skin was flushed like she had a fever and as Luka slowly removed her dress, she made small whimpering sounds that drove him crazy. He loved it when she allowed herself to let go like this, to be consumed by the pleasure he could offer her.

And she was so fucking sexy when she begged sweetly, driven past her pride to the tender woman beneath.

Already he could hear her breathy little pleas for Luka to touch her.

The fact that she wasn't talking dirty let him know that she wasn't quite desperate enough yet.

Walking over to a set of black-lacquered Asian cabinets, he looked through them until he found what he wanted.

A black latex deprivation hood lined with silk on the inside.

The hard pulse of desire that went through him had his dick dripping pre-cum onto the floor.

Luka let out a low whistle from across the room as he ran his thumbs along the edge of the chastity belt, making his beautiful wife moan and twist. "Good choice, Sir."

Once again Jessica's mouth opened as though she wanted to say something, but she pressed her lips back together before any words came out. Whatever was bothering her, it was preventing her from going any deeper into her subspace. As he walked over to them, he couldn't help but stroke his aching dick with one hand, and clench the latex of the hood in his other.

"You may speak, *prinsessa moya*. What is your question?"

She hesitated, then blurted out, "Is Luka a submissive?"

Amused at the flush of embarrassment turning her ears pink, he smiled and said, "Why don't you ask him that?"

He pressed up against her back, loving the way she arched into him with a sigh. Right away she relaxed, and as Luka helped her out of her heels, she said, "Luka, are you a sub?"

"I," he replied in a low voice as he slowly skimmed his hands up her legs while he stood, "am a hedonist. I enjoy sampling all the pleasures life has to offer and do not believe in labeling myself. With Alex, I am always a submissive. Is how energy works between us, yes? But you...I want to hold you down and fuck you into submission."

"Oh my," she whispered while Alex began to kiss the side of her neck. "All pleasures?"

"All pleasures," Luka replied in a tone that was a mixture of arousal and humor as he stood and wrapped his strong, muscled arms around her waist. "Even the forbidden ones that make sweet little girls like you so wet. And you are wet, Jessica? I can smell your cunt, and I bet if I removed your chastity belt you would be soaked with honey."

Alex unclipped one side of the belt, then the other, removing it as slowly as possible while Luka held Jessica to him. Right away she tried to press her legs together, but Alex made a clucking sound. "Do not orgasm. Keep your legs open."

Luka chose that moment to kiss her, and right away her legs pressed together as she gave a wanton moan.

"Bad girl," Alex scolded. "I see we will have to restrain you."

Easily lifting her into his arms, Luka followed Alex over to a sex swing. Together they quickly had her body in the sling, with her hands chained above her head with her feet strapped into stirrups that elevated them. Alex pulled the chain to her left leg and swung it out wider on the metal grid bolted to the ceiling above them. Giving the chain a jerk, he secured her left side, then her right, leaving her spread wide open before him. For a long moment he studied her pink flesh, imagining how good it would feel to penetrate her swollen lips with his cock. Luka joined him, stroking his dick while his gaze roamed over Jessica's body.

"She is exquisite, Sir."

Alex handed him the hood. "Put this on her."

She startled when the tie was removed, blinking in the dim lighting as she lifted her head to look around. When she caught sight of him, her gaze darkened further and she surprised him by giving him a small, almost drunken smile that vanished as Luka secured the hood over her head. It covered her eyes completely and covered her ears, but didn't leave her deaf. He wanted her to hear them, to know how much she aroused them. That was part of her kink, to know that she was bringing others pleasure.

After she was hooded, Alex drew Luka back to the cabinets and took out a pair of weighted nipple clamps. "Put these on her, then I want you to rub your cock against her pussy, coat yourself in her arousal and the oil. You will need it to keep up with my wife's sexual desires tonight."

"As if I need oil to help me with that," Luka laughed softly, then nodded. "Am I allowed to make her orgasm?"

"Yes, but make her beg for it. When she is desperate her language will become filthy, that is when you can make her come."

Licking his lips, Luka gave a shuddering sigh. "Yes, Sir."

Alex pulled out a good-sized butt plug made of stainless steel and some lube. The hilt of the plug had a large faceted topaz in it and he knew it would look beautiful in Jessica's bottom, right before he yanked it out then shoved his cock up hot little ass.

Her whimpers filled the room and Alex glanced over his shoulder, the sight of Luka applying a clamp while his wife sucked his cock through a hole in the black latex hood covering her face was one of the hottest things he'd ever seen. Her legs shook while the hazel-eyed man squeezed her red-tipped nipples tight in those clamps.

She must have been sucking him hard because Luka ripped himself from her greedy mouth with a groan. "Jesus, your mouth is so fuckable."

Luka positioned himself between her legs with a snarl and rubbed his cock over her cleft, making Jessica go wild in the swing. "Please, please, I need to come, please!"

Sweat dripped down Luka's face and Alex stood next to his friend, watching the dark-red length of his dick rubbing between her slick labia. "Tell me what you want."

"Your cock," she sobbed. "I need to be fucked so bad, my pussy hurts. *I* hurt."

Alex nodded to his friend, noting the almost desperate look in his eyes that increased Alex's arousal. "Tease her with your dick, rub her clit, but do not enter her."

While he didn't have an interest in men sexually, he did enjoy dominating them, controlling another man's pleasure. If Luka had his way, he'd be ejaculating all over her flushed body, but because Alex was in control of the situation he held himself back, pinching the base of his cock even as he tormented Jessica. His lovely wife went wild, arching and moaning, twisting her hips as best she could to try to get more friction from Luka's touch, unable to see because of the hood.

Alex smeared a large amount of lube on Jessica's ass, his knuckles brushing against Luka's tight balls, making the other man let out a strangled groan.

Positioning the plug against her anus, Alex growled, "Come for me, both of you."

In a matter of seconds they complied, Jessica screaming as he pressed the plug into her bottom and Luka's muscular legs shaking while his wife bucked in the sling, her slender body twisting as much as it could while she shuddered again and again. With a harsh groan, Luka jerked off onto her mound, coating her with his cum. The sight of them climaxing was so erotic, Alex had to look away to regain control of himself while the need to orgasm burned at the base of his spine.

"Lick her clean," Alex murmured.

Making an eager noise low in his throat, Luka did as Alex commanded, licking his freshly spilt seed from her soft belly and sex.

"Mmmmm, thank you," Jessica whispered. "So good."

Feeling as if his dick was about to burst, he went over to her head and rubbed the tip of his cock over her lips. Right away she lifted so she could latch on to him with her eager mouth, her hands grasping nothing but air as she tried to take more of him, until his dick touched the back of her throat. The burn was trying to inch down his spine again but he fought it, balancing on the fine edge between extreme arousal and climaxing.

With a gasp he tore himself away from her mouth. "Enough. I am going to come in your ass, not your mouth. Luka, unbind her."

They made quick work of releasing her from the swing and as soon as her feet hit the ground, she knelt. The sight of the black latex hood obscuring her features except for her lush mouth had his nuts drawing up tight. So beautiful, so kinky, his perfect wife in every way. He tossed Luka the condom package he'd grabbed earlier, grinning to himself as Jessica's breasts quivered with her pants.

He leaned over to whisper into Luka's ear, "We shall stand and hold her between us then fuck her."

Stroking his once-again-hard cock, Luka grunted. "I cannot wait to sink into that hot *pizda*."

"You will enter her first."

Jessica tensed as they neared, but didn't resist at all when Luka turned her to face him. "I am going to lift you, put your arms around my neck and your legs around my waist."

She did as asked, and at the sight of her sex spread open with Luka's dick nudging at her entrance, Alex helplessly thrust his hips into the air like it was *his* cock about to penetrate her.

"Hold her ass open," Alex murmured. "I will guide you in."

"Oh fuck," Jessica breathed. "Please, Master, hold his cock and put it in me."

Luka arched a brow in surprise, but Alex merely grinned. In her own way, Jessica was as hedonistic as the hazel-eyed man and not afraid to ask for what she wanted. Why would she be? He'd always encouraged her to be bold, to tell him what she desired, and he always rewarded her trust. With this in mind, he grasped the other man's cock and teased his wife's pussy with it, his thumb rubbing the sensitive part beneath the head of Luka's shaft while Jessica twitched and shivered.

"Are you going to climax without my permission?"

"No, Master," she squeaked. "I'm trying not to, but it's just sooooo good."

Alex nodded to Luka and began to twist the plug in her bottom. "Fuck him, *dorogoya*, ride his cock until you come all over him. Then we're both going to fuck you."

Right away she slammed herself down on Luka, both of them crying out while he filled her. Alex moved behind her, his cock rubbing against her back, his hands gripping her bottom along with Lukas. With a gentle movement, he twisted the plug in her bottom. "Give me your orgasm, *prinsessa moya*."

She screamed and Luka almost lost his grip on her, his voice shocked as he breathed out, "Fuck, fuck, *fuck*, her pussy is milking my cock."

"Do not come yet, Luka," Alex warned as he removed the plug from Jessica's ass and tossed it onto a towel he'd thrown on the floor.

"I won't, but you did not warn me how strong her cunt was."

Jessica continued to wiggle between them, incoherent words and noises coming from her as she lived in the moment, only reacting to their touches, operating on a primal level where her greed for pleasure ruled.

He positioned himself at her rear entrance and slowly pushed his way past the outer muscles of her anus.

"Ow," she yelped, stiffening between them.

"You will take my cock," he growled against her neck. "Even if it hurts, I am going to fuck you because you are my filthy girl and you like it. Can you feel that? My dick rubbing against Luka's, both of us stuffing you full?"

"I can feel you, both of you." She shivered and her body tightened around his erection. "Love it. Hurt me, please."

Despite his harsh words, he gently worked his way into her and they started a slow thrust and retreat, both of men holding her up so she had no control while they lifted and lowered her body. The sensation of the withdrawal then thrust of Luka against him, inside of her, sent sparks of pleasure shooting along his nerve endings and he had to grit his teeth as he fought his impending release. It was too good, the scent of sex in the air, the hot grip of her ass, the wild look on Luka's face as he gave himself over to the arousal building between them.

Grasping her hair in his fist, he bared her neck to him and sank his teeth into it, holding her still while he hammered into her body. Luka froze, his rough shouts of pleasure blending with Jessica's broken screams while she climaxed around him twice in rapid succession. By this point he was near out of his mind to fill her with his cum. Finally relaxing his control, he let his body take over and tensed so hard his hands shook. Against his cock, he could feel Luka pulsing as he came and that pushed him over the edge, his cries joining theirs as they all enjoyed a huge mutual orgasm.

Alex pulled out of her first, wanting to do it before her endorphins wore off and he caused her undo pain. Luka took a couple staggering steps with Jessica still wrapped around him, his back bracing against one of the large floor-to-ceiling black marble pillars scattered around the room. He was gasping and when his eyes met Alex's, he smiled huge.

"You lucky bastard."

For the first time in a long, long time, Alex thought Luka was right.

He took Jessica from Luka and nodded. "I am. Now, let us go clean up. I am not done with my submissive yet."

Jessica whimpered and he shared a smile with Luka that held the promise of delights yet to come.

Chapter 20

Jessica laughed as Tatiana told her a story about going to the Moscow zoo with her cousins, the warm morning light caressing her face while she walked around the garden area with her daughter. Alex had warned her that the warm weather was fleeting, and to enjoy it while she could, so she spent as much time as possible outside. Lord knew she needed a little bit of peace and quiet. Her life lately was filled with endless meetings, strategy sessions, and going over facts and figures about the Dubinski Empire. While she was often overwhelmed about everything she was learning, she was also enjoying herself. She'd asked Alex to be partners with her and he'd done just that.

They paused before one of the fountains scattered through the gardens and Tatiana lifted herself to the edge, the glitter on her purple top almost blinding Jessica as she helped her daughter stand up. Looking unbearably cute in her matching purple skirt and shiny yellow patent-leather shoes, she sang a song from a Russian children's show while carefully balancing as she walked around the rim of the fountain. Having now lived in Moscow for more than two months, Tatiana was beginning to naturally pick up the native language and Jessica was proud of how quickly she was learning.

Smiling at Jessica, Tatiana lifted one leg high, then the other, showing off her balancing skills. "Look at me, Mommy, I'm like one of those ballerinas."

Alex had taken Tatiana out on his own a couple times, once to the ballet, and ever since, the little girl was determined that she was going to be a ballerina. Or a ninja like Zoya. Their bodyguard spent an hour or so every day teaching them self-defense and Tatiana worshiped her. Hell, Jessica kind of worshiped her as well. That woman was a badass and even managed to take Krom down a couple times while sparring, despite his enormous size.

Her thoughts turned to Krom and she hoped everything was going okay with his sister. She was having trouble with postpartum depression and he'd returned to his hometown to try to help her out. At first he hadn't wanted to go, but having experienced herself firsthand the agony of PPD, she knew he had to be there for his sister. She missed him, but having him gone meant Oleg got to come out of semi-retirement to be her bodyguard.

These days her old friend ran the Novikov *Bratva's* Black Tier division and spent his days training Dimitri's top men, but he'd jumped at the chance to spend some time with her and Tatiana. Their reunion had been bittersweet but he'd been genuinely happy to see her again and instantly loved her daughter.

Tatiana carefully turned around so she could walk backwards. "Look at me, Oleg!"

"Very brave," came his deep voice from behind Jessica. "Much like your mother."

Lifting her arms up, Tatiana threw herself at Jessica, confident she'd catch her. With a soft "umph" she took the little girl's weight, then gently set her down. "You are getting so big!"

"Jessica?"

She looked up the path leading to the main building and smiled at the sight of Rya making her way towards them. Her long dark hair was back in a high ponytail and she wore a black wraparound dress that flattered her curves and went well with her camel-colored leather boots. Farther down the path, Maks' red hair burned in the sunlight and even though he wore sunglasses that hid his eyes, she could feel his gaze on her. She had to admit, it had hurt her feelings to learn that Maks was going to stay with Rya as her primary bodyguard, even though it made sense. He'd been with Rya from the day she'd arrived in Moscow and the two had formed a strong friendship, but that wasn't the only reason. According to Alex, Maks had some very confused and conflicted feelings as far as Jessica was concerned, and being the decent man that he was, had removed himself from temptation.

That didn't mean she was unaware of his intense focus on her whenever they were together, but she tried to pretend nothing was weird between them and treated him the same.

Tatiana spotted Rya first and took off with a squeal. "Auntie Rya!"

The smaller woman leaned down and gave Tatiana a big hug, her eyes closed and a peaceful smile on her face. "Hello, sweetheart. I heard you went to the zoo with your cousins yesterday. Did you have fun?"

At that, Tatiana went off on a tangent about all the animals she'd seen, switching between using the English and Russian words for each.

When they reached Oleg, the dark-haired woman looked up at Jessica, strain evident in her smiling face. "Can I talk to you, alone, for a few minutes?"

Oleg tensed. "What is wrong?"

"Calm down, nothing that you need to shoot." Rya patted his thick arm. "Girl talk."

"Girl talk is dangerous talk," Oleg muttered.

Jessica gave Tatiana to Oleg, warmth flooding her chest at the sight of her small hand being so carefully held by his big gnarled one. "I'll meet you guys over at the swings in a little bit."

He nodded, leading the chattering girl away. After he was out of earshot, she turned to Rya, her heart beating faster as the other woman led her farther into the gardens to a stone bench beneath the graceful branches of an elm tree. They each sat and Jessica braced herself for some terrible news that was going to destroy her world. It was a rather pessimistic way to view things, but she'd found if she expected the worst, it was better than being caught by surprise.

Rya looked over her shoulder, "You too, Maks. I see you lurking there and I know you have great hearing. Go skulk by the fountain. We'll still be in your line of sight, but you won't be able to read our lips. Don't think I'm not on to your sneaky ways."

Maks lowered his sunglasses long enough to give her a narrow-eyed look, but nodded and moved farther away from them until he was standing next to the fountain behind their backs.

"What's going on?"

Lifting her golden-brown gaze to Jessica's, she gave her a small smile. "Don't worry, it's nothing bad...just...I'm pregnant."

She stared at Rya for a moment, then laughed and grabbed her into a big hug. "Congratulations!"

Hugging her back, Rya whispered, "Shhh, I haven't told anyone but you yet. The only other person that knows is my doctor."

Taken aback by the sadness in the other woman's tone, she leaned back and studied Rya in the dappled shade. "Were you not planning on having children?"

"Yes." Rya blinked back tears while she fiddled with her enormous yellow diamond engagement ring.

"I mean no, we were planning on having kids. I've always wanted to be a mom and I know Dimitri will make a wonderful father."

"But?"

Taking a deep breath, Rya then let out a little shuddering sigh. "What kind of world am I bringing a child into, Jessica?"

"What do you mean?"

"This." She gestured around her. "I mean not this place, it's pretty sweet, I'm talking about the guards, the security, the crazy people wanting to hurt anyone who Dimitri loves. Deep down, I feel like a terrible person for exposing my child to all of this danger."

"I know how you feel, and worrying is a normal part of being a mom. My first thought every day is a prayer to keep my family safe, but I think that's most mothers' first thoughts. It doesn't matter where you are, or who you are with, bad things happen to people all the time. Yes, Tatiana's life is going to be different from the childhood I had in the United States, but not always in a bad way. She is going to have opportunities you and I never had, and she is going to grow up surrounded by people that love and adore her, men and women who would give up their own lives to protect her. Yes, the hard truth is our children will be technically surrounded by criminals, but my view of the world is not so black and white anymore."

Leaning back on her hands, Rya's gaze went to the high walls in the distance that encircled the property. "You would think having been raised by a biker gang, I'd be a little less worried about my kid turning out all right, but at least I had freedom growing up. Our children will never know what it's like to just hop on their motorcycle and go for a ride without having an army of people trailing them."

Laughing, Jessica shook her head. "I'm letting you know right now, Rya, that if you get Tatiana a motorcycle for her sixteenth birthday, I'm going to choke you."

"Awww, you're no fun." Rya's smile slipped. "That's another thing, how do I raise my children to value anything when they'll have the world at their fingertips? I know you and Alex had to deal with his spoiling Tatiana, I can't imagine that Dimitri will be any better."

"You deal with it like any normal couple having a child would. You talk about it, set some boundaries, and stick with them. If Dimitri won't listen to you, then I'll just feed Tatiana a bunch of cotton candy and send her for a sleepover at your place for Dimitri to deal with while we go out. That little girl can throw some epic temper tantrums and they aren't pretty. I think she even scared Alex."

Both women laughed and she noticed Rya's hand stealing to her lower belly as she cupped it in a protective gesture. "We've talked about kids, but always as an abstract future thing. We'd planned on waiting a few more years, but evidently someone at the birth control factory fell asleep at the controls when my last batch of pills went through."

She snorted. "You know Dimitri's going to claim that his superior Novikov sperm is stronger than any birth control. How far along are you?"

"I'm eleven weeks, give or take. I had some spotting a few weeks ago, but that's normal for me during my off days on my pills so I didn't think much of it."

"What tipped you off?"

"I have constant PMS." She sighed. "Poor Dimitri and Maks are walking on eggshells around me. Then my breasts started to get really sensitive and I broke out for the first time since high school. So basically I'm a bitchy hot mess with homicidal tendencies. A little bit of morning sickness, but nothing bad enough at first that I suspected anything other than an uneasy stomach."

"Sounds about right."

Rya grinned. "I actually went in to see if my birth control needed adjusting and when they ran the routine tests...well, let's just say I think I freaked out my OB by bursting into hysterical tears."

Knowing that Rya's doctor was probably on the Novikov payroll, she asked, "Do you think your OB will tell Dimitri."

"Not if he values his balls, which I let him know I'd cut off if he told my husband before I did."

She smiled at Rya, her excitement at her sister-in-law being pregnant starting to bubble through her. "How are you going to tell Dimitri?"

"I don't know. I've been looking on the internet and there are so many cute ideas."

"I'd tell him sooner than later."

"He's going to go crazy overprotective," Rya said with a slight whine in her voice. "I just got him to the point where I can leave the house without him having a nervous breakdown."

"Yeah, he probably will be." Lightly running her nails over the smooth concrete of the bench, she studied Rya. "But you also know that he's going to be over the moon with happiness, and will be a great father. You've seen how he is with Tatiana and Petrov's grandchildren, he's a natural."

A smile curved Rya's full lips. "Yeah, he is, isn't he? He has so much love to give."

"I know it's impossible, but try to stop worrying so much. It's easy to fall into obsessing about things you won't be able to control about your pregnancy."

"Shit, I'm already worrying if the baby will want to go to college in the US or in Russia." Rya laughed and fondly rubbed her belly again. "God, if this is what my mom felt like when I was growing up, no wonder she blamed me for all her gray hair."

"Excuse me, ladies," Maks said in a loud voice from not too far away, "but Alex wanted me to tell Jessica that it will be time to start getting ready soon."

Both women groaned, then looked at each other and laughed before Jessica yelled, "We'll be right there."

"Why," Rya said while standing up and brushing off the back of her dress, "does it take six hours and a team of people to get me ready? I mean, I used to be able to clean myself up just fine back home. I didn't need two hair stylists, a makeup artist, a clothing stylist, a nail technician, and all their assistants to get dolled up. And I'm so damn tired all the time. Wonder if they'll let me sleep in the chair and just move me around like a doll."

She looped her arm around Rya's waist and gave her a squeeze. "I know how you feel. At least after the big introduction-to-society party we'll be able to relax...ish."

Laughing, the women made their way to where Oleg and Tatiana were waiting for them farther up the path, and as they walked, Jessica reveled in the sublime feeling of being surrounded by a loving family, of finally being home.

By the time Jessica had a chance to sit down at the gigantic party Petrov and Vera had thrown for them, her feet were throbbing to the beat of her heart.

The evening had started out with a magnificent feast for their three hundred guests, followed by Petrov, then Alex giving an inspiring speech about the future of the Dubinski *Bratva* while she stood at his side. The navy beaded gown she wore was lovely, but it weighed a ton and her back hurt from standing so long. At least she didn't have to stand through the half-dozen speeches from various criminal lords.

But now, standing here listening to some man from Vietnam prattle on about his tech stock holdings to her, the whole lower part of her back was super pissed off and her feet throbbed. Thankfully, Vera must have seen the strain on her face, because she gracefully extracted Jessica from the people she was talking with and led her to an elegant powder-blue sitting room. Rya was already there in her gorgeous crimson gown, sprawled out on the couch with her shoes off and her feet propped up on the delicate mahogany coffee table at the center of the seating area.

Collapsing on the couch across from Rya, Jessica sighed and kicked her heels off with a blissful groan, "Thanks for the rescue, Vera."

The older woman smiled. "You looked like you were about to fall asleep."

She massaged her temples, wanting to rub her eyes but not daring to mess up her expertly done makeup. "I'm sure the Vietnamese technology industry is a fascinating topic, but my feet are killing me."

Rya wiggled her toes. "Think I could sneak away to go take a nap with the kids?"

The children had made a brief appearance earlier for everyone to ooohh and ahh over earlier in the evening. Tatiana had, of course, eaten up the attention and twirled around in her emerald-green party dress with her hair artfully curled, smiling at anyone who looked at her. Most people were eager to meet the little girl, but with Krom and Oleg standing guard over her, Jessica didn't need to worry about anyone messing with her. If anyone got what they deemed too close, they'd quickly, and professionally, let them know to back off.

"Maybe I could trade places with Gwen," Jessica mused. "Bet it's nice and quiet in the children's wing."

Vera chuckled, "Where do you think my husband is?"

"I thought he was out there in that madhouse somewhere?"

"No, he's down with the children on the pretense that they can't go to sleep without him saying goodnight."

The massive coming out party was being thrown at Petrov's country estate, basically a massive mansion with some impressive acreage to the east of Moscow. They were staying the weekend with Petrov and his family, and even though Alex's job never really ended, they'd managed to spend some time together as a couple with his family and friends. She smiled at the memory of playing poker and drinking with Petrov and a group of older men last night, their obvious flirting with her more charming than anything else.

Jessica groaned, really not wanting to move. "So Alex is out there alone? I should go find him."

Rya leaned her head back on the couch, her eyes closed and the silvery eyeshadow on her lids glimmering in the soft light. "He's fine. He's got Ivan and Dimitri with him. Let them do their male-bonding bullshit. You know half those sexist pigs out there would never actually talk about anything important in front of a woman. Our poor little brains couldn't possibly handle it."

Sighing, Vera nodded. "Unfortunately, that is true with man men, but it gives us an advantage. If you are quiet and blend into the background, men will often talk about things they should not in front of you. Is better to be the poisoned thorn on the rose, yes?"

Though she was pretty sure something was lost in the translation, Jessica nodded. "Still, I hate it when they talk to me like I'm a moron, or some pretty pet that has to be spoken to in a slow voice."

The door behind Vera opened and Jessica looked up with a smile, expecting it to be Alex.

Instead, a man she'd never seen before in a black gasmask tossed something into the center of the room and closed the door behind him. She screamed and tried to run to the window to maybe break it and get rid of whatever the smoke was that filled the air, but within moments she was sinking to her knees.

The last thing she saw was Rya feebly trying to fend off the man in the mask.

Chapter 21

Alex knew something was wrong the moment Maks approached him. The other man's face was pale and his blue eyes were wide with shock while sweat beaded his brow. Breaking away from the group of men he'd been speaking with, Alex had to resist the urge to run across the room. Never show fear in front of your enemy, and while most of the people in this room were his allies, he knew there were wolves in sheeps' clothing among his guests.

He caught Dimitri's eye and his brother quickly followed him, with Ivan in tow. They met Maks in the middle of the room and Alex's stomach dropped when he studied the other man's face. Whatever Maks had to tell him, it was bad.

Beneath the golden lights of the massive chandeliers, Maks said in a tight voice, "You need to come with me, now."

Members of his Black Tier guard spilled into the room, flanking him on all sides as he quickly followed Maks. "What is going on?"

"Not here." Maks voice cracked. "Not here."

Once they were in the hallway leading to the kitchens with their guards sealing it off at each end, Maks turned to him and placed his hands on Alex's shoulders, squeezing tight. "Brace yourself. Jessica, Rya, and Tatiana have been taken. Vera is unconscious and Petrov—Petrov is dead."

A ringing filled his ears and he found himself holding Maks off the ground by his suit while Dimitri roared in rage. "What the fuck happened?"

Ivan wrapped his arms around Alex, forcing him to drop Maks. "Easy, my friend. We will learn nothing if you kill him."

Maks remained on his knees, his whole posture curved in defeat. "We found an empty gas canister in the room where the women were. Their guards were incapacitated, drugged not killed. We aren't sure what happened with Petrov, but he was in the children's room and had been shot multiple times. Gwen was also shot, but it was just a graze and she's getting medical treatment. She managed to shoot and kill two of the men who came for the children before the gas they used made her unconscious."

With raw pain coloring his every word, Dimitri said, "Do we know who took them?"

"I—yes." He took a deep breath. "Your father has them. He left a note"

Dimitri had his phone out an instant later and put it on speaker as it rang.

"Hello, Dimitri," came Jorg's weak voice. "I have been expecting your call."

"Where is she!" his brother roared.

"Dimitri," came their father's frail voice over the speaker, "calm yourself. They will not be harmed."

Alex grabbed the phone from his brother. "I will kill you for this."

Jorg's weak laugh sent chills down his spine. "I am already dead. I can taste it, can feel it creeping up on me, but it does not matter. You will speak with me in person before I die, both of you, now. Come to the

Winter Manor. Do not bother to try and take my home by force, you will be wasting precious time."

"You took our women, my child, and killed Petrov so we would talk to you?" Dimitri's voice broke on the last word and Alex was only vaguely aware of Luka quietly speaking on his phone. "Petrov's death was not supposed to happen. He was not supposed to be there. For that I am truly sorry." He coughed harshly and Alex wished he would die while they were listening on the phone. "I have a helicopter landing on the back lawn. Alex and Dimitri, you will get in, no one else."

He didn't even bother arguing with the old man, not wanting to do anything that might upset him and push him into harming Alex's wife and daughter. The burning ache in his chest deepened and he was aware of Dimitri shaking next to him. This was their worst nightmare come to life and he struggled against the overwhelming darkness that wanted to swallow him whole.

He couldn't lose them, not again, not because of his father.

It would break him.

In a haze, he followed Dimitri outside, the aforementioned helicopter waiting for them.

Maks grasped his arm and shouted above the spinning blades, "We have spies in Jorg's home. They have confirmed that the women are there and are unharmed, but still unconscious. Oleg is with them."

He could only nod, then turned away and followed Dimitri. Once they were in the helicopter, piloted by a man he didn't recognize, his thoughts were consumed by not just the kidnapping, but by Petrov's death and what that meant. He was now the head of the Dubinski *Bratva,* one of the most powerful criminal syndicates in the world—and yet he couldn't stop his father from taking his family.

Their headphones were equipped with microphones and speakers, but he didn't use it to speak with Dimitri, sure anything said wouldn't be private between them.

The look of pain and rage on his brother's face must have reflected his own and he watched the world fly by, the occasional light of a house breaking up the darkness of the land below.

A battered Oleg met them at the landing area, his right arm in a sling and his eye swollen shut. As soon as they were far enough away from the helicopter to be heard, Oleg shouted, "I just saw the women, they are alive, but under heavy guard."

Aware that Oleg had been in the room with the children and Petrov, he said in a tight voice, "What happened?"

"It so quick, I am not sure. Someone must have been working with your father to get them past all the guards because they walked right in. I think they were surprised to see Petrov, but they were ready for myself and Krom. They gassed the room and went for us first. Petrov managed to get a few shots off, and they returned fire. Is he all right? I saw him go down and Gwen retrieved his gun, getting in a few shots of her own before I passed out."

"Petrov is dead," Dimitri said in a hollow voice.

Oleg stumbled. "What?"

Ignoring Oleg, Alex began to jog to the marble double staircase leading to the entrance of his ancestral home. The sooner he got to Jorg, the sooner he could get Jessica. Dimitri must have felt the same way because they were soon full-out running through the vast halls of the former palace, not stopping until they reached the doors leading to their father's room. Armed guards that Alex didn't recognize stood out front, but they stepped aside as soon as they saw Alex and Dimitri barreling down on them.

The man on the right lowered his gun. "Mr. Novikov, Mr. Dubinski, only you may enter."

Alex shoved the door open, surging into the big room that held their father's hospital bed and the large amounts of equipment used to keep him alive. A low moan broke from him at the sight of Tatiana laid out on the wide green-velvet sofa that had been placed next to Jorg's bed. She was on her stomach with a deep pink blanket pulled up around her, and he could see her little back moving up and down with her breath. Her hand was curled beneath her cheek and she appeared unharmed.

Across the room, two of Jorg's trusted men stood with their guns trained on Alex and Dimitri.

He started to go to her, ignoring the monster watching him from the hospital bed and his guards.

"Wait," Jorg breathed out. "Do not disturb her yet."

"Fuck you," Alex snarled, but stopped when Jorg pulled out a gun from beneath the covers and pointed it at Tatiana.

"You will listen to me," Jorg wheezed, his hand shaking, and Alex wasn't worried about his own life but feared Jorg's trembling would cause him to accidentally pull the trigger.

Holding his hands up, he backed away until he stood at Dimitri's side. "Do not punish them for my leaving the *Bratva*."

Jorg set the gun down atop the white sheets covering him, his hands almost skeletal. The cancer had eaten him away to next to nothing and Alex was reminded of an American movie with puppets he saw a long, long time ago, where the nemeses of the film were these emaciated-looking vulture-like creatures that were rotten to the core, yet surrounded themselves with luxury and wealth. That was what his father reminded him of, a dying vulture intent on devouring every bit of life he could before death claimed him.

His thin chest heaved as he sucked in a deep, rattling breath. "I regret Petrov's death, deeply. He was a good man, and a good friend. Know it was not my intention for anyone to be harmed. I did this for you, for both of you."

"What are you talking about," Dimitri snarled.

Jorg seemed to sink back into his pillows, his eyelids fluttering. "I have made many, many mistakes in my life but I love you both more than you will ever know."

"Love?" Alex spat out. "You have no idea what love is."

Not seeming to hear him, Jorg continued in a breathy, weak voice, "A great change is coming, one so huge you would never believe me even if I told you what little I know. I must protect you, give you a chance to save who you can."

Dimitri and Alex exchanged a glance, neither having a clue what he was talking about. "You are not making any sense."

"Silver Wood is the curse breaker," Jorg said, spittle dripping out of the corner of his mouth. "Had to find a way to keep it in the bloodstream, a way to make sleep until activated. She would only produce it for me if I helped hide her from the Vagrants, hide her so well even I cannot find her. This is my final gift to you both, a chance at survival. The tundra…is melting. Look at Tatiana's back. Such a beautiful child you have, Alexandr. Hair like your mother, Dimitri."

He reached out as if to touch the little girl, but Alex beat him to it and blocked his withered fingers from making contact. Across the room his father's bodyguards took a threatening step forward, but they froze when Jorg waved them away.

With great trepidation, Alex pulled the blanket down, revealing Tatiana's bare back. Seeing no obvious signs of injury, he scanned her again, then stiffened when he noticed three silver dots the size of his thumb starting at the base of her spine and going up, about an inch apart from each other. The skin around the circles was reddened, shiny with some kind of salve, and he struggled to understand what he was seeing.

"What did you do?" He looked over his shoulder at Jorg while Dimitri looked down at Tatiana from the other side of the couch.

The door behind them opened and a tall, skinny Asian man dressed in a cream suit with a pale orange tie came in, pushing a silver cart with some odd-looking equipment on it, and a small jar of sparkling silver liquid.

"If you do not allow him to tattoo you, I will order Jessica and Rya killed."

"No!" Dimitri shouted, and surged forward to attack Jorg, but Alex blocked him with his body.

"Don't," he snarled, staring into his brother's wild eyes.

"Get the tattoo, and I will let them go. Both of you."

"Swear it," Alex growled.

"I swear."

Desperate to do whatever he could to save his wife and sister-in-law, he handed his daughter over to his brother, giving him something to do other than kill their father. "Hold Tatiana, please."

With tears in his eyes, Dimitri nodded, cradling the little girl close while Alex stripped his shirt off.

The Asian man nervously licked his lips, but pulled over a chair and gestured to it.

Jorg watched all of this intently, his chest barely moving with each breath. At the first slight sting of the tattoo needle on his lower spine, Alex tensed, waiting for something to happen, but it was only the familiar scratching pain of a tattoo gun piercing his skin. The artist was quick, and after he was done he bandaged Alex, then gestured to Dimitri.

As soon as the needle touched his brother's skin, Jorg let out a long sigh that Alex prayed was his death, but the bastard kept polluting the world with his presence. Jorg pressed a button on the small pad next to him and ordered whoever answered to stand down.

"Where are they," Dimitri said while the Asian man put a protective covering over the metallic silver circles now dotting his spine. "What did you do to us?"

"Experimenting, unable to find way to make inoculation last without monthly infusion. Tattoos...answer. Vagrants don't know, but you both will see and shape the future." He sucked in a wheezing breath. "Forgive me."

"Never," Alex hissed.

The heart-rate monitor started to go crazy as Jorg struggled to gasp in a breath, then he began to twitch as a seizure racked his twisted body.

Ignoring the medical personnel and people streaming into the room as the machines sounded their alarms, Alex strode out of the room with Tatiana cuddled to his chest and Dimitri at his side, the commotion behind him letting him know that his father was finally on his way to the Hell he so richly deserved.

Oleg was waiting for them in the hall and he motioned to them. "Come, I know where the women are."

Feeling as if he was in a dream, Alex trailed after Dimitri, a bitter relief entering his soul as the monster he'd once loved with all his child's heart died behind him.

Chapter 22

Seven weeks later

Nico looked up from his laptop and sighed, taking away Alex's hope even before he spoke. "Still nothing."

Alex blew out a frustrated breath, knowing he couldn't vent his anger in a physical way among all the delicate lab equipment. They were in Nico's new private research facility deep beneath the earth. On the surface it was a normal, well-maintained pharmaceutical manufacturing plant, but four stories below ground, in a sealed and self-contained environment, Nico and his team of some of the smartest medical researchers in the world experimented with shit that gave Alex nightmares.

Anthrax, Ebola, some kind of flu that made a person's organs liquefy. Scary, scary illnesses that Nico worked diligently to cure. He wasn't in the business of designing the biological weapons, but rather disarming them.

Dimitri had been the first to remind Alex about Jorg's mysterious comments about immunity and they'd assigned Nico the task of figuring out if they were indeed now immune to anything, thanks to the introduction of Curse Breaker 2, or CB2, also known as Silver Wood, into their systems.

So far, test after test had revealed that the bacteria just sat inert in their system, like they were in hibernation, slowly consuming the minute amounts of Silver Wood in their blood. They'd tried to find out where Jorg had gotten the mixture from that was used in their tattoos, but so far they hadn't been able to locate anyone who knew anything, even under threat of torture. However Jorg had done it and whoever had helped him remained a mystery. He'd covered his tracks well and left no clues for them to follow other than the little bit of unused CB2 that had remained from the batch used for their tattoos.

Shaking his head, Nico rubbed his face with a frustrated hand. "The only thing that's different about the strain of CB2 that your father has and the one the Novikovs received from Lady Death, is that in CB2, Jorg was somehow able to encapsulate the Silver Wood to slowly release over time. The CB1 that Dimitri has will live for at least another sixty years, but eventually their food source will run out because they are awake and active, for lack of a better term, unlike the hibernating CB2. The bacteria in your body will live on long after you are dust if it remains within the circles of the tattoos on your back."

Trying to keep the frustration out of his voice, he said, "Do you have any theories at all yet?"

He was desperate to find some good news to give to Dimitri and Rya. They were very, very concerned that their unborn child would somehow be harmed by the foreign substance now living in Rya's body. Hell, he was terrified about the innocent-looking tattoos somehow killing his wife and daughter.

Drumming his fingers on the clear glass table that dominated his private office, Nico's jaw clenched, then released. "Looking at this from a logical perspective, I have been asking myself what would make this so valuable that Jorg would risk angering the Israeli mafia by basically stealing it from them. Mimi has no idea what it is, only that Jorg was uninterested in helping her until she mentioned the CB1, then he would have given her his right hand for it."

"We could always ask the Israelis why they wanted it so badly," Alex said with a grimace.

Nico merely snorted. "Back to the subject at hand, I have many theories, but a few that are more plausible than others. One in particular keeps coming to mind and I've been at this long enough to trust my instincts. I think that CB2 is an insurance policy against something, some kind of what I would have to assume is a disease or virus that I haven't yet run across that Jorg knew about. While I would like to think that I'm aware of every new biological weapon out there, I know it is impossible to predict what type of vile shit some insane chemist out in a jungle laboratory in Brazil is going to come up with next. I will say this, your father had more connections than God, and even if he was crazy, he went to a great deal of effort to get those tattoos on his family. He was not the type of man to waste his time, especially at the end of his life, on useless things."

Alex's stomach clenched as he considered the other man's words. "You believe my father was aware of some kind of future illness and he inoculated us against it?"

The dark-skinned man's broad shoulders fell, and he closed his eyes as he looked down. "I think that is the most probable explanation."

The sorrow in Nico's tone set Alex on alert. "What is it?"

"I believe we need to figure out how to replicate CB2, and we need to do it quickly."

"Why?"

When Nico met his gaze, the other man's dark eyes were filled with an edge of desperation. "Because I want to inoculate myself and my wife as soon as possible. If Jorg went to all that trouble to make sure you were protected, I want the same for my family, and it worries me greatly that I can't do that yet. We don't have the raw material, mainly the trees, to produce our own and I have a feeling we will need more than we currently have. With your permission, I would like to drop some of my research projects and devote more of my time to unlocking the secrets of CB2, specifically how to make more of the type that was used in your tattoos. I'll also need you to try to find out where the Silver Wood is growing, and secure some for the Dubinski *Bratva*. Someone somewhere has to be cultivating it, and perhaps if we find them, we'll have more pieces to the puzzle to put together."

Trying to swallow past his suddenly dry throat, Alex nodded. "If you truly believe that is necessary, you have my blessings and any resources you might need from the Dubinski *Bratva* to make that happen. We will find the Silver Wood for you, and you and Catrin will be the first to receive the new tattoos once we figure out how to do it. You have my word."

"Thank you."

One month later

Dimitri and Alex sat back and smoked their cigars on the large back porch of the Summer House that looked out over the frozen expanse of the lake on the Novikov estate, where their women were ice skating. He couldn't help but smile as Jessica wobbled on her skates, almost losing her balance, while a pregnant Rya literally skated circles around her with Tatiana. His wife was good at many, many things. Ice skating was not one of them.

Blowing out a puff of fragrant tobacco smoke into the chilly air, Dimitri sighed. "Do you think I could ask Rya to come inside without her biting my head off? She could fall and hurt herself and the baby."

"Not unless you want to spend Christmas in the guest house." Dimitri frowned and Alex patted his jacket-covered shoulder. "Relax, she is fine."

Crossing he legs at the ankle, Alex let his gaze roam the beautiful grounds of the Novikov estate, now covered in a thick blanket of pure white snow beneath the gray skies. While Dimitri had been left the Winter Manor as part of his inheritance, Alex had been left the Summer House by their father. At first they'd wanted nothing to do with it, both having too many bad memories here, but their wives had insisted they not turn their back on their heritage. The women had argued that generations of their ancestors had called this place home, and that they shouldn't let their father's memory destroy something that the Novikovs had fought to build and protect. Now they split their time between the apartment and the Novikov estates, where Rya and Jessica spent much of their time cataloguing the contents of both homes and working on restoring them.

Thankfully they had a built-in expert in antique architectural restoration in Gia and her renovation company. Ivan's wife was more than happy to take on the project and slowly but surely the buildings were coming back to life after decades of neglect. While they tried to restore as much as they could, Dimitri and Alex also had a number of safety upgrades done that had turned the estates into a self-contained fortresses with their own water and electrical systems that Mimi and Mike Anderson had helped them set up.

Guards patrolled the grounds at all times, and as usual Maks was lurking about, his attention focused totally on the women while Krom and his team were on outer-perimeter duty. After the disastrous evening of the party, Maks had changed, no longer smiling and always serious. Alex knew his friend suffered from immense guilt that he'd been unable to predict or stop Jorg, and even though Alex had told him time and time again that there was nothing he could have done, Maks still felt as though he let them down.

The sound of female voices coming closer snapped him out of his deep thoughts and he stubbed out his cigar as Tatiana raced up the steps.

Her pale cheeks were rosy and she placed her hands on her little jacket-covered hips and frowned at him. "Papa, smoking is bad."

"I know, *solntse*, I know."

Jessica came slowly up the steps with her arm looped through Rya's, the women giggling together.

From behind them, one of the French doors leading into the lavish Summer House opened and Gwen's cheerful smile greeted him. "Come on, everyone inside. I've got hot chocolate and snacks ready. That includes some homemade snickerdoodle cookies for you, Rya."

Alex had to hold back a laugh as his pregnant sister-in-law made a beeline for the door, scooping up a giggling Tatiana on the way, with Jessica trailing behind her.

Next to him, Dimitri ground out his cigar and sighed. "Did you ever think there would be a day where we would have such love, such joy in our lives?"

The scars on his heart from Jessica's supposed death were still tender and his gaze sought out the women through the windows looking into what Jessica had deemed the family room. They were all laughing and smiling while one of the maids handed out the hot cocoa, their contentment and happiness practically radiating from them. His chest swelled with pride at the knowledge that he'd done his job as a man and provided everything his women needed. He was aware of how brief these moments of peace were in such a fucked-up world, and he cherished every second of them.

Trailing after his brother, he followed the sounds of the women's merriment and knew he was home.

Epilogue

Rya Novikov
  A little over a year later

Letting out a loud whoop, Rya Novikov raised her shot glass in a toast, laughter ringing out around the room as the other women followed suit. It was rare that she got a chance to let loose and hang out with her girls anymore, so she was living it up while she had the chance. After many, many long days spent as the Queen of the Novikov Empire, and raising a very active little boy, along with a husband who still had the libido of a teenager, she was exhausted. So when her sister-in-law Jessica had called and proposed a girls' night out, she'd been more than ready.

Well, it was kind of a girls' night out. They were actually in the Novikov's private club in their apartment building, but it was about the only place they could all go without their husbands losing their collective minds. She gazed around the table, tipsy and amused at some of the most unlikely and powerful women in the criminal underworld all gathered in one place. Almost all American, and from as different backgrounds as possible. Hell, she was the stepdaughter of an outlaw biker, yet she sat across the table from Catrin, the daughter of a Russian Ambassador to the United States, and one of the most well connected women in the world.

It was all so surreal, but in the best of ways.

Even weirder, Sarah Rodriguez was visiting again from the United States with her husband, Beach. Rya actually knew the handsome older man from before she met Dimitri. The Iron Horse MC and the Ice Demons MC, where her stepdad was vice president, were friendly with each other. She'd met Beach a couple times over the years, but it had been more of a "nice to see/meet you" than actually hanging out. Sometimes she really missed home and being around her biker bitches, so it was nice to spend time with Sarah and Beach when they were here. Swan, Sarah's twin sister, kept promising to come visit, but her husband was super overprotective and didn't want them going anywhere while their boys were still so young.

Rya could understand that; she'd refused to travel to the US with her son yet.

Sarah had promised that she and Beach would put the pressure on Dimitri to go to one of the biggest motorcycle rallies in the world out in Sturgis with them. Evidently that was where they'd first met and they went back every year they could. The thought of riding into town on the back of Dimitri's motorcycle sent all kinds of warm tingles through her lady bits. Plus, she knew it would be fun as hell to party with Sarah and the Iron Horse MC. Rya was glad life, in its own weird way, had brought the other woman into her world.

Right now, Sarah was here as a consultant on building luxury prepper compounds, one of Dimitri's projects that he shared with Alex and the Dubinski

Bratva. Together, they were purchasing land all over the world and beginning to strategize which compounds to start first. Part of her worried about the men's sudden interest in surviving the end of the world, but she had too much other shit going on to lose any sleep over it.

While she hadn't been putting her nursing degree to much use, she had been helping Dimitri run the Novikov *Bratva* in her role as the *Pakhan's* wife. Thankfully, she had a wonderful mentor in Vera Dubinski, and she knew it gave the grieving widow something to do in order to keep her mind off the loss of her husband. Though she was still reserved, she loved what she referred to as "her girls" and they loved her right back. After all, her husband had sacrificed his life for them and their children.

The pit of Rya's stomach clenched and she refused to think about that night, refused to dwell on an odd dream she'd had while in captivity, where Jorg had told her that he'd had to wait until she was pregnant to give her the Curse Breaker, that she would pass on the immunity to her child. He'd blathered some more stuff, then apologized for kidnapping her and rambled on about how happy he was for his sons that they had found and protected such wonderful women. She hadn't told her husband about that dream, instead keeping them to herself. The last thing he needed was to stress out about her drugged-up mental fantasies.

So far her son, Petrov, was a normal little boy in every way. Yes, he had traces of CB2 in his bone marrow, but there didn't seem to be any ill effects from it among any of them. They still got sick from common stuff like colds and the flu, so if she did have some kind of immunity, she had no idea from what. Thinking too much about the fact that she had a foreign substance in her body gave her the willies.

Fear of what the future might hold for her son tried to claw its way out of the "what if" cage she kept it locked up tight in, inside her mind, but she forced her attention on the present and listened to what Gia was saying.

"So Ivan pulls me over to the side and tells me to calm down." She snorted a laugh, her honey-blonde hair glimmering in the cool lighting of the private club as she shook her head with a smile. "Like I could just, you know, chat with the Queen of Sweden like it's no big deal. Then he proceeded to tell me about some of the people who were at the coronation with us, and the kinky shit they're into. I thought he was full of it until I saw a few of them at a BDSM club that night. It took everything I had not to laugh when I saw one of the very hairy male heads of state from Greece dressed up like a little girl and getting spanked with a paddle painted like a giant rainbow lollipop. I mean, that's a *really* specific kink. What in the hell kind of shit was he into that it took all that to get him off?"

Smiling to herself, Rya toyed with her glass, rolling the edge on the table.

"I'm so jealous you get to play in public," Sarah complained with a huff that blew a strand of her white-blonde hair out of her face. "Beach never lets me do anything fun."

Reaching over, Catrin patted the other woman's arm. "That is terrible. He is jealous type?"

"Very, but in a weird way. He likes men to look at me and find me sexy, but only how he deems appropriate. Like, it's okay for him to show me off in some skintight dress and have a guy eye-fuck me, but if some random dude on the street stares too long, Beach ends that shit quick. He's like...possessive in a look-don't-touch way. Like the fact that I was in *Playboy* is no big deal because I didn't show my kitty—"

"Your kitty?" Gia snorted.

"Awww, pretty kitty, come here and let me give you a tongue bath," Jessica said in an unexpectedly loud voice.

They all looked at each other, looked at the bodyguards who were obviously trying not to laugh, then burst out laughing themselves.

"Oh shit," Catrin gasped, "I think Maks just came in his pants."

Jessica grinned, "Mmmm, I've made Luka come in his pants."

They all laughed again and took sips of their respective drinks. It was nice to be among women who owned their sexuality, who found nothing wrong with doing things most people would consider immoral. Knowing she could experience anything and everything with Dimitri added a heat to their sex life that continued to burn long after most couples fizzled. Yeah, it was kinda odd that she had no problem doing sexual stuff in front of her sister-in-law while they played with friends in the dungeon upstairs, but it worked for them because there weren't any attraction between them. Just a strong friendship and love.

"Bitch," Sarah said in a grumpy tone, but her teasing grin took the sting out of the words. "Don't get me wrong, sex with Beach is out of this fucking world every single time, but I've always been a free spirit about sex, and I love the energy rush I get from watching two people that love each other have a good time. I miss it."

Rya looked at Catrin cross the table, more than aware of her little smile that was nothing but trouble. Last time Catrin had smiled like that, they'd ended up swimming naked in the public pool of a very posh hotel in Tokyo at 4 am. Their impromptu swim hadn't lasted long. Maks, being the party pooper he was, ratted them out, and Dimitri hadn't been pleased. Then again, his punishment had been one of the best nights of her life.

Her nipples hardened and she crossed her legs, wondering when the men were going to return from whatever secret mission they were doing up in Siberia. They'd been gone for four days and were due back either late tonight or early tomorrow. She didn't like it when he was gone, but she'd had to learn how to deal with her separation anxiety. Well, separation anxiety and unfulfilled sexual desires. Even after a few years of marriage and a kid, their constant need for each other hadn't dimmed and she considered herself a very lucky woman.

"Sarah, your husband does not want anyone to see you naked, yes?" Catrin asked in a falsely sweet and innocent voice.

Gia and Jessica both whipped their heads around to look at Catrin with narrowed eyes. They'd also experienced Catrin getting them into trouble more than once, and recognized that voice. Ignoring them, the little blonde woman kept her serene gaze on Sarah, who didn't seem to notice the sudden tension in the room.

"Right, which is dumb, considering I'm freaking naked in a magazine that anyone can look at on the internet."

"What about watching?"

She grinned. "He can't stop me from watching at some of the parties at the clubhouse. We have some mighty fine-looking men in the Iron Horse MC, but it's not the same as going to a sex club or a private party. At the clubhouse it's just...fucking. A lot of the times there's no emotion, no connection, like these guys could be screwing a blow-up doll. That doesn't do it for me."

Having grown up in an outlaw MC in New York, Rya knew all too well what parties at the clubhouses were like. She avoided them at all costs because nothing was nastier than seeing a scraggly, but loveable uncle she'd known her whole life screwing a club slut with his flat old-man butt hanging out. Just the thought made her shiver and she swallowed hard as bile churned in her stomach.

Urk.

Clapping her hands, her eyes sparkling with mischief, Catrin said, "I think you should have some fun. Nothing that will get you in trouble, I promise."

Everyone except Sarah groaned and Catrin blinked her eyes at them. "What?"

"We'll get in trouble," Jessica assured a confused Sarah.

"Not always," Catrin pouted. "Besides, this is for our husbands. They have been working so hard while they've been gone. I just want to give them some...incentive. Is right word?"

"Incentive?" Gia asked in a dry voice.

"Yes, something to remember us by." Her eyes cut to Jessica, her look heated. "You know how much our husbands love pictures, don't you, Jessica?"

By the bright-red flush covering her friend's elegant face, she did indeed know, as did Rya.

A little naughty thrill of warmth raced through her and she met Gia's gaze, loving the way the gorgeous submissive instantly reacted to her. Tonight her long, wavy golden hair was down around her slender shoulders, bared by her white halter top. The color brought out the natural tan in her skin and Rya marveled again at how beautiful her submissive and best friend was. How lucky she was to have her. Slowly, Gia's full lips curved into a smile and she knew her girl was considering sending Ivan some naughty pictures. None of them were shy, and thanks to their amazing husbands, and they all had no problem acknowledging what their passions and desires were.

It was so freeing to know that there was nothing she could want that Dimitri would consider too perverted or obscene, and the fact that he loved watching her Top beautiful women was icing on the cake. Plus, he got the thrill of having two women suck his cock when she worked him over with Gia. The memory of their tongues twirling together over the head of his erection, then Ivan's, made her pussy clench.

Catrin let out a triumphant sound. "See, Rya wants to, so that means Gia's in as well."

"I'm in," Sarah said with a wicked grin. "I can't participate, but I can certainly take pictures for you. I might have to take a break with my pocket rocket, but Beach is going to shit himself. That is, as long as your husbands are okay with him seeing."

Rya shrugged. "Dimitri considers Beach a good friend, so yeah, he would allow him the privilege."

The other women around the table nodded and Sarah's eyes teared up. "You guys, that means so much to me—in a totally fucked-up way. Beach really admires your husbands so I know it'll mean a lot to him as well."

Catrin abruptly stood. "Oh no, we are not going to have drunk crying. Come, we will go upstairs to the Chambers."

"The Chambers?" Sarah asked while moving out of the booth after them, her amazing legs clad in a pair of relaxed blue jeans and her rather large breasts restrained by a tight black "Support Your Local Iron Horse MC" baby doll t-shirt. "What's that?"

"Come, is easier to show," Catrin said with a mischievous smile.

When they reached the exit of the club, Maks and two of Jessica's men stood there, along with a handsome black man named Hulk who was Sarah's bodyguard. They all had stern looks on their faces, but she wasn't intimidated. Much.

"Where are you going?"

Rya pushed her way through the other women and gave Maks a challenging look. "We're going up to the Chambers."

His eyebrows rose up. "I see."

"What's the Chambers?" Hulk asked in a low voice.

"Their private BDSM playground."

The massive black man's pale-green eyes went wide, then he grinned but shook his finger at Sarah. "Beach will lose his shit if you play with anyone."

"I know that." Sarah put her hand on her hip. "But he won't mind one bit if I give the girls a helping hand by taking pictures to send to their husbands."

Hulk shook his head while Maks looked towards the ceiling as if in supplication. "They'll be home soon enough. Can't your mischief wait until their return?"

"Maks," Jessica purred, and Rya almost laughed as the well-built auburn-haired man flinched. "I was hoping you could take pictures of Catrin and me."

He grit his teeth and Rya had to hide her triumphant grin as he said, "Someday, you are going to get me killed."

Catrin laughed and sauntered past Maks. "Do not be so grumpy."

After much laughter and whispers, they made it to the massive playground that took up almost the entire twenty-third floor. It had a magnificent view of the city, but the windows were specially treated with a variety of cutting-edge technology that not only made them blast-proof, but also spy-proof. No one could see or listen to what happened in this room, a rare luxury of absolute privacy that allowed Rya to be as loud and wild as she wanted.

There were five different rooms, but they all headed to the largest one, the common area. They often hosted parties here and the room itself was big enough to comfortably hold fifty people.

Dimitri and Alex didn't take them to the BDSM club to play anymore. They were too well known now and attracted unwanted attention. Here they could be as free as they wanted with people they knew wouldn't judge. They paused in the main foyer while Jessica took Sarah and Catrin into one of the theme rooms that held a variety of costumes. Rya led Gia into the women's dressing room and stripped her down, then covered her in sparkling gold body paint that was edible. It made her girl's slender body shimmer and she ran her palms over the tips of Gia's pierced nipples, groaning low in her throat as the other woman sighed and arched into her touch.

Gia then covered her in silver glittering body paint and paused to give her clit a quick suck that made Rya's knees buckle.

Laughing softly, she sank her hand into Gia's long hair and tugged her up, her grip just enough to sting. Instantly Gia's expression went dreamy. She'd never met a woman who loved pain as much as Gia, and it was a heady feeling to give her what she needed to fly deep in subspace. There was a great deal of trust involved in pairing with a masochist and Rya cherished the gift of Gia's submission. She planned to reward her girl well tonight. By the time their Masters arrived, the men would be savage for them, driven crazy by the need to reclaim what they considered theirs.

Her pussy clenched hard and she sucked in a quick breath, desire already burning her blood.

Hand in hand they strolled into the dungeon, both coming up short at the sight of Jessica with her arms stretched over her head, her wrists shackled and bound to one of the large black marble pillars scattered about the room. She was dressed in some type of outfit made of leather straps and metal rings, which highlighted her pale skin and flaming hair. Catrin was currently stroking her back while she whispered in her ear, a wicked smile on the curvy blonde's sweet face.

Catrin was totally nude except for her heels and a thick gold chain around her waist that highlighted her hourglass figure.

An evil plan began to form in Rya's mind and she led a complacent Gia to the other side of the pillar.

"Gia, reach up and grasp Jessica's hands in your own. Do not let go no matter what happens."

Doing as she was told, Gia positioned herself on the other side of the pillar and grasped Jessica's hands, the sight of her caramel-colored skin a nice contrast to Jessica's creamy tone. This position popped her spankable ass out and Rya couldn't help giving her a light smack, enjoying the way her girl sighed with pleasure. She was greedy for Gia's moans, flew high into her top space at the way the other woman softened beneath her touch. They'd been together long enough now that she could read her girl without safewords, but wouldn't push her too much tonight.

After all, once Ivan got his hands on her, she'd be in a world of pleasurable hurt.

Maks spoke up from the other side of the room. "Rya, Ivan wants you to plug her."

She glanced over her shoulder and looked at Maks, finding his gaze firmly on Jessica, as usual. "You told on us?"

He gave her an unrepentant grin, his erection pressing against his pants. "Do you really think I am going to face your husbands' wrath for not telling them about your play?"

Sarah's voice came from across the room. "Did you tell Beach?"

Maks' response came out in a strangled croak and Rya turned to see what was going on. At the sight of Sarah in a silky white bra and panty set, she understood Maks' inability to speak. Too bad Beach wouldn't let her play, because Sarah was magnificent. Lightly tanned with a flawless body, even her enhanced breasts looked real and they bounced as she walked.

A sensual challenge flared from her blue eyes and she gave them all a wicked smile as she strutted beneath their combined admiring looks. Oh yes, Sarah was an exhibitionist for sure. A light flush stained her cheeks and chest, revealing her arousal as much as her hard nipples and the cocky jut of her hips.

She held up her cell phone. "Okay, I have your husbands programed in to receive the images. You ready?"

Rya wrapped her hand into Gia's silken hair and tilted her head back, capturing her sweet lips in a loving kiss. "Are you going to endure for my pleasure, darling?"

A full-body shudder worked through Gia and Jessica let out an answering moan. "Yes, Mistress."

"Good girl."

She slid her hand down Gia's back, blending her silver paint with Gia's gold, a trail of moon dust invading a sunlit path. When she reached the other woman's pronounced buttocks, she gave her a swift spank, then another, working back and forth while Catrin was doing something to Jessica that had her begging and pleading. Energy filled the air and Rya took in a deep breath, swearing she was absorbing the sexual tension and adding it to her own. Her pussy was leaving a wet trail down her inner thighs, her nipples ached, but she ignored her own needs, fully in Domme mode. Sarah hovered around them, taking pictures without being obtrusive, her murmured compliments about how sexy and amazing they were adding to Rya's desire.

"Please, Mistress," Gia whispered as Rya stroked her fingers over Gia's swollen folds, teasing the hard clit hidden by her plump labia.

"Please what, Gia?"

Groaning, Gia's head fell back when Rya pinched her clit, hard. "That, oh please, that. Hurt me."

Sarah crouched down next to them, her pants audible while she got a close up of Rya's fingers playing with Gia's wetness. "Does she taste as good as she looks?"

Feeling wicked, Rya saturated her pointer and middle fingers with Gia's arousal then held them out to the kneeling Sarah. "Taste them and find out."

Sarah stared up at her with wide eyes, yearning in every line of her gorgeous body. "My *Papi* wouldn't approve."

"Come on," Rya cooed, always loving the lure of the forbidden, "just a little taste, I won't tell."

She held her fingers inches from Sarah's full lips, not forcing the issue but making sure the temptation was there. Sarah's nostril's flared and she licked her lower lip, a soft whining sound coming from her. "She smells so good."

"Do you like eating pussy, Sarah? Does it turn you on to have a woman grinding against your face, to feel the soft, wet flesh of her pussy quiver beneath your tongue? I bet you know how to service a Mistress well."

Another one of those pained whimpers and Rya gloried in the power she had in this moment, in the temptation she was presenting to the other woman.

A harsh male voice ripped through the soft feminine cries filling the room.

"Don't you even think about it, little girl."

All the women turned to look to the doorway, and at the sight of their men striding across the room to them, Rya let out a happy cry. "Dimitri!"

Her husband removed his shirt with quick, impatient gestures, his gaze filled with hunger. "You are trying to get Sarah in trouble with her Master."

Beach, stripped down to nothing but his worn jeans, wrapped his hand in Sarah's hair and lifted her to her feet with a pained cry. She stared up at him like he was her sun, moon and stars.

Rya's attention was drawn away from Sarah and Beach by the sight of a nude Ivan curving his body around Gia's, laying his hands over hers where they still grasped Jessica's shackled ones. The atmosphere in the room thickened, grew darker and hungrier with the addition of all the men's energy.

Dimitri collared her throat with his hand, forcing her to look at him. "I have missed you, *zaychik moya*."

"I've missed you too, *volk moy*."

Ivan joined them with an evil grin and Gia crawled next to him, her body moving with a lithe grace fueled by need and the desire to please her Doms. "Ladies, your pictures have inspired us."

She swallowed hard, then winced when Dimitri pulled out a pair of needle-nosed clamps from his pocket before removing his pants. At the sight of his thick, swollen erection, her pussy clenched hard enough to hurt. Oh fuck, she'd missed that cock inside of her. Missed his smell, his taste, his everything. Without thought, she sank to her knees before him and rested her head against her Master's thigh, a sigh of pure contentment leaving her.

Dimitri was here, he'd take care of her now.

He reached down and smoothed her hair back from her face, his voice soft as he said, "You will do whatever Master Ivan tells you, understood?"

"Yes, Master."

Gia crawled up next to her and rubbed her cheek against Rya's in an affectionate gesture. Off to the side of the room, Beach had Sarah strapped to a St. Andrew's cross while still wearing her underwear. His body was pressed to hers, but he had her chin firmly in his hand as he whispered into her ear, and her heavy-lidded gaze was focused on Gia and Rya. Giving the other woman a wink, Rya cupped Gia's breast in one hand and gave the nipple a hard pinch.

At Gia's loud gasp Dimitri frowned. "I see I have a willful girl on my hands. Perhaps we need to restrain you since you cannot restrain yourself."

"Jessica, Gia," Ivan snapped, "I want you on your backs, lying down with the top of your heads touching."

Now free of her shackles, Jessica scrambled to do as Ivan commanded while Gia did the same. Soon they were lying down on a thick black pad on the floor with their long hair spread out and mingling together in a fall of auburn fire and deep gold. They were both on the slender side, but their bodies were very different, each beautiful in their own way.

Rya startled as cold metal was slipped over her wrist and her right arm pulled behind her back.

Ivan checked the fit of her cuffs with brisk, efficient movements, but stopped to give her cheek a fond touch before moving away. Dimitri stood off to the side, fully nude, with Nico. When he noticed Rya looking at him, he gave her a smile that promised a rough fuck in the near future. She couldn't wait.

"Rya," Ivan helped her stand, "I want you to straddle my girl's face. Nico, do the same with Catrin over Jessica."

Alex's deep laughter filled the air and she couldn't help but smile. It was so good to see him happy, so good to see the darkness that had haunted him since they'd met finally lift. Alex adored Jessica and the feeling was entirely mutual. Just seeing them together gave her hope that despite the dangers of the world they lived in, despite all the evils trying to tear them apart, true love would win out in the end. And even if she didn't already love Jessica for how happy she made Alex, she would have loved the auburn-haired woman for the changes she'd made in Dimitri. Since Jessica's return, Rya's husband laughed more, smiled more, and in general had a more positive outlook on life. It was as if a great burden had been removed from his shoulders and Rya had never been happier.

Unable to deal with the depth of her emotions, needing to somehow let her Master know how much she adored him, she leaned forward as best she could and began to press soft kisses to Dimitri's thick thighs, loving the way the muscles twitched beneath her lips.

"When she isn't being a smart-ass, she can be quite sweet," Nico murmured as he joined Dimitri and gave her hair an affectionate stroke.

"My little rabbit is very cuddly," Dimitri said with obvious pride.

Ivan gently pulled on her arm. "Come, my submissive needs a pussy to muffle her cries."

She almost asked what he was talking about, but the moment she was arranged over Gia's eager mouth, all her thoughts splintered. Catrin was rubbing her sex against Jessica's lips with an erotic moan, her arms bound behind her back like Rya's. They were less than six inches apart, and soon Rya was leaning her head on Catrin's shoulder while Gia did her best to make Rya come.

The sensation of her clit being suckled had her shivering, and when she was forced to sit upright, she could barely support herself.

"Open," Dimitri demanded, and she did without thought.

Instantly a cock filled her mouth, but it wasn't Dimitri's—it was Nico's giant erection. The man was almost scarily hung and she marveled once again that Catrin could take so much dick. Eagerly, she licked and sucked at the head, aware that Catrin was doing the same to Dimitri's cock. Beneath her, Gia moaned loud and long, the vibrations traveling over Rya's pussy. When Gia shifted, she glanced over her shoulder to find Ivan had his wife's legs up around his shoulders and was slamming his cock into her.

Gia cried out again and Rya would have done the same if Nico hadn't grabbed her head and forced her mouth around his swollen shaft. "Suck."

Electricity tingled and surged through her, the nerves of her sex hypersensitive to Gia's ardent licking. Holy crap, her submissive could seriously eat pussy like a champ. Catrin whimpered against Rya's neck, then licked and sucked at the sensitive skin, making Rya cry out at the dual stimulation. Beneath her, Gia began to rhythmically moved and Rya knew her friend was now being fucked by Ivan, her Master. Sure enough Gia's efforts to get Rya off doubled and her thighs shook.

"That's it, my good girl, eat that cunt," Ivan growled, and Gia began moaning that low sound in the back of her throat that she made before she orgasmed. "When Rya climaxes and soaks your face, I want you to come all over my cock."

The taste of Nico lay heavy on Rya's tongue as she gently sucked some pre-cum out of him. He withdrew his cock and she cried out as Gia began to suckle on Rya's clit with a hard-and-fast rhythm that matched Ivan's rough fuck. Dimitri's big hands gripped her head as he fed her his dick and she almost cried at the overwhelming pleasure of serving her Master, of making him feel good. He used her roughly and when he told her to come, she did, screaming around his flesh filling her mouth.

Her pussy rippled and shivered, feeling empty even as she came. She needed more, she needed him.

Dimitri must have felt the same because he jerked himself from her mouth then plucked her from Gia's face with ease after removing her handcuffs.

Placing her on her hands and knees before Gia, he growled out, "Lick her clean."

The tang of her own pussy coated her tongue as she did as ordered, biting down on her lip as he slammed into her with a satisfied groan.

"Master," she cried out, bucking back into him.

Slapping her ass, he growled, "I told you to lick her clean. Now do it. Once she is clean, you may come."

Gia wrapped her hands in Rya's hair and their mouths fused as their Masters fucked them hard, their lips sliding while their bodies absorbed the impacts of the large men using them so roughly. Across the room, Sarah cried out, but she couldn't leave the pleasure of Gia's mouth to look and see what was going on. A smooth limb brushed against her arm and she knew Catrin was being fucked by Nico near them, the familiar scent of her arousal mixing with the other women's musk. Sex was so thick in the air that she was drowning in it, but she couldn't bring herself to care.

Lightheaded, she screamed out her release as Dimitri drove himself in to the root and grasped her hips hard enough to bruise. He roared, his thick cock twitching inside of her as he filled her up with his cum. As if it started a chain reaction, the other men snarled and growled out their climaxes one by one, each wild sound like a physical caress to Rya's trembling body. Her eyelids refused to open, even when she felt the lovely sensation of warm people she loved curled around hers, men and women.

They often did this, collapsed into a big puppy pile of sweaty limbs and satiated bodies after a particularly energetic night. There was soft laughter along with gently murmured words, heartfelt whispers of praise and thanks. She adored them, each of them in their own unique ways, and her heart filled with a joy that was even better than sex, the joy of loving and being loved, the joy of being surrounded by people who were an essential part of her life. An essential part that she would do anything to protect.

As their breathing slowed there was some murmured conversation around her, but she ignored it, content to snuggle up to Dimitri while he showered her with kisses.

"I love you, *zaichek moya*," he whispered against her forehead.

"You are everything to me, Dimitri." She gave him a slow kiss. "My husband, my lover, the father of my child, my everything."

He held her close, and as she drifted in the safety of his arms, she committed this perfect moment to memory, knowing somewhere deep inside that she would need these happy remembrances to get her through the hard times that were sure to come.

Dear Beloved Reader,

I hope you had a nice, happy sigh at the end and that you enjoyed Alex and Jessica's long journey to happiness. Many of you have been asking who will have the next book in my Submissive's Wish series, which sexy Russian will be meeting his match. Sorry, kittens, but I'm not telling. ;)

If you're curious about Beach and Sarah's story, please check out my Iron Horse MC series. The world of Submissive's Wish and Iron Horse cross over, and when those two series end, a third series about their children falling in love in the distant future will begin. If you enjoyed this story, please leave a review and thank you so much for giving me the chance to entertain you.

Ann

~ABOUT THE AUTHOR~

With over forty published books, Ann is Queen of the Castle to her husband and three sons in the mountains of West Virginia. In her past lives she's been an Import Broker, a Communications Specialist, a US Navy Civilian Contractor, a Bartender/Waitress, and an actor at the Michigan Renaissance Festival. She also spent a summer touring with the Grateful Dead-though she will deny to her children that it ever happened.

From a young Ann has had a love affair with books would read everything she could get her hands on. As Ann grew older, and her hormones kicked in, she discovered bodice ripping Fabio-esque romance novels. They were great at first, but she soon grew tired of the endless stories with a big wonderful emotional buildup to really short and crappy sex. Never a big fan of purple prose, throbbing spears of fleshy pleasure and wet honey pots make her giggle, she sought out books that gave the sex scenes in the story just as much detail and plot as everything else-without using cringe worthy euphemisms. This led her to the wonderful world of Erotic Romance, and she's never looked back.

Now Ann spends her days trying to tune out cartoons playing in the background to get into her 'sexy space' and has accepted that her Muse has a severe case of ADD.

Ann loves to talk with her fans, as long as they realize she's weird and that sarcasm doesn't translate well via text. You can find her at:

Website
http://www.annmayburn.com/

Facebook
https://www.facebook.com/ann.mayburn.5

Pintrest
http://pinterest.com/annmayburn/

Twitter
https://twitter.com/AnnMayburn

Other Books by this Author

Prides of the Moon Series

Amber Moon

Emerald Moon

Onyx Moon

Amethyst Moon

Opal Moon

Club Wicked Series

My Wicked Valentine

My Wicked Nanny

My Wicked Devil

My Wicked Trainers

My Wicked Masters

Virtual Seduction Series

Sodom and Detroit

Sodom and the Phoenix

Submissives Wish Series

Ivan's Captive Submissive

Dimitri's Forbidden Submissive

Alexandr's Cherished Submissive

Alexandr's Reluctant Submissive

Long Slow Tease Series (FemDom)

Still

Penance

Emma's Arabian Nights (FemDom)

First Kiss

Second Touch

Third Chance

Fourth Embrace

Bondmates Series

Casey's Warriors

Jaz's Warriors(Novella Coming Soon)

Paige's Warriors(Novel Coming Soon)

Iron Horse MC Series

Exquisite Trouble

Exquisite Danger

Exquisite Redemption (Coming Soon)

For the Love of Evil Series

Daughter of the Abyss

Princess of the Abyss

Sam and Cody

Want

Cherish

Adore

Chosen by the Gods

Cursed

Blessed

Dreamer

Single Titles

Blushing Violet

Bound for Pleasure (FemDom)

Sensation Play

Peppermint Passion

The Breaker's Concubine

Guarding Hope

Scandalous Wish

Pursued by the Prisoner

The Bodyguard's Princess

Summer's Need

Wild Lilly

Diamond Heart

CPSIA information can be obtained
at www.ICGtesting.com
Printed in the USA
FFOW01n1008201215
19833FF